Saleh's Children

Three Generations of Plantation Masters and Their Slave Women

A Novel

by

HOWARD BOTT

ISBN: 978-0-9862919-0-6

Printed in the United States of America.

Cover and interior design, editing and production by Joanne Shwed, Backspace Ink (www.backspaceink.com).

To my dear friend of many years Rich Bona, whose loving support always offered encouragement and honest, helpful criticism.

And most of all to my beautiful wife Nancy, who gave the same support and love to my writing that she has since the beginning given to every other area of my life: wonderful mother to our girls Jessica and Kelah and open-hearted Mimi to our grandchildren Hannah, Spencer, Eitan and Levi. Thank you, dear one, for being my life partner and best friend.

Special thanks to my editor Joanne Shwed. Her skill, long experience and tact combined to help me bring out the book I truly wanted to publish.

Introduction

PINEWOOD PLANTATION, VIRGINIA

It was April 1861. They were burying the ancient, light-skinned Fulani slave woman called Saleh, who was from the Senegal River and the lower margins of the Sahel grasslands in northwestern Africa, and whom George had, in the long ago, renamed Sally when he purchased her at Charleston. Because of the terrible events at Pinewood Plantation, nobody from the Leyland family supervised the sort of funeral the slaves gave her, so the slave carpenter made a proper coffin and a simply carved wooden marker board, instead of stripping her naked and dumping her without ceremony into an unmarked hole, as George had wanted. He was gone now.

Even the most enthusiastic Christian slaves did not offer to pray over her grave because Sally had hated everything to do with the Leylands, including their religion, and the slaves knew it. Nobody had any idea what Fulani words ought to be said over a grave either, even if Sally had wanted them, which everyone knew she didn't.

Neither daughter nor granddaughter was standing by her graveside at the far back of the slave burying ground where the new white marse, whomever he would turn out to be, would be least likely to notice it, assuming he would care—assuming he would even know any of the complex story that had been Sally's relationship with the Leyland family.

And even if daughter or granddaughter had been able to be present for the funeral, there was little they could or would have said about Sally that would have meant anything. She had been disliked by the slaves because she had always ignored them. She was tolerated and, in the beginning, coveted by the whites—whom she hated—because she worked hard, but even more because she had been so beautiful. Her death and burial at age seventy-six would only have had real, emotional meaning to George, but he had recently died in the unforeseen series of events that had overwhelmed the Leyland family and Pinewood Plantation, and there was really no one left who cared.

Which is exactly what Sally would have wanted ...

1861

PINEWOOD PLANTATION, VIRGINIA

There was a great stir at Pinewood Plantation. The man from Chicago—the city at the North where there was no slavery and where Negroes could work at trades as free men—was coming at last. This man, Mr. Thomas Bradford, had been corresponding with Young George about the possibility of going into the cigarette business up in Chicago. Young George invited him to the South to talk about being his tobacco supplier, sidestepping wholesalers; now, they had a telegram, notifying them that Bradford was coming within the next few days to discuss details.

Bradford said that he thought there was a lot of potential in this new and growing market—cigarettes—but, to make them, he couldn't use whole leaf tobacco. He wanted it processed, stems removed and the leaf finely shredded, and potentially he wanted a lot of it. Young George had to decide whether he would still make a good profit if he bought the machinery to do the processing or simply stick to what he knew: baled leaf tobacco.

Decatur, a middle-aged slave in the Big House, already knew of Bradford's planned visit, as he did almost everything else, but he had not been the first to hear it. As usual, it was Missy who first learned of this—as she did all new happenings in the House—directly from Little Master Will, and then hastened to send word of it through Decatur to the other slaves.

Decatur slipped out the kitchen door of the Big House and hurried to his quarters in the back. Like the other House slaves, he and his wife Young Sally had a small, single-room shack behind a stand of oak and pine trees, where the slaves were close to the House but screened from it by the trees. In this way, the white folks did not have to look out their back windows at a clear view of the unlovely huts they provided for their Negroes but could still control them by proximity.

The shacks of the field slaves—as well as those of the artisans, such as carpenters and blacksmiths—were cruder, though they had the advantage of being set a little further from the House, beyond the vegetable gardens, the wash house, the carpentry shed, the tall tobacco barns, the smokehouse, the dairy, the forge, the horse corrals, the stand of high grass and the large, mud-ringed pond where the hogs wallowed.

There, fronting one of the great tobacco fields that stretched toward a distant line of trees, was the long, double row of slave shacks, made of rough-cut logs that housed most of the hundred and fifty-odd slaves owned by the Leyland family at Pinewood Plantation. Like his neighboring planters, Young George knew that it was necessary to have the slave quarters as near to the House as possible. The conventional wisdom was that Negroes were inherently unreliable, living—as the planters believed they did—behind their age-old screens of obedience and good nature while secretly nourishing wicked feelings of anger and hatred toward their benefactors and masters, and forever plotting their escape.

"Anyone can see," the planters would say, "that Negro slaves were born without any capacity for gratitude and, as such, are different from and inferior to the true humanity exemplified by the white race."

This being true, it was necessary to keep strict governance over them.

But Young George's wife—called Miz Elizabeth by the slaves—was never comfortable having them live so close to her and had demanded, when she arrived as a bride at Pinewood Plantation, that they be moved much further away from the House.

Young George, in thrall to her beautiful features, soft voice and slim figure, and the novelty of what he called in his secret journal her haunting sexuality, nevertheless held firm. Placing them in more distant shacks simply created too much anxiety in him about what the niggers might be getting up to. He had insisted that Elizabeth give him at least one good reason why she wanted the niggers moved so far toward the back of his property.

She would only fix him with a stare so defiant as to be unsettling and say, "Across the many years ahead, I trust that you will ask favors from me. I *hope* that I will be able to satisfy you. I truly *hope* so ..."

At this, Young George's blood rose, but he felt proud of his ability to calmly resist even so visceral a threat to his sexual comfort as this and persevered. To be sure, even early in their marriage and contrary to his prenuptial expectations, relations with Elizabeth had been a great disappointment. This did not prevent him from claiming his rights with her, but he continued to feel cheated of the passion he knew other men enjoyed with their wives.

After giving the whole matter some thought, he came to believe that her coolness had nothing to do with where the slave quarters were placed but were rather an expression of her true, unsensual nature. Still, if the reasons behind her insistence that the slave houses be moved had been good ones, and if they were consistent with better slave management and plantation profits, he might have considered them.

But, as the main reason for her wanting the slaves so far from the House began to emerge, it shocked Young George that it was so annoyingly trivial. When all was said and done, she "couldn't bear" to be so "engulfed" by people for whom she played a part in holding in bondage, in perpetuating what was to her their truly "gruesome" poverty, in refusing to react to their universal if masked unhappiness and to do nothing about their miserable illnesses for which a doctor's care was seldom sought.

(The planters allowed these illnesses to be treated by the slaves themselves with herbal remedies and "witchings," which included spells and incantations brought over from their African roots. But the slaves did their best to hide their ancestral rituals from their masters because they knew these were seen as dangerous, incomprehensible and fundamentally un-Christian, and they dreaded the possibility of having them be revoked.)

The point was that these "humanitarian" ideas of Elizabeth's were dangerous to the way of life that Young George and all his ancestors had so successfully followed for over two hundred years. In Young George's heart of hearts, her ideas felt like "domestic treason."

He foreclosed any further present or future discussions of the issue by saying to Elizabeth, in as icy and calm a voice as he could find within him, " Henceforth, my dear, you will kindly allow me to manage all questions about the slaves while you confine your interests to the House. This, I believe, is the key not only to profitable tobacco planting but also to a happy marriage. After all, you were raised in a planter's family. Indeed, *your* family—the Jerrolds—occupy land formerly belonging to *mine.* Your father's plantation, as you well know, *adjoins* this one! I pass over any comments on how your great-grandfather obtained it.

"My point is that there is *nothing* about life among slaves being revealed to you now that you have not known all your life. If you have been all along a secret abolitionist, I will only say that, if so, you agreed to marry me under false pretenses, and that no Virginia court would deny me a divorce from you, under terms completely favorable to myself, including how much, if any, of your inheritance you would be allowed to keep!"

Here, Young George broke off, glaring in silence at his stunned wife. He was gratified to see her open her mouth, ready to argue, but then close it. This was, he realized, the first time he had ever been angry with her.

Perhaps, he thought, *my being so forceful with her this first time will preclude any future times.*

As it turned out, he would be proved not only wrong in this but naïve as well.

The slave driver, Black Sulla, had his house near the other slave quarters but set apart from the rest and of a better construction—planks instead of logs. It was also one room, but it contained a small and newly blacked stove, a window with glass panes, curtains and wood shutters, a proper bed with a headboard and straw-stuffed ticking that was resting on planks instead of on a webbing of ropes. It had a solid oak table and two handcrafted chairs, and pegs on the wall from which hung a red shirt, a blue shirt, an old swallowtail green velvet dress coat and a pair of brown trousers without tears or patches.

Black Sulla had a square of ancient carpet, which covered part of his dirt floor, and a lamp that burned either whale oil or coal oil. The other slaves had only mud and wattle chimneys over roughly fashioned stone hearths. Such chimneys routinely caught fire and burned the shack down, but always the shacks and the chimneys were rebuilt to the same cheap design. The other slaves had no clothes except bluish or brownish patterned homespun, and certainly none had a stove or a carpet. For light at night, they had a single tallow candle.

Black Sulla's comforts reflected the satisfaction that Young George took in his efficiency as a slave driver. In 1826, he had been bought from Muslim factors at Calabar on the African West Coast at age six and was smuggled like thousands of others into the country despite the 1803 ban on slave importation. He was forty-one now, unmarried, bald, very black, brooding and violent. To differentiate him from Little Sulla—a short, thin, sweet-faced mulatto who worked in the Big House—the other slaves called him Black Sulla. He had been a driver for fifteen years.

Since it was the middle of the workday, the House slaves were scattered about the plantation, either inside the Big House or at the wash house or the dairy, or bending over the sprouting rows of vegetables and flowers in the large kitchen garden. The field slaves were out far from the House, preparing the fields for the May tobacco planting.

But Decatur, Young Sally's husband in name, knew that she would be at home. It was understood now that she did not have to go to the fields or do any other work. Before Young George took up with her, she had been a House slave; now, she was freed of work but absolutely forbidden from going near the Big House. When Young George's infatuation with Young Sally was at its height, he had built for her a little cabin in the woods, with matching oak furniture, muslin curtains, a plank floor, warm carpets, a four-poster bed, a little fireplace and a chiming clock, where she stayed for the better part of eighteen years, occasionally coming "home" to Decatur for appearances.

Now, at thirty-nine years old, Young Sally had been turned out of her cabin, and her (and Young George's) nineteen-year-old daughter Missy lived there. Young Sally had been told many times over the years—by Elizabeth, Young George's wife—that, if she had her way, Young Sally would go to the field slave shacks, be given the hottest and dirtiest work and die in the tobacco rows, though Young George had thus far protected her. For years and years, Elizabeth had pushed him to renounce Young Sally but, for the past year or so, Elizabeth had said nothing and behaved as though the subject had lost interest for her.

It was speculated that, because Young Sally had been publicly rejected, it was certainly only a matter of time before she was sold. None of the slaves believed that Young George would protect her much longer or that he even wanted to, and most of them were glad of it. In her days of ascendancy, she had changed from a sweet, shy girl to an arrogant scold who put on airs. Despite warnings from her mother Sally and from others, Young Sally had gradually come to believe herself to have a superior skin color—a lighter tone—to the other slaves and was hated for it now.

Her mother Sally, who had had a "V" cut in her tongue long ago by white slavers, and who now frightened children when she stuck it out, and whose speech was so distorted by her injury that she was hard to understand, had told Young Sally all along what a mistake she was making in believing all that Young George had promised her.

"De onlietht ting yo kin exthpeck fum de white man ith trouble," Sally lisped. "An dey don' got ter promith yo dat. De white man ith trouble an nothin but."

But Young Sally would not listen and was now cast back into the house of her so-called husband Decatur, where she was brooding, depressed and beginning to act strangely. In the weeks following her downfall, she rarely spoke or stirred from her house. And, since Young George had rejected her, Black Sulla had been coming in from the fields during the day when Decatur was up at the House and was seen entering her shack.

Everyone knew how Young Sally hated Black Sulla and how long Black Sulla had coveted her. And they knew that, if Black Sulla were coming to her at all, let alone during the workday, and almost certainly forcing himself on her, he must have the permission, possibly the encouragement and—even though it stunned the mind—the out-and-out enthusiasm of Young George. Otherwise, slaves, even slave drivers, dare not leave the fields until the late bell at dusk called them in. Of course, to molest the marse's woman would be unthinkable.

Everybody could see, by Black Sulla's coming to Young Sally's shack so brazenly, where things stood now. Young George was plainly out to debase and humiliate her, and there was nothing anybody, especially anybody with a black face, could do about it. Decatur was as helpless against the marse's surrogate as he had been against Young George himself, and accepted everything with a quiet humility.

Young Sally felt as if she had been cast into hell. From her place of comfort and privilege—with her silk dresses, expensive furniture, warm carpets, good food, real coffee (not burnt chicory) and her own gold money, she had literally overnight been dragged out of her cabin and carried bodily by the hated Black Sulla to Decatur's shack. In the days immediately afterwards, Black Sulla started coming.

Then Young George paid her a visit at Decatur's shack. He demanded that Young Sally give him back "his" gold money, though it had been freely given to her by Young George over the years. When she claimed not to have it, he gave her a bad beating. After this, she started to talk to herself and wander about the plantation in a torn, blood-stained dress, both during the day and after dark.

The slaves were leery of her, as they were of all crazy people. Witchings were sometimes untraceable and the sorcerer unknown, and the spell might fall upon anyone unwise enough to offer aid, so the slaves avoided her. Since nobody knew who had witched Young Sally or why, it made sense to stay away.

At Pinewood, Young Sally's mother Sally was a known witch. But it seemed unlikely for her to be involved in this—the witching of her own daughter—so the mystery only added to the fear. Everyone was waiting for Young George to do something about Young Sally, but he was ignoring the situation as he did with most pressing matters. Decatur, Young Sally's husband, was the only one attempting to care for her.

1850

PINEWOOD PLANTATION, VIRGINIA

In her shack on the House slave row, Sally sat with her young granddaughter Missy. Sally had once again been brought in to serve at the family's table, George having admitted by his actions—and not for the first time—that his need for her outweighed his feelings of anger and frustration. He had moved Sally back and forth between the House and the field hand shacks several times already, according to whether she was in or out of favor.

"Yo know whut I tol yo bout thalt?"

Now, back once more in the Big House, Sally passed in and out between dining room and scullery, seeing to the white people's needs. The food was brought in hot from the kitchen, which was housed in its own small building close behind the Big House. Missy, eight, was charged with bringing the cooked food to the scullery, helping her grandmother pass the platters in the dining room and clearing away the dishes.

"Yes, ma'am. I know about salt," Missy said.

Her dark brown eyes seemed even more alive when contrasted with her nearly white skin. She laughed easily and often. Nobody had, since she was small, seen her cry.

"*Whut* yo know?"

The old lady—still striking, even beautiful in her mid-sixties—never cried either. Nor did she smile. Sally ignored almost everyone, living in a world of her own to which nobody was admitted. Missy came closest but only because Sally felt obliged to teach her witching, as her uncle Tenkaminen had taught her during the Fulani times in Tekrur, her tribal kingdom.

The gods expected that Sally would pass it on, which she was doing, even though her own love for the gods—as well as her fear of them—had ended on the slave ship. But the witching was a greater thing than either her or the gods, and it must be passed on. Her daughter Young Sally was a fool, so it had to be her granddaughter Missy. There was no other choice.

"I know it is bad luck to spill salt if it's by accident," Missy said, her soft brown eyes holding her grandmother's, which showed the beginning of cataracts. "But, if it's spilled on purpose, you can witch with it because you can point the spill at the person you want to witch."

"Thay yo want ter witch Marth Geo'ge. How yo gon do it?"

"I'd knock over the salt cellar when I was clearing off the table. I'd make sure it spilled toward him."

"Den whut bout yo? Will any of dat bad luck fall on yo?"

"It might." Missy showed no emotion, only a deep sincerity.

"How yo gon thtop it?"

"I have to say, 'Oh, Marse George, I'm so sorry. Let me get a tablecloth brush!' And then I take a pinch of the salt and run into the scullery, and right away I toss some over my left shoulder and some over my right. Then all of the bad luck will fall on Marse George."

"Dath right."

There was a silence. Missy sat on the dirt floor of the shack at the feet of her grandmother, who sat in a rickety chair. The old lady stared at the child for some time before she spoke again.

"Girl, I keep tinkin, 'How dat chile end up talkin tho white?' I turn my haid away an cain't tell any differenth tween yo an any of de white chillens in dith whole dithtrick. I know why yo thkin came out tho white, but why did yo *talk* come out white too?"

Missy's serenity persisted. "I don't know, Grandmomma. Maybe because I'm around Young Marse George so much at my mother's cabin."

Her grandmother was both reassured and annoyed. "He readth ter yo?"

"Yes, ma'am."

"Yo thit up on hith lap, an he readth yo thtorieth out yer bookth?"

"Yes."

"He ith yo righteouth fathuh. Yo know dat."

Missy's expression of polite attention did not change. "Yes, ma'am."

"Jutht don' ever b'lieve in anyting he thay. He ith jutht ath low a hog ath hith papa. He might read ter yo, an kith yo, an give yo a penny one day, an den drop yo daid ath down a dry well undah a load of rockth de nextht. That ith de way of de white man."

"I know," Missy said.

"Well, den. Thpill de thalt at Young Marth Geo'ge jutht lak at Marth Geo'ge. He don favor yo no more den a bear favor hith cub. A he-bear ith gon eat de cub if de thee-bear don bite him. Yo betht membuh dat."

"Yes, Grandmomma. I will."

Sally folded her hands, closed her eyes and was silent. Missy sat quietly on the dirt floor, waiting. One thing people noticed about Missy, beside her beauty and her white speech, was her calmness.

Finally, her grandmother spoke. "Theemth ter me dat my time heah in de worl hath bout run out. To tell de truf, I din want it ter go on thith long. But thure nuf now, it fixin ter be ovah. An dere ith thomethin yo got ter do fer me when I go. Yo mama ith tho lame in de haid becauth of dat Young Marth Geo'ge dat I cain't even trutht her ter eat when thee hungry. Tho now I'm tellin yo." Sally turned an unsentimental eye on her granddaughter. "Are yo hearin me good now, girl?"

"Yes'm. Just tell me what it is you want. I'll remember."

"All right. If I die in de day, yo kin do it right quick. But if I die in de night, den yo wait til day clean. Den, when de thun come up an de beeth be out, yo go an find dem beeth an tell dem dat I am daid. An dey will go on up ter Fulani heaven an tell de godth an de old folkth, de anthethtorth."

"What if you die in the winter?"

Sally smiled, showing strong, discolored teeth. "It good dat yo tink of dat. If it be winter, den build a little fire an tell de fire ter thend atheth. De atheth dat float up gon take de plaith of de beeth, an de atheth are gon tell heaven dat I be gone an waitin ter get in. Den the godth are gon open de gate."

Sally was wrong about the imminence of her death. It was another eleven years before the old lady passed. But she never forgot the instructions given that day.

Neither did Missy.

1861

PINEWOOD PLANTATION, VIRGINIA

Young Sally had never been Decatur's choice for a wife nor he hers. He had not sparked her, or even thought of her twice, though she was beautiful and many men wanted her. Decatur had loved—and still loved—Rhoda, who, once it was decided that Decatur must marry Young Sally, was sold away to Maryland.

Since reading and writing were forbidden to slaves, the two had not been able to remain in touch. Decatur had not heard anything about Rhoda for years. The last he heard was that she had married a man called Delboy's Arthur and had a child. As far as Decatur knew, they still lived on the Delboy Plantation on Maryland's eastern shore.

Decatur had only married Young Sally because Young George had ordered it. By tortured reasoning, Young George imagined that his relations with Young Sally would be less obvious if she were somebody's wife, even after he built her a cabin in the woods. This was the same reasoning that his father George had used in marrying off her mother Sally to Cicero.

Also, Young Sally being married offered Young George one very real advantage: When she got pregnant, there could be a presumptive father other than himself. However, it was common knowledge that Young Sally's marriage to Decatur was unconsummated, since all of her love and loyalty belonged to Young George, and Decatur would not have dared any sexual approach to her due to his fear of the marse.

Anyway, it was clear from her looks and lightness of skin that Young Sally's daughter Missy was not Decatur's child but Young George's, just as it had been general knowledge that Young Sally herself had been sired not by Sally's husband Cicero but by George, making Young Sally the younger George's half-sister—a fact that Young George seemed not to notice.

Sally was light brown, Young Sally was lighter still and some thought that Missy could pass. Missy had white features, very light-tannish skin, a tight curl to her black hair and fuller lips than most whites had. Still, white folks had to look at her twice to be sure and, even then, some couldn't tell. Maybe she was Spanish, they thought; maybe a white Mexican. Maybe she was a French Canadian with some Indian mixed in; maybe part Creole. But many were confused by her and couldn't be sure either way.

It was April. Decatur—excited at the news that he carried about Mr. Bradford, the man from Chicago, who was on his way to Pinewood to discuss large purchases of tobacco—first ran as far as the kitchen garden. There he told Little Sulla, the mulatto House slave, who was hoeing sweet peas. He knew that Little Sulla, accommodating and cheerful and, in his own smiling way, lived—as most slaves did—to confuse and defeat the white man, would be sure to pass the word on.

"Go on an tell Ol Uncle Jim," Decatur said. "He likely settin down at de dairy. He so old dat Young Marse Geo'ge don' track him no mo. He kin git on aroun an tell ev'body."

"Well," Little Sulla replied, "I speck nobody done tol yo dat Missy a'ready been talkin bout dis."

"Yas, I does know, but I jes want ter be sho dat ev'body else do," Decatur said.

"Well, praise God!" cried Little Sulla, excited. His thin face, creased by frequent smiling, was grave. "I jes hope dis white man know somethin. He fum right up in ab'lition country. I heah niggas up dere bout as good off as white folk."

Decatur shook his head. "Dey ain't no place in dis heah country where niggas is as good off as white folk. Fer dat we got ter wait til we gits ter heaven. Don' git stupid bout freedom, boy. De Norf ain't heaven. But it sho ain't slavery neithuh."

Little Sulla looked at Decatur in silence, and then said, "Yo right. I always git hopin an happenin mixed up in my mind."

"Hope's good," Decatur said, "but stupid ain't. Go on an tell Ol Uncle Jim now."

Little Sulla nodded.

Decatur turned and hurried from the long garden beds back to his own shack in the House slave row. He found Young Sally, lying on the bed and staring at the ceiling. She was dressed—not in the pretty clothes she had worn in the Young George's cabin days to reflect her lover's taste and generosity, but in slave homespun, like the field hands, with a patched sleeve and skirt, now torn and bloody, which she had not changed or washed.

As an eighteen-year-old House slave, before being taken as a lover by Young George, Young Sally and the other slave women who worked inside the House had worn proper white folks' clothes—dresses, skirts, petticoats, good shoes and stockings—at the direction of Elizabeth, who liked the House Negroes to look "more like servants than slaves."

But, for Young Sally, all that seemed long ago. Now it was homespun—and old, used-up homespun at that. She lay on her back with her hands folded on her stomach, as if laid out for a funeral. She was thirty-nine, still attractive but now, for many reasons, essentially useless and ripe for sale, although certainly not at a decent price. Gossip in the district always included items about master-slave sex relations because these were so central to everyday plantation life. So, of course, everyone knew about Young George's foolishness with his slave Young Sally.

"Young Sally!" Decatur said excitedly. "We sho now! De man fum up Norf be comin. Young Marse Geo'ge tell Little Marse Will, an he tell Missy!"

Young Sally did not move from her place on the bed or turn to look at her husband.

Presently, she said, in a low voice, "Missy … dat bitch slut. She ain't nevah done good or been good. She done took my life out fum undah me. Dat's jes whut she done …"

"Well," Decatur said gently, "Dat don' be de right way ter see it. An she yo daughtuh, no mattuh whut. Nothin dat happen be her fault noways. De white boy Little Marse Will started wit her jes like he daddy Young Marse Geo'ge done wit yo, an *he* daddy Marse Geo'ge done wit yo mama. Yo best git ovah it an move along, else you gon dry up an die. Yo too young fer dat."

"I ain't *young* an I ain't *old*," Young Sally said listlessly. "I's in de middle where de dead is at. I got no age an no life."

"Dat's *stupid*, woman," Decatur said impatiently. "Dis heah is important whut I'm sayin ter yo. Dis white man fum de Norf, he kin tell us de truf bout dis war dat seem fixin ter happen prac'ly any day now, if we goes aroun him right. If we git Missy on him. She know how ter git aroun white folk. Could be dat right terday de Yankee be fixin ter come Souf. Could be all de rumors is true. Could be we lak to git freed. Leastways, we kin find out somethin. Cause yo knows an I knows dat tween lyin an laughin, our own white folk ain't gon tell us nothin."

"Our own white folk is wicked as de devil. Dey jes de same lak de devil," Young Sally murmured.

She turned away from Decatur and would speak no more. He shook his head and hurried back toward the Big House. But, just outside his door, he nearly collided with stocky, muscular Black Sulla, the slave driver, who was walking toward Decatur's shack with the purposeful stride of a master. His hat was off, and he was mopping with a checkered handkerchief his bald, massive black head.

Decatur stepped back, looked at Black Sulla's hard eyes and nodded. "G'day, Black Sulla."

Black Sulla ignored the greeting. "Young Sally in dere?"

Decatur marveled that the man had not the slightest trace of shame. "Yas, she be in dere, for all de good it do yo or anybody. She jes body now, nothin else. Course, dat all yo wants off her, ain't it?"

"Whut I wants off anybody be gin'ally whut I gits," Black Sulla said with a little sneer. He could have stepped around Decatur, but instead, with his beefy hands, he moved the tall, thin, balding man roughly aside, looking boldly into his face.

Decatur said, "I don' wish harm ter nobody. But I do wish dat someday yo will git a taste of what yo gave out."

Black Sulla chuckled, as at a child. "Man dat kin stand up fer hisself don' need no wishes."

Then he turned and strode into Decatur's house without knocking and banged shut the door behind him.

Pinewood Plantation was a gift to Robert Francis Leyland by his grateful sovereign King George III after his service to the crown in the Seven Years' War, which the American colonists called the French and Indian War. Leyland had risen from a captaincy in the colonial militia to the rank of colonel in the British regular army—a rare thing in itself. He then distinguished himself by his courage at Montreal under Major General James Wolfe, and later by his ferocity when, on detached assignment, he led bands of Iroquois Indians, Britain's allies, against the French-sponsored Hurons. His Iroquois name meant "Bloody Hands" and was meant to be taken literally.

Because of their victory in the war, the British now controlled half of the North American continent, including French Canada, and all of France's former possessions east of the Mississippi River. Such a rich acquisition pleased King George so much that it inspired his generosity. After the war, the king raised Colonel Leyland to the peerage as Sir Robert Francis Leyland, Baronet. Then, in 1764, Sir Robert took possession of a square mile of land, southeast of Richmond, Virginia, which was the gift of King George.

But fighting as a British loyalist during the Revolution only eight years later, he fell into disfavor with his neighbors. Rejoining the British Regulars, he enjoyed winter comforts in Philadelphia as an officer on the staff of British General William Howe, while, at nearby Valley Forge in the Pennsylvania colony, fellow Virginian George Washington's ill-equipped army froze.

After Britain's defeat at Yorktown, Sir Robert prudently withdrew to England for a year and, upon his return to the newly independent, democratic republic of the United States of America, discovered that he had lost not only his nobility but over half of his land, which was confiscated for unpaid taxes by the state of Virginia and sold to a military hero of the late war named Francis Jerrold. At the time of Robert Leyland's arrival home, hero Jerrold was busy building for himself, his family and his slaves a new estate on the former Leyland property, which he called—perhaps as a sneer at his nearest neighbor—Liberty Plantation.

Pinewood Plantation itself was in disrepair and all of its Negroes had been taken from Robert Leyland by his patriot-planter neighbors, believing that, as a Tory who had fought against and killed Americans and then decamped to the enemy's country, he was only getting what he deserved.

Fortunately, the widow Suzanne Clarice Bidwill, proprietress of nearby Black Oak Plantation, did not hold his history against him but accepted his offer of marriage with some alacrity, though she knew him, as did everyone, as a faithless rake whose scandalous behavior had begun in his teenage years. Luckily, she did not need the permission of any parent to confirm the match, she being well past the age of consent, and of course a widow, and not at all a pretty woman, having considerable width at the hip, one breast visibly larger than the other and facial warts—though she was universally acknowledged to be kind.

More to the point, she had at her own disposal, free of the entail of any male relative, a fortune of two hundred thousand dollars besides the real property and slaves of Black Oak Plantation. This inflow of Bidwill money immediately restored Pinewood to its former potency and restocked the empty slave cabins. As an unlooked-for bonus, Suzanne—the new Mrs. Leyland—though a mature lady of forty-four summers, astonished her husband in two ways: by having a robust sexuality and by becoming pregnant in the first month of their marriage, giving birth in March 1782 to a healthy boy. He was christened George Leyland the First in honor of the British king to whom Robert Leyland had offered his loyalty and his life.

This little boy was fated to be Robert Leyland's only legitimate offspring (for the sixteen-odd children sired on his slave women did not, of course, count— other than when he sold them as income). As such, George received all of his father's affectionate attention and grew up learning but not loving the ways of a Virginia tobacco planter, having a fragile nervous disposition that often left him melancholy.

This same boy survived to a great age, having lived to see management of his plantation pass through himself to his son—also named George and referred to by the family as Young George and invariably by the slaves as Young Marse Geo'ge—and to celebrate the attainment of the majority of his grandson William, or Little Master Will, who was also called Little Marse Will by the slaves.

When his son Young George was forty-five and his grandson Little Master Will just twenty-one, George was seventy-nine years of age, healthy, melancholy, annoying, forgetful and unrealistic. Perhaps it was all due to the daftness that some people said came with such advanced years—though, to be sure, melancholy had been his companion for decades.

Often depressed in his heyday, but in his retirement with his mind rid of burdens and free to rise, George had come to inhabit the fantasy that, during his reign at Pinewood, he had created a golden age of plantation life that was being eroded now by the hot-headed younger male Leylands, who seemed all of a piece with their touchy, bellicose generation. All they spoke of now was war, honor, liberty and keeping the niggers down.

In George's day, the talk was about agriculture and profit. He had been comforted by the fact that the blacks had long accepted slavery as God's will for them and were easily managed. But now, to counter the ever more aggressive drumbeat of the rising tide of abolitionist sentiment at the North, everything had sunk into endless talk of southern pride, the blessings of slavery, the glory of war, the absolute need for secession by the South and the foundation of a new and separate country—not a Federal republic but a loose confederacy of states. It appeared that all ideas of seemliness, tradition and gentility were breaking down.

Still, the old man had the satisfaction of seeing his grandson Little Master Will reach manhood and show a talent for plantation management that was substantial if hard-hearted. But, as both the younger men, son and grandson pointed out to George, the days of coddling Negro slaves were long past. Now, the way of life they all followed—planters, farmers, merchants and factors, whose very livelihoods and well-being depended on African slavery—was threatened by a wicked northern coalition of Republican Unionists and mad-dog abolitionists, whose only purpose in life was to keep by force all southern states within the decaying and corrupt United States, and to set the undisciplined, ignorant and dangerous hordes of African slaves free to roam and ravage the land.

The younger men took it on faith that any southerners without the courage and will to stand against the Yankees did not deserve the benefits or the dignity they had so long enjoyed. They and all their friends—indeed, their entire class— believed they were being forced against their will into a war that would offer only a stark, frightening choice: either their survival with their way of life intact or ruin in a terrible and unthinkable new world.

George understood the passions that drove his son and grandson, but he was too old to share them. Privately, he thought both of them rough and unmannerly men. Neither treated the slaves with the tact and kindness he had shown when he was master at Pinewood. In his day, there was no talk of abolition or slave uprisings or even slave unhappiness. Back then, the niggers were happy and carefree, and he had provided for their wants and needs with such gentleness, such kindness, that discontent was unimaginable.

Satisfaction with himself and irritation at the younger men increased as the years passed. The further away George grew in time from the days of his actual governance of Pinewood, the more glorious and laudable he believed his reign to have been. Eventually, he came to see himself as a kind of planter-saint whose true goodness—and many mercies—would never be known to the world at large, but only to God.

He even said to his son Young George, "I do not understand all this trouble about slavery and secession. In my day, we never had it."

"Yes, sir, you did," said his son. "There's been secession talk for at least seventy years, and there's been trouble about slavery all along too. Somebody's always stirring up the poor niggers about freedom when they're no more able to be out free in the world than monkeys are. It's a damned shame. Now, the abolitionists have pushed us so far that we just have to start pushing back.

"And this jackass Lincoln—he's just making everything that's already bad, worse. He doesn't have any more give in him than a plow blade. Stephen Douglas, John Bell, John Breckinridge—any of them would have been better than Lincoln. At least the South could have borne with them while we tried to throw a rope over the runaway North.

"But it's too late now. There's war coming, sir. It's in the air, thick as smoke. There's going to be shooting down at Fort Sumter in South Carolina any day now … can't be avoided. The Yankees have seen to that. First Federal ship that tries to push past the Confederate guns and resupply that so-called Union fort is going to get fired on. And I say it's about time. Let's get everything settled once and for all."

George listened but did not care. The same thing that had preoccupied him for years preoccupied him now, screening out much of the urgency of the outside world. This was his sad, depressed nature, which was slow to cheer and quick to darken. By age fifty-eight, this lifelong melancholy had grown too burdensome to permit him to continue on in charge at Pinewood, and he had stepped aside in favor of Young George. Things had gotten so bad that every keen exercise of mind or hard discipline of his Negroes left him exhausted and anxious. Now, in his later years, he seemed to be seeing everything more clearly, his mind more at rest. But this clarity, though easing his burdens in some ways, only increased them in others.

Young George looked remarkably like his father. Both had large ears and noses, piercing blue eyes and fair hair, though the son carried twenty more pounds than the father. And certainly the old man had never been the fountain of loving kindness that he imagined himself now.

Yet, from Young George's point of view, his father had been a good and wise manager, being soft-headed, even blind, only in the case of Sally. With all the other blacks, he behaved exactly as slave owners must, seeing Negroes as property and being willing to make sound business decisions concerning their use or their sale. All of this nonsense that the abolitionists spouted—about "disrupting family relations" by selling parents and children apart or that "whipping Negroes is the greatest evil of the age"—made him sick.

"Let's just see," he often cried out to his father, "the goddamn *abolitionists* run a plantation without whipping!"

But Young George did not fault his father for his former meanness or his current mildness. He could see that everything shifted as a man aged. And, being a realist, he assumed it would shift for him too when the time came. But that was speculation.

What Young George knew for certain was that, at this historic turning place in American history when the country was splitting in two, he was forty-five years old, physically strong and completely in his right mind; that the South was breaking free of the North and forming its own government under former U.S. Senator and Secretary of War Jefferson Davis of Mississippi; that a war with the North must and would come, and the South would win it; that the state was a higher order of political being than any so-called nation; and that Negroes belonged in slavery under the rule of the white race. If that wasn't clear, then nothing was.

And there was plenty of scripture sanctioning slavery, though he had never researched it himself but took it on faith. The great Doctor Furman of Furman College in South Carolina had dug through the whole Bible at the South Carolina governor's request and written out his findings, so that white people could be properly instructed about it. Young George had that essay in his library and had read it carefully several times. Just imagine: There was abolitionist sentiment at the South itself … even a close neighbor might be a secret enemy! The more a man knew about the truth, the better.

Young George's wife Elizabeth (née Jerrold, whose family owned Liberty Plantation, the former Leyland land) was in her day a great beauty. When he married her in 1839, she was an eighteen-year-old girl, so trim and pert that he had lovingly called her "my sweet zephyr." Those days were long gone.

Now, twenty-two years into the marriage, she had gained a hundred pounds. This, for a woman standing only four feet eleven inches, was a great burden. She had become lethargic, lying for much of each day on a divan in the parlor, supervising and criticizing the House slaves, and complaining that, though she ate "next to nothing," she still gained weight.

Aware of Young George's relations with slave women—in particular, Young Sally—she had turned into a scold, taking out her resentment against her husband on the female slaves. It was not long before she was ordering whippings, though in the past she had always denounced them, saying that she was against any whipping of slaves and that Francis Jerrold, her father, had never done it. But the disinterest of her husband in their marriage bed turned her sour, and now she was easily offended and persuaded that the slaves' offenses were deliberate.

As she focused more and more on Young Sally as the cause of her troubles, Elizabeth had ordered Black Sulla, the heartless slave driver, to give the girl a good bullwhipping, and then felt restored and justified by it. But when her husband discovered it, he stepped in and, all pretenses discarded, physically struck her. Young George said that, if she did it again, he would send her to live elsewhere or build a separate wing on the house for himself and publicly abandon her.

This was a terrible shock. Besides the humiliation of the physical beating, it was as good as her husband saying that the nigger Young Sally meant more to him than his own wife and would be protected at all hazards to his marriage and his reputation. She stopped ordering the whippings but only hated Young Sally the more for it.

Still, Elizabeth did have at least one satisfaction: Young Sally's back now carried scars by which all future owners would know her for a troublemaker. And, at last, after many years of unremitting complaint and criticism by her, Young George had finally moved the slut out of her plush cabin in the woods and back into Decatur's shack where she belonged.

Truthfully, several years before this, things had gotten very much better for Elizabeth. None of the white people in her circle of friends knew exactly why (though certainly all the black people did), and she never said. But she had lost all the weight and started riding again, often with the handsome new overseer Wilkenson, who accompanied her to avoid the scandal of a woman riding out alone. She became again—as she had been in her youth—cheerful, gentle, an enjoyable companion and a forbearing mistress to her slaves. And, at last, as her highest good among many, her years-long campaign had succeeded, and Young Sally was on the outs and would soon be sold.

But, as satisfied with this outcome as she was, and as restored to good temper as she had grown these last several years, there nevertheless was a disturbing new development. She already knew that Young Sally had been moved out of the cabin in the woods by her husband, but then Young Sally and Young George's daughter Missy had been moved into it ... by Little Master Will, Elizabeth's son.

Sally had almost forgotten her life as Saleh. She had been having a nightmare for many years now, which brought her awake, sweating and shaking, about a life that had begun with slavery in 1801 when she was sixteen. It seemed like everything that came before slavery in her life—all of her Fulani years in the Senegal tribal land—had slipped into a fissure in her mind from which nothing ever returned.

She never dreamed of the sacred rock or the whirlpool in the deep, mysterious Senegal River. She had all but forgotten her uncle, the sorcerer Tenkaminen; Tekrur, her tribal kingdom, and the cattle that sustained it; and the great vastness of the Sahel grasslands, where the men took their cattle in the dry season, and the women and the unmarried girls awaited their return with impatience and excitement when the rains began.

Sally remembered the spells that her uncle cast, their power and effectiveness, and the fear they aroused in people against whom they were directed. But though he had taught her all he knew, she rarely used her knowledge anymore.

The plants she used in her spells, which she had found under her uncle's guidance in the forest and grasslands of Tekrur, likewise meant little now, though she had found others like them in Virginia.

She had long ago ceased loving the gods or fearing the ancestors. People still feared her, however, and she was content that they should. But, inside of her, everything had resolved itself, years and years ago, to one focused energy—her hatred of white men—and her life hung by the single spider's strand of hoped-for revenge.

If she could release herself from that, or somehow enact it with full redress and honor, she could let go of this worthless body and empty life, and rise to the holy place where were gathered the blessed dead of the Fulani. From the Fulani heaven, she knew that she would be able to make her way to where the departed of the Asante Empire were, and find *him*. And then, at last, she would have peace.

Her daughter Young Sally, sluggish and vain, was not fit to receive the teachings, but Sally had imparted them to her granddaughter Missy, who seemed to have been born already knowing them. Still, year after year, Sally had one unchanging dream.

When she had the dream now, and because it had come so often over so many years, it was no longer a trial and no longer made her weep or plunged her back into grieving. Instead, it had been so long since she had seen *him* in the flesh that she had forgotten his face. When he came back to her in the dream, the scene was as clear as if she were really seeing him again.

Sally had learned to accept that he always came back to her bleeding and legless, forever mutilated, forever dying. But at least she could again see into his eyes and again feel intensely the love that still lived in her for him. At least she could still draw from his strength, even after all these years among the white men, whose manifold evils continued to stream into her life like biting ants.

The dream was about Kano—the only man Saleh had ever loved—and it was always in two parts. She had come to terms with the first part, where the awful ship's captain, with his bright red stripe from nose tip to hair line, cut off Kano's legs, and it no longer ate at her.

But she was less at peace with the second part of the dream, where the demon captain, smirking as if he had poison in his smile, lifted his great knife, standing on the rolling floor of his terrible ship, and showed it to her, and then had her lashed against the tall barkless tree with her broken, bleeding head held, fixed by ropes.

The terrified slaves were chained and jammed together, standing on the pitching floor, with great wind-sucking cloths above them in the middle of an ocean most had never seen and some had never heard of—all being forced to watch what was done to her.

And some of the white men, wearing special red coats, laced white leggings and large, three-cornered felt hats, with guns that had knives on their ends, prodded the blacks away from the railings lest they jump. Then, the demon's assistant—the one-eyed, sad-looking man—gripped one side of her tongue with little iron pinching hooks and drew it out of her mouth as far as it would come.

Then the stripe-faced captain, taking sharp hold of the other side of Saleh's tongue with his dirty fingernails, dug in, held tight and, with his big knife, slowly carved a half-inch-wide, half-inch-deep "V" in the spongy tissue, its point toward the back of her mouth. Kano's death was so alive in her mind that she refused to scream lest his courage be dishonored, though the pain was like a riot or a screaming in her brain.

Saleh felt a stream of warm blood streak her naked breasts. But when she made no sound, the stripe-faced man frowned. He waved aside the glowing iron rod that the one-eyed man was handing him, its hot handle cloth-wrapped, and asked for something else. He was then given a salt box. Showing her his tense, ugly smile, he wet his finger, picked up a little salt, and then dabbed it lightly into the bleeding notch in her tongue.

She gasped and choked but did not cry out. Again, a frown knit the striped brow. Again, the finger dipped into the salt box and brought up a large pile, which he rubbed thoroughly into the wound. This time, the cry escaped her. Although inwardly she was clinging to her gods and ancestors, having not yet discarded them, a cry rose up from a place deeper than where they abided, beyond any human control.

The striped one smiled and nodded to the one-eyed man. Again, the red-hot iron was offered. This time, he took it. There was a searing and the smell of broiling meat. Saleh fainted.

Then, semiconscious, Saleh was untied, taken by two men to the striped one's large cabin, her limbs lashed to his bed's four corners and a rag stuffed into her mouth for the trickling blood. She lay waiting, swallowing the still-oozing blood, her battered face swollen from the beating that the whites had given her the day before at Cape Coast Castle before boarding her and the other slaves. Both eyes were swollen nearly shut, her crushed cheek and broken nose and mutilated tongue radiating waves of pain, like the eternal waves on this great and terrible ocean.

The two men left and the striped one came in. With trembling hands, he quickly undressed himself. A great excitement had hold of him. His penis was large and so hard that it was making little jerking movements toward his belly. The vertical stripe on his nose and forehead was glowing red, as if there was fire beneath the skin.

As he entered the room, he eyed her in what seemed to the bleeding, terrified and miserable girl almost an ecstasy of desire. He threw himself atop her and thrust his way inside her, not ignoring but apparently enjoying her dryness, and at once seemed lost in the most violent pleasure—humping, slapping her, growling, his eyes like mice running over her battered face, her mutilated tongue, his own face puffed in a mottled bloat, his eyes slits as he began a grotesque grunting that was the most repulsive thing she had ever heard.

This was the place in the dream at which Sally awoke, feeling soiled, humiliated and so angry that she could barely breathe ...

But, as the decades passed, she felt less, suffered less. She was sure that all those evil white men from the ship were dead now, did not imagine they could have outlived her now that she was nearing eighty. The dream was like a stage play seen too many times. And now she had it less often—less than once every few years. After all, it was about sixty years ago that those terrible things had happened, when they had killed Kano, sliced her tongue and raped her, and kept raping her all the way across that great unmerciful ocean whose gods in their hidden depths had ignored her.

She remembered the slave market in Charleston, with the white men in shining boots and top hats—cheerful, even playful—as they waited for the sale to begin, but growing long-faced and serious as the bidding for the blacks started. And that tall, spare, white man, very young, with the big nose and yellow hair and piercing blue eyes, staring unblinkingly at Saleh, refusing to be outbid.

Because of her sliced tongue and still-healing face, she recalled the bidding tailing off after thirteen hundred dollars, and then him getting her for thirteen hundred and fifty dollars; the shuttle ship north along the coast and up the broad James River to Richmond; and the wagon driven by the silent, diffident, old black man who took them down to Pinewood Plantation.

Then her immersion into the unending, ever-mutating acid of slavery, the forced learning of the white man's ugly language, coming gradually to understand the delicate folds in the all-covering fabric of his brutality: the slaves who came and went; who broke and died; who were born and sold away; who sassed and were whipped; who attacked the master and were hanged; who ran away and, when recaptured, were sent to the slave breaker's and returned all but dead to keen and breathing life.

And Cicero, that kind man, who took her for a wife despite the fact that she was deformed and lost to love. How little she ever had to give him.

And George, wanting her constantly, as often as he could get clear of the suspicious eyes of Martha Norton Leyland, his bride. He was obsessed by her, especially enjoying deep kisses when he ran his greedy tongue over her split one, until finally, after years and to her disgust, she bore him Young Sally.

This made George so deliriously happy that Sally was shocked and sickened and tried to abort. When she couldn't, she came within a heartbeat of smothering the child at birth. But, in the end, she could not do it, and had to bear George saying that the baby, Young Sally, looked just like him, and that it was a scandal, yet smiling as he spoke, cooing over the little girl.

He also teased Sally about her split tongue and her thick, spitting lisp, ordering her to say, "So swiftly stood Susannah up she swooned," over and over, and laughing until tears came to his eyes.

Saleh's reflections:

> *Kano nevah tol me whut I wath thupoth'd ter promith him. He wathn' in no thape ter thay, an I din athk. In dat dyin time, nothin mattered much. I woulda promithed dat man anyting he athked … an woulda done it too. But now I tink dat I know whut he wanted.*
>
> *He wanted me ter thtay thtrong undah de white man an not looth track of whut wath important: revenge on de white man, who done de coloredth wrong fer thuch a long, long time. It botherth me dat I din do nothin bout it in all de yearth thince. But I got reathonth, which ain't no excuth, but dey good reathonth.*
>
> *I got a chile by Marth Geo'ge, Young Thally. But thee ithn' of much account cauth thee lotht her way, an ended up wantin de white man ter love her. But her girl Mithy ith a diffrint thtory.*
>
> *Mithy ith a tharp girl, a cool girl, but ath thweet lookin ter de white man ath if thee made of thugar. Thee ith thuch a pretty girl, though almotht white-lookin, an de white man geth thtumped by her an cain't tell if thee nigga or white. Mithy can play on dat real good.*

Thee feelth lak I do but don' act lak me. I know dat I put fear in de white man wid my thtrong eyeth an hard faith. Until I got old lak now, I thtill thwung my hipth in dere faith cauth I know dat motht all of dem wanted me.

But none of dem—cept Marth Geo'rge—cared whut I thought bout dem. All dem treat niggath lak half-growed dogth dat dey feed an got de right ter kick. Mithy never let any white man know whut thee ith thinkin. I taught Mithy dat an ev'ting elth I know.

It theemth lak Mithy came into de worl a'ready knowin plenty. Thee an Young Thally are why I ain't done nothin. I needed to be theeing ter dem. An I cain't thtop tinkin dat, if I went ahaid an did whut I had a mind ter do, de white man woulda not jes have killed me, which I don' care if he did or not, but he woulda thold both of dem ter de Thouf, ter de hottetht bottom of Georgia, ter die in de cotton rowth.

Dat Georgia cotton field woulda killed Young Thally daid in a week but not Mithy. Thee hath pity fer no one an nothin, thtartin wid herthef. Thee woulda beared it an gotten round de white man too. Dey woulda never getht'd dat, behine her thmile an thpoony lookth, thee live a life wid no merthy in it. Cauth, at de thame time thee ith thkeeming on yo, thee ith thmiling lak an angel.

How yo gon be an angel wid no merthy in yo? But de white man ith thtupid an eathy ter fool. Dey nevah thee how dere own hatefulneth make de nigga thneaky and theecret. Dey tink dat niggath be jeth dat way by nature. An yet dey be tho thtupid dat dey tink all niggath love dem, ethpethially Mithy.

But, oh! If dey jetht know'd dere ith no way dat Mithy gon thtay a thlave. When de time come, thee ith gon raith up her fitht. Might be dat dith comin war time dere all talkin bout will be de right time fer her ter make her thtrike.

It might be de right time fer me too. Cause, ol ath I am, I haven' forgotten. Oh, no, I ain't fo'got. If I did, it would mean dat I fo'got him.

I won't nevah fo'get him.

No!

Thomas S. Bradford—businessman from Chicago, thirty-eight and married with two children—was a thin, almost fragile-looking, darkly handsome man, with deep brown eyes, wavy black hair and a neatly trimmed beard.

He, by his wife's design, was a believing Christian of the Baptist persuasion who, though loving his family, had repeatedly committed the sin of adultery, suffering on each occasion guilt pangs and experiencing fears of hell. But his compunctions were short-lived, and soon enough he had refreshed his hope of heaven. Then his taste for women—and his willingness to deceive—were splendidly renewed.

He was a successful manufacturer of scythes, shovels, picks and axes, but had taken an interest in the latest smoking fad: cigarettes. He believed that, if he could find a good, dependable tobacco source at the South, he could produce cigarettes fairly cheaply in Chicago and make far more money on them than he was currently making on garden tools.

He had been put in touch with a certain George Leyland, Jr., in Virginia and, after an exchange of several letters each, was on his way to see him, confident that a deal could be made for the supply of good Virginia tobacco, whether or not there was a war.

His journal entry on April 9, 1861, read:

> My wife is right. This is a peculiar time to be traveling South. With all the fuss down at Fort Sumter in Charleston Harbor, many say that a war is imminent. But I simply cannot put off a trial of my ideas until after this much-talked-of war. Anyway, I can't believe that such a war would be very serious or very long.
>
> The South is too economically interwoven with us here at the North and in too many ways to sacrifice all their prosperity to the ravings of a few secessionist lunatics. With virtually no heavy industry, how do they imagine they can survive on their own? They will have to trade with us in any case, will they not?
>
> Factoring in a system of tariffs, which of course do not now exist within the country, obtaining goods from us will cost them far more than at present, and buying from Britain or France even more. Are their politics so persuasive that they would bankrupt themselves to serve them? Surely not!
>
> Oh, I daresay they think that, because England's cloth industry depends on cotton, England will do anything to preserve the trade

connection. But this is fantasy on their part. Even the British clothmakers hate slavery, and more and more reluctantly use cotton produced by it. And if I can read in the papers that England is encouraging cotton plantations in Brazil and Egypt, and is already supplying fifteen percent of her cotton needs thereby, why cannot the southerners read it too and, by it, see which way the wind is blowing?

I simply cannot believe they are fools. They stand nearly alone in the Western World as keepers of slaves. Surely they know in what contempt the world holds them for this? Thus, to go against near universal modern social usage, economic advantage and the benefits of a whole and not a fragmented nation is to all but commit regional suicide. Would any men in their right minds and with an eye to prosperity and the respect of nations do this? I confess that I cannot believe they would.

This trip to Virginia will educate me in more ways than just about tobacco. I shall meet firsthand with these men, who demand independence from us and a national identity of their own, complete with a flag, an army, a navy, civil service, a congress, a president, a system of courts, a merchant marine and a postal service. All this is to be based on the continued legality of slavery, which is rejected as repugnant almost everywhere else in the civilized world.

Above all, I shall for the first time behold this beast of slavery with wide-open eyes and from a near range, so as to judge for myself its beneficence or iniquity. And, I must say, being little traveled but well read, I am very excited at the prospect!

1840

PINEWOOD PLANTATION, VIRGINIA

Young George loved the life into which he was born. Because of his family's wealth and social standing, he was looked upon in his Virginia plantation world in a similar way as the eldest sons of dukes or earls are regarded in England. Also, because it was known that George intended to retire soon from the management of Pinewood in favor of his son—an almost unheard-of windfall for a twenty-four-year-old man from a father only fifty-eight himself—and because Young George was handsome and grand company, there was not a girl of marriageable age in the Virginia district who did not wish to meet him.

Every week, it seemed, some little gathering or other was arranged, at which Young George's presence was most earnestly requested, and which, being vain, he was more than happy to attend. Granting himself the small conceit of an intimate and often shocking diary, he revealed, at the risk of snoops finding out, his real feelings and behaviors.

Of course, he hid the tall, flat book under a false bottom in a dresser drawer where he believed it would never be discovered. In it, he commented frankly on some of the young women who were deliberately put in his way by their mothers at these affairs.

Of one, a certain Sylvania Maria Morrow of Alexandria, whose grandfather had known General Washington and attended his church, Young George had this to say:

> Legs like a pianoforte. Looks a bit spotty and picked over, like cloth at a milliner's. Nice smile though, but too large a straw hat. Tricked her into removing it as we strolled the lawns because her raven hair was so very lovely. On pretense of a walk under the grape arbors, I took her instead

inside our maze hedge. There, I spoke of romance and the joys of love in order to encourage her intimacy. Gave her a few kisses and attempted a feel, but she proved resistant to every blandishment, and her heart was set on marriage, though she has the glance of a doxy. Besides, her conversation is insipid and her accent ugly. She was raised her first ten years in Boston and, because of it, her voice is nasal and thin, as if she spoke through an ear trumpet. So much for Miss Sylvania Maria Morrow.

Describing Miss Dorcas Lee Partridge:

Dear God: Thirty, thrifty and thorny. Her mouth looks like a crack in a dried lemon. But three thousand acres of tobacco and corn land and a hundred and fifty niggers come with her. Uncounted hogs likewise. I could not bear to test her in the maze but instead idled with her for an evening at my parents' fireside whilst they found occupation elsewhere, only looking in occasionally for the sake of appearances, I thinking all the while of her dowry. Then I had a large tot of a good rum punch and, despite her looks, grew lewd.

But she was not to be tempted into bawdy talk, as even the best girls can be if it be done with humor and grace. And, of course, rum. I soon tired of her but, as I was escorting her out to her carriage, passing through the dimly lit entryway, she, walking at my side, suddenly turned to me, put a limp hand on my arm and said, "I would not refuse a chaste kiss from you, sir, for it would serve to broaden our friendship."

In the near dark, I smelled her perfume and sensed her body heat. So, having nothing to lose, gave her the chaste kiss she requested, at the same time slipping a hand down her dress and cupping a teat. It was much like kissing and feeling a statue made of warm soap.

Miss Partridge, however many acres, hogs and niggers you bring, they cannot be enough.

Of his future wife, Elizabeth Gwendolyn Jerrold, Young George wrote:

Charming girl indeed. Innocent, shy, seemingly unaware of the fox hunt that has me as the quarry. All her life, she has been simple and sweet. Being near neighbors of ours, I have known her long. Kissed her once when she was ten. She blushed and ran away. Now I tried her out in the maze hedge, and she let me kiss her. But, when I reached inside her dress, she blanched, then burst out weeping.

"Oh, how wicked I must be for you to think so ill of me as this!"

I was shocked. "How can you call yourself wicked?" I cried. "Tempting, yes. But you must not blame yourself for your own beauty."

"Beauty, sir?" she sobbed. "It is no beauty that tempts a man away from his Christian decency. I pray you will forgive me for my wantonness, which has surely caused this. Pray let us return to the house. I must go home at once."

After futile protests, I did as she asked but begged to call upon her within three days, which she at first refused but then grudgingly allowed. I must admit that I am charmed by this innocent girl. And she has a nice scent as well—of violets, light and ladylike. Not to mention how handy her land lies to ours. No, I admit … especially that.

A later entry:

Ah, how I should love to poke Elizabeth! I never knew before how stiff a woman's innocence could make a fellow. But she has wept each time I tried to advance on her flank, accused herself of wantonness, and I see there is nothing to be done but marry her. And not only that I might fuck her.

I am enchanted with this little dimpled sprite. I feel as good in her lively presence as ever I felt anywhere yet in my life. And the fact that she, being an only child, will inherit Liberty Plantation, thus bringing home the lost Leyland land, which was taken from us by sham after the Revolution, only makes her the more attractive.

Of course, my mother and father, mad for the land, have been after me about her like niggers after a stray chicken. So it will please everyone when I shall propose to her, ask her hand of her father and have banns posted for the nearest date the church and families will allow, and then she will be mine.

I confess that I am happily certain my wayward days will end in her bed. Having her—in all her goodness and beauty—what more could I require? Thus I say, "Lust and sin, adieu! Thy match is met, thy purpose fulfilled in Elizabeth, my sweet mistress of pleasure, good temper and *joy—beside a half square mile of land, houses, fields and above a hundred niggers!''*

After one year of marriage:

At our supper party on Saturday last, Mrs. Myrtle Taylor—whilst her husband, the bloated sot, bellowed about his cleverness with his niggers, quoting DeBow's Review [the favored journal of the slaveholders] until I wanted to feed him an issue of it, and drinking wine like well water— reached beneath the table and between my legs. My God! Who could have foreseen a thing such as that! She is not pretty but has large, soft bosoms, the cleft of which is for all to see but the nipples forever secret. I resolved I must be in the secret.

She said to her husband, "Oh, Roger, how tiresome that you will be in Richmond tomorrow and the day after on business. How I wish I could go and divert myself in the city as you do. I am so envious!'' And then she gave me a look.

Roger Taylor said, "Ah, yes, m'dear, you deserve to go, and you shall go, but not this time.''

By ten in the morning next day, I was in her, and had her twice before the midday, and could not have been happier, tho' I felt some disquiet at the thought that Elizabeth should ever find out. It would break my heart to hurt her, sweet girl. Tho' to be sure, she is more lightly sexed than I had hoped but earnest and gamely willing, to her credit. There is so much to teach recently surrendered virgins, and they do not all have equal aptitude for learning, unfortunately. And it is not my imagination that she has got plump, though she swears it is not so.

Young George sat at breakfast in his dining room. An early riser, like virtually every plantation master who works his slaves "day clean to sunset," he liked his morning meal at six. Outside, his overseer Johnson was instructing Old Uncle Jim—the aging, toothless head driver—and young Black Sulla; upstairs, his wife Elizabeth remained abed.

Sometimes sitting alone had been irksome to Young George because he liked constant diversion. But, more keenly of late, he had been noticing the kitchen slave who waited on him—Young Sally—whom he had known all of her life but never before closely observed. Until very recently, her mother Sally had served at the table, as villainous an old pirate as can be imagined, with the forked tongue of a serpent and slanting, haunting, Asiatic-looking eyes, always tracking him out of their corners. How odd to think an old nigger like her "beautiful," but she was, though like an ancient marble palace, falling by bits to ruin.

His father George, as he had done more than once before, had abruptly dismissed Sally from among the House slaves to live in a field hands' shack alone, her husband Cicero having passed. Elizabeth, who liked Sally's calm, silent, deliberate ways, remonstrated with her father-in-law George to no avail. Though he had turned over plantation management to his son, George occasionally asserted himself and, when he did, would not be denied. In this matter of banishing Sally, he would neither reconsider nor explain; in the end, Young Sally took her mother's place. And now, aging and accustomed mostly to House slavery, Sally, in the cold or burning fields, chopped weeds and hoed and hauled tobacco.

Young George knew that George had sired Young Sally. Who did not know that? Even his mother Martha knew but was stoic, and now, of course, was dead. So was Young Sally his sister? Well, yes, but that was a technicality only. Real relationships arise out of a far deeper connection than a little casually shared blood. But it was odd to see a version of the old man's features looking at him out of Young Sally's beautiful, light brown face.

Still, that did not bother him. And he, like everyone else, knew or suspected why the old man, who no longer took much of a hand in things, had taken such a strong hand in this, sending Sally out to a cruel old age in the fields. Now that Martha was in the ground and George had a clear field with Sally at last, why not move her—not out of the House but actually closer to himself, upstairs even, as a personal servant permitted the run of the place? Was it that he could no longer rise to the bait of the old witch's persisting sensuality? Ah, well. It had nothing to do with Young George. His interest lay only in the younger woman.

She had a soft fall of hair, this Young Sally, unlike the other blacks, though the hair had a slightly different texture than some white women. But this girl had the kindest eyes that seemed like shining mystery windows to her soul, which God for her own good ought to have dimmed in her childhood but never had.

Of course, George had petted her, and she had grown up protected, like most all the mulatto children of planters. However, her father abruptly withdrew his interest and care when she reached her early teenage years, after the onset of menses, which had hurt and puzzled her. Nevertheless, a sweet, diffident, innocent self still peered out at the world through those gorgeous eyes, unable to hide itself, hoping for the best despite contrary evidence; loving despite every coldness, every heartbreak, every betrayal. Not that you could call what his father had done all of those things, of course. Merely a figure of speech. It's the way a man talks who is struck by a woman's beauty of body and soul and is falling in love with her.

Love? No, surely that is the wrong word, what with niggers being so crafty, ungrateful and primitive. And *slaves*, don't forget! They are nothing but *slaves!* This must never, *never* be forgotten, even for a moment. But this nigger girl's eyes … *damn!* It grated, using the word "nigger" on a girl like her. Dear God, you'd almost call her properly civilized, like a white woman—from the sweet, soft, loving look of those eyes. And the very long eyelashes that lay so fetchingly on the very light brown velvet skin of her cheeks when she closed her eyes in endearing confusion.

Her white blood, of course, meant that she was now and would always be ahead of the pack. And her carriage was straight (though she was not tall) and almost elegant, the simple elegance of the naturally beautiful, naturally dignified woman, regardless of color.

Regardless? Can color ever be disregarded? Surely, *surely* not! This is the very top of the slippery slope, is it not—this seeing of blacks as like whites, having white attributes, both races being of one flesh, one heart, one soul? He must not see her as a white who is part black but as a black who is part white. Anything else is madness.

More than one man has ruined his life and disgraced his name by going spoony on a black slave wench. Young George had heard of men actually imagining themselves in love and letting leak this madness to the wider world where it would spread like a pox and deform all they were and might have been. That would be a degeneracy he would never fall into. *Never!*

Six months later …

But still, anyone can see how a fellow might let himself slip. This girl now, this Young Sally. Lord, what a grace of person, what sweet humility—and not the usual sly, eyes-down of the typical House nigger. Her bosoms full yet in perfect proportion. Her lovely, feminine, sensuous hips. And he had seen once the light golden skin of her thigh when walking suddenly into the dining room and catching her with her dress hiked up, fixing a garter. Elizabeth insisted that the House slaves wear proper clothing and not homespun, which she thought drab and unappealing, so the House slave women had well-fitting shirtwaists and petticoats and stockings and garters, and the men dark trousers and starched, white shirts.

The sight of Young Sally's thigh above that garter—how shocked Young George was, how very shocked at the throb of pleasure that had shaken him. Made even more intense by the startled, frightened look in Young Sally's eyes when she knew he'd seen her, and then their eyes met and held. And, for that one long moment, neither looked away, and it seemed as intimate a moment as ever he'd had with a woman, and that too shocked him.

And this feeling of being drawn to her, despite his better judgment, intensifying over the weeks, morning after morning, as he watched intrigued, then beguiled, then enchanted, while she brought dishes in, carried them away, smiled, kept lowered her gorgeous hazel eyes, touched him by chance with her small, pretty hand, murmuring "Excuse me, please, suh."

And finally a feeling taking root in him. A feeling of wanting to rise from the table, reach out for her, bring her close, kiss her and confess all. *All!* Kiss her eyes. Kiss her hands.

He wanted to say to her, "I shall build a nice place for you, most lovely girl, most adorable girl, where you shall live all the days of your life whilst I worship you, and you bear me children to whom when the time be right I shall give my name. Yes, my name. And manumit them! With a settlement for each, in cash. Plus dowries for the girls, small farms for the boys. At the North!

"And you I shall call my real and only and perfect woman despite you being, in a manner of speaking, black. And more than that! I shall give this plantation to Little Master Will and remove to the North. There, my love, we shall live together. Well, perhaps not *give* the plantation but pass it down on the traditional terms.

"No, *wait!* How can I abandon my birthright? Rather, retain all rights but let him act as manager with a higher share of the income than at present. Yes, that's better. I shall keep the plantation's books with me wherever I resettle. He shall employ a trustworthy bookkeeper to send me his sheets of expenses and keep me at every moment informed. I shall visit Pinewood regularly, tho' leaving you behind at the North in placid safety, my own, my only love.

"In any case, I am ready to become a magnate in manufacture, slick as any Yankee, with you by my side, together with our children. I shall give Elizabeth a settlement. The old Leyland land. Put it back in the Jerrold family! Her closest relative being a distant cousin, a Jerrold, she can entail it on him, and let it go in that family across the generations."

Wait, no! What was Young George *thinking?* Certainly it must one day belong to Little Master Will and remain Leyland land, handed down only to a Leyland, again and forever as God intended. According to the law of primogeniture, since old Jerrold entailed it on Elizabeth, and he having no male heirs, that made it truly hers, which really meant *his* (Jerrold thinking no doubt of his seed going forward in Elizabeth and in her progeny for all future time but under the name, as it happened, of Leyland).

Young George felt certain that he would keep that land for himself when the time came. Women cannot own property—even their own inheritances unless unmarried with no male relatives—because a male, especially a husband, always takes precedence. Women have a hard time of it at law, true, but for good reason. If they had their way, nothing but confusion and ruin would result. But Young George was not heartless and would throw Elizabeth a sop—though he couldn't think what.

But no, wait a moment, *this cannot be!* The idea of removing to the North was complete hallucination. He could not bear the thought of it. He could never leave the South. It would be like living without air. Perhaps he would remove to very northern Kentucky, still plant tobacco but be close to Cincinnati in Ohio—a free state, where he and his love could fly were they persecuted and she threatened.

Ah, dear God, what a diseased fancy—just *imagine!* And yet the thought recurring and rising higher, spreading wider, of him taking her in his arms and confessing all, just as if she were white …

As if she were *white!* Oh, the utter, complete insanity of that! Having her, fucking her, yes! *Yes!* Why not let it go at that? Why go on treading dewy-eyed through this endless froth of mental clover?

Why?

1840

PINEWOOD PLANTATION, VIRGINIA

Young George confided to his journal:

Today, as it seemed an incubus possessed me, I could bear no more
dissembling and I, trembling, mad yet lucid, rose to go to her as she
busied herself, clearing dishes from the sideboard. I can tell (or at least
imagine) that she is drawn to me, but no words have passed between
us. I know she suspects but cannot even begin to guess the depth of my
feelings. It would shock her. It shocks me!

Her back was to me. I stepped quietly within her sweet cinnamon
aura as she worked at scraping my plate, putting dishes on a tray ... God,
the scent of her, so unutterably charming. I felt reckless as I took in the
comeliness of her form; the tossing about of her rich, brown hair as she
worked; and her girlish lightness on her feet. She is what?—eighteen years
of age?

And the ideal of the young niggers, all of them trying to spark her.
Word reaches me of these things, yet when before have I ever cared?
When before have I been—dear Lord—jealous? And she is not the first
Negro girl who has attracted me. There were Lucy and Harriet, Salome
and Amanda. With each, I found pleasure and gave each little gifts.
Jewelry, which they loved passionately. Where else might black women,
slaves, acquire jewelry but by the gift of a loving master? All I believe were
satisfied at our dealings, none resentful. Then I thought no more about
them, not who sparked them, fucked them or married them, except of
course as this touched on the slave quality of their children. To be truthful,
I assigned them all mates, having an eye to the best breeding. Simply good
business practice.

But this girl, this Young Sally ... this princess, this ideal of grace and feminine beauty ... how different things are with her.

I put my hands gently on her shoulders. Ah, God, the galvanic shock of her. It was as if she entered into my blood, a phantasm of clear good racing through my veins. Her utterly unique cinnamon-ness (but not really cinnamon—I don't know what it is).

She stiffened. I could hear her sharp intake of breath, feel her tension, but she uttered no word or made any motion. Stock still.

"Young Sally," murmured I, "you are beauty itself."

She hesitated for so long that I made as if to turn her toward me. She resisted.

Finally, in a low voice, not moving, her back still to me, she said, "Young Marse Geo'ge, I pray yo don' drag dis nigga inter sin. Yo church say de same lak mine. It ain't right. No good can come out er it."

"I am not looking for good," I heard myself blurt out. And now I did turn her and saw on her face such a look of fear mixed with shock as truly touched my heart. "Oh, dear girl, I have no desire to hurt you in any way. I am smitten by you. Can't you tell?"

I made to kiss her, but she turned her face quickly away, her hazel eyes showing tears.

"Don' talk lak dat, suh. It don' mattah if yo is smitten, an it don' mattah if I kin tell or I cain't. De end of a ting lak dis is me broke down an sold Souf, an yo sittin heah wif a new nigga ter wait on yo. Dey is nothin evah ought ter pass tween us two but words, suh. An dat is de God's truf."

I was astonished, as I gazed upon her, at the subtlety, the tiny shifting play of light in her eyes, on her face. Those hazel eyes had grown huge with her tears, which now spilled down her cheeks. I was filled with wonder at her crying. Did not crying mean an access of real affection? Was she not saying by these tears, as, in this moment together, that we exchanged with each other our first real and personal words as man and woman, and that somehow she cared?

"Dear girl," I said, raising a gentle hand to her face. "How utterly lovely you are. But why do you weep? Do you care for me? Is that it? Say you do, dear girl. Please say you do."

She shook her head quickly and turned away. "How kin I care, suh? Yo a white man an I is a nigga woman. Yo de mastah an I is de slave. How dem two evah gon join up, cept in a bed fer jes long nuf ter ruin my life? I cain't do it an don' want ter do it. I pray yo will jes leave me be.''

With that, she gave the tiniest curtsey and, taking up the tray of dishes, walked quickly from the room.

I felt breathless, charmed, humiliated, compassionate, angry—caught up in that powerful, insane surge of romantic feeling that unhinges the mind. Immediately, she was gone. I wanted to see her again. I was so delighted in her beauty and scent and strong-mindedness that I wanted to laugh out loud. But so annoyed at her refusal to be drawn out of herself that I ground my teeth. It struck me then that I, God help me, am serious! I am spoony, sotted, stupid about this girl. This madness of mine … it has passed from thought to action!

This is the greatest possible insanity. Yet so seductive that I want to forego the workday, find a secluded glade and wallow there in the soft, rich coils of it all. I have so completely forgotten my wife that it is as if I were never married. And this because of a Negress, a slave woman, an illiterate house drudge, that I have no reason to pursue and every reason not to, who has set me off my sane, sensible course as it seems, and has me thinking love. Is it only her physical beauty? Or also that quivering, childish, sweet, frightened fairy, peeping out from her hidden heart? I know I am florid and stupid. But I cannot help it. I am, more or less, actually in love!

How can this be? And she a slave and, so to say, black?

Well, there is nothing to be done. I must simply get past it and forget what happened this day. If I carry further I will be ruined and she brought lower than low. I cannot contemplate it.

Let it end … or, at least, if it continue, let me not be found out.

1800

SENEGAL RIVER, WEST AFRICA

The Fulani people of West Africa lived in the area near the headwaters of the Niger and Senegal Rivers. As cattle keepers and farmers, they eventually rose to power within what had been the old empire of Ghana but were soon conquered by their neighbors, the Mandinkas.

The Fulani were somewhat different from other West African peoples—lighter skinned and (they believed) more graceful and more physically attractive. Their kingdom of Tekrur touched the Atlantic Ocean at the most westerly point of Africa and extended far inland. They spoke a dialect of Senegalese.

In the hot, dry summer, a gold trader, who was from the Mandinka homeland to the southeast part of Tekrur, traveled from his home city of Mali to a village on the Senegal River, which was about four hundred miles inland from the Atlantic Ocean in the Fulani tribal land. He was hoping to collect a debt from a local cattle herder.

The agreement the gold trader had with the herder, entered into three years previously, had been to lend gold for the purchase of cattle to replace those lost to a persistent drought. Human arrangements being of necessity optimistic, it was assumed when the loan was made that the drought would soon be over. But it continued, year following year, and repayment of the loan, plus interest, was impossible. The Fulani herder suggested the Mandinka accept one of his teenage children—a girl—as a house slave in satisfaction of this debt, but the gold trader balked.

The Mandinka and the Fulani had been for centuries intimately aware of each other's ways. During this long period of Mandinka interaction with the Fulani, during which they had by turns conquered and ruled over each other, there had been continuous intermarrying and removal to each other's lands. The

49

Mandinka trader, being much traveled due to business, had long known the Senegalese dialect spoken by the Fulani.

Thus, the trader's discussion with his Fulani debtor proceeded easily, but he was not pleased at the herder's settlement offer of his young daughter. He already had enough slaves and did not want the trouble and expense first of keeping another one, and then, should she displease him, reselling her, probably by a laborious trip to the "slave castles" along the West Coast where, from the white slavers, he could expect to get the highest price. Accordingly, he refused.

"Why offer me such a useless thing as this girl?" the gold trader asked his host as they sat on the dirt floor of the herder's house in Tekrur. "Give me something of *real* value. After all, you bought cattle with the money I lent you, and it was in a mutually understood number of healthy cattle that you agreed to repay your debt."

"Yes, sir," replied the herder, an old man of fifty and very thin. "I deeply regret that I cannot. But this drought has beggared all of us Fulanis. How can we raise cattle without forage? And from where can we obtain forage when there is no rain? Look around you, sir. This is desperation that you witness. Our concern now is our survival, not the payment of debts. But I am an honorable man, sir, and will satisfy you somehow, even though it cannot be with the healthy cattle I promised you. My most precious possession is this girl I mentioned. She is worth all I owe you and more!" The herder slapped his skinny leg to show sincerity.

The Mandinka shook his head. "I pity your plight, my friend, but since when is a young female slave worth the ten fat cows and the full-grown bull you received from me? Come now, be reasonable!"

But, after much argument, the trader conceded that the man really had nothing else to give him unless he counted the lank, worthless cattle that still survived the drought. Finally, he said that he would agree to at least inspect the girl. The herder nodded to his wife, who left the house. In a moment she returned, leading the girl by the hand.

At the sight of her, the Mandinka was stunned. He had never before seen a creature of such exquisite beauty. She was tall, slender and strong, with high cheekbones, slightly slanted eyes and large, firm breasts. Her hair was worn very short. She seemed almost to glow in her golden brown skin. Her nearly black eyes met the Mandinka trader's fearlessly. Within a single cycle of breath, he fell in love.

The girl's father perceived this and began the process of altering the terms he had just proposed for the settlement of his debt. He now invited the trader to accept instead a number of scrawny cattle, most of the ones he still had left, and withdrew his daughter from consideration.

"Sir," he said to the trader, "I have had second thoughts about this whole matter. Did you just now see the look on my poor wife's face when she realized that our daughter was to be sent away into slavery? No, it is too much to bear. I must squarely face my obligations to you, sir. Though it will ruin me, I know the right thing is to give you my remaining cattle, retaining only a bull and two cows."

Just as he had surmised, the Mandinka passionately objected to this change. After two hours spent in offer and counteroffer, at every moment of which the father realized that he held the upper hand, the daughter was at intervals brought in to stand in front of the bewitched Mandinka before being led away again by the mother. Then the talk changed from the Fulani's settling his debt and giving his daughter into slavery to whether or not he would permit the Mandinka trader to take her in marriage.

At length, a new agreement was decided: The father would give his daughter to the Mandinka, and the trader would cancel all prior debts and give the father two healthy cows and a breeding bull and a leather bag the size of a newborn baby's fist, tightly stuffed with gold dust. He would provide forage for the new cattle and for the existing ones for one year or until the end of the drought.

All the while, the father pretended reluctance but, after the trader had departed with his daughter, he exulted to his wife, "From near disaster, we have been raised to wealth! I cannot believe our good fortune!"

His wife replied, laughing, "Who can say what a man will not do for love?"

The Mandinka trader regretted that he had paid so much for the girl but, as both her parents had clearly seen, his need to possess her was far stronger than his ability to strike a good bargain. The young woman was fifteen years of age. Her name was Saleh. And though she was indeed beautiful, she presented to any man assuming authority over her several distinct disadvantages.

First, she had ideas about almost everything and never felt that anybody else's ideas were as good as her own. For this reason, she was contentious and stubborn. Whenever her new husband directed her to do anything, she either criticized his orders or rejected them completely, seldom hiding from him her low opinion of his "slow-wittedness" and "lack of imagination." Her reaction to his requests were illustrated by their strained relations. For example, when he suggested that she alter her hairstyle to please him, the following exchange took place:

"Although I like your hair, Saleh, I would like it better if you wore it longer and arranged it as the women do here in Mali."

"Would you *indeed?* Well, I too have suggestions. I would like it if you behaved more as the Fulani men of Tekrur do, paying attention to their business rather than to their women's hair."

"*What?*" cried her husband. "How *dare* you compare me to those pitiful cattle keepers who cannot even feed their livestock! Have you forgotten that it was your own father who was about to sell you into slavery before I intervened and saved you?"

"No," said Saleh, her tone indifferent. "Neither have I forgotten that the Fulani are men I can respect, who have the true wealth of land and cattle, while the Mandinka do nothing but dabble in women and trade. And *never* say that you saved me from slavery. Instead, you bought me and thrust me into slavery of a much worse kind."

Conversations like this badly tried the Mandinka's patience.

But it was the second of the disadvantages Saleh presented as a wife that most discouraged her husband: her complete indifference to him in the marriage bed. She would lie under him with open eyes, staring into space, making neither sound nor movement while her husband thrust diligently into her, hoping for at least a tiny squeak of pleasure. But she gave him nothing, resisted his kisses, turned away from his tender touches.

The instant he had spent himself, she said, "Get off of me please, sir. You are heavy."

Also, beside the fact that she was slow to obey him, she imagined herself better than his other wives and declined to speak a single word to any of them in the Mandinka language—though, being quite bright, and already familiar with it, she spoke it well enough to serve.

She had contempt for his religion as well. He was Muslim, and she had no interest in anything to do with Islam but continued (insofar as he could see she had any religious feelings at all) to consult the gods that she worshipped in nature. Her continued unwillingness to speak the Mandinka language, forcing everyone to speak to her only in Senegalese, greatly irritated the other wives, who sneeringly referred to her as "the Queen."

And, worst of all, of course, was her sexual coldness and her refusal to make even a pretense of pleasure. It also greatly annoyed him that she was forever performing ceremonies of purification—for, aside from its being a heathen practice offensive to Islam, there was the unspoken but obvious implication that he and his entire household were unclean.

Finally, after living almost a year under his roof, Saleh had so exasperated the Mandinka that his fascination with her was gone and his other wives were in rebellion. He set about her father's original plan of finding a suitable buyer for her. He knew that he should be able to get thirty-five pounds sterling for her, which represented a profit over what he estimated he had invested in her and would provide more capital for his trading ventures in Mali. Besides, his three other wives together were not half the trouble to him that this Saleh had proved to be.

So, when on a business trip he was introduced to a black slaver middleman, he arranged for him to come to his house, inspect Saleh and make an offer. The sale was quickly concluded to his satisfaction, and Saleh was handed over. As she was being led away, to the jeers of the other wives, she ignored them and mutely stared at him with the same contempt she had shown all along.

The look in her dark eyes said, "What else should I expect from a man such as you?"

The Mandinka was furious, but at least he had the last laugh: He had gotten his thirty-five pounds sterling!

1801

CAPE COAST CASTLE, WEST AFRICA

The black slaver middleman took Saleh and sixteen other newly acquired slaves, lashed together and driven along by his assistants, southwest to the English at Cape Coast Castle on the Gold Coast of the Great Ocean, north of Accra and Anamabu. There, releasing the sixteen other slaves into the huge underground holding cells of the castle—the great, ugly, stone edifice in which the captives were kept locked until called for by the slave ships—he took her to his nearby house to enjoy her himself for a few days.

As she lay inert on his bed, the slaver frowned. "Your husband was right," he said with irritation. "Despite your beauty, you are graceless as a sow. What sort of man would want a woman who lies awaiting him, looking all but dead?"

"A man such as you," Saleh replied contemptuously.

And indeed she proved a disappointment to the slaver just as she had to her husband, and remained in open defiance of him. She so irritated him that he wanted badly to beat her. But, of course, he had to be careful not to harm her, especially not to cut or bruise her, for he was certain that the English would pay at least forty pounds for her and probably more.

So especially beautiful and compelling were her looks he was likewise certain that, at Charleston in South Carolina or Kingston in Jamaica, she would fetch sixty or even eighty pounds, though in Charleston the trade would be in American currency and would amount to about twelve hundred to sixteen hundred dollars.

This was a high price for a woman who as yet spoke no English and had no training in the white man's domestic arts—for they certainly would not make a field slave of her, at least not yet. It was also unknown if she could be successfully bred, though she looked healthy and perfectly normal.

Still, the slaver was convinced that Saleh would fetch a high price—partly because she was beautiful and stirred men's desires, but also because she was tall, strong, plainly capable of hard work and most likely good for at least ten years of breeding, which could yield up to six or seven high-quality baby slaves or, with luck, even more. Also, she was Fulani, who, as a tall, light-skinned race, were popular in Charleston as house slaves, where dealers were particular in preferring them and others like them, such as Gambians.

The slaver was scrupulous in knowing his own markets as well as his clients'. He knew, for example, that Calabars from further south on the Slave Coast were hard to sell in America. The Calabars' beliefs about a heavenly afterlife encouraged them to commit suicide at the first opportunity after capture, to the consternation of men like the slaver and all his potential clients. Yet it was almost as bad if they survived, for they were sulky, uncooperative and, coming from a culture in which there was much ritual human sacrifice, dangerous besides.

Paradoxically, a good Calabar was good as good can be. But they were so few amongst the dangerous many that it was a bad business decision to buy one of their tribe. Many a Georgia, Louisiana or South Carolina planter had rued the day he had ever bought a Calabar at the slave auction. Thus, Calabars were, except in those rare cases, a waste of time and money to capture or broker. He had not succeeded so well at his trade by remaining ignorant of the resalability of his own goods.

But Fulanis were a sure thing. They were little good in the fields but made excellent butlers, stewards, carriage drivers, ladies' maids, nannies, housekeepers, gardeners, animal handlers and cooks. A female of such beauty, strength and grace as this Saleh was rare and, assuming that she survived the sea voyage, certain to be vied for at auction.

The British Royal African Company's castle at Cape Coast stood about eight miles southeast along the inwardly curving African Coast from its sometimes bitter rival, the formerly Portuguese (now Dutch) establishment of Elmina. These installations were called "castles" because they were built solidly of stone with walls many feet thick to withstand attacks either by white rival slave empires— the Portuguese, the Dutch, the French, the Danes—or by local kings with a grievance. (The English referred to all tribal chieftains as "kings.")

The English castle at Cape Coast gave the appearance of disorder, even shabbiness, especially in comparison to the neat, bright and orderly façade of Dutch Elmina, where the interior hallways, courtyards and bed chambers reflected the solidity and elegance of an Amsterdam drawing room. But Cape Coast, though it looked disheveled and disreputable, was impregnable from the sea, standing over a narrow, rock-strewn beach with only a modest-sized pier along a seawall below one of its flanks.

The castle was built, like the castles of medieval Europe, around a huge, paved, inner courtyard that drained in the direction of the water. Inside were nicely appointed rooms for the English general agent and his factors, including the small garrison of His Majesty's marines on permanent duty station as security to the slaver businessmen. So, although there was a sense of general disorder, there was also a satisfactory amount of comfort.

Carved out of the rock itself under the castle were the great, cavernous dungeons that held a thousand slaves. And though these quarters were dark, filthy, wet and putrid, it was recognized that keeping the slaves underground was a wise arrangement since it better protected the white management against uprisings.

Rebellion, of course, was one of the two great risks for investors in the slavery business; the other was the tendency of slaves to die in the hot, airless holds of the slave ships during the long, transatlantic sail (the Middle Passage). The three legs of this grim triangle were New England to Africa with rum and trade goods, Africa to Jamaica and the U.S. southern seaboard with slaves and thence to New England with molasses or sugar. Slaves also, and frequently, had a tendency to actually jump overboard if not tightly bound when brought on deck.

Now, this African slaver middleman—a Mandinka from east of Mali, who managed to get by in five African languages, and numerous African dialects as well as English and Dutch—had, at the insistence of the English, taken a fetish oath (a vow backed by the power of a personal possession, such as a stone or a feather, which has spiritual significance) not to trade with the Dutch at Elmina.

With the English general agent at Cape Coast—a certain John Potts, assisted by his Fante wife Ti—watching him intently, he had brought forth his fetish. It was a small pouch of magically empowered items, such as bird feathers, sacred river stones, certain herbs and other little objects, including bones, whose provenance was mysterious.

The middleman swore never to sell slaves to the Dutch, at the risk of his fetish losing its power. He honored this undertaking whenever convenient, though he certainly never believed that African gods could be offended by a breached agreement with whites—who were, after all, ignorant, dishonest, smelly, brutal and untrustworthy men. He knew that the English thought themselves above fetish oaths, and only forced him to take one because they saw him as a savage whose whole life was driven by dread of his gods.

Yet they themselves wore the fetish of the Jesus god, keeping it always on chains around their necks and wearing it continuously—partly, he assumed, for protection, at night. Certain of the white men even tried to win him over to worship the Jesus god, saying that Jesus was the only true god, that he saved through love and the cross was not a fetish. But if Jesus saved through love, then no white man whom the slaver had ever met was saved, for they were all treacherous and violent and as far removed from love as fire from water. Thus, Jesus couldn't be much of a god.

And besides, the slaver's experience had shown him that all men possessed fetishes and, in some manner, swore on them, and that any man of any color would break his oath if given sufficient inducement. The slaver's only unshakable oath was one that he, like many other men both black and white, had made to himself: Never neglect any opportunity to do profitable business.

In the case of this female Saleh, he saw more potential on the British than on the Dutch side. The Dutch were not as inclined either to drink or debauchery as the British, who, in the matter of lust-provoking females, were easier to tempt to higher prices. The slaver thought that this greater clarity of purpose on the part of the Dutch—though, to be sure, they were dangerous and fickle, like all other white men—was responsible for their having displaced the Portuguese all along the Gold and Slave Coasts, even to occupying their great fortress of Elmina, while the British persisted on at Cape Coast Castle, slovenly, often drunk, their grounds unkempt and their apartments messy.

Yet despite this, there was one undeniable fact: The British had created and were able to service a much vaster world market for slaves than the Dutch, the

Danes, the Portuguese, the Spanish, the French or anybody else. Through their factors in Jamaica alone, the British provided slaves for all the sugar plantations in the Caribbean, which was a constantly hungry market. Because of the hot weather, brutal working conditions, poor quarters, bad food and uncontrollable tropical diseases there, even strong slaves lasted but a few years.

And after a particularly bad die-off, prices would skyrocket, which was good for everybody—for the slave takers of the African interior, for African middlemen, for the proprietors of the slave castles at the trading ports, for the ships' captains and for the slave dealers in the cities of destination, which for the English included, beyond Jamaica, most of the ports of the long American seaboard from Massachusetts all the way down to Florida.

At Cape Coast Castle, the slaver was able to get fifty pounds sterling for the girl, bargaining steadily and with good humor, for the British factor John Potts was unable to disguise the lust the slaver middleman could see flickering in his watery blue eyes. In the end, he went away feeling satisfied with himself for a deal well made and a job well done.

1798

THE FULANI LANDS OF WEST AFRICA

Saleh, though not descended from the kings of the Fulani, had in another way an almost royal lineage. She was the niece of Tenkaminen, the sorcerer. Because Tenkaminen was intimate with so many gods, it was assumed that their jealousy for his undivided attention had kept him childless with three different wives. Having neither sons nor daughters of his own, and his brother's—Saleh's father's—only son being dull from birth, it was to the bright, intense, thirteen-year-old Saleh that he found himself teaching what he knew.

It was the custom for grandfathers to take grandsons under their protection and tutelage and for grandmothers to do the same for granddaughters. The parents were not ignored, though it was understood—as it had been through all human time—that children should look for knowledge of their people and their heritage from their grandparents.

In Saleh's life, her uncle took the place of a grandmother, her own grandparents on both sides being dead. So the already powerful bond of his acting as mentor and advisor to Saleh was intensified by Tenkaminen's having chosen Saleh as his successor in sorcery and having for some years immersed her in the many-leveled initiation this entailed.

He could see that she was born for it. She was quick to understand everything he taught her. He was especially impressed at how she grasped and retained the intricacies of ritual. She also had, though still a child, an intuitive knowledge of people's hearts, which he had not mastered until he was forty years of age, practically an old man.

For example, when sick people came to him, seeking release from spells cast on them by enemies, Saleh sometimes would whisper in his ear, "Uncle, I do not think this one is under another's spell. I think a god is angry with him for some wickedness of his own. His heart is corrupt."

Often, the old sorcerer had already discerned this, but other times he had missed it. Upon a deeper examination of the supplicant, he saw that Saleh was right.

Of course, he also taught her about the healing plants. Every patient received from him herbs with instructions to prepare them for use as poultices or teas, or as charms against enemies. Everyone who came received something tangible to take away, or else they would have felt ill served.

Sometimes Saleh went alone to the river. There, more than at any other place, she imagined that she could hear the voices of the gods coming from a whirlpool in the river and from a great stone in its watercourse. She believed that she drew certain understandings about life from sitting so close to them.

The God of the Whirlpool revealed to her the radical twists her life was destined to take, while the God of the Great Boulder that lay in the stream below the whirlpool showed her how her life must be anchored inwardly. Her family and friends made light of her Little Gods, as they called them, thinking them mere cranky nature spirits whose ability both to help and harm was limited.

These others preferred the gods of the sun, moon and stars; of the thunder, the winds, the lightning, the mountains, the storms; and of the river's great rapids and falls, whose energies were manifest and clearly ruled the natural world. These gods, they felt, had the real power over human life and destiny and must be worshiped more than any others.

Also, and of even greater importance, was the consultation of the ancestors to whom it was absolutely vital to make frequent sacrifices and perform rigorously detailed rituals. If these were neglected, there was no hope for success, health or happiness in life but only the constant anxiety attendant upon any disrespect of one's forebears, who abided in the invisible realms and who could and did punish lapses. Saleh respected her ancestors and made appropriate sacrifices, even as her parents did.

But she was powerfully drawn to the intimacy she found with the so-called Little Gods. Sometimes she really felt that they spoke to her—not as audible voices but as inner ones that seemed to push her toward some thoughts and away from others. She was not afraid of them but felt them as a sort of loving force, and believed, against the teachings of her elders, that they were as powerful as any of the gods and, for her, the most powerful of all.

This sitting with the gods increased her intuitiveness so that sometimes she could divine people's secret inner selves and tell if they lived good or bad lives and what they might be hiding from the eyes of the world. But, as she used this intuition more, she tended—because of her arrogance—to exaggerate to herself the times she was right and forget the many times she was wrong.

The one thing Saleh had never learned was humility. She could not bear the thought that she might ever be wrong about anything. Never did she doubt herself, even when prudence or evidence required it. Nor did she respect others—elders included—although, of course, she feared the ancestors, for she was certain that they saw deeper and better into life than anybody else. It would be some time before she even began to realize how materially this attitude affected her. Meanwhile, despite her gifts, she and others suffered from her arrogance, never realizing that the very real limitations, which she could always see in others, were also and especially her own.

In due season, after Saleh passed through the painful initiation ceremony of womanhood, involving the removal by the women of her clitoris and a period of time in isolated retreat, her uncle said only, "You are a woman now."

Saleh was silent for a long time.

Then, turning away from him, standing in the open doorway of his house, and speaking as if to the sky or the forest, she said, "I hear that I will not be able to live as a grown woman in Tekrur. I hear that I will have to go away."

Assuming she meant that she had heard this from the gods, Tenkaminen said, "I see," but it troubled him. There was a silence, and then he asked, "What else have you heard?"

Saleh delayed answering, then turned slowly to him and met his gaze. As always, there was no fear in her eyes but simply, it seemed to him, an awareness, if not yet an embracing, of what she took to be her destiny.

"I do not know if any of this is true. These are only things I seem to hear when I sit by the great stone in the river or by the whirlpool. But it has happened many times now. Always it feels the same. It isn't really hearing, but hearing is the closest word I can find for it. It is more like feeling but as if feeling had a voice."

She stopped speaking. Her uncle waited. Then she said, "I hear that I will marry a man I cannot love, and love a man I cannot marry."

Tenkaminen nodded. "What further?" He did not know if she would or could tell him.

There was another long pause. He was prepared to let the subject drop. In this matter of intimacy with the gods, every man and woman is guided as to what can be spoken and what not and to whom.

At length, she broke the silence. "I hear that I will die in slavery," she said quietly.

He was shocked and almost cried out, "No, you must be mistaken!" Instead, staring at the hard-packed dirt floor of his house where they were alone together, he asked, in a voice as quiet as hers, "*Nearby?*"

"I don't know. Maybe far away. I keep imagining white men, though I have never seen one."

"When?"

"I don't know."

"I see."

Up to now, it had been the voice of a grownup speaking. Now, suddenly, it became that of a child: frightened, unsure, hoping for salvation.

"Uncle, do you think I am mistaken?"

He saw her lower lip trembling. His heart felt wrenched. Now, it was he who waited to reply, gazing at her beautiful, strong face and at the slowly welling tears.

At length, he said in an empty-sounding voice, "I don't know."

Without further words, she turned, softly crying, and left her uncle's house.

Saleh was thirteen years old. In two years, the Mandinka trader would come. And in three, she would be sold to the whites at Cape Coast Castle.

1860

PINEWOOD PLANTATION, VIRGINIA

After a particular and memorable encounter on the edge of the West Field at sunset one evening, Little Marse Will could not get Missy out of his mind. She was eighteen but seemed so much older, more mature. She was practically white and spoke like a white woman, and many times confused him as he watched her go about her duties as his little sister's nanny by how calm and sweet and unslavelike she was.

Miss Margaret Leyland (Peggy), Little Marse Will's sister, was tutored by the assistant minister of their Episcopalian parish church, Mr. Howard Parker Mann. He came twice a week and left lessons for Peggy to do between times. Missy sat with Peggy while she did these, though Missy was supposedly illiterate herself. But, one day, when Little Marse Will was passing down the hallway outside Peggy's room, he heard voices and stopped to listen.

Peggy, who was eight, was saying, obviously upset, "Missy, I just can't figure out this dang map! Everything's all turned around. Some of these words go sideways and some are upside down. I'm supposed to show Mr. Mann all the states and name the capitals when he comes again. Mr. Mann says Virginia's on this map, and all the other states too, but he's coming tomorrow and I still can't tell if these lines here are rivers or if they're boundaries. I just feel like the dumbest fool there ever was!"

"Well, Miz Peggy," Missy said in her calm voice, "let's just take our time and look." There was a pause, and then she said, "What's this word I'm pointing to?"

Another pause. Peggy cleared her throat. "Richmond?"

"Yes, exactly! And so what's *this* one? See, it's much bigger print."

A long pause. "Is that one Virginia?"

"Well, you tell *me*, now. What's this first letter?"

"That one? That's a 'V,' isn't it?"

"Yes, it is. And the next letter?"

"An 'I'?"

"So just look at the whole word and sound it out."

"Vir-gin-i-a?"

"Yes, Miz Peggy, that's *right!* It's not so hard, is it?"

There was warmth in Missy's voice. Little Master Will liked the sound of that. He liked that Missy was kind to his little sister. But it troubled him that she was reading. A state law strictly enforced at Pinewood was the law against teaching slaves to read.

Little Master Will stepped into the room. Missy and Peggy were sitting next to each other at a table with a map spread out in front of them. Both had their heads down and their index fingers resting on the map.

Peggy was blonde, a small edition of her mother and already a little plump. Missy had on the white shirtwaist and long, blue skirt she generally wore when she cleaned the upstairs or companioned Peggy.

Missy looked up, saw Little Master Will and immediately smiled, rose to her feet and made a full curtsey. Niggers usually did not curtsey, for this was reserved to white women. But Little Master Will found himself not minding.

"Good morning, sir," Missy said.

Peggy sat where she was but glanced up at her brother with obvious pleasure. "Willie," she said, showing dimples in her cheeks, "I'm learning about maps. I just now picked out Virginia. Before that, I figured out Richmond. See, all the words are printed cockeyed, and it takes some doing. But I *did* it!" Her smile widened.

Missy folded her hands at her waist, then smiled at Little Master Will. "Yes, sir. Your sister is a very intelligent child."

Little Master Will stood silent for a moment. A smile played around his mouth, but he did not give in to it. His gray eyes looked somber.

He was tall—six feet—taller than either his father or grandfather and strongly built. His face was pleasant more than handsome, for he had the family's rather large nose, but his smile was winning. He wore his curly blonde hair cropped at the collar and combed back over his ears. His shoulders were wide and his hands large. It seemed absurd that he was called "Little" Master Will. But the name referred to his place in the family, not his size. That was how things were at the South. At twenty, he might not even be finished growing. He could yet put on more bulk if not height. He already weighed close to one hundred and ninety pounds.

Finally he spoke. "How is it you can read, Missy? We've never had a slave here who could."

He was torn between threatening and accepting. He was coming to realize that there was something about this girl he did not want to alienate.

Missy did not seem disturbed, but her smile grew more modest. "Your father taught my mother to cypher, sir, and she taught me. Your father used to read me stories when I was very small. I sat on his lap. That was over at my mother's house. He would point to where he was reading, and it just seemed natural that I learned. I did not plan it. It just came about."

Her eyes held his strongly with no apology but with deference. Very nice indeed. But now, he had the choice to be silent or to reprove. He was struck by her naturalness in referring to her mother's house as though it was the most normal of slave accommodations and his father's presence in it completely unexceptional. Of course, she did not say "our" father's house. Only a mad-woman would do a thing like that. And it did trouble him, increasingly now, that she might be—no, she almost certainly *was*—his sister.

But then, as if reading his mind, she said, "It is odd, I admit, sir, because nei-ther my mother Young Sally nor my father Decatur can read a word, but here I am reading despite the fact that I never meant to learn."

Still, he hesitated. Then he said, "Just step outside in the hall with me for a moment."

Missy nodded and at once bowed her head as he preceded her into the hall. She followed, shutting the door on Peggy's look of puzzlement.

"You know this is a very bad thing, don't you? Our niggers don't read. Never have. It's not our custom here. And it's against the law. What do you say if my father finds out?"

"He knows, sir."

Little Master Will was shocked. "He does? My father *knows*? What does he say?"

"He says," Missy replied, softly but firmly, "that if it was anybody but me, he'd have them whipped. But he knows that my heart is completely given to this family, and that I would never hurt or humiliate him for anything in the world. Besides, he knows I can help Miz Peggy better if I can read."

Little Master Will frowned. "But my mother doesn't know, does she? Surely you realize that she has never been especially, uh, fond of you. And, if she knew you could read … my God, it would be a problem—*that* much I know."

Missy lowered her eyes. "I know there was a time she was not fond of me. But I have always loved and respected her. I think she realizes that now. She has taught me to sew—did you know that? I have a talent for it, she says. Just lately, she has had me make her a dress. I made one for Miz Peggy too. I love this family so very much!" Here, she raised her shining hazel eyes to Little Master Will's blue ones. "It distressed me when your mother would put me out of the House and away from Miz Peggy," she went on. "But always your father stepped in and had me brought back. Yet I knew your mother did not approve, and I was so torn, so hurt ..."

By now, Little Master Will had forgotten that the original subject was Missy's knowing how to read. It seemed to have shifted to how much she loved the Leylands, and how honored and joyful she was when they allowed her to serve them in even the smallest ways. For a moment, he stared into her eyes, taking in her sincerity, innocence, good-heartedness and warmth.

God, he thought, *she was barely a nigger at all!*

But then he heard himself say, "Well, never mind."

He had omitted to mention that she had not quite answered his question about whether or not his mother knew she could read. Perhaps he did not want to know. And certainly, you only had to take one look at Missy and Peggy together to know that Peggy would never tell on Missy, even if they twisted her ears or pinched her till she cried. And if his father knew—and approved—why should he interfere?

He looked at Missy's face for a few moments longer. He wanted to find a reason to stay talking to her. Then he had an idea.

"I want to make myself a room in the attic. There's plenty of space and nobody uses it."

Again, as if knowing his thoughts, Missy said, "Oh, sir, I hope you will let me clean it out for you! I'll wash the floors and windows and get up all the dust. And you can have anything moved in that you want, and I will see to arranging it nicely. That is, if you would like."

That afternoon, Little Master Will took Missy up to the attic. He had no more closed the door behind them than he found her standing so close to him, looking at him with such openness, such admiration. Before he knew what he was doing, he pulled her into his arms.

She came without reserve, passionately, whispering as their lips drew close, "I have wished for this moment!"

He locked the door and made love to her. She was not a virgin. He did not care or ask her to explain. He knew the realities of the quarters. And come to that, there were plenty of white girls who were not virgins either—some of them because of him. And he had no intention of getting entangled with this girl as his father had done with Young Sally and his grandfather with Sally.

But he was no more parted from her than he found himself thinking about her, not casually but with a burning inside his chest that oppressed yet galvanized him. So, the next day, he again invited her to the attic. And it was not long before it was "their place" as it had, many years earlier, been the place his grandfather George had taken her grandmother Sally.

He tried not to think that she might be his half-sister. When he doubted, he tried to remember her face as she said, "My father Decatur," and was for that moment comforted. He wanted to ask his father for the truth but did not dare. And he knew what his mother thought. She had not kept her opinion secret from anyone—although now Missy's grace and goodness had apparently begun to win her over.

So, despite knowing better and intending better, Little Master Will did just what the Leyland men before him had done: He fell madly in love with a slave woman; swiftly came to the place where he could deny her nothing; and had fantasies of fleeing to the North with her, having children with her and making her the center of his life. It was not long before he trusted her and told her everything he knew—every bit of Leyland gossip and every wayward thought, fact, opinion.

Missy rarely asked him anything but was so attentive and interested that he admired her all the more for her exquisite discrimination and reserve. He had experienced quite a few women before her—some slaves, a few white prostitutes in Richmond and a quite attractive virgin, who had expected but not gotten marriage. There had been a little trouble about that one, but it soon blew over, and he was left with his good reputation intact.

But nothing had prepared him for the passion and possessiveness Missy roused in him. Nothing …

1801

CAPE COAST CASTLE, WEST AFRICA

Saleh stood naked—except for a small loincloth—in the large, stone court-yard of Cape Coast Castle. Nearby, a group of exhausted, filthy, terrified black men were being released one by one from a middleman's rope, taken into custody by rough-looking, unsmiling white men and hammered into leg shackles on the spot.

The black men were muttering and moaning to each other, their faces pinched with pain and fear, their hands in constant gesticulation. They were short, dark men—nothing like Fulanis. Saleh could not understand a word of their rapidly spoken language, and the emotions under which they labored also distorted their speech. There were about twenty of them.

Saleh pitied them in their fear. She could see that they had not found a god like hers of the great river stone, who had taught her to make a strong anchorage within. Only one of them stood calmly, not even looking down at the white man who was securing his ankles in large, iron rings with a connecting chain. He was muscular, very dark, with a quiet look to his features, powerful hands hanging at his sides. Occasionally, he rubbed at his wrists where the middleman's ropes had chafed them.

His body was turned slightly away from her to facilitate the white man's shackling. He glanced in her direction, then suddenly turned his face fully toward her and smiled, and she, surprised, looked away.

What sort of a man smiles in a place like this? Saleh asked herself. *Does a man's lust never desert him? Will he womanize even in a fever, under torture, on his deathbed?*

Yet this man's smile was different. There did not seem to be lust in it. But of course, with men, you never knew. She glanced back at him.

Just then, another man, who appeared to be the overseer of the kneeling white man working on the shackles, shouted, "Stand still, you bloody nigger!"

And, raising a small lash with multiple thongs, he slashed the calm, smiling black man a hard blow across his shoulder and neck. Saleh had never seen a man whipped before. Nor—though she had heard much about them—had she ever seen a white man until she was handed over by the slaver middleman to this one with the whip. She gasped. At the same time, the other male slaves let out a collective shriek and began to run about clumsily, tripping over their chains, sprawling, screaming, looking with wild, desperate eyes for a way to escape.

The whip man began to stride about methodically, lashing each of them, yelling "Back in *line*, you goddamn black sons of bitches! Back in *line* … back in *line*," every phrase emphasized with a hard blow to one of the men's bodies.

The slaves were utterly terrorized, never before having thought of themselves as slaves or even likely to fall into bondage, but the white men ignored their shock because they were so used to looking at black men as slaves or slave traders—in every way inferior to them and perhaps not even fully human.

Other white men had been standing about. Some of them looked different from the rest and wore red coats and tall hats. Saleh would later learn that they were soldiers. They had guns. She had seen guns before. Now they moved leisurely forward, chatting amongst themselves and laughing, and began clubbing the black men with short, sharp blows of their rifle butts—not on the head but on the arms and shoulders and chests.

The frightened black men cried out in pain but allowed themselves to be herded back together, as they came to understand that the beatings would not stop until they did. The men in red coats then turned their rifles around. On the opposite ends were long knives. These they thrust out toward the black men, pricking at their skin, pushing, nudging, until the men were aligned again and quieting down.

One of the black men, hysterical, had rolled into a ball on the ground, from where neither whip nor rifle butt could move him. He was shaking, his face buried in his knees, crying out loudly, sobbing. He ignored the soldiers and the whip-carrying white man.

Finally, one of the soldiers gave him a sharp stab in his side with the long knife. At once blood flowed. The man leaped up screaming and, despite his chains, staggered and shuffled as fast as he could go in the direction of the stone wall that surrounded the courtyard. He tried to throw himself over it into the sea below, but the soldiers caught him and dragged him back. He broke free, lowered his head and bashed it against the wall. This made a terrible, gruesome sound, like a gourd being crushed with a club. He was staggering back to ram his head again when the soldiers surrounded him.

"Put the bastard on the ground, boys!" the white man with the whip shouted.

And, as the soldiers slammed the bleeding, dazed man to the paving stones of the courtyard, the white man with the whip rushed over and began to lay stroke after stroke on the black man's back.

"I'll teach you, you goddamn devil! See if you disobey my orders *now*. Just see!"

He whipped harder and harder. Blood began to fly from the gouges the whip was making in the new slave's back. As the blood flew about, the soldiers stepped away, keeping their knives pointed at the prisoner in case he tried to rise. But he now lay motionless as the blows descended and his crushed head bled freely, and the white man, tired out and red-faced, and covered with blood flecks, his breath heaving, straightened up, a triumphant grin on his face.

"There now, by god. *There* now. See how you like *that*, you damned villain!"

The soldiers chuckled. One of them said, "Good job, Mr. Potts."

"Well, get him up and put him in the cells," Potts, the man with the whip, said. But then it was noticed that a large pool of blood was spreading out from where the man lay. It was a very vivid red against the darkness of his skin.

"Damn it all, Sgt. Robertson, I hope you didn't nick his liver," said Potts to the soldier who had stabbed the man. "Get him up. Let's have a look."

The soldiers, four of them, took hold of the man from each side and tried to raise him. As the soldiers tried to make him stand, his legs were lifeless and his bare feet slid out from under him in the pool of his blood. His head hung down, gently swinging with the motion of his body being manhandled.

"Oh, son of a goddamn poxy bitch!" yelled Potts when he realized the man was dead. "Now there's twenty pounds gone. I might as well have thrown it in the sea as paid it to that sneering little nigger slaver. Look here! It's only two-thirty. I paid that twenty pounds at two o'clock!"

Turning angrily on the soldier called Sgt. Robertson, he shouted, "What in hell do you think you're about, stabbing him like that? Do you imagine that

HOWARD BOTT

you're in a battle with a bloody regiment of *Dutchmen*? This was just one stupid nigger, like the hundreds we have here every day. What do you want to go killing him for?"

"Well, I don't *want* to be killing him, do I?" Sgt. Robertson shouted back, cracking his rifle butt on the stones in irritation. "You don't think your beating the very *shit* out of his body had anything to do with his dying, I suppose?"

The soldiers let the dead body slump to the ground.

"Watch your tongue, you!" retorted Potts. "Remember who the factor is here and who is only a garrison soldier not fit for duty in England. *Remember* that!"

"Oh, yes, Your Grace," said Sgt. Robertson, sweeping off his hat and bowing. "I know what sacrifices Your Grace has made to come amongst us wretched bastards here in Africa. All the high positions in England you refused—the ambassadorships, the earldoms. There is no end to your goodness."

Saleh had noticed all this time the smell in the air of men who had been drinking. All of these white men had been drinking. And at least two of them—the two fighting, Potts and Sgt. Robertson—she could tell were drunk.

Inwardly, she spoke to her God of the Great River Rock: *Help me, Lord. Help me survive the madness of these demons.*

And inwardly, she seemed to hear, "Now you are at the ocean. Very powerful gods live within the ocean. They are my allies. Speak to them."

Saleh composed herself and reached out to the gods of the vast water world. As the drunken white men continued arguing, and the black man lay dead in his own blood at their feet, and as other white men chimed in and the arguing spread, and the black men chained by the ankles stood shaking with horror in this hellish place, Saleh began to listen to the unfamiliar sound of the waves as they broke against the narrow beach below the castle wall. Raised inland, she had never seen the ocean before.

Since nobody was paying attention to her, she moved carefully to the wall and looked over. For the first time, she beheld the long, blue combers; saw the surf; felt even through the castle's stones the echoing of the earth under the eternal pounding—and understood at once that this must indeed be the abode of very powerful gods. One of them—the God of the Ocean Shore—seemed to speak to her:

"Your gods have told me of you. Now, I will be your god also. In this place away from your home and your people, I will be your resource. There is no quiet here, only turbulence and sorrow. You will not find the peace you had at the river. But those times laid up a store of quiet inside you. Now, you must draw from it, even though all around you is fear and chaos. Turn your mind toward me in the night, and I will teach you."

Saleh glanced across the courtyard, over the bloody corpse and wrangling drunkards, at the dark muscular man who had smiled at her, had silently borne the whipping and accepted calmly the other slave's death. He stood, his arms folded on his chest, looking at her.

And, again, he smiled.

John Ebenezer Potts was born in 1753 in Dudley, Worcestershire, to an ordained minister of the Church of England and his wife, a low church, "chapel" Methodist who converted before marriage. Potts was schooled as were his duller siblings. But, unlike them, he received high marks in each of the three things he studied: mathematics, reading and composition. Once he could read, the world of the sea opened to him through books, and he thought of little else.

Being denied permission by his father to enlist in the navy where his learning would qualify him as a midshipman, he elected to go to sea however he could. Taking what little money he could find and a change of clothes, he left home in the night and made his way down to the London docks and signed on (to thwart any pursuit by his parents) to the ship with the earliest departure date.

This happened to be a slaver—the Mary Louise, eight hundred tons, twelve guns—that was sailing for the African West Coast on the next day's tide with a cargo of tools, knives, firearms and rum. Potts had been in the slave trade ever since and had obtained thus far a fortune of nearly fifty thousand British pounds, which would allow him to retire in comfort, at any time he elected to do so, on an estate in the County of Worcestershire, near Dudley, just across the county line from Tipton, Staffordshire.

He bought and paid for this impressive manor through profits from his slave dealings. He took it on faith that the estate was lovely and its house grand. He had never seen it nor been in England since he was eighteen years of age. He had intentions of seeing it someday and taking up residence in it. In the meantime, the agent who found the property for him was in residence there, on salary, as its manager.

Potts was the chief factor at Cape Coast Castle. He hesitated to leave Africa, was not sure if he wanted to or even if he could. He had a Fante wife named Ti who, miscegenation being against English law, would have to go home with him while posing as a slave. She would never agree to do this, being a king's daughter, whom the king of the Fante gave in marriage to Potts for three kegs of rum, a brace of pistols in a lacquered box, ten bolts of multicolored cloth for use by the king's ten wives, three pairs of scissors, an ivory-handled paring knife, a razor and a strop, a pewter chamber pot and an oil painting of an English castle.

Potts wanted a proper, high-born African wife, acquired fairly and honorably, as a means of connection to some of the African noble families, which he thought would benefit him in his trade. He married Ti in a Fante ceremony incomprehensible to himself but satisfying to the king and his family, which of course was the point. Potts would certainly not have married her in a Christian ceremony since God would have recognized the union, and he would then have been truly married to a heathen. He still harbored dreams of marrying well, at home, to an English woman of means, though this dream, like all of his other England-based fantasies, was fading.

The truth was that, despite drinking a bottle a day of good sack sherry, being forty-eight years of age, residing in a hot and debilitating climate and having a younger and highly sexed wife, he still enjoyed having intercourse with pretty slave women as often as he found one appealing.

He also enjoyed, when he chose to exercise it fully, the unfettered power he held at his Cape Coast station. He keenly relished the fact that nobody outranked him or could ever gainsay a single one of his decisions or criticize without consequences a single one of his acts. He was proud that the British Royal African Company, for whom he worked, valued and trusted him, paying all his living expenses of every kind as a sign of special favor and gratitude, so that he was free to save every penny of his earnings for himself, which came largely from the "tax" he imposed personally on every sale.

Also, his wife Ti was a shrewd, iron-hearted woman whom the young factors, even the soldiers, feared more than they ever did her husband. The reason for this was that Ti did not hesitate to use magic against them. On three different occasions, outraged at what she took to be the disrespect of someone at the castle, she had threatened them with sorcery and, if they did not "cease from their wickedness," as she said, she visited her father's court and consulted with a very powerful necromancer who lived there.

Whites sneered at this recourse of Ti's until the first of her opponents came down with the sweating sickness—dengue fever—on the very day she returned home from her visit to the sorcerer, and the man died from this fever after a month of agony. The other two opponents took sick with smallpox, recovered after months of recurring fevers and departed for England as invalids with miserably pitted faces. None of the free blacks who came and went from the town, and few of the whites who lived at the castle, ever again doubted her influence in the spirit world.

Beside her success with magic, Ti also drove hard bargains with the slavers who came to buy. Potts's margin of profit had risen since her arrival—a fact appreciated especially by his employers, who sent Ti a silver tea service in gratitude. She learned the proper brewing and pouring protocol from the English wife of a garrison officer and used her tea set proudly and often.

Ti was not attractive in the usual sense but was tall, muscular and large-breasted and had a pleasant face unless she smiled, when it was revealed that at least ten of her teeth were missing. This was because she had acquired the white man's taste for sugar to a degree few whites ever approached. Into each small cup of tea she drank, of which there were sometimes thirty a day, she put seven heaping teaspoons.

When the same soldier's wife taught her to make a candy out of vanilla beans, mint leaves, cream and sugar, she was so delighted with it that she gave the woman a bull and two cows, three acres of land, a hut and a boy to look after things—a conspicuous sign of her favor. But this monstrous intake of sugar led to tooth decay, chronic liver ailments and numerous painful extractions. And when Ti, always in discomfort from a toothache and ill-tempered, discovered that the black cattle keeper boy had taken the gift bull home to his father's corral for breeding, deeming the animal more potent than his family's bulls because of Ti's netherworld connections, she had him strangled and replaced.

Potts saw with gratitude and joy that in Ti he had a woman who would have been perfectly at home in any of the royal families of Europe. And, for her part, Ti wanted desperately to go to Europe where she could meet and mingle with her own royal kind. Naturally, Potts encouraged her in this, although he never had any intention of actually taking her.

For the truth was that, in England, Potts would be reduced from his African status of near royalty to a low-class commoner, having made his money from the sale of human beings whom he kept penned in subterranean dungeons where they lived in filth, like hogs or goats, and himself hobnobbing with brutes, pirates, other slavers and niggers—even being married to one of the latter.

So, considering these attitudes, slavery, though still practiced, was not quite respectable in England. Agitation against it was passionate and spreading. The memoirs of John Newton, a slaver who had been redeemed from his sin by a Christian conversion, had stunned the public, immortalizing his transformation by composing what became a beloved hymn entitled *Amazing Grace*. Newton's book was widely read, together with an ever-growing number of other slavery memoirs, which both repulsed and fascinated the British public.

Slaves were to be seen in England, of course, usually as the property of the rich, but were often referred to as "servants," and the practice of owning blacks had never caught on at home as it had in the Colonies. In England, Potts would be at best tolerated; here, he was one of the most well-known and powerful men on the whole of the West African Coast.

He could have all the women he liked at no cost to himself, and leave as many of the details of his work as pleased him to his wife who, conditioned by a different culture than Europe's, fully understood and sanctioned his enjoyment of young females. He could drink all he desired of the best Spanish sack and Lisbon port; not have to dress up except for certain selected slavers, who he knew judged him if he did not; and could flog any slave who annoyed him and kill any who threatened him. And, most agreeable of all, he was no more accountable under the law for any of this than a dog or a lion. Of course, if the targeted offender was white, he had to be careful, but even that could be managed by a man who knew what he was doing and had behind him a ruthless wife and the unconditional support of a superior sorcerer.

Truly, it was an ideal life, such as any man in the world would give up an eye to possess. So why leave it?

Really ... *why*?

From Potts's journal:

> I do not describe my condition as happy but rather as sated. All affections that abide in the heart of any gentleman anywhere abide likewise in mine. But in me they are satisfied to the limits of human imagination, whilst in other men they are gratified but fitfully, and the brief years of life slip away in restlessness and discontent.
>
> Likewise, other men must satisfy themselves with a single wife only, however disagreeable she be. They will have careless servants, for in England I hear there are now no other sort, and little opportunity to wield the authority that is every man's dream. Here, though a commoner in fact, I am a king in practice.

And though the weather be oppressive and entertainments lacking, my "wife" hath caused to be builded on the roof of the castle an ingenious hut, covered with foliage but open at the sides, so that, no matter how hot the day, a light air from the sea bloweth through, thus doth comfort stand in the room of diversion, and agreeably, since I am diverted enough elsewise.

I have had sunk in the cellar another deeper cellar, stone-lined, wherein ale and wine may be kept, as well as milk and butter, at an agreeable coolness. Outside it may be so hot as to near melt the varnish from ships, but in my cellar all remaineth cool and sweet.

Of course, my chiefest enjoyment, for which all men pine in vain, is the hundreds of nigar maidens by which I am made as pleased and contented as ever may be, having wished for such since first sailing to sea but having found it only here. Of course, in England, such a thing could never be, and a man who arranged it might be hung for a scoundrel for aught I know. There, also, the buying and keeping of nigars would be expensive, and replacing them with local village girls would perhaps be a disagreeable assault upon patience. In short, I have got so used to the life I live here that I could tolerate no other.

In England too, the church hath much more power to grind and shape than here. I hasten to say that I have not got out of the religious way and am still a believing Christian, even providing for the support of our church here and our minister and his family, and am glad to see him baptize the nigars as much as he likes.

But I have less equanimity than formerly in the matter of being interfered with. At home, I could not long abide the rude penetrations of my private life by a parson, seeking to redeem me from what I have been and mold to his benefit what he thinks I must become. Here, the church is silent about our work amongst the blacks, except it findeth scriptures that give blessing to it.

In all, I am naught but pleased. And if Captain Collins, now in port, take but five hundred of my blacks—though this be, I am sensible, a goodly number for his size ship, and the next master who cometh the same—why, I shall have things as much my way as even God's most holy and favored worshiper, on his knees in a monastery, could hope for.

Of course, I have mine own oppressions, as God intendeth all men should. I must needs deal, day in and day out, with the crafty, venal

African factors, who procure the slaves inland and carry them here to us at Cape Coast. These villains play upon our rivalries with the Dutchman as once they did ours with the Portugee. They force us to take their refuse slaves, who are too old or sick or half-blind or crippled to be disguised, with the sound ones; withhold slaves from us until we bend to their prices; or behave arrogantly, even with disrespect, knowing themselves immune to chastisement.

Likewise, the inland kings are fickle men, denying the Dutch in our favor one day, only to betray us the next. Yet, despite this, I prosper wonderfully and am sensible of the hand of God in all my affairs, which neither the wicked nigar factors nor the treacherous kings can upset.

So, I end these thoughts I write this day, as passages of scripture are ended, by saying "Selah," which meaneth "Amen, and let it be so."

1840

PINEWOOD PLANTATION, VIRGINIA

Young George pondered. The same day he declared himself to Young Sally and was rebuffed, he had intercourse with his wife Elizabeth. As always, she was calmly receptive but showed neither passion nor mystery. His very earliest experiences with her seemed to have had elements of both, but these quickly vanished and were replaced by mere warmth and a dull sort of contentment. Now, sex with her was no more exciting than having his hair trimmed by Decatur.

And worse, he could not get Young Sally out of his mind. Even as he was jogging dutifully in Elizabeth, he wondered why Young Sally smelled so exotically of—*whatever* that was. For it was a mysterious, erotic odor he could not identify, and it intrigued him. He had spent his whole life amongst the Negroes of Virginia and had never smelled the like before.

Perhaps Sally, still feared for her witching, had concocted it on purpose to enable her daughter to enslave him. He would put nothing past her and still felt uneasy at the sight of her notched tongue, her aging and beautiful face, her aura of danger and her still sensuous body. (Much later, he would learn that the odor was from something called patchouli oil, which Sally had got from a slave on another plantation as medicine for upset stomach, headache and skin miseries. Young Sally liked its smell and wore it as a perfume.)

If bewitching Young George was Young Sally's purpose, it had succeeded, although he of course knew that such thoughts were foolishness. The old woman had nothing to do with it. It was Young Sally's beauty, grace and sweetness alone that had won him—with no part being played by her intelligence! But he suspected that this was mundane at best.

Yet Young George did not care. He realized that he was more in love, more spoony and romantic about this girl than he had ever been in his life. He had experienced so many women and had countless brief fascinations, all of which faded away inside of days, if not hours. But never before had he felt such a yearning, such a feeling of ardor, such a burning in his belly about a woman as he did now about Young Sally, and never before had it lasted so long. For months, it had been building. And now that he had confessed himself to her—and been rejected—he felt desperate.

And it was so stupid. He could have her if he wanted her, at any time and on any day, and nobody—not his wife, father, mother, neighbors, friends or minister—could turn him from his purpose or change the thought that possessed his mind: *He was in love with her.*

After letting matters (as he thought of them) rest for a few days, contenting himself with merely tracking the supple movements of the girl as she went about her work of table service, catching her eye and noting with pleasure her confusion and basking in the husky sound of her voice as she answered but not asked questions, on the fourth day Young George spoke out again.

"Have you thought over what I told you, Young Sally?" he asked in a low voice as she leaned over where he sat, picking up his breakfast plate.

With the coming of fall, it was darker outside, and there was a chill in the air. Candles were needed in the early morning, their warm glow highlighting the soft, creamy tones of her skin. He wore breeches, boots and a warm jacket, but Young Sally was still in the short-sleeved dress of summer. Then he noticed goose pimples on her forearms and realized that she was cold.

"Dear Lord, girl, you are *freezing!* How dull of me not to realize. DECATUR!"

This consideration for her was such an odd thing coming from a white master that Young Sally felt a sudden rush of fear. She went stolid as he bellowed out the young House slave's name. The look on her face said that nothing Young George was now doing or saying had any connection to her. On Young George's orders, nobody but Young Sally entered the dining room when he was taking breakfast. This exclusiveness had already aroused suspicion in the slave quarters.

Decatur, confused, cracked open the door from the scullery and peeped through. "Was yo wantin me, suh?" he asked timidly.

"Yes, of course I was. Lay a fire in here at once!"

"Yas, suh. I knows yo don' want no niggas in heah when yo is eatin, suh. I sho members dat. An yo gin'ally don' want no fire till later on in de year, does yo, suh? Course, Miz Elizabeth lak one, an I has one fer her when she come down, but dat's aftah nine in de mawnin, an I ..."

"Oh, for God's *sake*, man," Young George snapped. "I don't want a *speech* out of you. I want a fire. Get about it!"

"Yas, suh," Decatur said and hurried into the room.

Decatur knelt by the wood scuttle and busied himself, laying a fire on the hearth. Young Sally, ignoring him and Young George, took the breakfast plate over to the sideboard, put it with the other dishes on a tray and carried them into the scullery.

Young George rose to stand behind Decatur, as if willing the fire to burn hotter and faster. He found himself feeling annoyed with the young slave's crisp white shirt and almost new black trousers. In his father's day, his mother Martha never had the niggers doll themselves up like Elizabeth had them do now. He thought it vain and presumptuous. What was the matter with old trousers and an old shirt? Too much of this specialness and the niggers would put on worse airs than they already did. Soon enough, they'd have to be asked instead of ordered to do things.

Then they'd think themselves above their station and begin to sass and slack, and the next thing you knew, they'd do what Alfred McMinn's nigger Cato did: turn on his master and mistress (who had shown him so much kindness) by setting fire to their barn to keep everyone occupied while he ran off North—led by a rogue black bitch, the nigger John Tubman's wife Harriet—where the goddamn abolitionists hid him clear to Canada. There Cato sat today—a sneering, free nigger, who ought to have his goddamn hands cut off and then be hung quickly before he bled out; instead, he worked as a carpenter for wages and had gotten married!

Suddenly, it struck him. Here he was, making his usual ruminations of dissatisfaction and suspicion about his niggers while at the very same time feeling spoony inside about Young Sally, who was as much a nigger as any of the others, and as uneducated and ignorant, and spoke in nigger talk just like the rest of them, and yet yearning for her to come back into the room and Decatur to leave so he could talk more about his feelings to her. Then she could thank him for the fire, and smile. And he could stand with her on the warm hearth, and enfold her in his arms without another word being spoken, and kiss her, and tell her that he loved her, and promise that from now on her life would be completely different, and that he would save her and take her away North and …

Oh, sweet Jesus, it was utterly mad! *He* was mad! Inside, Young George felt split in two. He was completely out of his mind and on the verge of ruining his life and his reputation and fortune and everything he was. Yet the heat in his body was so strong that he could barely contain himself. He wanted to rush into the scullery, sweep Young Sally into his arms, dash with her up the stairs to one of the guest rooms, lock the door and …

No! It would *never* do. He must remember himself, his family, his race, his class. It was nonsense. This drooling over a little nigger wench would ruin him if he let it run on unchecked. It had to stop … *now*. He must never give in to the thoughts again.

That was the trouble, you see—*those thoughts*. If he could force himself not to entertain them, he would be free and life would right itself again, and of course he could have all the affairs he liked with the planters' wives and the general run of slave women, but this matter of Young Sally must have a stop put to it once and for all.

Once and for all.

For good.

Forever!

It was as simple as that. And it must begin now, this minute.

Young George felt an agreeable inrush of sanity. Suddenly, he was able to distance himself from his obsession and see clearly how ruinous, how degrading it was to everything he stood for. Of course, his father had done it with Sally, and this had set him a bad example, but he needn't follow it if he chose otherwise.

And he *did* choose otherwise! As Decatur rose, dipped his head dumbly to Young George and went out the door to the scullery, Young George felt restored in his true manhood and clear-mindedness. Outside the dining room window, in the cool mist of the November morning, he could hear the white overseer Johnson, instructing the head driver Old Uncle Jim, plus the other drivers led by twenty-year-old Black Sulla, and all their gangs.

This Black Sulla would bear watching. He worked hard and long without complaint. He was very strong and strong-minded. Never had he uttered a word of sass. True, he was a Calabar, who were a violent, superstitious people, but Young George thought they'd got him young enough that it wouldn't matter. Calabars were difficult but not impossible, especially for a white man with a stronger mind than any of *them* had.

Young George wondered if Johnson even noticed how physically powerful and dependable a worker Black Sulla was. He thought fleetingly how useless most overseers were, how hard to train and trust and how short was the time each lasted, either deserting him for a better situation or being ejected by him for incompetence. Johnson was the latest. He surely would not be the last.

He—Young George, the master—would go outside now, add his own instructions to the overseer's and put this matter of Young Sally forever behind him. Also, he was determined to send her to the wash house or the kitchen and out of the Big House altogether, so that he would no longer be troubled by the sight of her.

Picking up his hat from the table, he set out with long strides for the hallway, leading to the back porch door. But, after only two paces, he heard Young Sally's soft voice calling to him, and he stopped so abruptly that he felt foolish. He turned.

She stood just inside the scullery door, which she was closing behind her. He found her eyes, and she did not turn away. Just as she had that one time, months ago, she held his gaze, and he could feel everything he had just resolved melting away inside him.

After a moment, she spoke again, her voice low. "I jes aks if dey was anyting else yo want, suh."

Young George hesitated. She stood calmly, holding his eyes. Tension quickly mounted. He knew, could feel that it was rising in her too (or was that only *his* wishful fancy?). For a moment, he did not know what to do. But then suddenly, like the sensation of ice breaking under his weight, he felt himself crash through every doubt and hesitation. Clear-sighted and settled now on his purpose, he walked swiftly to where she stood.

His voice shook as he spoke. "Yes. There is something I want. Something I know I will die for lack of."

Never before had this happened to him with a woman. It was one more proof—should he need any—of how different this woman was to him than any other had been. He was surprised and a little alarmed at how calm Young Sally was.

"Jes member dis, suh," she said evenly, looking into his eyes, neither passionate nor cold but quiet and wise, like a Sunday school teacher. "I said befo an I say agin now. Dis ain't right, an it ain't good. In de end, it cain't but ruin me. But I knows yo is set on it, an if it don' happen terday, it'll happen termarra. White wants an black gives. Dat's how it be. So I reckon yo kin do wit me whut yo wants ter. I jes hope dat, when yo is done, yo don' turn me out lak a mare yo is rode lame."

Young George felt such a rush of emotion that there were tears in his eyes. A great tenderness rose in him; a burning, deep resolve never to hurt or abandon this girl no matter what, but make her see that, against every fear of hers and bad example of other white men, he would be her true and eternal man.

He raised trembling hands to her face, cupped it and drew her into a gentle kiss. Young Sally's hands hung at her sides, and she did not close her eyes or open her lips. He fancied that her kiss tasted of raspberries and sunlight. His breath came short.

"Bes yo don' do dat right heah, suh," she said quietly.

"My dearest girl," Young George whispered, kissing her lightly again and again, on her lips, her cheeks, her eyelids, intoxicated by her scent and her beauty. "Nothing you fear will ever come about. I will make you the happiest woman who ever lived for I shall be the happiest man."

Young Sally said nothing. Her expression did not change.

Young George took her by the hand and led her up the stairs, she obediently following. They walked down the long hall, past the room where Elizabeth lay sleeping, to a guestroom at the very end of the hallway. There were no other occupants of this North Hall. Young George had his room off the South Hall on the opposite side of the House.

He opened the door, drew in Young Sally after him and, being as quiet as possible, closed and locked it.

Just then, downstairs, Decatur came in from the kitchen to stoke the fire in the dining room and saw that the room was abandoned. And immediately, in that moment, he could see the future ...

1861

PINEWOOD PLANTATION, VIRGINIA

George had never been able to get Saleh—or Sally, as he had renamed her— out of his blood. It was March 30, and all the young fools were bellowing, "War, war, war." The South was a confederacy and the North was beginning to threaten. There was this great dust up over a bit of sand and rock called Fort Sumter in Charleston Harbor. General P.G.T. Beauregard was swearing that he'd kick the Federals off what he claimed was now Confederate property.

George didn't care about any of it. All he thought of now, as he had for many years, was Sally. He reviewed his history with her. Something about her undisguised contempt, and the passivity with which she had always received his abuse as well as his ardor, had long fascinated him. He had always loved to look at her split tongue, even touch it with his fingers. He had also enjoyed making her say as many words with the letter "s" in them as he could think of, and had laughed heartily at the result. He knew that this was cruel, but she was cruel too. And, unlike him, she had no remorse about it.

Yet he also had tenderness for her, and some of his fondest memories of the sex he had forced on her for so many years were not of the ramming intercourse but of the times afterwards, when she lay on the bed, her face turned to the side, ignoring him and only awaiting his permission to leave, while he gently stroked her strong back and kneaded her round, beautiful buttocks.

Then it seemed, for a moment, as if she might be opening to him in some small way, taking pleasure in his touch. He loved her golden color too, was deeply stirred by the feel of her flesh when she had sweated, enjoyed the look of her if she dozed off and the feel of her breasts if he anointed and massaged them with scented oil. At those times, her nipples hardened—she could not help it, her body acted beyond her consent—and he took great satisfaction in it.

Yet she had told him many times, "Thith don' mean nothin. Yo don' mean nothin. Yo will nevah mean nothin. I cain't hep whut my nippleth do by dere own thef, an any time yo got a mine ter, yo kin thell or whip or kill me, an it will be all de thame ter me. I love only one man, an that ith Kano, an he ith daid, murdered by all yo white men. I hate all white men now, an I hate yo motht of all."

Why George should find such statements erotic he had no idea, but he did. Sally was the most erotic creature he had ever known. He remained obsessed by the belief that he could change her, and that hiding beneath her unfailing contempt was a powerful attraction.

For there was one fact that superseded all others of every kind. On a few occasions over the years, when he was in her, she had become stirred and passionate. She had clung to him and answered his thrusts. But afterwards, she subsided again into indifference, and there was nothing in anything she said or did to make him think that she felt any more for him than she did for a fly or a flower.

Yet those tiny moments of her response to him meant so much that he dared not examine them closely lest he discover that he had duped himself, and that the true scope of the awful idiocy that drove his life was grown beyond anything he could do or say to control it.

The other side of this relationship with Sally was that George had always taken pleasure in having her whipped, feeling she deserved it. How dare she be so ungrateful for the wonderful life he had given her as a servant in a Christian home, enjoying the love of a pure and decent white man? Part of his years-long equilibrium in the face of her coldness was the satisfaction he took in punishing her. But he made sure the strokes were not very heavy (though they stung, surely) and did not exceed ten.

Of course, he never laid them on her himself. And a real whipping should be just like in the Bible: thirty strokes laid on as hard as the overseer could wield the switch or the cane or the rawhide thongs or the bullwhip. But those he ordered for her were nothing like that. He never allowed a bullwhip to be used on her but only thongs or switches. He did not permit any driver or overseer to make her bleed.

Martha, George's wife, had always been offended by his relations with Sally and never tired of pressing him to sell her. But his strategy was to admit nothing. He always told Martha that she was imagining things and bought her gifts of clothing or jewelry to placate her. In his way, he loved Martha. She was the only woman beside his mother who had ever cared for him. She saw him through every illness, refusing to let any of the slaves wait on him despite that, when *she* was sick, he ignored her until she was well again, claiming that other people's illnesses dejected him.

Martha alone seemed to understand his unremitting melancholy and to pity him because of it. She held nothing against him—nothing except Sally—and he was skillful enough, and Martha willing enough to remain deceived, that he was able to keep her at bay about Sally for their entire married life together, which was fifty-five years.

During that great span of time, there were periods when George wanted Sally every day, and others when he would neither call for her nor speak to her for months. Over that time, he had taken a number of the other slave women—all of them far more responsive than Sally. He would get little crushes on them, make false promises to encourage them to a little passion, but soon tire of them and dismiss them with insignificant gifts. Sally he never tired of. She was a permanent irritant in his heart, a bite of delicious food that he could never quite swallow.

So many times he wanted to sell her but usually had her whipped instead. Once George actually did sell Sally to a nearby plantation, as nursemaid and nanny to a new baby daughter. But when they sent a slave to fetch her, he couldn't go through with it. She had tied up her few belongings in a shawl and was sitting impassively with her bundle on the top step of the Big House's front porch, wearing a blue kerchief over her head like any other slave woman.

When the slave from her new master arrived, Sally rose and walked toward the gig he was driving. Before climbing in—her exotic, slanting eyes deep and challenging—she glanced over at George, who was sitting on a rocking chair on the porch behind her.

At that moment, George was overcome with such remorse and panic that he cried out to the black man driving the gig, "Go on back home, and tell your master that I've changed my mind!"

Then he took Sally upstairs to "their" room—the locked attic to which he held the only key—and cradled her in his arms as they lay on the bed and wept. She hadn't wept since Kano had held her in his arms in the slave dungeon.

Sally said, "Marth Geo'ge, yo be de biggeth jackath dith nigga evah theen!"

These words, which might have meant a bad whipping from another man, did not seem to register on Sally's master. Instead, he lifted her rough dress, buried his face in her breasts and, still weeping, murmured, "I know … I know … I know …"

Eventually, as he aged, George wanted Sally's body less. Martha noticed and thought he had finished with Sally. He had not, but rather had moved the entire relationship from his outer to his inner world.

Martha died and Sally remained in the House but, though Young George had long been in charge at Pinewood, George took it on himself to order Sally moved from the scullery back to the dining room as the table servant, something that Martha would not have liked. George had, over the years, placed Sally there to be near him, and banished her again when he was angry with her, many times before. Young George, who rarely interfered with his father's whims, accepted the change without comment.

So, once again now, day after day, George watched Sally, seeing age taking her over even as it had taken him. And though, all around him, the country was only days away from bursting into the flames of war, he thought mostly of her and all she had meant to him.

But, as he studied her, not speaking to her but simply looking deeply at her as at a slide specimen or a piece of ingenious taxidermy, day after week after month after year, a toxic realization gradually dawned on him. He began to suspect that, over these many, many years, he had not really seen her. Instead, because she fulfilled so perfectly some inchoate longing in him, not for a woman but for *woman*—primal, sexual, tempting, denying—that is all of her he ever saw or could see.

Her coldness was the very thing in the whole blind masquerade that kept it fresh and tempting. Should she ever have really embraced him, shown him tenderness, loved him, stayed passionate in his arms, she would soon have become merely another woman, though a comely one, and he would have tired of her as he had every other. Instead, he had spent most of his grown life pursuing a phantom goddess through an imaginary forest. And, painful as it was to touch on this in his very belated new awareness, he now knew that what had kept him involved so powerfully, so madly, and for so long was her very disdain.

Why in God's name had it been so dearly important to him to break her cold and storm her heart? This was a woman who, as far as he could tell, cared little for her own daughter, even her own life; had told him hundreds of times that she did not care what became of her; was dead to happiness; and would never forgive white men for all the wickedness they had done and still did, and that he could whip her to death, if he liked, for saying so.

Why, after a disclosure like that, would he become so aroused that he would enter her with an angry, almost savage yet tearful desperation? Why, as he slammed away at her, weeping, his tears falling on breasts he thought could suckle baby gods, did he count even an involuntary grunt as a hint of passion?

Why?

This retrospection in his old age, beside painful, seemed unnecessary. Why now, so late? What *good* was it? Why not let it lie, let it die with him? But he could not. Like suds in a tub, it now overspilled the place in his mind where he had always kept it contained. And, as he followed it deeper and deeper through all the unexamined areas of his life, he realized with a sinking gut that it was as if he had been looking at this woman through a telescope from the big end to the small but had now turned it around. In the fuller picture, she had never been a goddess, and he had always been a fool.

The humiliation of finally accepting things as they were pushed him deeper into depression. There were different levels of his long-term melancholy, but those precipitated by his relationship with Sally were especially painful and long-lasting. Why had he not accepted all this before? Were these the sorts of things that only an old man could discern? Perhaps it was nothing more than the fading of his potency that gave his higher mind a chance to peer through. He did not know. All he did know for certain was that a substantial part of his life had been lived as if underwater, inside a powerful, unremitting, drug-like fixation.

But there was more. Seeing deeper his own part, he could see deeper hers as well. And though she had always been frank in her rejection, he saw now that she had also taken care to perpetuate her attraction.

As George studied her dining room movements, and her still powerful sensuality, a nauseating realization took hold. He understood now, as if God-struck by truth, that her sexual beauty had all along been displayed by her only to show him that what he desired most he would never have. He suddenly had the thought—which, like all of these new and disorienting thoughts, was of a sort unknown to his commonplace mind—that Sally's entire life in the Big House was an unending rebuke mixed with tease.

He saw, as if through lifting clouds in his old age, that there never had been a single moment—since first she noticed him staring at her in the slave pens at Charleston until this present day—when she had felt anything for him beside revulsion and contempt. The only "desire" she ever felt was the desire to attract, so as to frustrate and enrage and confound him.

Yet, for all these years, he had, he now realized, nourished the fantasy that she secretly loved him; that she knew, when he had her whipped, it was only because he loved her and was frustrated by her aloofness; and that, when he spoke of selling her, it was only because he wanted so desperately to keep her. But the truth was that, through her pervading coldness, combined with her exotic, flouted beauty, she meant to hurt him as badly as she could, to the depth he was fool enough to desire her.

Gradually, over weeks, these understandings first unbalanced and then soothed him. His racism, which had exempted her, now turned on her with force. Bitterness at his own cupidity fueled a burning hatred at her for her unwavering dislike. He heard words in himself that he had routinely uttered about other blacks but never applied to her before.

Now, he thought, *What else can you expect from a nigger? They are the most ungrateful, vicious people in the world! Lifted from the ignorance of their mindless idolatry in Africa, where they imagined spirits in every tree trunk and mushroom, gifted with the benefits of the Christian religion and the blessings of a civilized society and a loving home, they yet are wicked, guileful, selfish people. Goddamn the niggers! They do not deserve all we have given them and give them to this day. Goddamn them all to hell!*

Almost charmed by the novelty and sense of liberation in this thought as applied to Sally, George held onto it for days. Then, to his disgust, the old desire arose in him to excuse her, to offer her yet another chance—one last chance to show even a trace of kindness. He had to master this impulse if he ever was to live a life, however short it would be, that was free of her.

George ruminated on the matter for weeks. A lifelong hallucination could not be disposed of in a day. Over and over, he played the melodrama of his Sally years. Again and again, he forced himself to entertain the conclusion that had been obvious to everybody else for decades. For the first time, he acknowledged his bitterness, always before hidden by hope. And no sooner did he admit it than it swelled up inside him like a blowfish, crushing every surviving need to excuse her.

He read his Bible for guidance but quickly scorned the path of forgiveness and love he found laid out there. He had not the slightest desire to follow it. The newly acknowledged anger flooded him to his eyes and fingertips. The thought of her rejecting him for so long—he who had truly loved her—almost maddened him. At last, he was forced to admit what he never dreamed he could accept: *He had failed with Sally from the first day he knew her and had wasted his life.* The more his mind played over this realization, the more heated it became.

He now recalled and reviewed in detail every humiliation he had ever suffered from her, every gift she had tossed aside, every compliment she had scoffed at, every plea she had rejected, every favor for which she was ungrateful. As the weeks passed, he had what he came to think of as a "blessed realization." Now, at last, he could punish her—truly, truly punish her—to the extent she had always deserved, releasing himself from every compunction or human feeling but entertaining instead a set of vengeful fantasies he now understood had been there from the beginning.

He comforted himself with this thought for weeks as he watched her movements around the dining room while she, as always, ignored him. The anger built, and he welcomed it. It was salvation, belated but blessed. How good it felt now in his old age to experience a power that could set him free!

When he felt certain in his mind what he wanted to do, he sent for her.

Sally came, as she always had, walking with slow dignity. She still wore her hair short, though it was now gray, nearly white. Despite orders and beatings, she would not let it grow as he desired. And finally, like everything else about her that she would neither change nor explain, it stayed as it was. That was the problem in dealing with someone who placed no value on her own life.

"Yath, Marth Geo'ge."

He thought, *I am staring for the last time at her goddess's eyes. Little good has it ever done me until now. Little good will it do me in the future.*

George sat in a large, brown leather, high-backed chair in the parlor. At his side was a small table with sherry in a decanter and a little crystal glass from which he sipped. He wore his burgundy coat, white breeches, old-fashioned but dashing white shirt with scalloping at the throat and shiny black boots.

But he had outlived the ability to take on a persona lent by costume. He had avoided clearly seeing in the mirror how his face had become wrinkled parchment, but now the vision forced itself on him, and he could no longer deny it. He had kept his lower teeth but for uppers wore a misfitting plate. He admitted the truth. He was a used-up, old white man in an armchair, looking at a nigger slave woman who had defeated him.

"We have known each other a long time," he said at last, while she silently, comfortably stared.

He felt anger like a separate life in his breast. He did not want to let her see it lest she once again be satisfied. He knew that he was reduced to enacting emptiness, both as strategy and comfort. But at least that much control was in his hands now … at least that much, after so many years.

"Yath, thir," she responded, as always, impassively. Simply staring and answering, just as she had these last sixty some years.

"We have a child together."

"No, thir. Yo got a chile on me, an I couldn' hep but puth it out. I din want it. An, thure nuf, it turned out dat thee wath of no account."

Sally's stare was as calm, as unwavering, as on the first day he had ever seen it. Why for so many years had he not believed this stare, not accepted its unvarying message? Why now, when death must lie close for both of them, could he finally *see*? Was it all—was it *only*—because the madness of lust had died away? Is there no learning in life whilst the prick is yet wakeful?

"Why have you never appreciated anything I did for you?"

Again he felt anger roiling, again suppressed it. Why had he always chosen to see her insults as coy little charades, ironies … even *jokes*? And why ask her—again now—to explain herself? How many times had she told him the answer, which never varied? This prying was not letting her go but was only holding on in a different way.

Enough. It must be ended.

In a quiet, impassive voice, Sally said, "Thir, I tol yo many, many timeth. I hate de white man fer whut yo all done ter me an my kind an my color. How yo killed an crippled an brought thlavery on tho many of uth niggath. How yo killed Kano, de betht man who evah lived. I nevah kept any of dat theecret fum yo. I nevah cared if yo killed me. I tol yo dat.

"Yo thittin dere now, an ol man, actin like yo din know anyting bout my feelingth. But I tol yo ev'ry time yo athked me, ovah tho many yearth, jutht how I felt. I din care if yo killed me or thold me, an I don' care to thith day. De betht I kin thay ith dat, oneth or twieth ovah de many yearth, yo acted lak a dethent mathter, but yo got no right bein a nigga mathter to begin wid. Yo got no right bein who yo are or havin whut yo got. No white man doeth."

At this moment, a great number of thoughts streamed through George. Like monkeys holding each other's tails, they dashed across his mind's eye, and he noted each but could cling to none. He realized again, more deeply, that he had wasted his life, and the person he had wasted it on had told him all the while and very clearly that he *was* wasting it, and now she was a gray-haired, old woman not worth a nickel in a sale.

Suddenly, he wished he had been kinder to Martha. He wished he had not loved Young Sally and petted her. He should have sold mother and daughter the day the baby was weaned. He was sorry that Young George had been with Young Sally for so long, who had been shy and open-hearted but had become, in the end, a sneering scold. She was destroyed now and drifting because her sustenance—position, power, precedence—had been snatched away. Still, if Young George sold her quickly enough, she might recover herself in new surroundings to suit a new master. Perhaps he could sell her to a broker for the Louisiana market, for good money ...

But Young Sally's mother would certainly live on. Sally had that gift of dogged, clinging life, in calm or chaos. And George still felt the pang of sexual heat, despite his age, despite the emptiness of the thousands of times he had been with her. Sex was why he had always kept her, spoiled her, whipped her, mocked her, begged her, sent her out into the fields to die, only to bring her back, restore her to grace and favor, so that at last she might respond, soften, love him, and then he would be justified.

Saved.

But no, never. Indeed, if George had not sent her away that one time from the dining room, Young George might never have started with Young Sally. It was his decision that willy-nilly threw them together alone, day after day, until Young George had his way with her. *His own sister!*

Still, George knew that if Young George felt about Young Sally as he had felt about her mother, it was fate; it was inevitable. Stopping it would be like trying to head off the sunrise, the high noon, the rain. So stupidly was he enchanted by

Sally, so eternally did he want to penetrate her, so much of his sex imagination did he lavish uselessly on her.

Martha had been far more sexually adept. She had powerful spendings where she would weep afterwards and quiver for a quarter-hour. More than once she had spent from George merely touching her nipples. Yet he never much wanted Martha, always wanted Sally, and Sally wanted nobody but a dead, legless, black son of a bitch of an Asante murderer.

Ah, the injustice of it—the dreadful, stupid nightmare of it all. George—a wealthy Virginian, of good family, a Leyland indeed, whose Toryness was long forgiven—ending up the slave of a slave. And rutting in her over decades to coax out a single grunt of delight. Which she denied him as she denied him everything. *Everything!* He had again as he had often before the urge to shoot her, which he could do with impunity. He also wanted to shoot himself, walk out to the far North Field, kneel in the tobacco stubble and ...

In the silence, Sally looked at him with her strange, empty yet saucy stare, just as always. And George knew what she had said was right. She had never hidden anything from him. It was he who had done the hiding. But the truth was exactly what she had always told him—that she was just a comely nigger with a murderous grudge. He felt as empty and fragile as a man recovering from a long illness.

At length, he said, "You will move from your House cabin back to the field hands' shacks. You will not come into the Big House again."

"Yath, thir."

She looked at him steadily, giving him the chance to say anything else he had on his mind. Then, as he kept his silence, she turned her back on him, showing him her haunches, which he had for so long worshiped. She did not ask his permission to withdraw. At the door, she did not glance back. She did not say goodbye. He noticed that she walked a little stiffly. Rheumatism? Perhaps. He hoped so. That would add to the pain of her last days, which he intended should be substantial.

Right then, he took his little pleasure. It was small enough recompense for so much wasted effort. But at least now the feeling was pure, undiluted, in some way empowering. For this one time, at last, he was going to punish her—not regret or seek to temper it, but enjoy it.

"Sally," he called out, just as she reached her hand toward the door.

She turned, impassive.

Well, George thought, *let us see how long her impassivity lasts!*

For once, and finally, he was going to test her on her assertion that she did not care if she lived or died.

"You will work in the fields," he informed her. "I shall instruct Black Sulla exactly how to employ you. Perhaps at last you will prove worth a little of all that has been invested in you. Or perhaps you will get your wish to die. Time will tell."

Saying this to her, he felt more satisfied with the words than any he had ever spoken to her in his life. He smiled.

Sally looked at him as before. She nodded, again turned away and passed quietly out the door.

And this is the end of her, at last, in my life, George said to himself. As she closed the door, he thought, *I will never so much as see her again. Now let her see how calmly and happily she will abide in the tobacco fields—now, approaching the backbreaking planting time.*

Let her see how satisfied she is on the fare provided for the field slaves.

Let her see that suffering did not end on the slave ship.

Let her see what she has lost by her vileness.

Let her die and be buried with the other niggers in a cheap shroud or even naked.

Let her bones clutter his graveyard but not her memory his peace.

At last, let the madness end, and let me now turn to God to prepare for my crossing over, where Martha will be awaiting me and where I can make her sweet amends and enjoy the glories of heaven.

Sally will live now far from my sight, in a bare hut by the fields. Forever, now, I am done with her!

But, though he could not know it, he was fated to see Sally again … once more.

1801

CAPE COAST CASTLE, WEST AFRICA

Ever afterwards, Saleh remembered this day as the one time in her life when it seemed possible that she might lose her reason. First, she too was hammered into shackles, while several of the red-coated white men came strolling over to inspect her, shamelessly running their hands over her breasts and belly and laughing. Then, with the twenty trembling black men, she was pushed down a ramp to a corridor where the stone walls sweated, the floor was slippery and the smells of urine and human excrement were overpowering.

As they descended the ramp, the sound of the murmuring sea receded and a new sound replaced it—also a seething, rippling current, but of people's voices in which were mingled wails and sobs and cries muffled by the stone walls.

They stopped before a low, thick, wooden door, which the white man Potts unlocked with a key from a large ring of them, hanging from a thong on his belt. As the door creaked open, a terrible roaring sound rose, like the voices of the murdered dead who haunt their burial places, crying out to the gods and the living their rage at the injustice done them.

The opening door revealed a huge cavern lit by only a few small windows high on the walls. In the dim light, Saleh could see hundreds of naked, filthy, black people crowded together. At the sound of the opening door, they rushed toward it, shouting. A few tried to push their way out but were quickly stopped by jabs from the long knives fixed to the soldiers' guns. Wailing, they went stumbling back into the mob.

Saleh could see in a quick glimpse into the hell of this dark, stinking cavern that many of the people were still bloody from the chafing of the chains they had worn while being driven by snapping leather thongs to Cape Coast Castle.

As soon as they saw the white men, the shouting rose to such a pitch that it was painful to Saleh's ears, all the more frightening and confusing because at first she could understand none of the words they were crying out. But then, amidst the awful bawling roar, she caught a word of Senegalese, another of Mandinka:

"Water ... food ... air ... we are dying!"

Jabbing cruelly with the knives, the soldiers drove the people back and, as they yielded a little space near the door, John Potts and several other white factors began pushing the new captives in. Cries of rage rose now from the people inside as they saw that more were to be forced in with them.

Potts's voice was high and shrill. "Get in there, you bloody buggers! Get in there *now!* Make way, all you bastards! Shut your damn *mouths!* Make way, I said!"

Prodding and shoving, the whites pushed the black men headlong into the huge cell where at once they were sucked into the body of the seething mass, and one by one disappeared, like people being lost to quicksand.

Now, there were only two left: Saleh and the muscular, dark man, who was just ahead of her. As the man's turn came, he suddenly reached toward her, grasped her wrist and, attempting to shield her by absorbing on his own shoulders as many of the white men's blows and knife jabs as he could, he lurched forward and drew her in after him.

Immediately, the door was banged shut and locked. The new slaves' screams of horror now blended with those of the others. The stink and press and sweat and filth and heat of the crammed-in bodies engulfed Saleh. Immediately, she began to tremble. In the wretched light, she saw the desperation and madness on the faces all around her and gasped as her lungs failed to find enough air. Suddenly, the horror of her situation rushed upon her like a rapist.

She began to scream. Never before in her life had she heard in her own voice the notes of such panic and despair as she heard now. Even though it became harder and harder to breathe, she could not stop screaming. It seemed impossible to stop because screaming was a weapon or a lever ... the only one she had. Screaming might pry open the door or shatter a wall or melt the iron bars off of the small windows, which she could see high on the stone walls of this dreadful pit. It seemed that in screaming lay her only hope and strength and solace and safety, and that, if she should ever have to abandon her screams, she would disappear into an indescribable abyss where every devil she ever dreamt of awaited her with bleeding smiles and fingers of sharpened bone.

The heat generated by tightly packed bodies immediately oppressed her, her breath felt crushed out of her chest and her screams began to wane in their power. As they did, the rock inside her that was her legacy from the river god, the rock that had secured her a foothold in the mystery world where the shadows of both past and future took on meaning, began to dissolve.

And now, because her screams were failing, she could feel the rapid approach of death—or even see it, as if it were a giant, murderous sorcerer, striding toward her along a dirty, disappearing road. It was not like the dignified, white-robed, slow-moving death in which people died in her village in Tekrur or in the Mandinka city of Mali, but an insane, raging death, all mouth with hot breath and crusted tongue, opening wide to swallow her like a crocodile swallows a calf.

With the last of her strength, Saleh pushed her screaming to such a pitch of terror that her breath failed completely. At once, hot and sticky blackness licked at her like the tongue of a dog.

That was the moment at which she almost lost her reason.

But then she felt strong arms encircling her, and in her ear she heard Fulani words spoken strongly, in an accent she did not recognize.

"Wait," the voice said. "Hold on." Like a rope thrown around her soul, the voice embraced her. "Hold on."

Dimly, she realized that somehow she had split in two, and that one Saleh was clinging doggedly, at the center of her being, to all she had been and was, holding fast to her uncle's love and to the power of the God of the Whirlpool and the God of the Great River Rock. But another Saleh, one she had never seen before but who was powerful and insane and murderous, was trying to force her way out of Saleh's head, to press through brain and bone into freedom and oblivion.

The voice continued. "Hold on."

The Saleh that seemed to be leaking out through her head paused in its flight. This Saleh—who had forgotten the river god in the whirlpool and the god in the rock and the ocean god in the waves, who was oozing out of the side of her head like porridge, and who would in another few heartbeats leave her empty while it climbed the cool airshafts leading to home and the river and the land of the blessed dead—hesitated.

"Wait," the voice said again. "Hold on." The strong arms tightened. She stopped screaming. "Wait ..."

Blessed silence and a cool darkness came ... and she knew nothing more.

Another great empire had arisen after the fall of the empires of Ghana and of Mali, of the Fulani and of the Mandinka. This was the empire of the Asante.

From their capital at Kumasi, one hundred miles to the northwest of Cape Coast Castle, the Asante conquest, beginning in the eighteenth century, had radiated outwards in all directions for hundreds of miles, encompassing much of the territory that would later become British colonies. At about the same time that the Dutch were displacing the Portuguese in West Africa, the Asante Empire was on the rise. It was natural that the two ascending powers—the Dutch and the Asante—should become trading partners and allies.

Over the years, Saleh had heard much about the Asantes, but she had never seen one. The first Asante she met was the stocky, smiling man who, in the stinking, crowded hole dug out of the rock at Cape Coast Castle had, by embracing and encouraging her and lending her his strength when she had lost touch with her own, saved her reason.

His name was Kano. He would become one of only two men Saleh ever trusted (though the trust came hard); the other was her uncle Tenkaminen.

And Kano would be the only man she ever loved.

"Listen to me carefully."

Kano spoke to her in a ragged but understandable Senegalese on the morning of their second day of captivity. He spoke quietly, barely audible to Saleh over the constant, restless muttering and wailing of the prisoners' voices. They sat huddled together on the slimy floor on the side of the great stone room, farthest from any window. It was less crowded here, for people insisted on pushing as near to the windows as they could, thinking that they would find better air. But Kano believed that the opposite was true—that air was best where it was least crowded, however far from the window this might be. This was the first lesson of captivity he taught to Saleh. Whether or not it was true, it comforted her. He kept his voice low. Saleh had to lean close to hear him.

"I know these white people. I was taken by them once before. I learned their ways. Before they could put me on a ship, I escaped and returned to my home in Kumasi.

"I was elated by my escape but, when I returned home, I learned that all was not well with us. A debt hung over our family that my father had been unable to repay. So I entered slavery again two years ago—this time of my own free will—to settle this debt, which was to a fellow Asante. Never did I imagine that I would end up in the hands of the whites again. My term of service to my Asante master was to be three years. But he was a sly and dishonest man. He sold me to a Whydah middleman for twice what my family owed him in the first place. And my master had already gotten two years of service out of me before he sold me!"

"Who are the Whydahs?" Saleh asked. "I have heard of their name before."

Kano snorted. "The Whydahs? They are a wicked, stupid people who live on what the white men call the Slave Coast, to the south of here. They were among the first blacks to sell their own kind into the white slave ships. It is because of them and others like them that there is such a thing as the Slave Coast."

"The Whydah slaver sold you to the whites?"

"Yes. My master had brought me down to the city of the Whydahs on the coast near Jaquio and Lagos, three hundred miles south of here. There, he sold me. The Whydah middleman who bought me faced a glutted local slave market, so he brought his slaves up here.

"But, before the journey, he put me in a pen with the other men who were brought here with me—the same men you saw when you arrived. They are from Benin, and I could not understand their language. Besides, they were frightened and behaved stupidly, wringing their hands and shouting constantly. I knew they would be of no help to me.

"When you lose your courage, you lose everything. Even in the slave pens—even here in this filthy hole—you must have courage and remain calm. Only then can you accurately gauge opportunities when they arise. Only then can you plan. Only then can you act."

Looking into her eyes, Kano suddenly grinned. Saleh was surprised, even shocked. This man was *grinning*. In this awful, evil place, he was grinning! What good would it do him? He was still here, was he not? Still crushed into a dungeon, still without enough food or water or light or air, and with no reason she could see or imagine for holding any hope for the future.

She frowned. "How can you be lighthearted in such a place as this?" she asked snappishly. "It makes me wonder if you are truly a serious man. It seems to me a serious man would not be smiling but chafing with rage at the injustices being done to him."

At this, Kano laughed.

Saleh was offended. "What is the *matter* with you?" she cried angrily. "Don't you see where you *are*?"

Kano grew quiet. He stared at Saleh. Then he asked, "Where do *you* think you are?"

Saleh shook her head as at a gnat. Her annoyance grew. How could a man who seemed sensible act like this man Kano? True, he had saved her yesterday from the fear madness that had seized her, and she was grateful. But had not the moment now arrived to grow sober and forget smiles and lightheartedness until freedom could be restored? Was this not the right time for serious men to deeply reflect on the injustices done them, and organize a resistance by which they could gain both their liberty and their revenge and, if they failed, an honorable death?

As she spoke and got caught up in the passion of her feelings, her voice rose. "What do you mean by that? I know very well where I am. I am in a filthy pen, held captive by devils. Against this situation, nothing but a great uprising can prevail, and such a thing must be carefully planned and be led by a man who is serious and worthy of leadership. Not by one who acts important but grins like a fool!"

To her great irritation, Kano snickered. "I think I begin to understand your husband," he said, for Saleh had told him her history. "The poor man! No *wonder* he sold you. You must have nagged him to distraction!"

This shocked Saleh. She put her hand to her mouth as if it had been she who uttered it.

"Do you insult me like this intentionally?" she cried. "What have I done to deserve it from you other than to tell you a truth worth hearing?"

Kano did not reply directly but waited a moment before speaking, the trace of a smile still on his lips. His voice was very low pitched but now took on an edge.

"You are a beautiful woman and perhaps an intelligent one. But obviously somebody has spoiled you, for you seem to think that you may chastise men as if they were children and you their mother. This grows out of your bold nature, which, besides making you shortsighted, arrogant and uncompromising, also renders you unable to see that your hasty evaluations of things are not wisdom, as you so smugly think, but ignorance—and dangerous ignorance at that."

Here, Kano's voice took on a rasping intensity lacking before. He leaned so closely that he was almost speaking into her ear. He whispered but the anger and offense in his words shocked Saleh out of her false righteousness, as if being dragged from a dream.

He continued. "For should you be overheard by any one of the desperate people who surround you—all of whom, believe me, would eagerly trade your life, and mine too, for a bowl of yams—you would not live another hour. There is one thing a black man can say that will *always* be taken seriously by the whites: *a warning.*"

Saleh gasped in shock, but Kano ignored her.

"Let me tell you what would happen if the words you have just so carelessly uttered were passed to them by an informer. First, after driving you at the point of their little thong whips to their quarters, where they will feel comfortable and secure, every single one of these white men would rape you to their heart's content, being as rough and brutal as they liked, for you would have lost the one thing that protects you: your value to them as property.

"Lacking that protection, and for having shown yourself to them as a dangerous rebel, they would rape you until your mind was blurred with terror and your vagina dripped blood. They would put you at backbreaking tasks, humiliate you, beat the bottoms of your feet with sticks and rape you again. Sooner or later, your will would break, and you would belong to them forever. This—or worse—is how they deal with those who openly plot to rise against them. You will be dead to yourself but useful to them. For you will not die but mindlessly serve them for the rest of your worthless life."

Kano's smile was gone, and he sat staring at Saleh, presenting to her a picture of a terrible reality she could not refute. She hung her head and began to cry. Kano put his arm around her, and she leaned against him as she wept. She did not know why she was crying, only that a terrible reality had again invaded her soul and spirit. Inside, she felt so stained with the evil and impurity of this place and these people that she did not think there could ever be a ceremony powerful enough to cleanse her.

At length, Kano spoke again, in a softer voice. "Perhaps you were speaking so foolishly only as a way of keeping your courage up. But I had already told you that I had fallen captive to the white men before and knew their ways. Yet you did not ask me what I knew, or what I believed ought to be done, but only showed yourself to be a scold and a fool. You must not do that again. I began this talk today by saying that you must listen to me carefully, but you have not done so."

As Kano spoke, Saleh, still sobbing, nevertheless listened. She realized that he saw her clearly and that she had always looked down on and discounted all men, save only her uncle Tenkaminen. But now, in this man, she had found a power and a clarity greater than her own. And so, mixed with her humiliation and the feeling of resentment that he was right and she wrong, there was also a gratitude to the gods that he had found her.

"And so I must ask you," Kano continued, "you who have questioned my seriousness: Are *you* a serious woman? Do you wish to be guided by my knowledge and experience or go your own ignorant way? As you see, you have managed to provoke me and have caused me to wonder if I was right in believing that you might be a useful ally."

Saleh replied in a quiet voice, her face wet with her tears, her lip trembling. "It is true that someone spoiled me—my uncle. He saw and encouraged my spiritual gifts and never rebuked me when I was too bold or too proud."

"Then," said Kano, "I must wonder how wise he was, though I am sure he was adept in sorcery. As to spiritual gifts, they are useless without humility. In fact, there is a saying among the Asante: 'Knowing the gods makes you either better or worse but never leaves you the same.' You it has made worse. And it is not up to the gods to make you better, just as it was not they who made you worse. It is up to you."

Saleh said nothing else—not "I am sorry" or "Please forgive me" or "Do not abandon me," and her saying nothing was not lost on Kano. But he realized that she had said all she could.

She continued to rest her head on Kano's shoulder as they sat, leaning against the sweating stones in the ugly, stinking slave pit of the white men. He suspected that this wordless resting in his strength was her apology. He hoped it meant, by this action, that she admitted he was wiser in these matters than she was and that she would allow herself to learn from him. He told himself that he would have to wait and see …

But, the very next morning, she disappointed him again by consulting her arrogance instead of her wisdom. And this time, he was not disposed to overlook it.

"They will come for you very soon," Kano told her.

In the night, she had quieted herself enough to open to the ocean god, who had also seemed to convey something of this message to her. The white men would come for her. The reason was the same reason that men always had for fetching into their private spaces attractive women who were under their power.

Kano went on. "I saw it before when I was a captive of the whites. Their chief takes the pretty women for himself, and then passes them along to his assistants and to the soldiers. They will be gentle, even jolly. It is not in their interest to be rough, for they want to preserve your value.

"They will make you small gifts of food. They will give you their beer to drink, to loosen you. But this is rarely needed for most women are too terrified even to protest. So it is a simple thing and quickly done. Eight or ten of them will have you, and then return you here to the cell. The next day, they will want you again. Eventually, they will tire of you for the supply of women is endless, as you see." He spoke in a passionless voice, the voice of a schoolteacher reciting the details of a lesson.

"But it will not go on for long," he continued, "because the ships will come very soon. There are so many of us here now that one ship will not suffice. At least two ships will be required.

"I think what has happened is that the white men here have held out for higher slave prices from the ship captains, which the latter have refused to pay and so have sailed away along the coast, looking for cheaper slaves elsewhere. This has left these white men with too many slaves, which they must dispose of quickly lest we all die, which to the slavers is the second worst thing that could ever happen. The worst would be an uprising in which the blacks murdered them all, threw their corpses and their guns into the sea and carried away their treasures along the forest trails leading to their homelands.

"You have seen the bodies dragged out every morning, as I have. To the white men, we are not people but investments withering away before their eyes. The fact is that there are far too many of us jammed in here, and the white men know it. So I do not think we shall be here too much longer. It could be as little time as a few days. I doubt it will be longer than several weeks.

"They will settle quickly with the next few ships that come at prices favorable to the captains. New captives are being brought in every few days, and there is not an inch of space left to house them. That is why I think we shall find ourselves at sea in very short order.

"But, in the meantime, they will come for you. You are one of the most beautiful of the women. I am surprised they have not come already."

Saleh's eyes narrowed. Forgetting her resolve of yesterday to learn from Kano, she brushed aside the fear that his rough whispering had raised in her in favor of her own hot temper, which, she believed, was what had always made her resilient and strong.

She looked at him with disgust. "You speak so casually about it. If it were you they were coming for, I doubt you would be so detached." Her whisper had the intensity of a shout.

Kano sighed. "Your ill temper always betrays you into stupidity. How else should I talk about it? With wailing and wringing of hands and weeping? With a frightened face and trembling lips? Show me the good in *any* of that!

"I am telling you that they will come for you. But, as before, you only wish to carp and whine. You seem to imagine that you have some sort of great inner force, which can upset the arrangements of even powerful men. But, in fact, you are at their mercy, and if you do not learn to turn even that to your advantage, you will be dead in very short order."

Against her own instincts, she snorted at Kano's words. Something in her refused to be governed by anyone. It was a trait that was to remain with her the rest of her life.

"I do not claim to be wise," she snapped. "But I am behaving in a more human fashion than you."

"Again, your voice is rising," Kano said, irritated. "Again, you allow others to overhear and thus threaten both our lives." He did not smile. His dark eyes were expressionless.

Saleh saw the tension in his compact, powerful body as his hands gripped tightly together. She dropped her voice and leaned closer.

"So you say. And, in case you might be right, I will comply. I yield to you. But I will not give in to the white men. When they come for me, I will fight. And before I let them put their filthy penises in me, I will die!"

Kano shook his head and sighed. He turned away from her and did not reply.

Saleh soon grew impatient. "Do you mean to say that you *want* me to let them have their way with me?" she gritted in his ear. "I cannot *believe* you would want me to be so cowardly."

He delayed answering for a long time. He seemed deep in thought. Although she did not show it, Saleh felt alarm. But her face wore an expression of contempt.

Kano took this in, and then said softly, in her ear, "I see you are a fool who cannot be saved. I must release you to fend for yourself. Hereafter, I ask you to remain apart from me. I do not wish to be seen talking to you again."

With that, to Saleh's shock and dismay, he turned and moved immediately into the mob of packed bodies, disappearing from her sight in seconds.

She stood unbelieving, feeling as if kicked in the belly. Minutes passed, but Kano did not return. The minutes became hours, and Saleh again felt plunged into emptiness and fear, crushed by the hopelessness of this nightmarish new life. Too late, she realized that her sharp tongue and impatience had severed the one connection she had to what might prove to be her only hope of salvation.

Outside, it was growing dark. In the cells, the stench and the heat, the noise and the crowding, the hunger and the thirst pressed in on her. It seemed that the darkness was also creeping into her insides, and the feelings of despair and longing for death returned.

Again, she felt the stirrings of the maddened Saleh of that first day, but now she was able to stand against them. She pushed her way into a corner and began to speak silently to the god of the sea whose breathing today was so loud that she could hear it through the tiny window above the voices of the trapped and desperate people with whom she was caged.

And it was just then that they came for her.

1861

PINEWOOD PLANTATION, VIRGINIA

The latest overseer John Bryant had gone. He was dismissed because he was too rough on the Negroes. A thin, dull-eyed man with long, stringy moustache and a useless left hand, he had used the whip too often with his good right arm and persuasion too little.

He had even wanted to whip Black Sulla, which was too much for Young George, who thought that Black Sulla represented the constant, perfect, eternal values of African slavery: loyalty, ruthlessness and, though continually moving between modesty and violence, no threat to whites. He had been a slave driver for fifteen years; carried out orders without a moan or a murmur; was never late for the morning assembly of the work gangs; never excused himself from work on account of illness; never sat down during the day; never ceased to nudge, cajole or shout at the slaves he supervised, who were bending over the tobacco rows in the hot fields—sometimes he even sang or chanted with them; and was not hesitant to whip, and whip hard, anyone he believed deserved it.

Unlike many black drivers, he did not simply put on a show of ferocity for the overseer's pleasure and relent the minute no white man was looking. He enjoyed power for its own sake and used it as other men used liquor, always aware that, without the white man, he would not have it.

He was unmarried and uninterested in marriage. His one defect from Young George's point of view—and it was sometimes a substantial problem—was that he used his position of dominance to take certain slave women, both maidens and the married, against their will. This caused severe tension amongst the Negroes. Several times, Black Sulla's depredations had been brought to the attention of Young George, and Black Sulla was warned, but he would only desist for a day or a week, and then return to bullying and violating others.

Then came the day he went too far.

It was March. Black Sulla had been trying to seduce Lucinda, a field slave, but she resisted him. She had given in to him in the past but, since her marriage, had refused. Her husband Barton had at last stepped in and argued with Black Sulla. Their argument rose to shouts, then blows and, to everyone's surprise, Barton beat Black Sulla badly. But none of the slaves thought it was over. Many warned Barton to be careful because now, whipped and humiliated, Black Sulla would be more dangerous than ever.

They were right.

Black Sulla arrived at Barton and Lucinda's field cabin one late night, just as the tallow candles were being blown out all along the row of slave shacks that edged the great South Field. In what followed, anybody, even a white man ignorant of the slaves' inner lives, could see that Black Sulla had gone too far—much, *much* too far—and now Young George would have to act. Or so people thought …

Lucinda—attractive, modest and robust, with skin the color of Black Sulla's own—was in her night shift; Barton, a muscular, good-natured man, was in just a shirt. Without a word or a knock, Black Sulla pushed his way inside, carrying a wooden club.

Barton, surprised and angered, cried, "Black Sulla, whut in *hell* yo tink yo doin?"

Lucinda, who instantly knew, screamed out, "Git on outta heah, Black Sulla! *Git!* I tell Young Marse Geo'ge directly, sure as Christmas I gon run an tell …"

But, even as she tried to rush out the door, Black Sulla struck a terrible blow to Barton's head with the wooden club and, as the big man slumped down, seized his shirt collar with one thick hand and heaved the muscular, bleeding slave out the door, face first into the mud.

Then Black Sulla dragged Lucinda into bed and heaved himself on top of her. Lucinda's cries could be heard all the way to the Big House, but nobody came. The other slaves dared not intervene lest Young George side with Black Sulla and Black Sulla take a leisurely but certain revenge.

In the bed, Black Sulla pulled down his work pants to just above his shoes, which he still wore, and stripped Lucinda of her wrap. Her cries had become screams, but it was as if Black Sulla could not hear them. For a few moments, he glared down at her, sucking in great deep breaths, his penis large and frightening. He was so stimulated by her beauty, her helplessness and, above all, her fear that he began to make little animal noises deep in his throat.

"All right now, girl," he said in a growl. "Now I'se gon fuck yo pretty cunt till I bust through clean ter yo ass."

Then, as Lucinda whimpered and cried out, she turned her head desperately to the side to see Barton visible through the open door. He was lying frighteningly still in the darkness, his face pushed into the nearly liquid mud that looked as if it must surely suffocate him if nobody came to help.

Lucinda could not see any movement in Barton's limp body and began shouting, her voice becoming a screech. "Barton! *Barton!* BARTON!"

At that moment, Black Sulla grabbed her hair and forced her to turn back to face him.

"Jes keep a'lookin heah, girl. I'se de one yo gots ter see. Gots ter see what I be doin wit yo. Gots ter see all of dis. So yo gon member. An member good. An don' nevah fo'get. *Don' nevah fo'get!*" Black Sulla forced his way inside her and began a series of thrusts, repeating as he rammed harder and harder, "Dis be gittin' it good, girl! Dis be whut yo needs! Good! *Good!* GOOD!" with a shouted "good" riding every thrust.

The gathered slaves, who were drawn to the uproar and now daring to peer inside, stood mute, as if they were bewitched by horror. Some tried to help Barton, but Barton, even when his mouth was cleared of mud, remained unresponsive.

Besides ramming Lucinda, Black Sulla rained slaps and punches on her. All of his movements resolved together into a primitive, heartless dance. Very soon, Lucinda's eyes rolled back in her head and only the whites showed.

Black Sulla kept chanting "Good! *Good!* GOOD!" as his voice thickened.

Lucinda's body seemed to be buffeted by some terrible inhuman force that could have no being except in the thick blackness of evil. Then a shout rushed up from Black Sulla's loins—hellish, ugly, triumphant. To the slaves' horrified eyes, he seemed to explode. In that instant, any will to ever oppose him, in any way, died out of every heart. From great and deadly turbulence, he plunged into collapse, the dark force spent but its spirit casting its eyes savagely about the room.

Then he smashed his forehead down onto Lucinda's. In the crush of bone on bone, Lucinda went quiet. He rested but a moment, and then jumped back and away from the woman's still body, his large penis wet and dripping.

"Lookie heah, niggas!" he cried out, his voice eerie, terrifying. "Dis heah be de truf. All dis heah dat y'all sees be de truf. Y'all sees now whut yo gots ter do ter jes live inside of de truf. Den tings be fine an y'all be happy."

He nodded, a sort of mystical endorsement of what he had done. His try at an explanation explained nothing. But it did add something. It showed them Black Sulla had grown so strong and so bold that he now—all on his own, without so much as informing Young George what he intended to do, much less asking if he was permitted to do it—had killed a fifteen-hundred-dollar nigger and disabled an equally expensive breeder.

(In fact, Lucinda was never again right in her head. She stopped speaking and responding and, in a while, to get rid of her, Young George sold her as a refuse slave for two hundred dollars—a fine bargain for any master who could manage somehow to "bring her back.")

The witnessing slaves could make nothing out of all this except that it was so ominous, it made them sick with dread. What *else* could this man do to bring fresh suffering into the world?

Anything he liked.

Black Sulla walked out of the cabin, stepping over Barton's body without a word, and returned to his cabin. In the morning, Lucinda's terribly beaten face was a swollen, slit-eyed mask. In a few places, the skin had been torn too badly to begin healing, and blood still trickled from them.

Sally put a cold poultice on Lucinda's face for the swelling. She also gave her a tea to drink for the pain, but Lucinda was so withdrawn that she could not speak or even assist others in her care. It was Missy who fed her the tea in spoonfuls and gently stroked Lucinda's throat to get her to swallow. Her bleeding vagina was treated with bees' honey mixed with herbs, and it too began to repair itself over the course of days. Barton was lying just where Black Sulla had thrown him, the blow from the thick club having crushed his skull.

Young George, almost beside himself with anger over Black Sulla's rampage, struggled to control his temper. He knew that Black Sulla's dark side was the currency he paid for his matchless good side. He talked the matter over with his overseer Bryant but was not hopeful that the man would have a single helpful idea to offer.

"Bryant," he said, as they spoke in Young George's study, the walls lined with mostly unread books but also well-thumbed back numbers of *DeBow's Review*. "What do you suggest we do with Black Sulla?"

"Why, whip him, sir," Bryant said without hesitation. "Whip him near to death, and then make him just a work gang slave and put Decatur in his place."

Young George frowned. "Decatur's the head House slave. What good would he be in the fields? And do you think for a minute that, if you put him over Black Sulla, he'd live out the month? You'd find him with a broken neck, head down in a stump hole. The only man we could put over Black Sulla would have to be a greater brute than he is. And we have none such."

Bryant shook his head, nervously licking at his long, wet moustache. This habit of Bryant's repulsed Young George, who had disliked this overseer from the beginning and now was disgusted with him.

"Then sell the goddamn nigger, sir. For every good you see of his, there's a bad you don't see. Who knows how many of these young buck niggers he's terrorized? And, as far as the women—hell, the niggers is so a'feared of him that he could have had all the girls and women twice, including the old aunties, and we'd never even know about it.

"He belongs down in Georgia or Texas, gittin drove hisself, jest a common cotton slave. Or, if you want the *real* truth, he belongs dead. I'll tell you this, sir. If the Yankees ever come down here and free the niggers, the very same day they turn Black Sulla a'loose, he'll have a hatchet in your head. There ain't no more human in him than there is in a boar hog."

Young George turned a hard look on Bryant. "So, it's either beat him near to death or sell him. Is that it? Bryant, I've always suspected that you had little sense, but now I know it. Do you have the slightest idea how hard it is to find a driver like Black Sulla? Hell, I could hire a *dozen* overseers like you in the time it would take me to find another driver half as good as him. I don't see where you're helping me solve this matter at all. Black Sulla's about as close to a white man as a true nigger can get, by which I mean that he's got my interests at heart all day, every day. Which is more than I can say for *you!*"

"Well, now," Bryant said, anger in his voice, "all due respect, but your being so easy on him is what's made him like he is. If you don't ride a horse till he's done kicking, you'll never gentle him. This nigger ain't never been really rode hard. You just turn me loose on him and, in a month's time, I'll show you a tame nigger."

Instead of being encouraged by Bryant's words, Young George was offended. What he was being offered was a certain prescription for ruining the best nigger he had ever had.

Young George rose from his chair behind his wide, walnut desk and said, "You're a fool, Bryant. In a month's time, he'd be gone in the countryside, I'd be at the expense of tracking him down and you'd have the trouble, without the ability, of making a good head driver out of one of these stupid, lazy field hands. I think it's time for you and your family to pack up and move on. Be out of your house by sundown tomorrow."

Bryant squinted, his good hand furiously grasping his sweaty, wide-brimmed hat, crushing it against his chest, and his voice was a little unsteady. "All right, sir. And I'll call here at the House in the morning to collect my quarter's pay. The quarter's up next week anyhow …"

Young George said, "*What?* Pay you for a week you didn't work? No, sir. I'll deduct that week, you may be sure."

"No, sir! For I'd be working it except for you."

Young George snickered. "That's like saying, 'I'd be dry except for the rain.' You serve at the owner's pleasure, Bryant. And I can tell you that I haven't been pleased in a long while. Just consider yourself lucky that I'm being as generous as I am. Now go on along."

Bryant still controlled his anger and stood, head down, looking at the oval rug that slaves had braided in the founder Robert Leyland's time. "Well, sir, I can't make you do the right thing. Folks like me don't have much power against folks like you. It ain't worth my time to fuss with you about it. But at least you can give me a letter." Bryant glanced up and looked steadily into Young George's eyes.

Young George let out a bark of a laugh. "You want a *letter*, Bryant? Very well. Here's what it will say: 'To whom it may concern: Please be advised that this applicant for employment as an overseer on your plantation is a dim-witted, violent rogue, who will swiftly ruin your niggers and try your patience. You have my word that he will faithfully live up to all I have written here. Yours in relief that he is your problem, not mine, George Bidwill Leyland, Pinewood Plantation, Virginia.'"

Bryant stood where he was for a moment before speaking. As if both admitting and defying defeat, he put his hat on, though Young George allowed no hats to be worn indoors.

Again, mastering his anger, and looking at the carpet, Bryant said in a quiet voice, "You didn't need to insult me that a'way, sir. There was no call for that. I done my best by you. You just don't like my ways. But you have stopped me from really using them and faulted me because they didn't work. You and me both know, sir, that the honorable thing is to pay me my full quarter's wages and give me a decent letter. That's what an honorable owner would do."

Young George said, "I agree, Bryant. That's what an honorable owner would do for a competent overseer. But, for the likes of you, an honorable owner would do as I am doing. Now get along to your family and start packing your wagon before I decide that you haven't done enough this last quarter to deserve any pay at all!"

The Bryants departed. Still, Young George was left with the vexing problem of what to do about Black Sulla. And now he faced, again, the ever-recurring, almost maddening situation in which he was without an overseer and in despair of ever finding a good one.

So, in the absence of better advice, he thought that he might remove the carpet from Black Sulla's slave shack as punishment and scold his driver, who would look at him out of black, unreadable eyes, saying an occasional, "Yas, suh," and life in the slave quarters would go on just as before.

Young George simply had to accept the fact that Black Sulla had killed a perfectly healthy, fifteen-hundred-dollar nigger. He felt sick and inadequate at the weak way he had decided to discipline Black Sulla yet did not think he could risk doing more lest the slave be offended and lose all drive and effectiveness. God, what a sickening picture that made!

Suddenly, Young George remembered something that Young Sally had told him about punishing Black Sulla when next the driver would stray particularly far from his owner's control. It was a simple thing but bristling with emotional implications that would hem Black Sulla in, at least for the moment—and, with Black Sulla, all you ever had was the moment. After mulling it over for several days, he called Black Sulla to the house and put Young Sally's suggestion into action.

"Black Sulla," he said, "you have overstepped your bounds and not for the first time. As a punishment, you are to remain in your shack without food or drink for one day clean to the next, and then come out repentant and submissive again to my authority."

Black Sulla frowned, his broad face going flat to contain his anger. Young George realized, and not for the first time, that Black Sulla made him extremely nervous. He was, when all was said and done, in many ways a wild animal. The idiot Bryant might have been right about one thing. If Black Sulla were ever freed, his first act might be to kill his master and, at liberty to do as he pleased, run North.

But, on this occasion, Black Sulla contained himself, took his master's order in silence, finally said, "Yas, suh," and stalked away. Young George could hear his heavy bootfalls as he crossed the back porch. But he felt relieved that he had acted and that, for now, Black Sulla was neutralized.

However, the daunting, almost overwhelming task of finding a good overseer remained. But, the very next day, as if in answer to a prayer not yet uttered, there arrived a letter with a Macon, Georgia, postmark.

Young George opened it and read it through. It was admirably brief:

May 10, 1861
Dear Sir,

   I am acquainted with Mr. Garret Holliday, who advises me that he was at Washington College with you. At present, I desire to remove to Virginia or Maryland from Georgia. I seek employment as a plantation overseer.

   Through Mr. Holliday, I have learned that you have a large and flourishing tobacco farm and wonder if you could use my services. I have references as to competence and character. I am a Christian man, forty-two years of age with seventeen years' experience in managing Negroes, and enjoy good health. I stand six feet in height and weigh one hundred eighty pounds. I am a recent widower with no children. I do not use alcohol.

   Yr. Obed't Svt.,
   Jared Wilkenson

Young George was heartened by this letter. He knew Holliday for a sensible man who would not steer a wastrel his way. He liked this Wilkenson's economy with words and his apparent intelligence. He knew that some overseers—less these days, thank God—could neither read nor write, though claiming they could do both until unmasked.

Also he liked the fact that the man was unmarried. Of course, a recent bereavement might work against the owner's interests, but there was no hint of mawkishness in this nicely brisk letter. Elizabeth held unmarriedness against a man, thinking a single overseer more likely to be a rogue. Young George believed the opposite—that a single man had far less demand upon his time as a matter of daily course, though he might disappear into a nearby city upon occasion and be brought home drunk in the bed of a wagon. But, with a single man like this Wilkenson, in mourning and a teetotaler, there was little chance of that. So, unless the man was a liar or gone mad from a pox or in flight from the law, he seemed a godsend.

At once, Young George sat down and wrote a note to Jared Wilkenson, telling him that the position of overseer was presently available and inviting him to come to Pinewood to apply for it. A week later to the day, Wilkenson rode up to the plantation on a hired horse from Richmond, where he had arrived by the train of cars and taken a room at the Planter's Inn, pending his interview with Young George.

Young George, looking out a front bedroom window, watched him approach up the wide carriageway from the Richmond Road, sitting tall and square-shouldered on his horse. He wore a buff-colored coat; dark blue shirt and trousers with a broad, black tie; shining black boots with spurs; and a tan, wide-brimmed hat. He had a military look to him, like a cavalry officer. He was clean-shaven and seemed much younger than his claimed forty-two years, with clear, innocent-looking blue eyes and shoulder-length brown hair.

As Wilkenson's horse walked past a couple of slaves, who were digging out a dead tree, he nodded and smiled. This to Young George was another good sign since Bryant had been a sour, violent man whom the slaves had hated. On the other hand, Young George hoped that this smile of Wilkenson's did not presage an equally ruinous laxity. He could only hope for the best.

Decatur, the head House slave, now wore at Elizabeth's direction a long dress coat and dark trousers. He answered, with an impressive dignity, Wilkenson's discreet rapping with the brass knocker and admitted him.

"I expeck yo is Mistuh Wilkenson, suh?"

Wilkenson smiled. Decatur found himself attracted to that smile. It seemed to light the man's face.

"That's right. And what is your name?"

"*Mine*?" Decatur was surprised. "Why, I'se Decatur, suh, de haid House man. Miz Elizabeth say I'se de butluh."

White men usually were not interested in, and did not inquire about, the identities of Negroes. Decatur was favorably impressed.

"Well, I'm pleased to meet you, Decatur. Is Mr. George Leyland free to receive me?"

"Yas, suh. I b'lieve he is, but I'll jes go in an aks him."

"Thank you," said Wilkenson, again smiling. He had removed his new-looking hat upon entering and now held it in his big hands. "Maybe you could drop off my hat someplace on your way?"

"I should of aks yo dat my own sef, suh," Decatur said, a little embarrassed by his oversight. He took the hat.

Wilkenson smiled wider and winked. "Don't tear your shirt over it."

A few minutes later, Wilkenson was ushered into the study where Young George sat behind his desk. Young George did not rise to greet him or offer his hand or encourage by his expression Wilkenson to offer his.

Young George always liked his overseers to know right at the beginning that there would be neither friendship nor good will offered by him as part of their working relationship. Civility, yes, and respect if earned. But everything was contingent on one thing: the overseer putting his owner's interest first. If that was done, everyone would profit; if it was not, nobody would. Most overseers were too stupid to know that and had to be first shown and then reminded. Young George was willing to do both.

The smile Jared Wilkenson wore into the room disappeared as he took this owner's measure. The change made him look more formidable—a shift that Young George did not fail to notice. Which was all to the good. Find out as much as you can as early as you can was Young George's motto. See who this man really is to whom you are offering a good wage, a comfortable home and respectable employment. For there was no worse experience for an owner than surprise—except for treachery.

"Good day, sir," Wilkenson said.

"Good day. You are Jared Wilkenson?" Young George did not offer him a chair. He liked his supplicants to stand.

"I am."

"How do you know Mr. Holliday?"

"He is the brother-in-law of Mr. Alfred Stroud, my last employer, owner of Oak Leaf Plantation near Macon. I often saw Mr. Holliday when he came to visit."

Young George stirred in his chair. "Alfred Stroud? The former attorney general of Georgia?"

"Yes, sir. He retired from public office upon the death of his father when he was needed at Oak Leaf."

"Well, I must say, Mr. Wilkenson, a reference from Mr. Stroud would carry weight with me provided it is a wholly positive one."

"I have it, together with others, here in my coat pocket, sir. You can read them and decide for yourself."

"Who beside Mr. Stroud has recommended you?"

Wilkenson's tone was respectful and brisk. "Mr. Holliday. He has often observed my operations on the plantation and has formed opinions as to my worth. And Mrs. Mariah Wells, a widow for whom I worked before I came to Oak Leaf. Upon the death of her husband, she hired me to work closely with her, sir, to manage her crops and her Negroes, in which work she had little experience. Her plantation flourished. When she remarried, I felt relieved of my obligation to her and accepted an offer of employment from Mr. Stroud. I have been there these past three years."

Young George liked his businesslike attitude. "I see. And it was cotton you grew in Georgia, I assume?"

"It was, sir."

"And you have experience growing tobacco?"

"No, sir."

"You don't? I'm curious how you expect to get along without experience."

Wilkenson stood calmly before the desk neither nervous nor shifting about. His arms, which had hung easily at his sides, were now folded across his chest.

"Sir, I do not think the key to plantation management lies first and foremost in knowledge of a crop. This, with all due respect, can be gained very quickly by anybody of good resolve and intelligence. I can sit down with you—or, to be honest, your head driver, sir—and, at the end of two hours, know everything that will be required of me for the next year.

"What *cannot* be gained quickly—and you know yourself, sir, that by many it cannot be gained at all—is the secret of managing Negroes. A balance must be struck between hard discipline and carelessness, so that the Negroes, though in no doubt as to who is overseer, will yet be willing to work hard for him.

"I do not think cruelty can stand in the place of competence. A Negro is not a fool. He can see as well as anyone else whether or not his overseer knows what he is about. He can see whether or not the man has a backbone He can also see every weakness and will use it to his own purposes.

"A good overseer constantly corrects his own mistakes and learns to amend whatever in him his Negroes might seek to exploit. He must then turn the blacks' every effort to undermine him against the ones responsible for it, so they are undone and his position is reinforced.

"But, in chastening, he must not humiliate. A humiliated man is a lifelong enemy, no matter how much he may smile and grovel. As he chews on his discontent, he will become progressively more creative in avoiding work. And, in his own way, to the level of his skill and courage, he will take his revenge. The net result, sir, is that the owner's troubles rise even as his profits fall. That is the exact opposite to what is desired."

"Indeed," said Young George, impressed. "You speak very well. But I cannot imagine that you have been much educated? Overseers do not require education."

"You are right, sir. But neither do owners. Yet every man of true ambition becomes educated as best he can, regardless of his birth. That is our national promise and our great strength."

Young George frowned. "Well, that may be true, though our national promise means less as the days pass and the Federal rogues at Washington City forfeit all rights to the respect and obedience of the South—but I certainly don't agree that a planter can do without education. Not unless he also wants to do without success. As you know, I am a graduate of Washington College."

"Yes, sir. And I respect you for it. I have had no such education myself but have always learned all I can, everywhere I have ever been placed, which would be of advantage to myself and to any employer. If you consult my references, sir, you will see that I have not entirely failed in that regard."

"I dare say."

Young George fell silent and sat back in his chair, staring at Wilkenson, who still stood comfortably before him. There was something a little too glib about this man. An owner wanted intelligence in his overseer, yes, but not cleverness. Cleverness was sure to end up working against an owner. But what was the alternative? Another moron like Bryant with a chinless wife and a brood of dim-wit children, who looked as if they'd been sired on his sister?

Well, perhaps that was not a good illustration. In the common run of things, although one shouldn't be intimate with one's sister, there are very clear exceptions. For example, where there is only a half-parental connection, together with a goodly racial divide, it is no different than any other relationship, more or less. Possibly better, for where good blood meets good blood, nothing but good can result. Look at Missy! Certainly white-fortified Negro blood is good. Simply behold Young Sally's beauty, charm and intelligence and say that she hasn't good blood. What a laugh! Why, it's nearly the same as white. But, damn it, in this matter of overseers …what's to be done?

After some time, Wilkenson said, "You seem deep in thought, sir. Shall I come back another day?"

"*What?* No! I'm simply considering matters. These references will prove genuine, I trust?"

"I can't imagine what good false ones would do me, sir."

"And you are prepared to sign a statement of allegiance to your employer?"

Wilkenson hesitated. "I am, sir, unless I deem it to interfere with my right to act in my own interest."

Young George frowned. "But that's the whole point, Wilkenson. The owner's interests must be paramount. I don't see where your interests enter in at all."

"I understand your words, sir, though I can't say they reassure me. But please remember that I am a free man and not entering into slavery on anybody's plantation. I am sure there are many overseers' jobs I can find that will not disempower me. I am in no particular need of your position here. Nor, as our discussion advances, am I much desirous of it. I want to come to Virginia or Maryland to escape the extreme heat of Georgia, sir, and to better attend to a personal matter—not to be a blind donkey on a planter's treadmill. Yours is the first place I have visited. It will not be the last."

Young George sensed the sinking in the belly an ordinary man feels upon realizing that he has encountered a strong spirit. He was annoyed. And now that Wilkenson was indifferent to being employed by him, Young George was suddenly determined to have him.

"Well, you needn't be rude, Mr. Wilkenson. Nobody has any notion of *enslaving* you."

"I trust not, sir. But, speaking of rude, you have kept me standing here like a driver. I've yet to work for a man who demeans me. The former attorney general of Georgia offered me both a chair and a refreshment many's the time. He never once acted indifferent to my interests or expected me to. He was a man of breeding, sir."

The inference in this was so close to insulting that Young George drew in a quick breath and considered carefully what to say. He was smart enough to know that he had pushed Wilkenson into pushing back, but now he wanted to avoid further confrontation. Anyway, all he had wanted in the first place was a strong, dependable overseer to whom he could relinquish the day-to-day tedium of a great farming enterprise. This Wilkenson, for all his sauciness, seemed a good man. Certainly Young George could steer him in a better direction over time. But it would have to be done with caution. This was no Bryant. That was very clear.

He tried another tack. "Well, you are right. I have overlooked a courtesy. Please to have a chair." Wilkenson nodded and sat down in the single chair that faced the desk. "What would you want as wages? I generally pay forty a month over and above your house and your food. You'll have a nigger to cook for you and look after you too. You can use one of the horses, so long as you're careful."

"I have my own horse, sir. And only a fool treats either his horse or his slaves carelessly. As to wages, I was twenty years old the last time I worked for forty dollars a month."

"*What?*" cried Young George. "Hell, I can get a good carpenter for ten!"

"Yes, you can, sir. And a plasterer and a shingle maker. What does that signify? Will a carpenter operate your plantation? How many niggers do you run?"

Young George felt his breath coming short. This Wilkenson was very bold and impudent. But already he could tell that he was head, shoulders and belly above any overseer he'd ever seen in his life. He steadied his temper.

"About a hundred and fifty, if nobody's died or been born today." He smiled to show that he really was a good-humored man.

Wilkenson smiled back. "Very well. What I'll want is seventy-five cents per nigger per month. You want me responsible to you all day, every day, putting your interests first, making your fortune grow. Fair enough. But, for my part, I too want to be able to show something for all the hours and days I'll give in your service.

"What I'm asking comes to about one hundred twelve dollars or so a month. I'll accept one hundred twelve dollars and fifty cents. But not paid by the quarter. That method puts a little too much of my money in another man's hands. I like to be paid monthly, in advance, on the first day of every month. If I'm fired or leave in mid-month, I'll refund the difference. Today's May 3rd. If you hire me any time this week, you'll pay me for the full month, will you not?"

Young George wanted to cry out, "Get the hell off my property, you insulting son of a bitch!" But, instead, he held his tongue. Like every planter in the Virginia district—indeed, everywhere at the South—the chief, recurring problem of plantation management was finding a competent, intelligent overseer. Because the pay was low and the job thankless, most men of quality shunned it. Instead, it attracted fools, bullies, ne'er-do-wells, drunkards, drifters and even criminals.

The occasional man of substance was immediately snatched up and jealously kept by a discerning and grateful planter. Of course, this meant that such a man would have to be paid what he was worth, not what was commonly given to the flotsam of the trade. In this case, with a strong-minded, intelligent man like this Wilkenson, it meant one hundred twelve dollars and fifty cents plus the house, the nigger and board. Jesus, it was galling! But did he really want another like the string of incompetents before him? Forbid it, almighty God!

Soothing his temper, Young George said with a sickly smile, "I think I can agree to your suggestions, Mr. Wilkenson. Though I confess they are a bit, let me say, *unusual.*" (He had made them into suggestions, not demands. He could not bear to give in to demands!)

Smoothly, Wilkenson replied, "They are only unusual if supervising the gangs in the hot fields week upon week is unusual; or working long hours in the stifling, tobacco-curing barn while the tobacco stakes are turned or the leaves stripped; or being awake and active all night if a rain threatens when the leaf is drying next to the fields; or pitching in at the harvest if hands are short.

"If these are all unusual, so are my … *suggestions*. But, if they are not, then why quibble? I will—and you know I will—sacrifice for you. Why will you not do the same for me? If you will not, though expecting it of me, then I conclude that you see me as a fool. I have never yet allowed any man to think of me as such."

Momentarily stymied, Young George snapped, "I thought you said you knew nothing about tobacco farming. How is it you know all the things you just said?"

"All due respect, sir, but I did not say I knew *nothing*. Your question was if I had experience, which I don't. But no experience is very different from no knowledge."

Hells bells! Stymied and chastened. But damn it, Young George wanted this man. He could sense how good an influence his common sense and clear-headedness, not to mention his strength of character, would be on the niggers. No more sniveling, moustache-sucking, nose-wiping thrashers like Bryant for him!

Besides, with a good man in residence, Young George's own workload would drop. He could spend even more time with Young Sally. Of course, that was a mixed blessing now, what with she having got so high-nosed and proud. Who would ever have thought that such a girl as sweet as she had been, and as inno- cent, would ever have … well, that was a different matter. This was overseer business now. He had to take it in hand.

"What did you mean before, Mr. Wilkenson, when you said that you had come here both to escape the Georgia heat—by the way, there's heat a'plenty here—and to see to a personal matter?" He sat back into his chair, as if resuming control.

Wilkenson looked at him for a moment, and then shook his head. "It's Vir- ginia hot, sir, not Georgia hot. And a personal matter is just that." He thought to leave it at that but saw the gathering cloud on Young George's face and decided to say a little more. "It is a case at law, sir, which is going forward in a Baltimore court and has been for several years past. It will not affect you or in any way concern you. I prefer to keep the details of it private."

This was literally true. But if Young George—or any other planter—knew the details of the case, it would affect them emotionally. It would gnaw at their guts, worry them and make them suspicious, fearful, even though it had nothing in the world directly to do with them. For they would think—in fact, would be sure—that it did.

There was a long pause. Young George again leaned forward in his chair; Wilkenson sat easily in his.

Finally, Young George said, "I am afraid that will not do, sir. If I am to take you on here, I must be assured that nothing will arise to upset our arrangements or cause you to leave suddenly, with me and my plantation in disorder and dis- may behind you."

"I can and do assure you that it would never happen, sir."

"But that is not good enough, Wilkenson," Young George said sharply. "Assure all you like. I need to know why you are at law, and with whom and over what, before I will feel free to hand you a key to a fine house, let you next to my niggers and give you the run of the place! I need to know if you are a plaintiff or a defendant in this law case and exactly what it's about. This is not a matter that you can keep a mystery to your employer. I daresay there's nothing in it. But I must be the judge of that. You must tell me."

Wilkenson's face hardened. His look found Young George's eyes and bored in. "This is coming pretty close," he said slowly, "to calling me a liar, sir."

"No such thing," Young George said quickly. He was distressed that his voice sounded a bit choked and thin.

"Well, here I think we disagree, sir. And I must say I do not much care for how our talk has gone today. So I'll thank you for your time and be on my way."

With that, Wilkenson nodded to the surprised Young George, rose and left the room, leaving the study door open behind him. He retrieved his hat from Decatur, not neglecting to thank the slave, and went immediately out the front door, unhitched his horse, swung up into the saddle and, before George could so much as call out to him, kicked her into a canter and disappeared into his own dust.

1801

CAPE COAST CASTLE, WEST AFRICA

journal entry from Nathan Collins, ship's captain:

I, Captain Nathan Collins, am forty years old and the commander of the Lady Dora slaver out of Charleston in South Carolina. We are at sea and our port of destination is Cape Coast Castle, West Africa.

Today, I received a very unsettling suggestion from my second mate Badger, who rarely speaks and then only with mildness. But today, he made a strange proposal—strange not in its novelty but in its disturbing oddness. He and my first mate Will Grainger sat with me over breakfast in my cabin, and we discussed our hopes for a favorable sale of our cargo of Boston rum and a good buy of slaves at Cape Coast Castle, and also for a clean voyage home with most of the slaves surviving.

Badger said, "Aye, sir. But however harmonious things may be, there will always be wrongdoers, and wrongdoers must be punished severely as an example to the other niggers. I mean the rebellious slaves, ones such as we always encounter, though we show the patience and kindness of saints."

"How mean you—'punished severely,' Mr. Badger?" asked I.

"Why, such as I've seen done on other ships in our sort of trade," he replied.

"And what exactly is that?" asked Grainger. Neither Grainger nor I felt at all nervous of his answer, Badger being always so bland a man.

But then he said, "Why, cut off their legs, sir! Next, to prolong somewhat their wicked life, cauterize well the stumps and stitch over them a flap of skin. Then, suspend the rogues in baskets of netting fixed to the mast, so as to astonish and cow the other niggers. Quick as one such malefactor dies simply, if still needed, supply another, for there is no shortage of 'em. Thus, peace and harmony are maintained, no matter the conditions in the ship's hold. For everyone knows, sir, that even men who laugh at death lose heart at mutilation."

I sat quietly for a moment, believing he must be in jest, tho' I'd never seen levity in him till now. And the stripe of rash on his face from nose to forehead shone a fiery red, indicating that a strong passion was driving him. His mouth was set and his shoulders braced as if, had we troublesome Negroes now aboard, and were I to order him to enact his desires, he'd dismast them all in the wink of an eye.

Grainger was appalled. His mouth drop't open in shock. I myself could scarce believe that I'd heard Badger a'right. But then he went on.

Drawing out the great sharp knife he wore always on his belt—a nasty, wide glinting blade, fully fourteen inches long—he said, "You see, sir, I've a whale flensing knife for the flesh, and there's the surgeon's saw for the bones. I'll have the buggers' legs off before they can blink."

Now, I myself wear a dagger of the Arabian kind always on my belt, more from pleasantry of fashion than need. But, beside this monster of Badger's, it is a mere paring knife. I shuddered to think what awful meat that blade would make of men's legs.

For a time, Grainger and I sat silently, at a loss what to say.

Finally, Grainger said, deeply affected by Badger's words, "Surely you can never think that we would do such a thing on the Lady Dora, Mr. Badger!" Grainger looked to me for agreement and found it.

"Aye, Mr. Badger," I said. "We are not brutes here. Nor is there value in dead or disabled slaves at Jamaica or Charleston."

Badger grew a bit turbulent, so unlike his normal mien. He made to argue. "But I have seen it done, sir! On the Whydah, Captain Sloan, out of Kingston. Also on the Queen of Calabar, Captain Owens, Bristol. It worked wonders, sir. The niggers were docile and the voyages profitable. I should not like to think that we were foreclosed from judicious practices, sir, because of false notions of humanity. These are niggers, after all. To think them human beings like us is the gravest error. And I—"

Feeling both anger and a nameless discomfort, I silenced him, my voice raised. "That will do, sir. We'll have no more such talk. We shall use the methods we have always used to discipline the Negroes—denial of rations and the lash, temperately applied. We are not barbarians but Christians, Mr. Badger. Pray remember that."

At once, Badger's face, which had been enlivened, even avid in the grip of his vision, returned to blandness. "Aye, sir," he said with his wonted quietness. "'Twas but a suggestion. For as always, sir, you know best and shall be obeyed."

At this, Grainger sighed, having evidently been holding in his breath. He looked toward me. Our eyes met, and I could see that the same disquieting question now troubled us both. We turned our gaze on Badger, but he had reclaimed his customary diffidence and look of harmless calm.

I had not then, nor have I now, any idea what to think about that very strange and disturbing conversation.

There was a rattling of keys, and then the thick door of the slave dungeon creaked open. Sgt. Robertson was standing there with three other soldiers behind him, peering into the packed mass.

Gesturing with the gun that had the bayonet on the end, he shouted, "Move aside, all you niggers. Move *aside!*"

Nobody understood his words, but the back-and-forth swinging of the great knife at the end of his gun indicated that he wanted their ranks to part so he could see into the mob. Amidst the shouting that always erupted at any appearance of the white men, the slaves complied.

As they did so, Sgt. Robertson's glance darted about the room until it found Saleh, who was crouched against the back wall. "Wait—there! *That* one!"

He pointed at her with the knife and made jerking motions back toward himself. The slaves saw that he wanted Saleh and began to push her toward the door. Immediately, her instinct to resist flamed to life, and she started to scream and struggle. But the momentum of the massed bodies was so great that she was helpless and was pressed steadily forward, like a stick before a slide of rocks.

Near the door, she thrust her heels out and tried to stop the surge, casting desperate eyes around her and screaming, "Are there no *men* here? Are you all *cowards*?"

Then, her eyes flashing about in despair, she saw Kano.

He was staring at her. Instantly, she found herself locked into the powerful gaze of his dark eyes. He shook his head, so subtly that she was not sure she had really seen it. But something of his clarity and detachment seemed to flow into her as his eyes pierced her depths and, suddenly, to her own surprise and relief, she stopped struggling. The voice and presence of the God of the Great River Rock seemed to well up inside her.

"Stand firmly," it said. "Not against them but for yourself. None of this will harm you. If you stand firmly, it will only make you stronger. To survive, you must grow stronger every day. These white men will test you as you have never been tested before."

The calmness and solidity of the hours she had spent at the river returned to her. She fell silent, raised her head, disengaged herself from the pushing hands and walked calmly forward. The door clanged shut behind her and, surrounded by the red-coated soldiers, she mounted the ramp, naked but for her loin cloth, and filthy, her strides shortened by her leg irons.

After crossing the courtyard, she was halted by soldiers who struck off her chains. As night was falling, she was taken up a flight of stairs to a room, brightly lit with oil lamps, where a silent, thin, very old black woman with the facial scarring of a people unknown to Saleh awaited her. Seeing this black woman, and finding herself alone with her, hope rose in Saleh.

"Grandmother," she said in a whisper, in case these white men were spying on her, "how can I get away from these devils? *Help* me, Grandmother."

Without replying or looking at her, the woman drew her toward a large wooden tub filled with warm water. There, the dirt of the slave pen was carefully washed from her hair and body, and the silent, old woman dried her with a large piece of absorbent cloth of a softness Saleh had never experienced. Her short hair was anointed with a sickly sweet unguent that the slave woman massaged methodically down to the roots. Afterwards, noxious perfume from a small, blue phial was dabbed on her thighs and breasts. Her dirty loincloth was discarded. She was given a new one to replace it, and the woman wrapped a piece of sheer muslin around her upper body, covering but not concealing her breasts.

Saleh tried speaking to her again. "Grandmother! Why will you not *answer* me? Do you not understand Fulani?"

Saleh asked the question again, this time in Mandinka. Finally, the old woman met her gaze. Her scarring—three upward-slanting marks on each cheek—made her bony face with its wide forehead look catlike. She stared at Saleh.

Her eyes were pale with the beginnings of the blind sickness. But, despite the sickness, her eyes spoke. It was as if she, for a moment, allowed the girl to look into their depth to see, in a way, all she had seen, and the completeness with which it had broken her. All that remained was the part that moved, ate and worked. Everything else was dead. The shock to Saleh was like a physical blow.

Just then, Sgt. Robertson pushed open the door and motioned to her. "Come on."

Saleh, not moving, continued to stare at the old woman, whose dimming eyes were still on the girl, open books for the new slave to study to the deepest level she had the courage to look.

Impatient, Sgt. Robertson took two steps into the room, grabbed Saleh's arm and pulled her out into the corridor. "I said *come on,* you stupid little nigger!"

Saleh's eyes did not leave the old woman's until the closing door came between them. She was taken to another room—this one also well lit and luxuriously appointed but messy and stinking of alcohol. Standing in the room, wearing only loose breeches and an open shirt, and drinking out of a large goblet, was the agent Potts. Saleh now noticed the lines in his weathered face; his watery, grey eyes reddened from drink; and his thinning, gray hair combed down to his shoulders.

She refused his offer of beer but accepted a large tumbler of cool water and a dish of cooked yams. The water she drank immediately, and its effect on her was soothing and regenerative. She did not look at the white man but over his shoulder toward a window through which came a little fading sunlight.

"Aren't *you* a pretty thing," Potts said. His voice was thick from drink.

Saleh had no idea what he was saying but realized that it was meant to reassure her. She picked up a yam from the bowl and raised it to her mouth.

"Ah, what a *lovely* face. I saw a Chinese girl like you once. Those same high cheekbones, same sort of dark, slanting eyes …"

As he spoke, he was stripping off his breeches. She saw his small, stiff penis and was not frightened.

Saleh had only taken a single bite of her yam before Potts pushed her down onto a disordered bed, on the sheets of which she saw what she thought were the stains of dried semen. While she was yet chewing, he snatched off her wrap, lifted her loincloth and pushed inside her.

The calm of the river god remained as Potts enveloped her with his liquor breath, seized hold of her head, grunting loudly, and humped at her as she had seen a lion hump a lioness. He was not in her a minute before he spent himself and collapsed onto her.

After resting for a few moments, he climbed off, now ignoring her, and shouted, "Sgt. Robertson!"

The door opened and Sgt. Robertson came in, without his gun, his coat off and his shirt open. Potts, pulling on his trousers, lurched toward the open door as Sgt. Robertson began to strip off his.

Suddenly, Saleh felt comforted by a sense of deep understanding and serenity. It was as if the river gods themselves had come into the room behind Sgt. Robertson to help her direct her thoughts and breathe up courage out of her heart. In that instant, she knew beyond any doubt that she would never be like the old grandmother and die in despair, and that these white men had no real power over her unless she yielded to them inside herself. Now she understood Kano's detachment and what he had been trying to teach her about remaining calm and clearheaded and aware.

What Kano had said was true. Courage was everything; nothing could be accomplished without it. But she now saw that courage came in many forms, only one of which was defiance. The courage she needed with these white men was not defiance but the quiet solidity of the inner self, the river-rock self that could never be breached by even the most violent batterings against her outer shell.

She now knew that she could bear their indignities and insults without reacting, while remaining, deep inside, steadily fixed on and certain of the day—which she knew *must* come—that she would take her revenge.

As Sgt. Robertson stepped from his trousers and turned toward her with his large, pink erection bobbing, Saleh's hand darted out toward the plate of yams on the table beside the bed. She grabbed hold of a large one and, as Sgt. Robertson lowered himself onto her, already grunting with anticipated pleasure, Saleh stuffed the yam into her mouth.

It turned out to be worse than Kano had predicted, for there were not eight or ten men who had her body that day but at least twenty. She could not be sure. After Sgt. Robertson, there were six more soldiers; the rest were men, who were not soldiers or at least not dressed as such. She had no idea who they were.

Some of them were black. For all she knew, they were merchants or Fante tribesmen the English were cultivating from the little town that lay just beyond the castle walls, or perhaps slaver middlemen. She knew instinctively that all of them had great value to the white men or they would not be granted such a privilege as this. All smelled of drink. Some insisted on kissing her. Some talked to her in words she was grateful to not understand.

Gradually, as she saw how a strong, healthy mind could operate even in such filth and disorder as this, she felt and noticed each successive man less than the one before. She did not look at their faces. She wanted nothing of their identities to remain on her as the juice of a rotten fruit remains on the skin it has stained. Inwardly, she said the prayer of purification, releasing herself from each man's evil as he departed. One of the men struck her, though she had no idea why. He said something two or three times in a harsh voice and, when she did not respond, the blow fell.

To herself, she said, "Perhaps I will not be able to repay this man personally. But I will make other white men suffer in his place. And I will trust that the gods will not let this one escape the fruits of his evil."

Her ordeal lasted about an hour and a half. And, by the end, she had finished the yams.

Kano was proved right in yet another way.

The very next day, a ship appeared and dropped anchor about a quarter mile out from Cape Coast Castle. She was the Lady Dora—a huge, wallowing slaver of two thousand tons, eighteen guns, out of Charleston in South Carolina, painted a gay blue and yellow, Captain Nathan Collins commanding. Apprised of this, Potts ordered the seaward guns fired in salute. Shotless but fully powdered, the great naval cannon roared out the factor's welcome.

Answering with a barrage of her own, the Lady Dora at once lowered a boat containing four men, two of whom sat astern while the other two rowed through the smooth seas to a pier projecting out into the little cove from the shingle below the castle's flank. The rowers wore the loose, knee-length breeches, bloused shirts and headscarves of sailors everywhere, while the two being rowed wore dress coats of blue, despite the heat, and three-cornered hats also in blue. One of the two had white piping on his hat; the other gold.

They had no sooner tied up their dory amid the welter of the castle's boats drawn up at the pier than a large, stout basket on thick ropes, threaded through pulleys, descended down the wall to them, so that the honored guests need not laboriously climb the stone staircase. There was room in the basket for all four, and quickly they were hoisted up by sweating slaves over the parapet, with its long line of massive cannon, to the courtyard, where they were greeted by John Potts.

The chief factor was clean-shaven and dressed in an out-of-fashion, dark green velvet waistcoat over a cream-colored shirt with ruffles at the throat and sleeves, and tan breeches with strings tied in bows behind the knees, such as had not been seen in England for thirty years. His gray hair was tied at the nape with a black silk ribbon.

Sgt. Robertson and the detachment of His Majesty's marines were drawn up in the full sun, sweating in their red dress coats, at attention nearby. Captain Collins, a surprisingly young man—he looked no older than twenty-five—with a cherubic face, blonde hair worn long and tied back, smiled. (He was the one with the gold piping on his hat.) He bounded out of the basket and held out his hand to the chief factor.

"Mr. Potts!" he cried. "It is so good to *see* you again!"

"Captain Collins!" Potts replied. "How you stay so hearty and youthful in such a taxing business as ours I shall *never* know. And you, a ship-owning captain of forty, who looks no older than a midshipman!"

Captain Collins laughed and wrung Potts's hand affectionately. "Well, my dear sir," he said comfortably, "it is all by the grace of a just and loving God. As you know, I take neither liquor nor tobacco and spend time daily seeking the guidance of the Lord in prayer. I am fortunate to have—as do we all—agreeable and useful work, sanctioned by Holy Scripture, which is also a great boon to the poor benighted Negroes. Owing to our interventions, they now can enjoy the blessings of the Christian religion and the advantages of civilized society." The radiance of his smile testified to his sincerity.

"They can indeed," said Potts. "And it so happens that I have some on hand to whom you can extend those advantages beginning today—provided, of course, that we can reach agreement on price, which I confess, given our prior relations, I have no doubt that we shall." He too smiled, as still his and Captain Collins's hands were joined.

"And I, sir," said the captain, "have a cargo of New England rum, fine or finer than any ever seen before on this coast, the distillers in Boston having perfected the taste of the beverage to such a high degree as was formerly thought impossible. Tho', as you know, I myself abstain from drink for reasons of religion, I have tasted personally the rum we have now on board, for I would not carelessly sell anyone a blind pig in a poke.

"And I must say, Mr. Potts, that if alcoholic beverage may become nectar, this of ours has done so. And, of course, I have brought with me a goodly sample of it for the delectation of yourself and your factors, which you may like to enjoy whilst we discuss the details of our transaction."

Here, Captain Collins opened a large satchel that he had carried aboard, showing the factor the glistening bottles of rum it contained.

Potts smiled. "I doubt it will be prudent in me to try it *whilst* we discuss our business. But afterwards is another matter entirely!"

Captain Collins bowed.

Negotiations had begun. They removed to Potts's quarters in the cool interior, where juices and fruit and a sweet cake had been set out on a thick-legged table. Potts's Fante wife Ti, who was accustomed to being present during all discussions of trade, was on a visit to her family a few miles up the coast. Captain Collins was grateful for this, since in Ti he had found a trading adversary superior to Potts, and one who, moreover and unlike her rather diffident mate, was inclined to fits of ill nature.

One of the other three men—the first mate Will Grainger, who had come ashore with Captain Collins and who also wore dress coat and hat—remained with his captain but kept silent during the ensuing discussion. Like every other first mate in the trade, he sought the captaincy and ownership of a vessel. An owner-captain's profit share of every voyage was naturally much higher than a mate's. It was to these high shares that every sober man in the trade aspired. Drunkards may have aspired also but would lack the clarity and energy required to bring them about. Grainger, like his captain a nondrinker, possessed both.

Today, first mate Grainger's role was, as usual, a passive one. Should he discover anything in the sale under discussion that he thought would be a disadvantage to his captain, he would of course discreetly advise him on the chance that the captain had not seen it himself. But, for the most part, Grainger listened and continued to learn. Soon, he would have enough money saved to lease a ship from an owner's consortium, when his share would be higher than now but not yet a full owner-captain's share. That too would come in time, the natural fruit of unremitting industry.

Meanwhile, he gave the service and loyalty to his captain that was the latter's due and made it his business to keep alive as many slaves as possible during the rigors of the two-month Atlantic crossing by seeing that his crew neither neglected nor abused them. Grainger had served on slavers where these two managerial principles were ignored, to the great detriment of profits. He simply could not fathom carelessness of that sort and did not permit it on ships whose crews he supervised.

Of course, mixing with the darkies in the stinking hold was onerous work, especially releasing the dead from the long chain that threaded through all their shackles, because it meant moving among the suffering, sweating and shouting live ones, and through scattered piles of excrement and puddles of urine, which no crewman liked to do.

Of course, once the live ones saw their dead wives or husbands or children being hauled topside to be cast overboard, they could grow ugly. For this reason, some mates, all of whom Grainger thought idiots, simply left the dead in place, only culling them once or twice during the whole voyage. This resulted in completely unacceptable levels of stench and disease in the hold as well as rage—and panic—amongst the survivors, and might cause a dreaded uprising or such a general die-off as to make the trip profitless and a losing proposition.

The thought of losing money on any voyage where he was first mate was such a poisonous one to Grainger that it made him melancholy and ill. However—and this was the reason Grainger sought to serve under him—with a man like Captain Collins, such a result would be unthinkable. No, Collins was as sensible a man as any in the trade. And, on the fundamental principle of slave management, Grainger and his captain were agreed: Care equals condition, and condition equals profit.

The other two men who had come ashore in the dory were simple crewmen. But, beyond the undemanding role of rowing, Captain Collins liked them to mingle and drink with the marines and the factor's assistants, and try to learn with some reliability how long it had been since the last sale.

If recent, he knew the factor would not be worried about the slaves' condition and would hold out for higher prices. But, if it had been a long time since he had made a sale, the slave dealer would be concerned that effects of the crowding and poor diet would show. Also, he would need to clear space for incoming captives. Thus, he would be apt to let the slaves go more reasonably because of the eventually unacceptable crowding. Knowing this fact at the beginning was of great value to the captain. And indeed, he had already been discreetly informed by his men that the cells were overcrowded and the black mob was in desperate need of culling.

Everything seemed to indicate a good sale at good prices. Of course, Captain Collins could guess how long they had been in the stone cells from their general appearance, although Potts would never permit him to inspect them in the pit itself but only in groups in the courtyard—and only after they had been made "presentable." So, careful man that he was, the captain bided his time before concluding anything. It was this very carefulness that made Captain Collins such an agreeable master to a profit-minded mate like Grainger.

One other person, who had remained aboard in command while his superiors went ashore, possessed some small authority on the Lady Dora. This was Andrew Samuels, the second mate. He was a short, broad-shouldered man, much marked by the pox. And, with his wide-set eyes, small, rounded ears and long, blunt nose, he resembled a badger. He was also marked by psoriasis, though not broadcast but in a ragged line running along his nose and up his forehead. This striping made him especially badger-like.

Captain Collins, though an exemplary Christian and faithful in his daily habit of prayer and scriptural reflection, did have a singular fault, which, though burdensome to others, he tended to view indulgently: He had a tendency to tease.

One seaman, who wore a peg leg below the knee, Captain Collins called, to his face, Mr. Stump. Another, Carlson, who had lost an eye in battle while serving in the British navy, the captain enjoyed referring to as Mr. Cyclops. And second mate Samuels, owing to his unique markings, he invariably addressed as Mr. Badger.

Grainger, to please his captain, did the same. The rest of the crew, though they were Samuels's subordinates, felt encouraged by these officers' liberties to take liberties of their own. So, quickly and permanently, Samuels became Mr. Badger to all, just as he had on every other ship on which he had sailed before the Lady Dora.

Now, second mate Samuels was neither a good-humored nor a forgiving man. Having been made fun of his whole life, he was raw and ugly at his core. In a long career—he was forty and had sailed to sea at age thirteen—he had heard far too much about badgers.

It was known that he had never married and had little to say of women. But he had a secret life ashore, in the lowest neighborhoods of the port cities, with desperate, disabled women—scarred, broken-limbed, even bleeding women, some prostitutes and some ale sellers and the like—who appealed to no other men. He loved their suffering and helplessness, the readiness with which they grasped at his money. The sight of them brought him a great sense of well-being, strength, vigor, even something like cheerfulness. Looking down on them spread out in their ugly powerlessness—sores visible, missing teeth, smelly— summoned his maleness with a rush. At every port, he had taken at least one such woman, and often more, and nobody knew.

Nor was it known that, in sailors' taverns in each of the cities of Liverpool, London, New York and Kingston, he had killed a man who had teased him. In each case, he had sat alone in a saloon, quietly drinking—often after having satisfied himself in a dark lane with a sick or bleeding woman to his liking—and suffered the arrival of a mean-spirited stranger, heard all about badgers, smiled faintly, left casually.

Then he had waited in the darkness outside the tavern, hours if need be, until the offender emerged. He followed him, surprised him from behind, dragged him by brute strength into an alley and cut the man's throat, making a terrible, deep and satisfying slash with the great flensing knife he carried in a sheath on his belt, cutting from behind so that the victim's body shielded Badger from the spurting arterial blood.

To each of the astonished and horrified victims, as they lay dying in the filth of the alley, feeling the lethal outrush of their blood and the shock of coldness from the downward plunge of blood pressure, Samuels leaned over and said the very same words: "Never thought you'd be killed by a badger, *did* you?"

Not a single living soul besides himself knew of these killings or of these women. Because he was so quiet and passive, nobody was afraid of Samuels. And second mates, having only limited authority, and he being apparently mild, there was little thought and no apprehension about how Samuels would behave should his situation drastically improve. And, all things being equal, Samuels should never have presumed to rise so high as a captain's chair, with its prerogatives and unimpeachable powers, since he lacked both the intelligence and ability required to fill it.

Unfortunately, the world being what it is, all things are never equal.

The men were restless for shore leave, but the captain had denied it until he had sold his rum and bought his slaves. In case the price of one was too low and the other too high, he would cast off at once and sail further south. There were many slave ports from which to select, where rum was wanted and slaves were for sale. Indeed, rum was the one thing most demanded by the African nations, they having been resolutely brought to a yearning for it by generations of white slavers. And, Captain Collins feeling in no way obliged to or especially fond of Potts, his dory might at any moment now be seen pulling for the ship.

But no. There came no sign of his returning. Samuels assumed that a sale must be in process. He would leave the rum barrels lashed in their places on the shelves below deck where, once they had been passed topside and put into boats for transport ashore, and the decks cleared, hundreds of chained Negroes would take their place. That was not yet, however. Nothing distresses a sailor more than wasted motion. Samuels would bide his time and await the captain's orders.

Just then, the one-eyed sailor Carlson, whom Captain Collins had named Mr. Cyclops, called out to him: "Mr. Badger!"

Samuels looked down from where he stood on the quarterdeck to Mr. Cyclops, who was leaning casually against the footing of the mainmast. The black patch that Carlson wore over his empty eye socket made him look dangerous and pirate-like. But, in fact, he was a quiet, decent man, no longer young, with a strong taste for rum.

"Aye, Carlson," Samuels replied.

He never addressed Carlson as Mr. Cyclops. Inside, Samuels felt the familiar lurching to life, at the word "badger," of the huge mass of resentment that lived forever in his chest, always growing as it seemed larger and more turbulent, never lightening, never shrinking back. It made a thrusting, that hot mass, like a battering ram inside him. The only thing that ever eased it was a man's blood on his shoes. Then, for days or weeks, he had a cheerful, good humor in him and lovely mental pictures to sort through and a blood-bubbling, begging voice to hear and rehear in the dark of his hammock.

"I know you can't let us go ashore, sir," Carlson said. "But won't you give us a rum ration at least? Our work's done, and we've but to wait, sir. It won't hurt nothing."

He was decent enough—if only he hadn't said "badger."

The thought of rum flashed through Samuels very agreeably. He loved rum, as it was an ally in his shedding of redemptive blood. But he rarely drank while aboard ship lest his mind stray or his tongue slip. Instead, he stood aft while others drank, leaning on the rail, looking at the ship's wake as it glowed silver in the ocean dark, dreaming his private dreams.

He thought of how badgers had been known to dig down to newish graves, being both powerful and creative animals, to get at the rotting meat inside the coffins. How too they penetrate the dens of skunks, slaying skillfully, swallowing the reeking musk sacs and clean flesh together, with good relish; how easily they kill dogs set on them; how invisibly like night shadows they drift through yard and cote, with such strength undermining heavy coop doors, with such stealth killing unheard, departing unseen.

Perhaps, without his knowing it, Samuels had fallen under the badger influence himself, just as the Negroes all had animals whose spirits instructed and protected them. Perhaps there was even a great tribe of badgers in the invisible world that called to their own, as the Negroes believed that lions, hyenas and crocodiles did.

Many times, Samuels had found himself thinking well of badgers before recalling the shame they represented to him. There was nothing that could correct it. That question was settled, and four dead men with slashed throats proved it.

Yet, at the same time, he was forever finding good in badgers and traits he could emulate. He found the paradox odd. It was even burdensome because, if he could simply embrace his *badgerness*, he could cease from killing. But he knew that he did not want to. Love of killing was detached from the badgerness now; spilled blood had wakened it to be a governing voice and revealed a self too deep to die.

That great mass of resentment, swirling with hates and rages, had become his real self—the "him" that was truly Samuels, with his history, parents, pride and passions. Yet it was a new sort of Samuels too. To his knowing, never had a man of his name murdered anyone. But it was also true that he no longer cared who lived or died, so long as he retained dignity and an ever-deepening pleasure.

He was greatly charmed, reassured, by the maturing of this force that had remained untouched in him since first he felt it, dimly and distantly, even before he had ever sailed to sea. So, even if he appeared outwardly the same, he knew that he had been cleft with half of him joyful in blood, pain and death, and the other half putting itself to sleep at night just as always with the Lord's Prayer.

However, that balance was being lost. The dark was eating the light, and the light remained only as a mere misleading shell. For beyond bringing justice against the scoffers and teasers, beyond the alchemy in his man's body, which seemed at times to turn him into fire-hardened oak, the smell of blood itself was now exotic. The thought of any violent, bloody death intrigued and comforted him, and *called* to him …

Samuels had begun yearning of late to openly act out the maiming and slow deaths of strangers, which came as a keen surprise, a delightful marvel to him. How this taste to publicize came to inhabit him, he never knew or cared. It seemed that, day by day, the most real, most hidden of all his inner selves was breeching—a great Leviathan from unseeable depths. And how good it was at last to see and know the truth, to find in his murderous revenges the keenest liveliness, the sweetest gifts of spirit!

Inside him, he heard increasingly a voice detached from his own, as if a god's. It spoke in a rich, almost biblical language, demanding appeasement. It asked questions he could not answer except by the voice's own promptings.

Today, standing on the quarterdeck, pondering Mr. Cyclops's request for rum, this voice whispered in his soul: "Was there peace in any place ye have ever set foot? Nay, say ye? Know ye where there may be found peace that ariseth not in the shedding of blood? If so, recollect it and hie thee thence. If not, then act the man's part, be neither coward nor fool, but shower me with the blood that bringeth the good peace, that it may please me and release thee, to the limits of all desiring. Let it be done for pleasure as always. But let it be done under the gaze of men in the guise of justice, and I promise ye a pleasure till now unimagined …"

And Mr. Badger said, "Aye, Carlson. Issue the rum."

1840

PINEWOOD PLANTATION, VIRGINIA

Against his every expectation, Young George did not have intercourse with Young Sally that first day or the second or that week or the week after or the week after that. Instead, he felt when with her as if he was in an enchanted fairyland, where all former practices of his own were exposed as shallow and patience took hold of him like a drug.

"Don' yo want me ter take off my clothes, suh?" Young Sally asked him that first day in the guestroom at the end of the hallway.

She was sitting on the bed by his side, letting him kiss her but not responding. Her eyes were clear, he noticed, and sad. Their being sad sent a pang through him.

"Are you frightened, sweet girl?" he asked, touching her face.

"Yas, suh. I tol yo no good kin come fum dis fer me. When I tink on it, I git trembly inside. Niggas kin get hung fer de lak of dis." Again, tears stood in her eyes.

Again, they confounded Young George. "*Hung?* What madness is this, dear girl? Do you imagine that I would ever let anything happen to you?"

Inside, he felt a jolt of happiness and the desire to compulsively self-disclose. His caution warned him not to, but he rushed ahead anyway and was proud of himself afterwards.

"Young Sally, I don't know what has come over me, but I have fallen in love with you. All I want is to be with you. Whatever happens between us—I say *whatever* happens between us—I shall free you. I shall free any children I am fortunate enough to have by you. I shall set you up in a home of your own—in Richmond, in Baltimore, or at the North somewhere, Washington City, New York … it is up to you. You will always be provided for."

Young George suddenly felt a little current of alarm. *Dear God!* What undertakings was he making to this slave girl? None of it was necessary. He had only to throw up her dress, cast her down on the bed and fuck her. Yet the mere thought of that sickened him. *He was in love!*

Young Sally stared at Young George just as he had once seen Decatur, the black playmate of his childhood, stare at a rabid dog. "Suh, yo don' be needin to talk dat way ter no nigga. Yo kin git whut yo wants widout lyin. Man lak yo don' belong sittin heah lyin to no House nigga. Dat beneath yo, suh." The rebuke was strong in her voice.

"Ah! So you think I am *lying*? Well, I don't blame you. But I swear I am in earnest. How can I convince you?"

He wanted to embrace her but instead pulled his hands back and, not knowing what else to do with them, joined them at his waist, like an effeminate dancing master. If she only knew, really knew, how clumsy, how nervous he felt!

"White man don' got ter convince no nigga of *nothin*. Why yo talkin lak dis, suh?"

An edge was creeping into her voice. In his whole life, he had never seen a slave raise her voice to a white man without getting whipped. But the thought of whipping Young Sally made him ill. Yet, right at that moment, had he realized it, she was revealing a contrary, even disrespectful part of herself, quite at odds with her normal shyness, which would later, encouraged by her growing sense of security, bedevil him.

"I don't think of you as a nigger," he said at last.

Young Sally's eyes widened. "*Why* yo don', suh? I ain't nothin, but yo kin see dat as good as I kin."

"I know," he heard himself saying, another proof of his unbalanced state. "But, if I admitted that you were a nigger, I couldn't feel about you as I do. And I have no idea why I feel this way. But watching you, as you came and went in the dining room, listening to your quiet voice, seeing your modesty, and your beauty … your eyes, for example … your very beautiful hazel eyes … so expressive … your grace … your … intelligence …"

He was going to say, "Your perfect hips and bosom," but he stopped.

Young Sally stared at him, still disbelieving but now a little intrigued. "Yo nevah tol me yo was feelin all dat, suh."

"*Told* you? My God, how *could* I have? I knew it was wrong of me. Must you call me sir?"

Young Sally frowned and fear took back her face. "Oh, dear Jesus, don' start on *dat* now, suh. I feels lak I is standin on de top step of hell a'ready. Don' start bout not callin yo 'suh.'"

"Of course. Mad of me. I apologize. I don't know what to say or how to act. I don't want to force you into anything. I don't want you to be afraid." He paused, and then pushed on, intense and irrational. "I have had Lucy. Did you know that?"

Young Sally dropped her eyes, hesitated. "Ev'body know dat, suh."

Young George was annoyed. "*Everybody?*"

"Yas, suh. Y'all tink niggas is stupid. I don' mean no disrespeck, suh. But—"

Young Sally checked herself. Next, she would be giving away secrets of the quarters, secrets that a white man was never meant to know. She could not do that. Not even if she came to trust him, which she was sure she never would. But her first loyalty must always be to her own kind. She could not bear to think that she would put into a white man's hands more weapons than he already had. If she were to be brought low, then she would not take any other slaves down with her. She would give away no secrets. Never. Not even to her ... *brother.*

"You charming creature! What did you stop yourself from saying just now?"

Young George impulsively reached for her hand, raised it to his lips and kissed it. The mystery scent again.

Young Sally gasped. "Oh, *no*, suh. Dat dere's courtin." She pulled her hand back. "Yo don' belong courtin no nigga woman. I cain't *stand* dat, suh. Yo gon make me *crazy* now. Dis heah's got all bent out from no'mal shape, suh. I cain't abide it. I aks you please ter let me go now."

Astonished, Young George sat speechless. Then, "Because I kissed your hand, you want to go?"

"Yas, suh."

"Because it's *courting?*"

"Ack lak, tho I know it ain't. How *could* it be? But I jes feels lak I got set down in a country where I don' know dey langwich. I don' know de words. It all ain't settin right. I jes wants ter git away. Please, suh. Please leave me be, Young Marse Geo'ge. Please jes leave me work lak I always done, an me stay wit my own folk an yo stay wit yers. Yo a married man, suh. Yo kin even put me out in de fields if yo wants, an I won' git in yo way no mo, suh. Jes keep me out'n de House an I won't trouble yo no mo." Again the tears, but now of fear and frustration—above all, of confusion.

Finally Young George asked, "Do you know why I mentioned Lucy?"

Young Sally, her eyes lowered, shook her head.

"Because I wanted you to know that I don't want you as I wanted her. I wanted her for her sex. But with you—I want *you*. I am in love with *you*."

Sitting on the bed, Young Sally looked at her master unbelievingly, as if he was speaking and she listening in a dream. Then she abruptly raised her hands to her face and burst into sobs. In a minute, she was gasping and breathless as the crying took hold. She fell over onto her side on the bed, brought her knees up and cried so deeply that Young George was shocked.

He noticed that, as she brought up her legs, her calves were revealed. Young George stared at their silkiness and light brownness while Young Sally wept. He marveled that they were plump-looking without Young Sally herself being plump. No, they were not plump. Shapely. Yes. They were shapely. He was very strongly moved to rest his hand on her calf and gradually stroke up under her dress.

Now that he thought about it, that was how he had taken Elizabeth for the first time. Weeping on her wedding night in her bridal nightgown, he had stroked her legs while she sobbed, and then moved to her quim. In ten minutes, she was on her back, guiding him in, though virgin as a nun. And what a fine fuck *that* was! One of the best with Elizabeth he ever had. Indeed, it had inferred a promise that was never kept. But with Young Sally? *No!* Instinct be damned! He'd rather grope his mother.

In his journal, he wrote:

> Thus ended the time, I folding her in my arms whilst she wept.
> Then she crept out, saying, "If Miz Elizabeth find out, I might as well be daid, suh."
> I forewent the midday meal and, at dinner with Elizabeth, avoided looking at Young Sally, though glancing covertly. She behaved as if she were waiting on the King and Queen of England. I must be out of my mind! Perhaps I ought to let it lie, as she has asked. Put it behind me. There is no doubt that would be by far the best thing.

1822

PINEWOOD PLANTATION, VIRGINIA

All along, Sally had been trying to prevent conception. She never let Cicero, to whom George had married her, touch her, though she knew it went against his rights. But she felt that her own rights went deeper and arose from a greater truth. With George, she had no choice, so she took the precautions she had learned from her uncle Tenkaminen. Even though she had lost all love for the gods on the slave ship, she knew that a sorcerer's spells were binding on the powers both in this earth realm and the ones higher. So she did what she knew to do.

Sally drank haw tea at each new moon, lay motionless during coitus and turned onto her left side immediately afterwards. And she wore a yarn string soaked in coal oil around her neck for nine straight days, twice a month. When, despite this, she got pregnant, she tried to abort the baby. She drank a brew made from blue cohosh, but it did not work.

She tried the strongest remedy she knew of: infusions of powdered cotton root in very hot water with a spell spoken over it. She spoke the spell in the required way, in a single breath without the tiniest gasp, pause or in-drawing of air, and then drank. But when that too failed, she realized that the gods wanted this baby in her belly—a girl whom George named Young Sally. This meant that she could not strangle the baby at birth either, as many other slave women did unless the master discovered and stopped them.

So she bore Young Sally.

And, ever afterwards, bore with her.

1801

CAPE COAST CASTLE, WEST AFRICA

John Potts (the general agent), Sgt. Robertson, and the soldiers and factors and tradesmen had only two days to enjoy Saleh before they had to turn their attention to the arrival and accommodation of the Lady Dora. Saleh was grateful on the second day when she was returned to the cell where the slaves were after the white men had finished with her.

Kano came and touched her shoulder. He spoke in a voice so low, his lips so close to her ear, that she felt every tiny exhalation of his warm breath.

"I noticed your restraint and admired it," he whispered, though in his usual blunt manner, which, now that he had chastened her, she no longer dared resent. "You not only have saved your life by it but showed me that you can be useful in my plan to escape. Are you interested?" His voice was soft, indicating that he had forgiven her, as well as low, to escape being overheard. And he smiled, perhaps to see if she would still chide him for it.

She did not. Instead, she felt glad to be with him again, with the chance to look once more upon his strong body, handsome face and dark, fearless eyes. The impulse to scold arose, as it always did at any sign of another's strength, but now she curbed it. She had come to understand that, with Kano, her peevishness worked against her. She had been forced by her fearful circumstances to accept that no situation could be understood, much less judged, without careful study. She knew that this new perception of hers was true, for with it had come such a sense of solidity and self-possession as could never accompany sham. She knew too, and clearly, that Kano was her benefactor, and she wanted to know more from him now that she was certain he could teach her.

And beyond that, there was something in the man that called to her—to a part of her that she had not before experienced.

"Yes, I am interested," she whispered back. She was conscious of barely moving her lips. "I am honored that you can still trust me. I ask your pardon for my willfulness."

"You have it." Though he was so close to her ear that she could not see his face, but his voice told her that he was smiling "And if my plan works as I hope, you can have your revenge against the ugly white man with the long, gray hair."

At this, Saleh brightened. To give voice to the elation this brought, she wanted to shout but only whispered, as before, "I had never thought I would have such a chance!"

"Yes, good," Kano went on. "But it's not his death I'm looking for. Actually, he will not suffer much except in his sense of security and in his reputation, which to him will be bad enough. Oh, I dare say I can let you cut him just a little, to punish him and terrify the others. But it is not to our advantage to harm him much. I shall explain why presently. However, no such prohibitions exist as regards the captain of the slaver. In fact, he will have to die if our—I do say *our*, as you see—plot is to succeed."

Saleh was grateful for this but still felt moved to question him closely. But she did not because of how awkward it was speaking to him under these conditions and because she had come very quickly to trust him and fear his rejection.

Instead, she asked cautiously, "How do you mean?"

Kano took her arm and, without answering, pulled her through the press of bodies to a place against the wall of the cell where, by pushing people back, he managed to clear a space where they could nestle together, face to face. Many of the slaves, given enough food and water to calm them, instead of pacing about in rage and fear, now sat on the floor listlessly, exhausted and crushed together.

But it was impossible for Kano to separate them enough to feel confident of secrecy, so he pulled Saleh very close to be sure that she would catch his words. He spoke in a quiet, intense voice for five minutes, telling her, among other things, an important fact that he had learned about this slave ship captain. He wore a dagger on his belt. Then Kano told her all of his simple plan, repeated it in slightly different words and then fell silent, looking questioningly into her eyes.

A little time passed.

At length, Saleh said, as intensely as he, "If you are waiting for my assent, you have it. I shall be very happy if we succeed, and I can go home to Tekrur. And I am also willing to die if we do not."

Kano looked surprised. "*Home*, you say? Would not your father have to remit your bride price if you did that?"

"No. By selling me into slavery, my husband breached the agreement he had made with my father. Thinking that my father was sincere in all his wailings about not wanting me sold, that Mandinka offered to agree, all on his own accord, never to sell me to the slavers. My father, of course, gave a great sigh, with a show of relief and, in truth, I think he did care, though his desperation outweighed his sentiments. But now it has worked to my advantage, should I ever want to go home."

It was not lost on Kano that she had quickly moved from saying she *would* go home to saying she *could*. Nor had she chosen her words by chance … though now was not the time to make anything of it.

What Potts thought of as "the Great Rigmarole" now began in earnest.

He knew that, to empty his badly overcrowded slave quarters, he would have to name a lower-than-desirable price at which he would consent to trade his slaves for the rum. Although actual money never changed hands, both sides had to agree what, in fact, each slave was individually worth and how much rum had to be offered to satisfy it.

This arrangement was agreeable since the price inland for rum that he resold to the blacks was always much higher than what he could get coastside. Though it meant relying again on black middlemen and their crews to carry it in and sell it, with all the vexations and uncertainties attendant upon such an arrangement, still he knew that, allowing for what they would steal, his profit would be high, for his market was constant.

Potts even condescended, to flatter Captain Collins, to sip a tumbler of the touted brew, which of course turned out not to be "nectar" at all but only the ordinary, run-of-the-mill, flavored alcohol that was cheaply produced with undiscriminating blacks in mind. Still, he complimented Captain Collins on it. And, their bargaining over rum concluded, he sent Sgt. Robertson out to the plaza for a squad of marines to begin bringing up the blacks, still in their chains, from the slave pits.

Potts, Captain Collins and Grainger walked up from the cool meeting room into the hot brilliance of the plaza. The baking sun, radiating from a blinding sky, heated the paving stones until their sweating feet soaked their stockings inside thick-soled shoes. The blacks, now being led up and out of the near dark, having gone always barefooted, walked on skin as impervious as leather and, though discomforted by the hot stones, were not much injured—except for the small children, whom the mothers lifted into their arms to spare their tender feet and quiet their cries.

The sale went quickly since Potts's immediate need to part with his slaves was greater than Captain Collins's need to procure them. However, Potts had done all the usual things to make his wares attractive. The instant that the Lady Dora was descried in the offing, Potts had quickly set his whole establishment to work.

Any gray hairs on the slaves were hidden with shoe blacking. Those with diarrhea were cut off from water and fed bowls of cooked oats mixed with rye flour, dry tapioca and crumbled ship's biscuits, in the hope of stemming the flood of excrement until after the sale. (For these unfortunate ones, thirst soon raged, though they were assured by Potts's workers that water was soon to come. But water usually did not come until hours later when they were being stowed in the slaveholds.)

For those displaying the worst, most ungovernable diarrhea yet still appearing robust, Potts employed a novel intervention: He ordered that these slaves have their gushing anuses blocked with oakum, which was a mixture of shredded rope and tar, commonly used aboard ships to stop water leaks in the hull. From all he had heard, this stratagem would serve to get the slaves out to sea before it was discovered, provided the oakum was tamped well up into the anal tube. Also, those with skin blotches were rubbed with a brown dye, and all the slaves were wiped from forehead to toes with palm oil to impart a healthy, glistening look.

After examining minutely the merchandise for sale, and after some intense haggling, Captain Collins bought three hundred slaves at an average price of twenty pounds each. He reasoned that he should, when he sold them on the American coast or at Jamaica, make a profit of at least fifteen pounds on each of these—unless, for reasons beyond his control, they deteriorated in transit.

Of course, some of them would die; this was unavoidable. It sometimes almost seemed to Captain Collins that the Negroes died to spite him, for though he lavished care on them as few captains did, he would be sure to find, day after dreary day, dead men and women in the hold whose only use now was to feed the fishes.

This turn of events could badly discourage a man. Especially as he knew how greatly he was improving the blacks' lot by taking them to a civilized country where they would live amongst Christians and have a hope of heaven. To die while being carried to such a haven as this seemed to Captain Collins almost perverse of the Negroes. He did not ask much of them, after all. But was it unreasonable to expect them to live long enough to appreciate the great good that he was bestowing upon them?

Another hundred Negroes—younger, stronger, radiating a greater life force—went for twenty-five pounds each, and the captain thought that if, at his destination, he was firm in his bargaining, and if the Jamaica market—he had by now decided to offload at Kingston to escape the losses of a longer voyage and reluctantly forego the higher profits at Charleston—was not glutted, he could get fifty each. These slaves were of a decent quality—not the best by far but certainly not the worst—and he had made up his mind that he would absolutely not let them go in a "scramble" sale.

In such sales, the Negroes were herded ashore to a large slave yard and, on a signal (usually a drumbeat or the blowing of a horn), the white buyers and their assistants would rush in amongst the astonished blacks, each team of two or three rounding up and forcing together those they liked, much as a male reebok or zebra does with females at the mating season.

Often, a rogue slave from the town would creep aboard the slaver, riding at anchor, descend to the slavehold and, to tease and frighten the new arrivals, tell them in their own language that the white men—whose palates, he said, favored Negroes over any other meat—have brought them this great distance so that their new owners could eat them. Thus later, in the slave pen ashore, when the white buyers would rush, shouting amongst them, the blacks were overcome with horror and would run helter-skelter in all directions in terror for their lives. This greatly amused the old slaves and the town idlers, who looked on from the sidelines, pointing out the most desperate ones and laughing heartily.

But Captain Collins disliked the disorder of such proceedings in which it was not uncommon for slaves to be injured and lose value, or even escape over the wall, after which it was necessary to sift the surrounding forest, at great trouble, to recapture them. Thus, even as the sale at Cape Coast proceeded, he was already preparing his mind for the most advantageous way to present his bondsmen to the market at Jamaica.

The next fifty slaves that the captain bought would, he knew, fetch higher prices. These were the highest quality slaves of all: agreeable, healthy, handsome, young—even, he admitted, intelligent looking, fit for work in the great houses among the slave owners' families, where they would act as maids, cooks, gardeners, butlers, carriage drivers, nannies and, in the case of the youngest ones, companion slaves to the white children of the household. For these slaves, Captain Collins paid forty pounds each, an enormous sum. But he was confident that he could sell them for sixty at Kingston and a few of them for more.

There was one girl he noticed in particular. Potts had paid more for her and would not let her go for less than sixty pounds. Her beauty was so startling, so ravishing, that he thought he could certainly get eighty pounds for her—or rather, sixteen hundred dollars American—at a minimum. Probably a lot more. If she survived the trip looking as she did now, she might bring two thousand dollars. Hers was a beauty rarely seen: the golden glow of her skin; her dark, Asiatic eyes; and her strong, shapely body and self-possessed carriage. Enchanting!

Watching the parade with Grainger, Captain Collins said, "She's the sort of girl any owner would be anxious to have so as to take to his bed, paying whatever price necessary to outbid competitors at the slave auction. For, quite aside from the enjoyment she'd certainly bring—mind you, I speak not for my own ideals but from an owner's point of view—a man could sire mulattos on her who would be comely and intelligent, and fetch high prices when sold off.

"As we know, mulattos are always in higher demand and bring better prices than the pure blacks, owing to their white blood. Who knows how many little mulatto slaves a strong, beautiful girl like that could produce? Ten would not be a number beyond possibility. And, even figuring an average sale price for them of fifteen hundred dollars each—less, of course, what the owner would have to spend to feed and house them until sold off at age ten or even younger—there's the prospect of an extremely attractive profit."

Grainger said, "Aye, sir. I thank God, sir, that we ship and trade in them, for the money is good if a man knows what he's about. Of course, some die in infancy. Death is the unavoidable risk in any slave investment. Dread of it keeps the faint of heart in the grocery business or other piddling pursuits."

Captain Collins smiled. "While men of courage, like you and me, Mr. Grainger, dare all, and suffer losses and heartbreaks. But, in the end, we grow rich. For wealth is God's way of rewarding the brave."

Grainger nodded as to a universal truth, and together they watched, self-satisfied and cheerful, as the slaves trooped by.

Of course, Collins, the captain, would not profit as greatly as he would wish from the slave auction, more's the pity, if he took them to Charleston or to any other American slave port, owing to the commission he would have to pay the slave dealer/auctioneer. The dealer/auctioneer would then, having again prettied and preened the slaves for the sale, get every dime possible for them, using his keen auction skills and playing upon the rivalries that he knew existed among the local buyers. This fact made Captain Collins even more determined to offload at Kingston and squeeze the slave dealers there as hard as he possibly could, for some of the merchandise he was offering was really top drawer. Refuse slaves aside—who he was forced to take, by custom, with the rest—this lot was as high in quality as any he'd ever shipped.

That girl, for example. The more Captain Collins looked at her, the more money he thought she would bring. She was so exquisite, so sensuous—was even twenty-five hundred dollars possible? He had to admit to himself that, even though as a faithful Christian he did not hold with adultery, he was eager to claim his captain's right to enjoy the fairest of the fair. He had already decided that he would keep her in his cabin during the weeks of transit and have her as much as he liked, thus protecting her value by her good condition and enjoying her charms at the same time. Any sin committed with a Negro was not really a sin, anyway—certainly nothing as serious as if committed with a white woman. Any Christian minister worth a dime would tell you that!

Yet, still pondering the question, he asked his first mate, "Do you, Mr. Grainger, believe that the blacks are human beings like us? Can relations with them be occasions of sin?"

"Well, sir," said Mr. Grainger, gravely shaking his head, "there are—so I have heard—doubts amongst the clergy as to whether the Negroes are human at all.

Whether they have souls or are only—as I myself believe, if you want the truth—members of the lower orders, like hogs, cattle and apes, though with a larger brain. As such, interactions with them carry no spiritual penalties. They have been provided by God—so I believe—for the use of the white man, like horses and sheep, and not being quite human themselves are incapable of being occasions of sin for others."

Captain Collins received this opinion with a wise nod. "Naturally," he said, "it is expected that one would treat them decently, as anybody with a keen self-interest would treat any sentient creature in which a good deal of money is invested. But, I tell you, to worry and fret about them beyond that is idle. The abolitionists must be daft! There are even those amongst them—I have talked to some of them myself—who believe that the Negroes should have equality with whites! You know, Mr. Grainger, this sort of thinking is criminal, and people daring to teach it ought to be imprisoned."

"I could not agree more, sir. Yet, in all our dealings, we must show patience, even mercy when required. In fact, I see it as our Christian duty."

"Exactly. For even if not precisely human, they are sentient."

Still—though Captain Collins did not share this view with Grainger—in some ways, they looked human enough. Especially the attractive ones. Like this girl, for instance. It would be lovely indeed to entertain her in his cabin, wash her, dress her up, scent her, give her wine, make her lusty and enjoy her delights to his heart's content. After a few days of such pampering, he was sure that she would begin to enjoy it. He knew these simple-minded Negro women were quite often swept off their feet, so to say, by men such as himself, and far from resenting the attention given them, gloried in it.

The other crewmen would have their pick of the black women as well. Since slaving was such an onerous duty, and the men who sailed its ships were low characters who expected absolute access to the women, he knew that to deny them their fleshy desires would be dangerous, like snatching the meat from feeding dogs. No, the men would bring the women topside, take them to their quarters or, at night, have them right on the deck under the great white moon of the tropics.

To these goings on, Captain Collins always turned a blind eye (as did Grainger, who likewise patronized the comely) since he obviously could not, as a Christian, sanction them, though how his own conduct might be seen by others he did not examine. But he knew that, if he interfered with them, he would face in his own angry men a greater menace than the slaves themselves could ever present. So, it was a comfort that he did not trouble himself by recognizing how far his own practice diverged from his principles.

It often happened that a few of the Negro women developed passionate attachments to particular crewmen and believed that they would become their wives and live easy lives in the white world, where clever men, using machines and contrivances unheard of at home, would pet and pamper them, give them children, beautiful clothing, exquisite food and slaves of their own.

Nor were the whites at any pains to dissuade the black women from these fancies, for they could point to instances—so rare as to be marvels—of white men, once ashore at home, actually taking black women as mates. But not wives, certainly. For such things were considered unnatural, wicked and against the laws of both God and man.

The last fifty to be sold were refuse slaves. These Captain Collins bought at twenty-five pounds for the whole lot, both he and Potts knowing that he would be lucky indeed if half of them reached Jamaica alive and a half of that half not die in the first ten days ashore. It was more like gambling than investing. And yet Captain Collins would never forget a lot of refuse slaves he had once bought at Anamabu, who actually grew healthier on the ocean voyage.

"Do you recollect them, Mr. Grainger?" he asked smugly.

"Indeed I do, sir. There were sixty-five in that group. But only ten died on the ship, and the rest, for whom we had paid a shilling each, we sold for more than a pound. One—you recall that scrawny Yohimbo, no doubt—had got sleek on the horse beans fed to him in the slavehold and went for ten pounds.

"And that man still lives, to this very day, as far as I know, and has become a slave driver on the plantation that bought him. He has, by his owner's liberality, been permitted to marry, and has taken an Ibo woman offered to him by his master, and she has produced a baby slave a year ever since. All this I learned when last we docked at Jamaica.

"So, from experiences like this, we learn that prudent men—like yourself, sir—do not sneer at refuse slaves but remember that even dangerous gambles can sometimes return great windfalls."

Captain Collins, greatly pleased at the memory of that Yohimbo, and in a mood to take full credit for all the man's subsequent accomplishments, nodded benevolently. "You are most kind, Mr. Grainger."

Left unspoken between them, however, was another truth of the trade, having to do not with the cargo but with the crew.

It was this. So valuable were captives brought safely to market that many captains, confronted suddenly while at sea with a life-threatening emergency, did not favor their white crew over their black slaves. Why should they? If food ran short, they would feed the slaves before the crew, for the crew were worth nothing on the market, so to speak, and, in fact, cost the captains in wages and trouble. If crewmen died while aboard ship, their relatives were owed nothing, even if they died one day short of reaching port. That was the maritime law and owner-captains thanked God for it. Indeed, the closer the ships got to their destination, the less these captains cared about their men's health or welfare.

After the slaves were landed, at Jamaica or elsewhere, they needed only half the number of men than they had while slaved to sail the ship, which was laden with sugar cane, to New England or Virginia. Truth to tell, a very agreeable outcome would actually be for a die-off amongst the crew, in the days just before landfall in Jamaica, from a cause that did not affect the slaves.

Trouble was, such a thing was mostly a sweet fancy—although, in very rare cases, it happened that most of the slaves had already had, for example, smallpox, while most of the crew had not. Jolly good luck then should the sickness flash through the ship! Indeed, slaves with pocked faces fetched higher prices from the buyers since they were clearly immune to the dread ailment.

But, in the horrid case of any epidemic among the slaves, one had to act quickly and throw the infected overboard. For the insurance companies—all of them hard-hearted, unreasonable men—would not cover slaves lost to illness or the wounds of capture. But they *would* pay for slaves lost overboard, probably not imagining that anybody would casually commit scores of living but infected men, women and children to the deep, only to protect profits. Many, and growing louder, were the voices of people, both in England and America, who whined about things of this kind. But what did these humanitarian, abolitionist meddlers *expect* a man to do when faced with the loss of such great sums of money?

Captain Collins had never confronted a situation such as this, although he certainly sympathized with and understood men who had, and did not rule out the possibility of someday having to do such things himself should dire enough conditions arise. For the sad truth was that the murdering of Negroes and the paying out of so many hundreds of dollars to crews were two of the most disagreeable tasks with which any captain of a slaver had to cope.

After all, the crews had their own small share of the profits, did they not? Why else indeed would they ever sign on to a slaver? Everyone who sailed to sea with slaves aboard took risks, often grave ones, did they not? Why should the crews be spared whilst he and other owners had to suffer? He knew this attitude was hard-hearted but, in fact, a common one in his line of work. And he did strive to be reasonable and just, despite the wickedness so general and so discouraging throughout the trade.

Ah, well. Captain Collins knew that one could not throw off completely his Christianity for the sake of profit, though at times his religion did seem to press down upon him so heavily that he was tempted to set it aside until, at an advanced age, when the need to avoid hell reclaimed him, he could be reconciled to God just in time to be whisked to heaven at his last breath. Then the rewards awaited him that awaited all men of character, honor and liberality.

When that moment arrived, he knew that all his toils and sacrifices would be recognized. And he, in the presence of the venerable and beautiful archangels, who stood arrayed in light and sang marvelous hosannas, would see revealed before him in such brilliance as astonishes the mind, the very throne of the eternal god, upon which would sit the Father, his arms extended, his presence radiating the most pure, the most unimaginably wonderful light, sending out a flowing river of love, to enclose and transform him as he, Captain Collins, was received into glory.

1858

PINEWOOD PLANTATION, VIRGINIA

L ittle Master Will was looking at a very agreeable sight—namely, Missy, who was standing by the edge of the West Field, watching the sun go down on this summer day. He was concealed by shrubbery some little way behind her, looking at the sun shining through her dress.

She seemed completely unaware of him. Such a modest, self-contained girl she was! It was almost a crime to creep up on someone so unsuspecting so as to see her lovely body outlined against the glare of the dying light. She had never detected him yet, though he had spied on her before. She seemed very fond of standing just here at sunset. Not only that, she often turned slowly, as if posing for an invisible artist, so that in profile he could see her breasts. She would stretch, laze, turn—all the while the sun streamed through her clothing, revealing her. It surprised him that Missy did not seem to wear petticoats like the other House slave women, but she was only the more interesting for that.

Of course, she was just sixteen and certainly innocent. He had been keenly aware of her all his life, had watched her grow even as he grew and now marveled at her white-girl beauty. There was so little of the nigger in her that it was a shame she couldn't just "pass" her way out of slavery. Should she ever get hold of enough money to buy herself, he would certainly be a liberal enough man to let her go, if the choice were his.

But she seemed attached to Pinewood—and even to him, personally. Sometimes, when passing by her in the House, she turned her innocent smile on him, and he had to admit that he was taken with her. But he had seen his father's disgraceful ways with Missy's mother Young Sally, who he even yet kept in luxury in that cabin in the woods. As a slave, Young Sally did progressively less work, sometimes abandoned her tasks for her special cabin at midday and did not return. She was now forbidden in the House by Elizabeth, which included the scullery and the truck garden, so Young Sally mostly spent her work time in the wash house or the dairy.

For years now, Young Sally had looked down on the other slaves as "common," stared haughtily at Elizabeth, who was forbidden to whip her, and even on occasion refused to do something Elizabeth ordered, if she felt that it was beneath her, secure in the fact that her mistress was helpless to punish her.

But Little Master Will was pleased that Missy had no such airs about her. She spent far more time with her grandmother Sally than with Young Sally, her mother. Indeed, Sally had raised her, Young Sally wanting to be available to Young George much more than she did to her daughter. Something about that arrangement had produced a beneficial effect, though it seemed odd because Sally was such an implacable hater. But Missy appeared as content in slavery as she could ever have been in freedom. She was polite—even sunny—to everyone, slave or white, and was everywhere loved. And she grew more beautiful by the year.

Little Master Will—though fully aware of how badly his father Young George had erred in the matter of Young Sally, how cruelly he had treated his wife Elizabeth (Little Master Will's mother) and how scandalized the neighborhood felt with his mooning over his saucy nigger—was beginning to think that, with someone as intelligent and compliant as Missy, a man would have none of the troubles his father had with Young Sally but all of the pleasures.

Indeed, Missy, looked at honestly, was a white man's sister … *his!* Of course, he would not make the mistake his father had made—for that matter, his grandfather too; everyone, it seemed, pitied the Leyland men for their bondage to their women slaves—but Little Master Will privately thought himself a far more intelligent man than either of them, with a much keener awareness of what was really important in life. He knew how and how not to dally with a nigger. And himself only eighteen!

Now, Missy did one of her slow turns but this time came all the way around until she was facing where he hid. Suddenly, her comely face paled with shock.

She put both hands over her mouth to stifle her cry, but he still heard her words: "Oh, my Lord. Little Marse Will!"

At first, he was embarrassed and annoyed but, as Missy stood, still staring with wide eyes at where he crouched—apparently ill concealed, damn it all—he laughed, stood up and stepped out into the open.

"Clever girl!" he said, as if good-naturedly. "You have found me out."

Still with her hands to her mouth, Missy flushed and came running to where he stood. "Oh, Little Marse Will, I am sorry. I was just so surprised!"

He liked it that she was flustered. If she were white and told on him for spying on her like this, his reputation would be tarnished and she justified in her pique. This girl, though but a nigger, was pleasingly abashed, in just the right way. *Very nice.*

"Never mind. I was strolling in the area and saw you, and you discovered me just as I was on the verge of speaking to you."

"Oh, yes, sir! I do apologize for being such a ninny!" Again, she flushed.

He had never before stood this close to her, alone. Never before seen the great depth of her brown eyes that had little flecks of gold in them. The softness of her light brown hair and the almost indescribable color of her skin—something between thick cream and the very lightest caramel. Suddenly, he felt a little shy in her presence, which, as soon as he noticed it, he corrected.

"Well, well," he said briskly, now all business. "You must not neglect your duties."

"Thank you, sir," Missy said, holding his gaze with her soft eyes. "You have the kindest way of directing your niggers. Perhaps that is why we all love you so much." She dropped a nice curtsey—a full one, not sham—and walked rapidly back toward the House.

He liked her walk, the unself-conscious swaying of her hips. And he never failed to be surprised when she spoke, for there was not a trace of nigger in her speech. If you were not looking at her, you could not tell her voice from a white woman's.

He had mixed feelings about that. It was certainly not what you expected from a nigger. The white voice coming out of a slave, however light-skinned, was unsettling. He had no idea how she alone of all the niggers on Pinewood Plantation had learned to talk like this, unless it was an unintended side effect of her years as his little sister Peggy's nursemaid and companion.

That had been an odd arrangement, come to think of it, given his mother's feelings, but Peggy loved Missy so and got so distraught whenever Elizabeth said it was time that Peggy learned to do without her, that Young George let her stay, however much Elizabeth sulked.

Little Master Will knew that Missy was not only his father's child but also his father's joy. It was natural then for his mother to hate her, since Missy was visible proof of her husband's lust for his Negro mistress. But, after a time, even Elizabeth found it hard to dislike Missy or be cruel to her. The good-hearted girl offered herself so sweetly to the family and was so plainly attached to Peggy, now six years old, and so loving and serviceful to Elizabeth herself, that Elizabeth occasionally forgot she ought to hate Missy and found herself warming to the lovely young girl, making excuses for her and telling herself that it was not the girl's fault that Young George and Young Sally had played her falsely.

Little Master Will was on the verge of calling out to Missy to come back and tell him more about how he was loved. But, remembering his father's sad muddle, he did not. However, after that, his thoughts turned to Missy more often than they had in the past. But he never once thought to ask himself why Missy had discovered him so easily this day when she had apparently never even suspected his presence before.

I, Jared Thurlow Wilkenson, am thirty-nine years old. At first, I regretted my decision back in the spring to change my mind, accept Mr. George Leyland, Jr.'s apology and enter into his service as overseer. But he had come all the way to the Planter's Inn in Richmond in person, which impressed me, though his apology it seemed only redeemed the past, whereas I had hopes it might secure the future as well and foreshadow a better behavior.

I soon became aware that Leyland was no more capable of respectful conduct toward his workers than he was toward his poor wife Elizabeth. That lady seemed in miserable health and mood. When he took me into the House to be introduced to her, she was rude and ignored me. Leyland preferred to meet with me out of doors and only brought me into the House that once, when I met her. Afterwards, I had few occasions to come in her way.

Leyland has a great need, it seems, to stay at a distance from others. At first, I thought his attitude was out of annoyance that, when he visited me at the Norfolk Inn, I had withdrawn my offer to work for him at one hundred dollars per month and reinstated my original claim of one hundred twelve dollars and fifty cents. But, soon enough, I saw that it was his personality, not his pose, to be churlish, and I found that his staying at a remove suited me.

That one time I did see Mrs. Leyland, though she was unkind, I had felt drawn to her. She was so much like my late wife Constance—even to the blonde hair and very fair complexion—that I may have stared at her too closely, for she seemed disturbed as much by my look as by my presence.

Like Constance, she is heavy of flesh, but this in no way reduces her attractiveness. Many men would disagree, I know, but I am more touched by a woman's soul than her substance. And besides, I sensed a tenderness in Mrs. Leyland that has gone for some time unappreciated.

But it was a few months later before this intuition of mine was proved right. It happened thus: I saw her walking in the carriageway one morning as I stepped out of my house, near the plantation's front gate. She was advancing slowly, carrying but not leaning on a cane.

We saw each other at the same moment. She appeared ready to ignore me and continue on, but then, as it seemed changing her mind, stopped and turned to me as I stood on the little porch of the overseer's house. She was wearing a lemon-colored dress with a white lace bodice, which made her look youthful, though I knew not how old she actually was.

"Good day to you, Mr. Wilkenson," she said.

I noted, as I had before, the sweet tone of her voice, so much like Constance's, which, she being so recently departed, I still heard within me.

"Good day, ma'am," I said, and smiled.

Since I had that day to leave for Baltimore on my court business, I had dressed and preened a bit, shined my boots, brushed my coat and oiled my hair. Others have told me that the look of my dark hair, shining with the lightest application of a sweet-smelling oil, is a pleasing feature of mine. Never one for beards or moustaches, I had just had a good bath and a shave. For the first time I saw her smile, which was lovely indeed.

"You look very nice today, sir."

"Why, ma'am," said I, "in just those few words, you have made me very happy." I hoped my tone conveyed sincerity as well as good humor.

"In times such as ours, Mr. Wilkenson, when everything is so uncertain, even a moment's happiness is a precious thing."

Her smile disappeared, and she seemed to turn her gaze inward, her thoughts not on the outer world but her inner one.

Why I dared say such a thing as I next uttered, I simply cannot imagine, but words came out of me that I had not anticipated even one second before they, as by magic, emerged.

"I gather that happiness for you has been an infrequent visitor?" I was shocked at my own forwardness.

At once, I braced for her rebuke, which I clearly deserved. But, instead, her look grew very serious, and she stared at me.

Then she asked in a quiet voice, "How can you tell?"

Again, words came, as it seemed, independently of any plan or intention of my own. "Because I see sadness in your eyes and hear it in your voice. And I notice that you walk with difficulty and are likely in pain, and wonder how long you have had to bear it."

"You are a very perceptive man, sir." She seemed about to turn back toward the House and walk on, which I, in guilt, attributed to my rude manners. But then, instead, she advanced a step toward where I stood on the porch, and asked, "Might I rest for a moment in your house, sir? I am a little fatigued."

At once I came down the porch steps and stood by her side. She smelled agreeably of violets. Up close, her eyes were a deep sea blue, just as were my late wife's.

"Of course, madam," I said. "I will be honored. Please take my arm."

I had planned to ride the fields before leaving for Richmond and the train of cars for Baltimore. But, instead, I now guided Mrs. Leyland inside my parlor and offered her a seat on the faded blue settee provided for me, together with all the other jaded furnishings, by her husband.

The house had gone a little beyond run down, having apparently passed through much travail. The place evidenced the unrepaired damage done by twenty years of overseers' children. I had no need to apologize to the wife of its owner because of it, yet I wondered if she had ever been inside. She sat down heavily onto the settee and immediately my question was answered.

Looking about her with some displeasure at the threadbare rug, scratched table and overstuffed furniture with holes in the arms—not to mention the dilapidated settee upon which she rested—she said, "My, this is a dingy place, sir! I'd no idea my husband served you so poorly. We must remedy this at once."

In this care for my comfort, she was so very like Constance that I fear I was too ardent in my reply. But she was pleased by it.

"Madam, I assure you that I am comfortable enough. Please don't trouble yourself." (Though, had it been her husband, I would have said, "Right you are, sir. When can I expect improvements?")

"Well, you are a generous soul, sir. I see that plainly," she said with that lovely smile, so like that of my departed wife. "But we must address the sad state of this place. The truth is that I enjoy such little domestic tasks as decorating and furnishing. If you've no objection, I should like to take this upon myself, for your benefit but also as a diversion for me."

"Oh, madam, how kind you are! As if I could object to anything you were good enough to offer. I consider myself a fortunate man indeed."

At this, she smiled again, a little girlishly now. It struck me then, not unpleasantly, that in truth we were, though harmlessly and with due decorum, flirting with each other, though how it had come about I did not know. It seemed that, from the moment I saw her standing in the carriageway opposite my door, I felt as if I were being visited by an angel who wished me only well—which, I must believe, encouraged my liberties.

"Might I offer you a refreshment, madam? I know it is early in the day, but perhaps you would like a sip of something restorative? I was given a bottle of very fine Madeira by my late employer and only await a special occasion on which to open it."

"Oh, that is so kind of you, Mr. Wilkenson. I do like a glass of good Madeira. We keep mostly sherry, port and, of course, the French table wines. But it has been so long since I enjoyed Madeira."

Constance loved Madeira too, and I was always at pains to be sure I had some in the house for her, though it was expensive. I was happy to let her have all she liked, in which, of course, she was the soul of temperance. Now, with Mrs. Leyland, I thought to have a little whiskey myself. But it did not matter. To a man who drinks but rarely, one thing is as good as another.

With a jolt, I suddenly recalled I had told her husband that I did not drink at all, which, when I wrote to him, was the case, for I feared that in my grief I should overdo it. But now, I had returned to having an occasional glass. I have never been drunk in my life. I wondered if Leyland had told his wife that I was an abstainer.

I looked at her as I stood closely by where she sat, noting the creamy complexion of her cheeks; her clear, blue eyes; her pleasant, ladylike scent; the delicacy of her hands folded in her lap as she rested on the shabby settee. She was heavy, it is true, like Constance. Yet a sweeter, more giving lover than Constance I never knew nor ever wanted.

In that instant, the thought of Mrs. Leyland as a lover flashed through me, and I was chagrined. Rewarding goodness with lustfulness is the trait of inferior men. I made haste to cleanse my mind.

As I moved to the cabinet in which I kept my few wines, she said, her tone soft, "I hope you will join me in a small glass, Mr. Wilkenson."

"Ah, madam," I said, working to unwrap and unstop the Madeira bottle, "I fear that I cannot, since I must be in Baltimore about my legal affairs. And I admit that traveling after taking drink makes me somehow uneasy."

"Mr. Wilkenson," said she, unwilling to be denied, "the trip to Baltimore takes some hours, during which you may recover your serenity should the wine affect you. But surely a strong, intelligent man such as you could never be in the least influenced by a sip of wine. I confess that I would feel strange if obliged to take wine alone."

I hesitated. The look in her eyes was very earnest, though she was smiling. We seemed to have instantly got on such a footing of intimacy as befits friends of long standing, not new acquaintances such as we were, and I nothing to her but her husband's employee.

"Well, you are right. I am being too cautious. I should be happy to join you!"

So, pouring myself a glass of the rich, deeply brown Madeira, I took hers to her, went and got a kitchen chair, which I brought close to and facing her, and sat down. It then struck me what a liberty I had taken. Why had I not sat on one of the parlor chairs across the room? Yet she did not reprove me, only smiled and sipped from her Madeira glass, and I, feeling ever more comfortable, did likewise.

Then she made gentle reference to an earlier comment of mine, and again I felt alarm, which once more swiftly departed as I saw that she was at ease with it.

"Mr. Wilkenson," she said, "you mentioned before—when we were outside—that you heard sadness in my voice and saw it in my eyes."

"I did, madam. And it was forward of me. I apologize."

"Oh, please don't," she said. There was now more energy in her voice, and her eyes were bright and resting on mine. "It has been so long since anyone noticed what I felt, or cared …"

Here, she lowered her head, raising a hand to cover her eyes. I thought perhaps she had got embarrassed by her disclosures.

I said, once more feeling that I had blurted rather than considered, "I cannot imagine why this would be so, madam. You are so lovely a woman and so agreeable—I cannot understand how anyone could neglect you. I—"

But here I broke off, certain now that I had overstepped. In the next breath, we would be discussing her husband, for if it were not he who had made her unhappy, who then? And, as his overseer, I felt a clash of loyalties. The man certainly had the right to expect discretion from me.

Yet I yearned to press on with the subject. I recalled suddenly that I had experienced a similar discussion with Constance not long after she was widowed from her first husband, and she opened to me vistas of her personal life I never would have guessed at. But that made me feel somehow more obliged to her and determined to supply what I could of the happiness her previous life had denied her.

"Mr. Wilkenson," Mrs. Leyland said, shaking her head as in annoyance at herself, "I pray you will forgive me. I am speaking amiss and placing you in a very awkward position. My happiness is not your concern. I fear that I have overstayed my welcome. I must go."

As she raised her face to me, I saw why she had covered it: Tears were wetting her cheeks. She handed me her wine glass, which, together with my own, I placed to one side on the floor. Standing, I held out my hands to assist her in rising, at the same time chagrined that I had unthinkingly caused her to weep.

"Please, never think such a thing, madam. Your company is the most agreeable I have had these many months, and I only wish there could be more of it."

Now she was standing, taking in hand her cane, and I realized how close together we were. I felt flowing from her the unmistakable current of feminine affection so comforting to men.

She raised her tear-streaked face—which I now, so close to her, saw to be quite beautiful—and smiled, though there was an unnamable tension in the smile, and said, her voice gone a little husky, "Then there must be more of it, sir."

"But I am not to be invited to the House, am I, madam? Mr. Leyland has made that clear from the beginning."

Both of us were ignoring her tears. I had no idea what to do beyond that. Anything else on my part seemed an unacceptable liberty.

"I was not thinking of the House or of Mr. Leyland," she said. "I shall be coming here to make new decorating arrangements. Surely there will be time for us to talk."

"Nothing would make me happier. Depend upon it. Nothing."

Despite myself, I squeezed her hand; she returned the pressure. She was not wearing gloves, and the feel of her flesh was soft and warm. I thought again of Constance and how uncannily like her she was. Then, though I had no right to assume so much, I bent over her hand and kissed it. As I raised my head from doing so, and found her face very close to me, I hesitated.

And then, suddenly, she dropped my hand and burst into sobs.

1801

CAPE COAST CASTLE, WEST AFRICA

The loading of the slaves began directly. They emerged, chained from their large holding cell, attempting in vain to shield their eyes from the sudden hot, blinding sunlight and driven by little prods and shouts of encouragement across the plaza to the stone stairs leading down to the boats.

"There's a good tide at six tonight, Mr. Potts," Captain Collins told the chief factor. "If we've finished loading provisions and slaves, I'd like to ride it to deep water if I can be ready to cast off by then. The men won't like it, for they always want shore leave, but extra rum and the new black women aboard will comfort them. And, your factors having delivered to the ship fresh water and rations for the return voyage, there is no reason to remain even an extra hour."

"Right you are, sir," said Potts comfortably. "We have done as brisk a business as any man could wish, with satisfaction on both sides."

This Collins, Potts mused, was a very unusual man. Most captains dawdled, hung about their anchorage for weeks, idling and drinking, denying their owners due diligence. But not Captain Collins. He was the owner and as fine a one as Potts knew. He smiled.

"You are right, sir," said Captain Collins, "and you have given me even more sanguine hopes for future collaborations."

Grainger, the first mate, stood with them. As was his habit, he kept quiet. Instead of joining in this smug, post-sale chatter between Potts and his captain, he was watching the line of slaves being urged across the plaza to the boat portal very close to where the three of them were standing.

The refuse and lower-priced slaves had already been put in the boats, and the quality Negroes were being driven past now. There was the usual wailing amongst the blacks as they realized that they were to be taken away—perhaps forever—from their homes. Because of the Negroes' fears, the boarding of sla-vers was always noisy and turbulent, but practiced men could make a good, brisk job of it, and Potts's slave handlers at Cape Coast were among the best Captain Collins had seen.

Grainger even felt moved to admire them. For, although Potts was an unpleasantly used-up sort of man, like so many in the slave trade, it surprised Grainger that Potts's organization could be so skillful. They had black men standing by the wide doorway through which the slaves emerged from the underground pits into the dazzling sun.

Just here, where they were most disoriented and fearful, Potts's blacks were chanting, in several different languages, "You are going to work on large, pleas-ant farms. You will be well treated and made rich. Then you can come home, bringing wealth and blessings to your entire family."

Next to the blacks stood the whites, smiling and nodding, endorsing every word. This practice made for an orderly sale and boarding, and the first mate wondered why every slaving station did not adopt it.

Grainger now caught sight of the beautiful Fulani girl approaching. She walked with her exquisite head held high, looking about her with the dignity of a queen, ignoring the shouting blacks and nodding whites, who kept up their false reassurance to the last. He wondered if she was some sort of Fulani royalty.

The man walking closely behind her was handsome also—darker, muscular, not a Fulani, perhaps a Fante or an Asante. To Grainger, this man looked like a servant to the poised, beautiful girl who walked in front of him. Yet he doubted, thinking about it, that any such relationship could exist or that they so much as knew each other.

Speculations like this were of interest to Grainger. Where other men who went slaving thought only of profit and animal comforts, he imagined the inter-relations of those he held as captives. And, despite his avowals to the contrary, he sometimes had a hard time remembering that they were not human in the same way he was but only marvelously elaborated beasts in whom, according to the teachings of old and wise Christians, the fire of humanity burned, if at all, with only a low, smoky flame. Yet, like every successful slaver, he had no com-punction against strong—even bloody—discipline, wherever it was needed.

Just then, the lovely woman, trailed by her seeming acolyte, drew abreast of him. She turned and looked into his eyes. Grainger, expecting a proud but soft beauty, recoiled inwardly from the terrible fury he saw burning there, and involuntarily took a step backward.

At just that moment, the woman leaped out from the slave line, threw the chain connecting her manacled wrists around Captain Collins's throat and drew tightly. The captain gasped, choked and began to struggle violently. At that same moment, the man behind her reached for the Arabian dagger in its richly gold-ornamented sheath, which the captain wore at his waist, drew it quickly forth and, in the same movement, raised and slashed it across Captain Collins's throat. A great shower of blood shot out from the gruesome wound, and the captain's legs at once gave way.

As the captain sank to the burning stones of the plaza, John Potts shouted in a high, screechy voice, "Sgt. Robertson … help! MUTINY!" and then turned to run.

But, in an instant, and despite leg irons, Kano was on him. He threw his wrist chains, which were wet with the captain's arterial blood, around Potts's throat, drew the chief factor back against his body as a shield and turned toward the shocked marines.

Shouts erupted all across the plaza. A cry of triumph mixed with dismay went up from the line of slaves, for they sensed that, however this turned out, in the end it could only make things worse for them. Yet to see a blow struck against the whites was a marvel, a blessing. It reassured them that, even in this slave castle hell, justice could still survive.

Sgt. Robertson bellowed to his marines, who were paralyzed with astonishment, "Fire. *Fire!* What are you standing there for? *Kill* the bastard!"

And John Potts, choking, tried to scream, "No, you'll *hit* me!" but only gurgled, madly gesturing with his arms.

The marines hesitated. Muskets pointed at Kano, they turned to look at Sgt. Robertson.

Saleh, her bare breasts wet with Captain Collins's blood, stepped away from his slumped body and joined Kano, taking from him Captain Collins's knife. Her eyes shone as she seized Potts by his long, gray pigtail, pulled his head roughly back and passed the bloody knife from his left ear to his right, opening his skin but only deeply enough to loose a thin curtain of blood.

Abruptly, Kano slacked the chain so that Potts's animal cry could be heard all the way beyond the castle, to and past the dirt street and mud huts of the town. All of this took only seconds. But, on the plaza, it was as if time had stopped. Marines, slaves, factors, sailors, black middlemen and townsmen all stared, mute, uncomprehending, at what was taking place.

Kano raised his head, looked around at all the stupefied white men on the plaza and barked out a question in Asante. Though he knew at least two other languages, he chose his own. From this moment on, live or die, he would do nothing else to accommodate the white men. When he was not instantly answered, he repeated what he had said.

At this, a slaver middleman stepped forward and said in Asante to Kano, "I can do it. I can pass on what you're saying."

"Very well," said Kano. "Then tell these white men that this ugly slave trader will die immediately, just as that captain died, unless the soldiers put down their guns. I will count one, two, three, and then this woman will cut, for we have nothing to lose, as you see."

Though the whites could not understand him, they could tell—by his hot eyes, and by how deeply the knife's blade in Saleh's hand pushed into the bleeding crease on Potts's throat—what he had said and what he wanted. The slaver middleman translated his words into English.

Kano then began his count, each word echoed by the translator.

Not hesitating, Sgt. Robertson shouted, "Guns down!"

At once, the muskets clattered to the paving stones. The marines, never having seen or heard of such a thing as this, stared helplessly about them, as if in search of the salvation that must surely be near at hand, since the great Christian god could never countenance such a calamity as was unfolding before them.

"Release us from these chains!" Kano ordered.

"Do as he says, whatever it is!" John Potts screamed, his voice thin and rough from the crushing of his throat by the chain. "Give him anything he asks!"

"We will take this man with us as we leave this place," Kano said, giving Potts's gray hair a shake. "If we are not followed, we will release him at the proper time. If we are interfered with, we will kill him and ourselves."

As the translator spoke, Saleh grinned fiercely. Only a fool could imagine, looking at the two of them, that they were not in earnest.

Grainger, seemingly as shocked as the rest, now stepped forward. "I have a shackle key," he said, sounding calm.

Saleh turned to look at him. Her eyes met his, searched, probed, narrowed. Though he reached into his pocket and drew forth only a key, she began to shake her head.

Suddenly, she turned to Kano. "Not this one," she cried. "No, I don't trust this one."

Kano looked at her, the beginning of a frown on his face. "Why?"

"I don't know. I DON'T KNOW!" Her voice rose.

At that moment, Grainger pulled a pistol from his wide-topped boot and shot Kano in the throat. As Kano fell, Sgt. Robertson, his hands shaking, snatched up his musket and fired. The shot struck Grainger in the forehead. The ball exploded out the back of Grainger's head, in a shower of bone and brain and blood.

Instantly, a dozen men leaped upon Kano and, punching and kicking madly, brought him down. Saleh too was dragged down, as infuriated whites beat her with their fists and kicked her with their heavy boots. Kano lay on his back on the hot stones, a froth of blood bubbling in the hole in his throat—badly hurt but alive and conscious.

A great commotion ensued in which the turbulent, terrified slaves were driven with whips and shouts into the boats. Potts was quickly freed and tended to; Kano and Saleh were again beaten and kicked. All of the white men began shouting in a frenzy of relief and rage, and a vigorous argument immediately burst out amongst them over who was most to blame for allowing this evil thing to happen and what should be done with the rebels.

Word of the tragedy was instantly dispatched to the Lady Dora, to notify the abruptly promoted captain of his new dignity and to summon him ashore that he might directly confront the tragedy, aid in its further resolution and make himself better known to the shocked and furious factors and slavers of Cape Coast Castle.

This was of course the Lady Dora's second mate, Andrew Samuels. With the deaths of Collins and Grainger, he stood next in line for the captaincy. He was little seen ashore but, aboard the Lady Dora, he was of course well known to everybody by his other name: Mr. Badger.

Once ashore and consulted, Mr. Badger took command. First, he saw to it that the slaves were boarded and stowed below decks in the cramped, hot slave-hold. He also gave orders that the bodies of Grainger and Captain Collins be caused to lie in American flag-covered, rum-filled tin coffins, soldered against leakage, in the Lady Dora's 'tween decks, among the sick slaves who were usually the only tenants of that place, where they were stowed to prevent any disease they might carry from spreading. Then Mr. Badger was free to make any decisions and direct any punishments that now lay within his power—and, it much pleased him to realize, his alone.

In the plaza, he no more took in what had happened and looked into the cold, defiant eyes of Kano than he turned to the excited group of white men surrounding him and cried out, "I now see with my own eyes what horror these damned wretches have brought upon us here, and instantly into my mind has come the only punishment that could even begin to redress this base and hateful crime. An example cries out to be made, and I am the man to *make* it!"

He turned, sneering, toward Kano, who looked back at him, lying with his flesh broiling on the hot tiles of the plaza but showing only contempt, despite the blood running from the hole in his throat, despite his pain and shock from the bullet and from the beating. He beheld Mr. Badger's striped face and, twisting his lips in scorn, gave a weak bark of laughter.

Seeing this defiance, Mr. Badger's face darkened. His eyes took on an ugly, slanting squint, alarming to his watchers, who wondered from whence it came within such a harmless soul as he, seeming to belong more to a wolf than a man.

He raised his voice in a ragged shout. "I see this hateful nigger, lying here, sneering at us, at the very men who have sought to rescue him from the darkness and savagery of the nigger life, and I am outraged! By God in heaven, I am *outraged!* If we let his infamy stand, if we do not strike him down with the great strength of our righteous wrath, then we show ourselves to be weak, idle men who do not deserve the dominion God has given to us in the world. We admit that we are mere poltroons, standing by mischance in a place divinely intended only for the powerful and the fearless, who are not cowed by evil but rise against it with the hot blood of true Englishmen!"

Here, Mr. Badger broke off, casting his eyes aggressively around the circle of shocked, angry men who, with every word spoken by their new leader, were rising into flights of fresh courage and beginning to feel all through their flesh the holy justice of a magnificent hatred.

"I am determined to cut off this damned evil nigger's legs just below the hips, and show him off still living to his fellows, so that such a terrible fear will rush into them as will shape their lives from this day on and forever!"

This acid bath of words visibly stunned even such jaded men as these, whom the years-long embrace of slavery as a great good had spiritually reduced to a level far below that of ordinary men, though they themselves never so much as noticed. They would have been enraged to be told that they were mere blind drudges, who were heart-willing in their work and content, even proud, within the poisonous fog of sanctioned human bondage—and were all of them sunk in a wickedness so deep, so vast, that it was devouring them as a spider does its silk-bound prey, by sucking out their moral insides.

But, in Mr. Badger, there was no sense of this. In him resonated both happiness and satisfaction at this chance to do what he believed was good, and that he could stand forth a righteous hero, in public, so that he might have "the greatest pleasure of his soul's desiring." He would, of course, use his efficient blubber-flensing knife to do the necessary work and, if a surgeon's saw for cutting the bone was not handy, a carpenter's ripsaw would do.

The instant his eyes fell on Saleh, however, and when he was told that it was not she who had actually killed Captain Collins, though she had very coolly assisted Kano, he decided to let her live but punish her in such a painful and lasting way, in front of all the assembled slaves, that the lesson would be indelible, unforgettable and so terrifying that they would not, even if they could, ever forget it.

And then, of course, once at sea, he would have her as often as he liked. For she was—or soon would be—the very sort, the *only* sort—of woman he truly desired: maimed, terrified, bleeding and powerless, whose suffering was deep enough to rouse him. Indeed, looking at her facial wounds caused by the beatings she had already received, and imagining her coming torture at his hands, he even now felt the stirrings.

At once, Mr. Badger set about what he had decided must be done. The morbid excitement attendant upon this action made him breathe faster and more shallowly and experience such little, subtle shudders as were invisible to others but immensely thrilling to him.

Demanding the grudging aid of Mr. Cyclops (Carlson), Mr. Badger charged him with heating a metal plate red hot and, when the time came, applying it to the leg stumps to sear veins and arteries closed, and then stitching loosely with a sailmaker's dexterity the large skin flaps that Mr. Badger would prudently cause to be left in place.

The job would be done right there in the plaza under the gaze of all the fascinated and justified whites, horrified resident slaves and freemen of the town. It was bizarre that Mr. Badger proposed to leave skin flaps, for that is what a surgeon would do in a proper amputation in which the patient is valued and his survival desired.

Mr. Badger had his reasons, however, which he presently explained to Mr. Cyclops. "With a good sewing up of the stumps, one of these buggers can last a few hours or even longer. In those few hours, the niggers who watch his suffering and death will learn the lessons of it. This is the whole reason we do it. But I must say I doubt that this one can live very long, seeing his throat wound. Still, let him have his desserts, leaving to God his length of life ..."

Everyone was intensely interested in what the response of the badly wounded Kano would be to his mutilation. The general expectation was that he would die during the "surgery" and that, since no anesthetic of any kind was offered him, he would first beg for his life upon seeing what Mr. Badger intended, and then scream and twist while strong men held him down.

But they were greatly disappointed when they saw that Kano neither begged nor screamed. Nor could they comfort themselves that it was because he was already insensible, owing to his wound.

Instead, he lay quietly, a look of contempt making more striking his strong face, blood bubbling in the hole in his throat, while Mr. Badger's great knife was honed, the metal plate heated, a large table brought out and Kano, securely bound, placed upon it and strapped down.

Mr. Badger turned to the tense crowd to make a few more remarks. "You see here, in this vicious nigger," he proclaimed, holding out to them his knife, "the very sort of slave we must stamp out. If we are to continue this way of life, which has been so good to us, we must take care to defend it against all destroyers.

"The former captain of our vessel, may God rest his soul, was blinded by his kindness. Now, two good men lie dead, and this scoundrel"—and here he indicated the defiant Kano—"must be made an example to the rest. As you love and revere the way of life we follow, I charge you to spread far and wide what you will see here today, taking up a like practice yourselves when you, in your turn, assume authority, so that our calling may be made again safe and wholesome for all of us, as God intended."

The stripe of rash that ran up his face glowed bright red, and his eyes retained their eerie, heated look, as the savagery lurking just behind his little smile suddenly showed itself unmistakably on his radiant face.

With that, he turned to his work and, in Kano's muscular thighs, made the deep circular cuts required—about ten inches below the crotch, taking care to leave flaps. Since it lies within the province of very few men to remain silent under such terrible insult, a groan issued from Kano, a groan he neither willed nor controlled. It seemed to be ripped from his guts—a primal, keening sound that raised the neck hairs even of the hardened white men who watched, and registered on the black faces as an explosion would, an assault unforeseen and surreal.

Kano's face twisted to animal, all humanity bypassed. But his was not the look of a herd beast or a scavenger run to earth but of a predator, pinned by pygmies in a sink of his own blood, his air and life vanishing but not his will. The bloody sucking hole in his throat likewise diminished his voice but could not still it.

Saleh, dazed, her face swollen and bleeding, her body aching from the hard blows and kicks, watched Kano's agony, knowing that she would be next. She tried to prepare herself by taking hold of the solidity of the river and ocean gods and by calling on her ancestors to assemble and witness.

Lords, grandfathers, grandmothers, she whispered in her heart, *surround Kano, surround me. Give us courage to die, sneering at these brutes who demean humanity. I willingly give up my legs, my arms, my nose and eyes and ears. But let me keep my lips. Grant me only that, lords and blessed ancestors. Let my last act be to spit blood in their ugly faces.*

The rasping of a carpenter's saw now sounded across the hot plaza. Fixated white men stood bareheaded in the deadly sun, their skin burning, indifferent to the sun and to everything beside the awful ceremony unfolding before their eyes. They perceived and studied the tiny movements in his body of Kano's gasping breaths. Black men dared not turn away for they knew that this deranged captain with the striped face was demonstrating their own possible fate to all the other white men here—a cautionary tale written in blood and agony that all blacks, to gird themselves against what these madmen were capable of, were obliged to witness and, above all, remember.

First one and then the other of Kano's muscular black legs were cast aside onto the flagstones. The left leg fell extended, the knee locked, and so rolled a single turn, like a roped length of carpet. The other one fell bent, struck the stones at the point of the knee, sprang open, turned over onto its side and lay still.

At the fall of each leg came the loud spattering sizzle of hot metal against raw flesh. To everyone's astonishment, Kano did not lapse unconscious or scream out. Instead, he raised his head, as far as he could, to watch his immolation. He then turned his tortured face slowly aside. His huge, red-veined, bulging eyes found those of the other blacks. The keening sound in his throat had become a wild, low growl, as if his soul were speaking in a secret language.

Like a firebrand being passed over areas of darkness, his suffering gaze touched them all, one at a time. Some could not bear it and, at the last moment, averted their eyes; some let themselves be baptized in his pain, taking it deeply into their lives.

All of the blacks who gathered there saw revealed in that moment the true nature of the white slavers and of slavery itself. Never, from that day on, could they imagine that they did not know the truth.

Finally, with everyone enveloped in the terrible stink of blood scorching on hot metal, the mutilation ended. But, for Kano, the agony was not yet over.

And, for Saleh, it was just beginning.

To the astonishment of the sailors, Kano did not die. Instead, he was moved into the shade—not in mercy, of course, but in the hope that carrying him out of the broiling sun might extend his life a little—where he lay on the stone walkway, now semiconscious, to await Mr. Badger's further plans and continue to provide a terrible spectacle for both blacks and whites as he died slowly before their eyes. He was ordered wrapped in a sheet of netting and then hoisted up, with the netting nailed to the sole sturdy tree in the plaza, a great pine.

It then became clear that Mr. Badger's hopes were being rewarded: Kano lived on. His buttocks held his weight while the seared, skin-covered stumps of his legs, blood leaking through the wide-spaced stitching, protruded forward. His breath, shortened by the throat wound and by blood loss and shock, was growing shorter still.

Saleh was chained to the tree almost at his feet, for Mr. Badger had instructed his crew to be sure they positioned him high enough so "she and all the rest of them had a damned good view," and they did. They had raised and secured Kano to the thick trunk of the pine a good three feet above the stones of the plaza, displaying the tortured man, where all the slaves—especially the males, the most likely rebels—could see everything that would be done to him.

She strained to listen to Kano's words over the rustling of a fitful little wind in the tree's needles, the cawing of crows and the babble of slave voices. Even now, as death slowly took him over, Kano was trying to instruct her. But first he spoke to the other slaves, in Mandinka, the most widely known of the West African languages.

"Do not be frightened by any of this … Stay strong and vigilant …" His voice was weak but his heart strong, and they could see this. "Remember this day and, when you must, sell your own life dearly …" He paused, squeezing his eyes shut. His faced twisted into the very mask of pain, but he pushed on. "Make them pay for our blood with their own … Make slavery painful for them—so painful that they cannot continue it …"

His voice dropped to a whisper as other slaves translated what he had said, and gradually the meaning of it passed through the screen of languages to every slave ear that was listening. Then, overcome with exhaustion, he stopped, hung his head, his breathing rough and labored, sweat dripping from his nose and blood from his throat. For a moment, he rested.

The slaves stared at him as at a holy man. Even before translation, they all in some way understood him. These were tribal people, separated from each other by geography, language and custom, with little idea of coalition or confederation, and none of "national" allegiance. They had no such concept as "African." That would be an understanding that only came into being in the holds of the white man's slave ships.

They left Africa as Ibo, Fulani, Fante, Calabar, Asante, Mandinka, Whydah and a hundred others. In the ships, their common suffering and shared courage built bridges over chasms of religion, belief, ritual tribal scarring and language. Those who had shipped together formed lifelong bonds, regardless of tribe. The reality of the plantations quickly solidified what had begun in the slave ships: an African identity.

In men such as Kano, they could see the gifts of courage and resistance raised far above the threshold of tribe. They could see that, whether or not they could understand him, he spoke *for* them. They had been separated from their lives and homes by white men because the color of their black skins somehow convinced the white men of their inferiority, even of their insensibility.

Now, the slaves began to understand that this very blackness would bond them together, and they would come to see that, however far they could be marginalized and mistreated because of it, to that same extent they could unite around it and become strong. But little of this was as yet dawning in the minds of the black men, women and children, who were being carried into the unknown by the white sailors of the Lady Dora.

And the focal and flash point of it all was Kano—hanging legless, bleeding, tortured by thirst and dying in the netting, nailed to the tree where all the men could see him and speaking to them in the voice, though weakened by his pain and his dying, of a man afraid of neither death nor his captors.

Kano spoke to Saleh. His face was badly damaged, his lips swollen from the beatings. Her own eyes were all but hidden by the swelling around them, her lips split, her cheek throbbing, her jaw radiating pain—a pain that was just beginning to set in. She was shivering and dull with shock but determined to listen, to hear him.

"They will not let pass what you did," he told her, his broken voice now barely audible. "But the moment when they would have tortured and killed you has passed. That would have happened by now, but all they have done is beat you. So I think you will live. Though you humiliated them, you did not kill any of them. But certainly they will punish you further, but not in a way that mars your beauty.

"Now that they have you in chains to take you aboard their ship, still undamaged except for wounds that will heal, it is to their advantage to get you to market where you will fetch a good price. Nor will they hurt your belly or loins for, if you are scarred there, the buyers will fear that you cannot bear children, which will reduce your value. They will not remove any of your fingers or toes either, or put out an eye.

"I think what they will do is cut out a piece of your tongue. I have heard that is one of their tricks. By doing so, they can punish you and inflict great pain and deformity but not spoil your looks. And you will be able to talk, learn their language and speak respectfully to them. But the flaw in your speech because of your slit tongue will forever remind them that you are a rebel whom they have broken to their purposes and now control. It will be up to you whether or not they are right about that."

Though she tried to be as stoic as Kano, as these words were uttered from his cracked lips in an impersonal croak, Saleh gasped. "My *tongue*?" As she spoke, her swollen jaw radiated pain.

"I think so, yes," he said, his voice fainter. "It will hurt very much at the time, for the knife bites terribly, and they will put the hot iron to you for the bleeding. You will be in great pain for a few weeks, but then it will begin to mend. I know a man whose tongue was cut. Prepare yourself. Try to give them no reason for satisfaction with themselves.

"Of course, they will have your body during this voyage, just as if nothing had happened. And though you are restless with the pain of all your wounds, and repulsed and terrified of everything on their death ship, they will persevere in their desires.

"That is how they are. They are not human beings like us, but demons. Expect nothing good from them. Never let them surprise you. Do as they say, but inwardly keep to your gods. And even if they take out all of your tongue, it will not matter. It will even be to your benefit because, afterwards, they cannot expect you to speak to them." Exhausted, Kano broke off.

They had given him nothing to drink, and his mouth was so dry that his voice was thick, his tongue swollen. Thirst now brought a worse misery than his wounds. His body slumped in the net, his arms useless from exhaustion, his head drooping to his chest. Then he roused himself and stiffened, like a man being crucified who thrusts himself erect against the pain in order to breathe. In this way, time after time, he refused the seduction of death.

"Promise me ..." he said, his voice now fading and close to its end.

Saleh beheld him in silence. As she did, love for him overwhelmed her. It was the strongest thing she had ever felt, overriding both pain and fear. Her heart suddenly ached in her chest, tears coming to her eyes. It was as if, all at once, she had seen him truly, as all of himself. Because of her willfulness, she had never let herself accept or even see other peoples' strengths and goodness. But now, with Kano, as she watched him dying, she realized that she had taken all of him inside her. He had become rooted in her, been made a part of her, more than if he had married her, more than if she had opened to him in sex, more than if she had borne his children.

Her eyes and his clung together. She let him see past her tears to her heart, where she had at that moment given him anchorage. He tried to tell her what he wanted her to promise. But his voice failed. All he could do was hold her eyes with his.

"Yes," she said. "I promise."

They lived their entire life together in the next few breaths, flowing into and out of each other, so that they no longer had boundaries between them. Kano's breath faltered, but he held Saleh's gaze as long as he could.

Finally, it was finished. He closed his eyes, fought to open them and then closed them again. His head dropped, and he was still.

At that exact moment, two white men pushed forward through the crowd and, removing the weeping, grieving Saleh from her chains, dragged her across the plaza and toward an open door.

1840

PINEWOOD PLANTATION, VIRGINIA

Some time passed in what Young George came to think of as his courtship of Young Sally. Every day, he would steal minutes or a half-hour alone with her, tell her that he loved her, kiss her, promise her freedom and predict ease and happiness in the future for both of them. But the girl's fear and resistance remained.

One cold autumn day, Young George told Young Sally to meet him in the thick woods that connected the Leyland and Jerrold plantations, at the edge of the South Field, and she came in her old, threadbare jacket. He, self-conscious in his own warm coat, impulsively removed it and draped it over her shoulders.

Her eyes widened as she stared at him. "Young Marse Geo'ge, dese is courtin ways. I don' see why yo go on botherin to court no nigga. I done tol yo a'ready yo kin git whut yo wants widout it. Doin all dis make it feel lak yo jes buildin up a big trick. I gits a baby an sold, an yo gits a new nigga gal of which dey's plenty mo where I come fum. Whut yo troublin bout me fer? I don' expeck it, an I tol yo I don' want it. Dey don' be nothin' dat I wants from yo an nevah will be …"

Young Sally shrugged out of Young George's coat and handed it back to him. Again, he felt pride in her spunk and frustration at her skepticism. Yet, if he were in her place, would he not be the same—or worse?

Suddenly, he had an idea. The frugal planter in him twitched at the thought, but the lover would not be denied. Taking the coat from her small, graceful hand, which he forbore to kiss though the urge was on him, he once more held it out to her.

As she again drew back and frowned, Young George said, breaking out in an almost boyish grin, "Look in the pocket. See what you find."

Young Sally stared at him a moment, and then shook her head, but Young George could see she was intrigued. A little smile fought to emerge on her pretty lips, but she resisted. Yet, like a child encouraged to open a brightly wrapped package, her eyes had brightened.

"Go ahead," he said. He turned the coat so that its large side pocket was toward her and, with his other hand, he opened wide the top of it. "Reach in. Don't be afraid."

He was grinning and, for the first time ever in his presence, Young Sally forgot herself and giggled. She was staring at the open pocket. Young George could see that she was aching to reach in and find what was there. But she still held back, still mistrusted him, still was persuaded that nothing good could ever come for a slave from the white man. After all, look who her mother was and how bitterly she scorned all things Leyland! But he could also see her rising curiosity and perceive the thrill of being offered something like this—an experience that probably was unique in her slave's life.

She raised her eyes to his and looked carefully at him. She was silent awhile, then suddenly smiled. "I shouldn' do dis, Young Marse Geo'ge. Sho'ly I shouldn'."

"Well," he said, encouraged now by her lifting spirit, "I do things I shouldn't do all the time. This once won't hurt you. I promise." And again, he held out to her the coat with its gaping side pocket.

Suddenly, she went shy and little-girlish—not from coyness, he was certain, but from being caught up despite herself in excitement. Her face flushed. She suddenly clasped her hands, as though to restrain them.

"It ain't a spider, is it?" Again, she giggled.

Young George was charmed. He smiled at her, reached out and touched her face. "Oh, dear girl, the very thought of tricking you upsets me. Don't you yet know that I would never hurt you?"

Young Sally did not answer. But again she looked into his eyes … and again smiled. "Oh, Lawd," she said nervously, "yo reckon I should?"

"Believe me. I would be very disappointed if you didn't. There's nothing in there that will hurt you in the slightest, but rather something that will do you a world of good."

Young Sally stood, still clasping her hands, blushing. He could see that she had forgotten the cold and was caught up in the mystery of what she might find in that fascinating coat pocket. She glanced again at his eyes, reached one hand a little way out, pulled it back and did something that completely captivated him.

She suddenly clapped her hands together and cried out, "Oh, Young Marse Geo'ge, yo done caught me. I cain't but reach in dere, but I'm scairt ter an dat's a fack!"

Then she burst out laughing but immediately covered her mouth and looked quickly around where they stood in the late autumn woods. But they were alone in the afternoon's slanting sunlight. All through the stand of leafless hardwood trees, nothing could be seen between where they stood and where the oaks and elms ended at the edge of the fallow South Field.

Young George was so delighted at her laughing, at the dimples that appeared in her cheeks then, at the flush on her face and the excitement in her eyes, that he could not forbear saying, "Ah, Young Sally, dearest Young Sally. You charm me so. Your beauty is a wound in my heart. I simply have no words to express my love for you."

For once, his saying this to her did not appear to cause her discomfort. Instead, he could see that, for the first time, she seemed to be wondering if what he said might really be true. He could feel his heart flooding with hope.

"Go ahead, dear girl. Please, *go ahead!*"

Young Sally lowered her head, eyes closed, as if in prayer. But Young George suspected that she was only recruiting herself, as a soldier does, who for the first time steps from cover into the deadly whiz of musketry.

He waited.

Slowly, she opened her eyes and studied him again. Then she reached out her hand, touched the pocket rim, drew back, touched it again and, her eyes closing, let it creep down inside.

There was a clinking sound as her fingers encountered and grasped the pocket's contents. He heard her sudden intake of breath. Then slowly she withdrew her fist, which she opened to reveal on her light-colored palm a small number of gold coins.

Her eyes darted to Young George's face. To his surprise, she did not speak, giggle, shriek. Instead, she searched him out in his depths, her eyes agitated, caution discarded. Gone were her smiles, her shyness. A strange feeling crept into Young George's inside—a feeling of finding something unexpected in her that altered her air, her look, her potential. He did not know what to make of it, was a little unnerved by it. Then it was covered again, as a vista by drifting clouds. But still, there was something barely showing in her that he had never guessed at.

"I nevah touch money lak dis befo," she said, her voice very soft. "I nevah see no money lak dis."

There was no sign of distress. Only a great seriousness, her agitation dying back into a quietness he could feel, a shift in the whole spirit and vibration of her vitality. Again, he was surprised that she didn't cry out or laugh or thrust the coins back or begin weeping or run off or say it was all a trick. Some of his enjoyment drained away at her sudden calm. He realized that he had wished for … well, not hysterics perhaps, but at least a gratifying excitement. Instead, she stood looking at the coins, and then at him, pensive—dear God, *calculating!*

"They are yours, dear girl," he said, though feeling against all expectation a growing disappointment.

Again, her reply surprised him, shocked him even; her face was grave. "How much money is dis heah?"

Somehow they had passed, in only a few heartbeats, from levity to an atmosphere of commerce. Young George now questioned his wisdom in starting this game.

"You can see for yourself, dear girl. The coins are marked."

"I cain't read none. Yo knows dat."

She had not said "sir"! Before, this lapse would have reassured, even encouraged, him. But now, a strangeness had arisen in her that could turn out to be either barrier or bridge. Certainly, it was unexpected, completely beyond his range of fantasy. Feeling slightly threatened but not sure why, he turned an equally sober look on Young Sally and frowned. But now he could see a little smile peeking through her cool gravity. This somewhat relieved him even as it puzzled him.

"Two hundred dollars," he said.

The money was meant for his neighbor Wilson, to whom he owed it for a young brood sow, a mature hog, two piglets and a lame jackass that Black Sulla claimed he could cure. But now he was determined she would have all of it.

"Whut fer did yo aks me ter reach in yo pocket aftah dis money?" Her voice was very quiet. A little of her diffidence was back. Not much, though. Window dressing.

He had loved that insecurity of hers. But still no "sir." How mad he seemed to himself, wanting both shyness and worldliness from her, and at the same time.

He felt a passing nausea. God, how swiftly things had gone beyond what he had thought of as sense and reason!

"You can have it. To keep. As your own," he told her, now in a very low voice.

Again, a long silence.

Her eyes moved from the money to his face and back, a tiny smile playing across her mouth. Her eyes deeper than he had ever seen them. He felt the queasy oddness once more—the sense that she was suddenly, unaccountably, something … *other.*

He was not a very perceptive man, he knew that; Elizabeth had often told him. He looked most clearly only at what he wanted most, and cared little about the others in his life—their needs, moods, ways. In most people, things he did not understand simply annoyed him. What was important was only that his needs be met. That was all he had ever wanted from anyone—even, after he married her and exhausted her novelty, from Elizabeth.

But now, with Young Sally, he wanted more. He wanted to understand her, penetrate her mind, so as to be sure of her. And sure of her in a way new to him, beyond anything he had wanted from a woman before. Now, he saw something in her that he could not even name, let alone understand. It troubled him that, despite this, he still was warm to plunge on blindly. But he was.

"Do yo truly mean fer me ter keep dis money, Young Marse Geo'ge? Cause if yo do, it scare me an it cheer me." She started to say more, then changed her mind. And the look she now gave him was not bold as much as earnest. It was the look slave dealers wore as they weighed the offer. Still, her tiny smile played.

"Why 'scare,' dear Young Sally?"

But of course he knew why. Because fear in her was the right—even the righteous—thing. But cheer. How odd a word, how *mysterious.*

Yet, carrying it all forward, if she were to receive him inside her, for money, which bore its own sort of passion, cheer would be an appropriate word, would it not? It would stand in the place of love. But this was precisely what was so disappointing!

Then, once again, her voice unbalanced him. "'Fear' cause now I owes yo mo den I kin evah pay back. Now I be yo slave in my soul, not jes my body, if'n I goes on an takes dis money fer my own. Free nigga don' earn dis much in years an years of workin hard as she kin work. If I takes it, den I sells yo my soul."

He saw that she was serious. Her smile dropped away. It struck him with force that, until now, she must have seen everything he had tried to build between them as a frightening game, a sort of dance. If he had put candies in that pocket, it would be so even yet. And she would go on with the game because he was the white master and she, the black slave, had no choice. This was the very definition of slavery, was it not? That to be a slave meant to have no choice?

But he now saw that Young Sally *really* did not care for him, was truthful when she had said so many times that she did not want him, only wanted peace, to be left alone. He could read this in her face. The undisguised self-interest, showing both in her gravity and bold little smile, the constant shifting of her eyes from him to the money, showed him her train of thought.

If he had forced her, the most she could hope for was to turn his selfish mind toward a genuine caring, one she could rely on to save her when she would fall under peril from the white women. But already, obviously to her great surprise, absent artifice or manipulation by her, he had offered money—a great amount of money. Truly, for her, a *lifetime* worth of money.

Instant changes in Young Sally arose like brushfires under lightning. He, witnessing them, could neither understand nor track them. Yet he could feel them, feel their heat, as if a coal oil lamp had flicked on in his belly.

For the first time, though a lifelong slaveholder, he realized what it meant to *really own someone.* In that moment, he learned something about himself. The feeling was so expansive, so joyous, that he nearly laughed. He was ravished by this sudden power, which was made perfect by the paradox of Young Sally's innocence on the one hand and her unexpected—as he saw it—greed on the other. Instead of daunting him, it only called him deeper. It offered a complexity that would flavor sex as nothing else ever had before.

A question flashed through him but did not linger: *Would he not be better off, since money was the focus, to find and keep an already bad woman in Richmond than to ruin a mostly good one at home?* But no, the issue was not any woman but Young Sally herself. And yes, it would hurt Elizabeth. And yes, it would make him look a contemptible fool should it all get out. But he did not care.

As he looked at Young Sally's beauty—made more rich, more tempting somehow by her willingness to sell it—he lost his uncertainty. Instead, a veil was lifted in his mind, and he saw that this was the only way it could possibly be, if he were to really invest himself, to persevere. Otherwise—if Young Sally had no wiles and no will but was merely his victim—it would be like and feel like fucking a child. And, in the end, he would be disillusioned with himself and with her.

But this way would bring them close! Money always brought people close, as long as they were agreed on price and timing. Perhaps she would come to love him. Why not? Was it so impossible? Who could predict the impact of large sums of money on the inner world of a dirt-poor Negro slave? Who would deny that all the possible ways money could be offered expanded the possible ways it could influence? If she did not come to love him, he would have lost nothing. And if she did, it would confirm in him another, a different but even greater power …

As he stood, breathing in her mystery scent in the cold air, he foresaw the interest; the complexity; the unsampled, even unknown pleasures that awaited him with Young Sally. It would launch a new phase of his life. It would be a new career, in a way—a separate compartment of life in which he would ceaselessly sift experience, investigate, analyze, meditate. At the very least, it would be an avocation on a level of challenge with, say, model shipbuilding, or the study of astronomy …

"What madness are you speaking, dear girl?" he murmured. "How can you say I am buying your soul?"

Young Sally looked at him, saying nothing. But he could see that now everything was clear to her, and she knew it was clear to him.

They waited. They each knew that what happened next must come from him.

He stepped forward, folded her hand tightly around the coins and kissed her.

She closed her eyes. Her arms, the money held tightly in one hand, crept around his neck. He was engulfed in her scent, her softness, her mystery, her aura of being untapped and unknown …

He, entering into the kiss, drew her closer.

And she, ever so slightly, opened her mouth.

1843

PINEWOOD PLANTATION, VIRGINIA

A journal entry from Young George:

I am astonished that I have let so long a time elapse ere I took up my pen. It was so long ago that now, it is a different man sitting here writing his adventures. So I shall just go on as before, filling in as needed.

Three days ago, the "house" was completed!

Elizabeth is in a glowering sulk: "Your nigger baby was bad enough, but now you've built your whore a beautiful new cabin for herself and her brat. What will be next? Shall you divorce me and marry her, so she can have the entire estate?"

Here, she snatched a breath while staring at me with—I am forced to admit—apparent hatred! This was annoying but, since I could not in all justice deny anything, I stood quietly and let her vent her rage.

"Believe me, I am tempted to withhold the Jerrold land from you and sell it to as great a set of ruffians as I can find!" Elizabeth glowered at me, but then some of the spunk seemed to go out of her. "I would love," she went on more calmly, "to sell it to rich, free niggers from the North. But, of course, my threat is empty. I cannot sell it."

Here, she seemed dejected but then pressed gamely on. Despite everything, I can even yet admire her ... a little!

"It is your property now as well as mine. More yours than mine. To sell it now, I should have to divorce you, expose your dalliances with niggers and, claiming the land as my patrimony, wrest it from your control by court order."

I could not repress a tiny, satisfied smile.

Seeing this, and flushing in anger, she returned to the attack. "But, of course, as you know, there is far more to it than that. To be a divorcee is to incur the contempt of my circle and my class. I would end by living as a marked woman among friends who have become strangers. This would please you, I am sure.

"But, even then, there is no certainty that I could reclaim full title, for the law is such that you claim everything of mine while I claim nothing of yours. In this country, men have everything and women nothing. You may have as many black whores as you like but, if I should ever seek solace from a kind friend—let alone a Negro—I should be abandoned by everyone I love.

"You are the most heartless and evil man I have ever known!" She was heating up again. "Because of you, we are all laughingstocks and pitied by every right-thinking person. I am certain that, when you die, you will go to hell, and I only hope that you will be able to see me resting happily in heaven and finally realize all you have LOST!" She put the period to her outburst with a stamp of her foot.

I had to own to myself that she had given quite a speech. But I was more economical in my reply.

"Very well, madam. You have had your say, and much good may it do you. But now, let us look at things as they actually are. You are a lukewarm woman with a great, fat arse. How do you expect any man to be tempted by the likes of you? You have no more passion in you than a watermelon. Now, madam, I have made the arrangements that suit me. Your carping will not change that!"

At this, she hissed "villain," then turned her back and stormed out.

Now, if this "round" of her behavior mimics the past others, she will go a week or two in silence, then fling herself at my feet, weeping, amorous, apologetic and forgiving. After a night or two of passionate (for her) beddings (for I am kind enough to humor her), she will relapse into sloth and creep again into her place of sulky silence where she will remain until enraged again by some new twist, just as a sow in very hot weather will not leave the shade unless thunderclaps drive her out.

Ah, but what matters it now? Young Sally grows in sweetness by the week, almost the day. How different are things now than when we began!

At first, she was so charmed by the money that nothing else seemed to touch her. We were established in the West Woods in an old cabin that was painted and properly floored, in which I placed a bureau, a mirror, a table, two chairs, a lamp and a bed.

With her "own" money, she bought linens, a bedspread, a crystal oil lamp, a mahogany lamp stand, a chesterfield, an overstuffed chair, a thick blue rug and other flubdubs that pleased her. She also bought gowns, garters, stockings and perfume, and, in the end, crammed herself in so tightly with furnishings and possessions that it was hard to so much as walk about.

Poor Elizabeth was beside herself, as she is still. And Sally, stalking about the dining room of the Big House like a murderess, eyeing me, frying me with her hot-coal gaze, carped in private at Young Sally to end it, act up, get sold but save herself.

Young Sally has told me about this. Less and less did my Young Sally listen. Now she is earless and eyeless under the pouring spite of the comely old bitch. Now she belongs—not to her mother, not to the blacks, not to any friend—but only to me!

The first time I had her, it was awkward. She was a virgin and wept, tho' the Negroes have a very different attitude about sexual matters than we do. I am told that, in some nations of Africa, the girls are purposely deflowered just after their coming-into-womanhood ceremony, which is observed after their first menses, and thereafter taught that the enjoyment of intercourse bears no moral taint or interferes with the divine relationship.

I know full well that many of our young slaves here at Pinewood have congress before they are married. This, I must say, is one thing about the Negro civilization that seems very wise. Neither Lucy nor Amanda nor any of the other slave girls I have had was a virgin, tho' neither was any of them married. I think Young Sally's weeping was because she still at that time thought that, by becoming intimate with me, she had sold her soul to the Dark One. But, soon enough, everything changed.

The first time happened in the guest room down the hall from my and Elizabeth's room. She bled on the coverlet, which shocked her almost to death for she was certain that Elizabeth would see the blood, instinctively realize its origin and have her whipped and killed.

There was a fire on the grate, it being the cold season. To Young Sally's amazement, I simply tossed the coverlet on it and kissed her as it burned.

Her eyes were wide with wonder. "But, suh, won' Miz Elizabeth miss it?"

"She might," said I lightly, "but it will not miss her."

Young Sally ignored the humor, although I stressed it. In those first few months, even as a little passion took root in her, fear was never far away. It did not begin to disperse until it was clear that everybody knew the truth, including Elizabeth, but that no punishment was going to follow.

Young Sally was dismissed from the Big House, of course, but was much happier in the wash house, where she washed and rinsed and wrung and told her gossip to the Negro girls and bathed in their fascination. Out on the grounds, in the wash house or the garden, she wore her cotton homespun. But, whenever she could, she brought the girls into her cabin to display her treasures—her nacre hairbrush, her tortoise-shell combs, her silk gowns—and let them try on everything, sit on the furniture and lie on the bed, enjoying their cries of astonishment and envy, and their gratitude for allowing them this entry into her suddenly "magical" life.

Elizabeth, of course, immediately learned of the new use to which the cabin in the West Woods was being put. It was originally the overseer's quarters but had long been replaced by a larger house very near the front gateway of the plantation and had stood empty for some years. House slaves are such great tale bearers! I suspect it was Sally herself who put Elizabeth wise. What business would Elizabeth ever have had personally out in those faraway woods?

Ha! But, soon enough, Elizabeth found everything out. I made neither pretense nor defense but told her plainly that now things were on a new footing, and she might feel more comfortable in residence at Norfolk or Charleston where the sea air could "restore her to health." This shocked her into silence. But then she began having the slave girls who visited Young Sally whipped, at the same time ordering a whipping for Young Sally herself, though I had warned her against it.

Young Sally said to me, "Young Marse Geo'ge, Miz Elizabeth gon have me whupped de minit yo leaves fer Richmond. Black Sulla done tol me, an grinned when he said it, cause she aks him ter do de whuppin his own sef, an dat man be bout de hardest nigga in Vuh-ginia. He'd whup he own mama, daddy an sistuh, all three ter death an laugh when he done it!" Her pretty lips were quivering and her little hands were clasped together, as if in prayer.

In all truth, a whipping by Black Sulla is a sobering thing. But he is of great value to us precisely because of such heartlessness as this.

I hastened to reassure her. "Never waste a tear or a fear on this, dear girl," said I. "You shall never be whipped. Never as long as I live. Elizabeth knows this. I have told her explicitly. But I shall remind her, never fear."

"But Black Sulla don' know. Nevah mind how yo remine Miz Elizabeth. Dat skeemin nigga wants ter whup me out he own pleasure."

"What do you mean?" I asked.

"I means dat nigga be sweet on me an have been dese tree years. He fo'evah brushin wid he big rough hands at my behine an, as many times as I tol him I hated de sight of him, dat many times he laugh an say, 'Well, girl, if'n I don' git yo one way, I'll git yo anothuh.' Now he say he gon' whup me soon as Miz Elizabeth say ter do it, an he'll do it hard as hard kin git, but he'll do it lightah if'n I says he kin have me."

I felt a quick upspring of annoyance. "I will put him straight. He shall never bother you again. I am sure it is all Elizabeth's doing."

But no more did I say it than I forgot it, since I was departing for a business trip to Richmond to look over a new lot of slaves at auction that very hour, and my mind was preoccupied. I did not think to caution Black Sulla. For it never occurred to me that Elizabeth could be so defiant.

And indeed, I went to Richmond. When I returned the day after, I found Young Sally, face down on the bed in her cabin, breathless from crying. Her lovely, smooth back was opened in a series of short diagonal slices from her shoulders right down to her buttocks, and now all of these wounds were crusted with dried blood. This was the result of an expert bullwhipping—the work of Black Sulla.

I comforted Young Sally, then sought out Elizabeth. She received me in her bedroom with a smug look, sitting cross-legged on her bed, like a great three-chinned frog on a lily pad. But all smugness vanished when, without a word, I snatched hold of her hair with my left hand and hit her with my open right palm very hard eight or ten times in the face. She screamed.

But I attacked her with such force, and so unexpectedly, that her scream trailed off, and she tumbled under my blows, down off the bed and onto the carpet. There she lay, woozy and terrified. It pleased me to note blood coming from her nostrils and to see a nice, vivid redness on her left cheek and around the eye. (The next day, there was a swelling in both places.)

I said to her, "If you whip her again, I shall build a wing on the house and live in it, and have no more to do with you. But before I do that, I shall bring an overseer's whip here to your bedroom and use you exactly as you have used her. If you doubt my word, test it."

Elizabeth was so astonished and horrified that it took her a moment to speak. Cupping her swelling cheek with both hands, her eyes wide and wild, she lay on the carpet, staring up at me, and stammered, "You have completely thrown up your life for a nigger slave woman. I cannot believe you are the same man I married and was so in love with."

"I am not that man," I replied.

And, saying no more, I turned and left her. Even a year since, I would have accused myself for a like behavior. Now, I congratulated myself on such restraint as prevented me from really injuring her.

After that, I took another bedroom on the same floor—my "Young Sally room"—but separated from my wife's by an empty one. I am now in the very room where we two went together when I first had Young Sally. I have slept apart from my wife ever since, and most nights I am with Young Sally in her cabin.

The first few months of my sexual life with Young Sally were strained and disturbed by little tremors, as if my plucking her from her only known life had been an earthquake and all that followed tiny aftershocks. She tried—knowing, of course, that it was in her interest to be a well of sweet passion—but could manage little, though I judged her intentions to be of the best.

She often wept. Sometimes, she would let me hold her; other times, she would curl up, facing the wall, saying that, sure as the rain, sun and stars, she was going to hell. The one thing that restored her to a certain equanimity was the sight and handling of her slowly growing treasure of gold coins, which she would take out from their hiding place in a dirty stocking behind a chimney chink that I had fashioned for the purpose.

As I allowed her to spend her money to suit herself (within decent limits)—taking her personally into Richmond and accompanying her to the stores where, of course, as a slave alone and without my presence, her custom would be questioned—she decorated her little cabin. I confess that I was charmed and surprised by her natural taste.

Though unschooled even as far as reading or writing her own name, she was yet sensitive to the blend or clash of colors, of furniture styles, of rug patterns, of the subtleties of one design—say, of the carpet—echoing another in the coverlet. The colors she chose were by no means all of a piece but quietly reflected one another, even as each broadened the canvas as a whole. She had no words to describe the process she was in.

The most she could say about it was, as she did about the coverlet she selected, "I tinks dis cullah be lak ter please me good."

"But," I said, "the carpet has checks in it. So the coverlet you buy can't have stripes, like this one. The two will clash, won't match at all."

Her face fell, but she said, "Yas, suh. Jes as you laks, suh."

"Well, they won't. Do you understand what I am saying? I know you have no experience in this."

"I does unnerstan yo, suh."

"But you don't agree?"

A pause. Then a little smile played about her lips. "No, suh, I don' gree."

"You actually think the two together will be harmonious?"

"Harmonious mean 'look good,' suh?"

"Yes."

"Den I say yas. Dey look good!"

"But how can you say they will? The coverlet is here and the rug is at home."

"How kin yo say dey won', suh?" Her smile broke through. "Dis heah really is my money, ain't it, suh? If it ain't, den yo buys whut yo sees fit. But if it are, den I wants ter take my chance wid dis heah culluh an dis heah pattern."

The proprietor stood by, wearing an anxious look at this easy interchange, clearly wondering why a Negress was speaking so familiarly to me, clearly her white master.

"Is everything in order here, sir?" he asked.

I couldn't think what he expected me to say. "Indeed, yes. I will take this coverlet, if you please."

Young Sally slipped me "her" money when his back was turned, and I paid. She had quickly learned her numbers, though I felt odd teaching a Negro even this much. I do agree with the wisdom of keeping the general run of them ignorant. But, as to Young Sally, I simply have never seen her as I do all the rest. To me, she is the exception to every rule.

At home that night, in the light of a low-wicked lamp, she lay in her soft bed in her nightgown of sheer material, a pale yellow, revealing the sweet flesh beneath. She was preoccupied, lying with one arm flat on the sheet beside her and the other resting on her breast, head propped by a pillow, her glance roaming amongst her treasures and now and then over to me. I sat, still dressed, in an overstuffed chair, looking at her beauty, feeling that I never would get my fill of it.

Then, her eyes drifted slowly to mine and held them—a rare thing for her—and she said, "Yo done make me happy. I nevah been happy lak dis."

Her quiet seriousness touched me. As always, she did not use my Christian name unless it had a "Marse" in front of it. But simply the dispensing of "Marse" and "suh," as she had, except when saying my name, was a deep intimacy.

I did not know if I even wanted her to use my Christian name alone, for that would be the greatest imaginable departure from the master-slave relationship, far more so than sex. Sex does not need to touch on identity, while names were identity itself and everything they stood for.

Young Sally held my eyes. Hers seemed luminous. Her gaze was as strong as a voice in my ear.

I rose and slowly undressed, thinking that, if I had misread her, it need not raise my hopes but only my patience. But her eyes stayed soft and open to me. And, when I climbed in beside her, she did not ask me to put out the lamp as always before. She extended in the most sweet, most tender way her arms above her head as an invitation for me to slip off her nightgown. Then she pressed herself into my embrace, sighing. And, when I kissed her, she engaged my tongue; when I entered her, I found her wet and receptive.

It was the beginning of our true life together.

It was not necessary—I had not even thought of doing it before we embraced—but afterwards, I leaned out of bed to retrieve my trousers and out of my pocket took a twenty-dollar gold piece, which, for a reason I still cannot quite understand, I brought up to my lips, as if to kiss it, then held it in my lips as I leaned out toward hers.

She opened her lips to take it, extending her tongue as though to receive the host. For some reason, this was so erotic to me that at once I entered her again. Now her ardor was raised also, and it was an intense and prolonged coupling. I, being in no danger of spending too soon, thrust so strongly and for so long that her breath came short.

She wrapped me tightly around with her legs and spent for the first time in my arms, making lovely, deep-throated sounds of the sort more expressive than words, still with the gold coin shining between her lips.

And this night, as I held her afterwards and whispered "I love you" in her ear, she did not lie silently and passively but sighed once and brought her cheek next to mine. That was the moment at which I realized that I was now happier and more content than I had ever been before. And I realized too that, against usage, religion and law, I was truly and deeply in love with her.

When she became pregnant, she was at first dismayed. All of her old fears of my abandoning her arose again.

"Sho'ly, sho'ly yo gon sell me now, me an my baby. Dis gon be too bad a ting fer yo ter face. All de white womens gon be gossipin an Miz Elizabeth won' stand fer it. She gon carry me an de baby up ter Richmond an sell us fer any price us kin fetch. Someday, when yo be gone away, dat's jes whut she do. An me an my baby be gone Souf to Geo'gia or Loozianna an nevah see none of y'all no mo."

Fear cannot be talked away but only reduced by events that counter it. The baby came—a delightful, beautiful girl whom Young Sally named Missy because that is what my father always called her when she was a child, and I agreed. It was splendid to me that her fondness for those days persisted. So, Missy it was!

I doted on her and brought them both little gifts. Eventually, Young Sally became convinced that I would not sell them and, relaxing into this new depth of security, began to show me attentions never dreamed of before. It was at that time that I first became aware of Young Sally's considerable intelligence as well as what I can only call her "worldly wisdom."

Fear makes children of us all. But absent it, the true mind emerges. In some cases, such as Elizabeth's, there is not much to emerge. In Young Sally's case, there was and is a great deal. I found myself beginning to discuss with her the problems that faced me as a planter responsible for a great plantation and near enough a hundred and fifty souls, white and black. In this way, my attachment to her, and hers to me, deepened.

1801

THE LADY DORA

Saleh found the pain ebbing day by day. Though Mr. Badger (the second mate Samuels) refused to minister to her, and seemed to want her perpetually bleeding and suffering, the man with the eye patch—Mr. Cyclops (Carlson)—rubbed her bruises and cuts with an ointment when the captain was elsewhere detained.

Through making signs and being patient, Mr. Cyclops conveyed to her that he had heard about others who had also had their tongues cut, and that much of the pain would be gone in a month or two, and all of it in three. She must not chew things in the meantime but mush them in a bowl with water and swallow them. She must let her tongue rest on the floor of her mouth rather than ceaselessly touching it and sucking at it out of nervousness or pain.

To help Saleh remember to do this, Mr. Cyclops gave her a shiny green stone, which he took out of a small leather bag he wore attached to his belt by a leather thong. It was the size of a large pea and, in her former life, she would have thought it beautiful. He told her to hold it on her tongue, so that it would remind her to let the wounded tongue rest. He kept telling her not to become careless and swallow it. And, afterwards, he told her that she could have it as a keepsake.

"You're to keep yer tongue as still as a female can, young one, though I know I ask too much." He smiled. Then his face grew grave, and he said, "Ah, what a shame we've hurt ye so. And you so luv'ly."

Saleh stared at him, as she always did when he spoke to her. She had no idea what he was saying unless he accompanied his words with signs. She accepted everything he did for her with no show of gratitude, though neither did she reject him. She tried not to think much about him lest she have a kind thought about a white man.

As she healed, Mr. Badger wanted her less, but she was forced to remain in his cabin. He made her sleep naked on the bare decking, however, enjoying from his nest of warm blankets her teeth chattering in the night with mid-ocean cold, and only unlocked her chains and took her into the bed when he wanted her.

But her being free of the slavehold gained her great advantages. She knew that the blacks down below suffered with the trapped heat, the poisonous air, the tasteless food and diarrhea. When they were allowed on deck for the occasional airing, she saw how they were suffering. Every day, she saw dead bodies brought topside and, without ceremony, cast overboard. She wished that she could jump over the rail to join them, but Mr. Badger, anticipating this, kept her chained.

But at least she remained easily accessible to Mr. Cyclops, who continued to bring her medicines, including laudanum, which much eased her pain. He also brought meat for her, chopped into a bean mash in a wooden bowl and stirred runny with warm water, when Mr. Badger was not nearby, and urged her to swallow it down.

And, despite the fact it seemed that the heart had been ripped out of her life, and life itself forever spoiled, she slowly mended, and even found herself not actively hating Mr. Cyclops. But that was the most she could allow him. From that point, and for the rest of her life, there was no longer anything like love in her with which she could attach to anybody else. And certainly not to a white man.

Yet, day after day, as the ship drove through the seas headed toward the west, Mr. Cyclops continued to look after her. He did not touch her body, except to apply unguents, or leer at her as she had seen all the other white devils do or take any advantage of her.

Sometimes, as he ministered to her, his voice had a soft, cooing sound, like a mother's: "There now, young one, *there* now. It's healing nice and sweet, ain't it? Just look at yer pretty face with the swelling down. In God's good time, I do hope ye'll be sold to a nice farm with a good master and be happy. I pray ye will, young one. After all ye've seen and all that's been done to ye."

Sometimes, when Mr. Cyclops was gathering his creams and cloths together, wanting to depart before the appearance of Mr. Badger, he would lean down and kiss the top of Saleh's head as she sat in her leg chains, naked but for a dirty loin cloth, on the rocking deck of the captain's cabin. When he did this, a chill shot through her blood. But immediately then, murmuring his strange English words, he would depart.

His kissing her head left her angry and frightened anew that he would soon drop his pose of caring and come at her with his penis bobbing. And, if by chance she would lose for a tiny moment the keenness of her suffering history, and feel even a little grateful to Mr. Cyclops, the vision of a bleeding, dying Kano instantly pressed itself upon her, and she was flooded again with the rage that only intensified her emptiness.

Then came the day the lookout called, "Land ho!"

Gradually, a green shoreline rose from the blur of blue water, and the entrance to Charleston Harbor could be seen in the distance. Mr. Badger, on the Lady Dora's bridge, called for soundings as they rode easily on the incoming tide.

Just then, Mr. Cyclops came to Saleh one last time. "I wish God's protection on ye, young one. This voyage is my last in a slaver. I'm going to work a merchantman home to England and go no more to sea. I've sins to atone for. Many, many sins. Some of the worst are against you and your man. The Sisters of St. Benedict have a convent in London. I know they'd let me live in a small room in the cellar in exchange for my work. Then I can go to mass every day. Let go of strong drink and the evils of slavery. End my life a decent man, perhaps with a small hope of heaven. Pray each day in the chapel for all the souls whose lives I soiled with my greedy hands. Yours most of all ..."

Mr. Cyclops's face was very somber. He walked close to Saleh and stood leaning over her, murmuring his incomprehensible words. Saleh—cut adrift from the river and the rock, abandoned by the sea gods, alone and broken in a world filled with pain, rape and death—had lost all her intuitive abilities. Never in her lifetime would they return. Their place inside her was so crammed with rage that everything she had learned—sorcery, healing, intuiting and speaking with the gods—felt like a sickness instead of a blessing.

What good had any of it done her? What good was it to talk to impotent, even deceitful gods, whose revelations were only about the pains she must suffer? Where was any single promise of good? What advantage was it to be able to see into men's hearts when, despite what she saw, the information was useless? Life was a sham, a bitter joke. Black people were powerless and white people evil.

There was no meaning beyond pain, and the very idea of trust—let alone for-giveness—was an obscenity.

She grew tenser as Mr. Cyclops spoke softly to her, then pulled back inside herself, as if coiled snakelike. After leaving off talking, he leaned over her and once again kissed the top of her head.

She said to herself, *I cannot bear this. I cannot let him touch me again. He must not!*

But he did. After he kissed the top of her head, he put a soft hand to one cheek, and—now so close to her that she could see the dirt on his eye patch, the grease on his hair, the lines in his face, a missing bottom tooth and the vein in his nose, and smell his repulsive, white-man odor—he kissed gently her other cheek.

She cried out in Fulani, "You filthy dog! May you drown in *shit!*"

And, her hands being unfettered, she simultaneously struck at his head with her fist and spit in his face. As she did so, the small, beautiful stone he had given her to ease her tongue's misery struck his forehead, and he staggered back, shocked.

It had been, she later learned, an emerald.

1859

PINEWOOD PLANTATION, VIRGINIA

Missy was seventeen now and being taken up by Little Marse Will. Young Sally could see it all unfolding in her daughter's life as it had in her own. Missy was like Young Sally had been at the same age—outwardly cheerful but inwardly cautious, even fearful.

At least she thought so. Missy was such a hard girl to understand. She outright denied being connected to Little Master Will at all, even though Decatur had told Young Sally that Little Master Will had taken Missy many times to the attic room where George used to take Sally, and locked the door. But Missy swore that nothing had happened there, that Little Master Will had only wanted her to sweep and dust and mop the place since he wanted to use it for a private study, to get out of the way of both his father and grandfather. But, if that were the case, the preparations were lasting a very long time.

Young Sally had been denied access to the Big House for so long that she had lost touch with what went on there (even Young George no longer told her anything). She was dependent on the other slaves for news and, in recent years, she had found them less forthcoming. She thought they might be hiding things from her because of her position of intimacy with Young George, who had opened his life to her almost far enough to make her the mistress of Pinewood Plantation, if things had been different.

Over the years, Young George's disgust with Elizabeth had become palpable. Even the youngest, dimmest field slave, who never went near the House from one year's end to the next, knew all about how Young George had brought Young Sally close and pushed Elizabeth away, and knew everything that was said and done by the involved parties every single day.

The slaves at first felt a great pride in Young Sally's rise, since it proved that the white man's assertion of the Negro's stupidity was a lie, and that one of their own had gone inconceivably high in the world. But then things began to change. From the sweet, generous soul she had once been, Young Sally gradually became haughty. She still went to the wash house to work a few hours each day, though now in a bad spirit, and only because Young George insisted on it—"for appearances."

The other slave women there no longer chatted with her as in the past. They had stopped telling her news of the quarters. And Young Sally had abandoned the practice of inviting them "home" to try on her pretty clothes and admire her things since she had moved into the spacious cabin that Young George had built for her. Now, she did not want their unwashed bodies to touch anything of hers or their broad, dirty, bare feet to track in mud. She became impatient of their opinions because she realized how ignorant they were. She began to reprove them, and they fell silent and shut her out.

As she more and more identified with the concerns and perspectives of white people instead of black, Young Sally found that she could still bear the lighter-skinned slaves, but the darker ones made her feel angry and hateful. And the ones who were so black that their skin shone and whose palms were glove-white, she loathed and shunned.

In a world where whiteness was valued and blackness a curse, many black people now wanted to disguise or change or deny their color. Wiry hair, wider noses, more everted lips were deplored in the hearts of black people who yearned to be white.

Young Sally wondered why indeed they would not yearn. What were the advantages of black skin over white? Did any exist? No! Then, to gain freedom— and after it, respect, social status, success, wide community, financial power and, most fundamentally, acceptance as a full and proper human being—how could anyone not wish they were white? And, when freed, how could they not act white, think white, dress white, learn to talk white, so as to rise with white's lightness and not sink to oblivion with the dreadful muddy heaviness of black?

Such thoughts possessed Young Sally and infested the wider slave communities like germs. Within black people—side by side with pride of African family, kingdom, heritage, language, art and story—lay the antiblack virus, eating souls. Those with white blood had lighter skin, sometimes a yellowish tan, and were called "yallers"; those with very light skin were called "high yallers." If a yaller had soft hair and narrow lips and looked almost white, then he/she had status over the blacker ones and dominion over the blackest.

That is just how things were.

As luck would have it, one of the latter—a newly purchased, nineteen-year-old slave named Phoebe, crippled from birth, recently almost given away to a broker when her master's plantation in North Carolina went bankrupt—had been bought very cheaply by Young George and was put into the wash house where Young Sally could not avoid her.

Immediately, Young Sally spoke to Young George about it. She was lying on the bed in a filmy nightgown the color of jade, her back against pillows, her arms folded, body tense.

"How come yo put dat black nigga inter de wash house nex ter me? I cain't stand de look or de smell of her!"

Young George frowned. "Well, dear girl, I certainly can't run my plantation to suit *you*, can I? If I did, I'd have to sell off every nigger with darker skin than yours. Not that you go to the wash house much yourself, no matter how often I ask you to. I can't imagine why Phoebe bothers you. And you will admit that I let you have your way in most things. But you'll just have to accept that there are some things you can't change."

Young Sally's face was grim. "Well, dis yo kin change if yo wants ter. It jes mean movin dat nigga out'n de wash house an inter de fields."

Young George, sitting across from the bed, shifted in his chair. "I don't think she's fit for field work, sweet girl. She's lame. I'm sure you've noticed that. Her left leg is shorter than her right, and she is very thin. Her left arm is affected too, though she still uses it. She's good-natured and gets along well. I got her for a very good price. Fifty dollars, if you can believe that! But she's not strong. Still, she can dust and wash dishes and, eventually I think, be able to help Black Rowanna, the cook."

"Yas, I notice, but lame don' mean nothin. Lots of mastuhs puts out lame niggas in de field rows."

"Well," Young George said, impatience creeping into his voice, "I'm happy if they're happy. But I do not put lame niggers in the fields simply because they cannot keep up. And if they don't keep up, the work suffers. And if the work suffers, so does profit. If I put out a hundred lame niggers in my fields, in a year I'd be at the bank borrowing, and in two I'd have all my niggers and my plantation up for sale, and you'd be in Mississippi, and I'd be in the poor house!"

"Oh!" cried Young Sally, clapping her hands in annoyance. "I hates it when yo talks lak dis. Sometimes yo treats me lak I be de most iggerant nigga in Vuhginia. We ain't talkin bout no hunnert lame niggas or nothin lak. Dey jes dis one, lame, stinky nigga gal dat talk screechy lak a blue jay fum day clean ter dark.

"If yo gon keep her in de wash house, den I ain't goin in dere. No, suh. An besides dat, I knows how good yo's fixed fer money. Yo could raise a dead crop five years runnin an Miz Elizabeth still be coverin her fat ass in silk. If yo don' want me ter know somethin, den don' tell me. But if yo *do* tell me, den jes membuh dat I *knows* it!" She folded her arms more tightly and looked away from him.

Young George rose slowly from his chair. He stared at Young Sally until she felt the pull and met his eyes. He looked at her in silence for a minute until she could see by his face that she had overstepped herself. In the past, he had found this serious, almost threatening look of his to be more effective than scolding.

But, apparently, she no longer really noticed it—or worse, was not cowed by it. Less and less as the years went on did Young Sally acknowledge anything that was apt to limit her willfulness. In the end, she got her way, and Phoebe was removed. But Young Sally's imperiousness continued.

This annoyed Young George, the more so as it continued to get worse. Conversations like this one had become, instead of rare, almost routine between him and Young Sally. The sweetness of the bedtime was drifting more and more into the past. The intimate moments when he revealed the problems of plantation ownership to Young Sally and heard her sensible, uncomplicated suggestions were likewise diminishing.

On the other hand, Elizabeth, miraculously slim again, had completely changed her tune. Instead of carping, she had been saying for some time now—in a detached voice, not nagging but as if commenting on some interesting neighborhood gossip—that Young Sally had grown ruder and now was almost ungovernable. Elizabeth had even begun visiting Young George in his bed every few weeks, and he found himself enjoying her again.

Elizabeth told him, "Despite that we are intimate again, I realize that our marriage is not as sound as it might be, since the trust and fidelity that would sustain it are strained. I accept that. I think I have behaved very well, given the circumstances.

"My fear now is that, because Young Sally will so alienate the Negroes, they will rebel. They will march in a group up to the House and complain. You know yourself that slaves have done such things, when one of them has alienated the rest and gotten too bold, too above herself and, worst of all, too above the others. And, once they have banded together over one thing, it is easier to do so over another, more important thing. And, of course, that is the seed from which uprisings grow."

She said this in a conversational tone, as she knitted a shawl for Old Dorcas, a Jerrold House slave whom Elizabeth had brought with her to Pinewood and who was now blind and infirm.

Young George was irritated. "Don't be so sure of what I know and don't know. Worry about what *you* know."

He did not know exactly when it had started, but he was listening to Elizabeth again.

Elizabeth knitted on, nodding at her husband. "Of course, you are right. I spoke amiss. But this about Young Sally is not just what I know. *Everybody* knows it, black and white, slave and free. Everyone from here to Richmond and beyond. The little joke around town is, 'Did you hear that a nigger's running Pinewood now?'

"Of course, I pretend not to hear such things, but I do. *Everyone* does. I know that you are indifferent to others' opinions. You have told me this many times, and I know a man of your strong character does not easily change his mind …"

Young George was irritated that what Elizabeth said was true. And the very word "uprising" brought such a cold, ugly contraction to his heart that, immediately after she said it, he was plunged into fear. But he did like it that Elizabeth at last admitted what a strong character he had.

And more often now than he liked, he had to correct Young Sally, warn her, argue with her, even threaten her. And though he could silence her for the time, she constantly renewed her willfulness, again and again. And he kept thinking of the Turner uprising in the Virginia Tidewater in 1831.

Nat Turner, a Negro slave and preacher, had felt that he was being instructed by God to rise against the white oppressors and kill them. He, with a few other like-minded slaves, began the revolt by killing his own master and his family, then went from plantation to plantation, enlisting new slaves, killing whites with knives and axes, raping and burning.

Over a period of two or three days, Turner butchered sixty white men, women and children. The countryside rose up in terror and outrage. A posse was formed to hunt him down. Turner and his men were run to earth, his men killed, and Turner tried and hanged as a public reassurance.

But Nat Turner changed permanently the way white people saw their slaves. Fear replaced complacency. Many slave owners now routinely locked their doors at night because fear of the black people, whom they kept enslaved, was endemic, a natural byproduct of slavery itself.

None of the whites killed by Turner and his men had experienced the slightest intimation that any one of their own slaves was capable of such horrific acts. This being true, other slave owners all across the South wondered how they could trust even their oldest and mildest Negroes, and began taking protective measures against them.

Locked doors and loaded guns at the bedside became the rule. The once merely unpleasant thought of uprising became a terrible specter, which hung like smoke from a fire that never died, over every farm and plantation where slaves were kept. The thought of abusing the slaves to the point of their rising up was now terrifying.

And, to be sure, Young Sally's preferment represented an abuse to the slaves. The Negroes made no secret of that. They hated her. Hated her high-handed ways. And they had even told Young George. Well, Decatur had told him.

Even Black Sulla, in his humorless, blank-faced way, had said, "Yo bes look ter Young Sally, suh. De niggas gittin dang sick of her. I jes says dis ter let yo know, suh. I don' mean no kind er disrespeck by it."

But the look on his brutal face as he spoke was chilling. Was this a sly, purposely horrifying hint of an uprising? *Dear God!*

The thought of being murdered, in some ghastly way, by Negroes, because of something a snotty slave woman had done, was nauseating. But such things had happened, would happen again and could happen to Young George.

And Elizabeth, in her calm, detached way, was reminding him of this constantly.

The new northern Republican Party, which had replaced the Whigs, had taken up antislavery as a cause. Gradually, their views spread South through their political web, making their way to the slaves through southern Republicans and other sympathizers, and through smuggled abolitionist newspapers.

Now the northern abolitionists were louder and more strident than ever. The moron William Lloyd Garrison's damned newspaper, *The Liberator*, infested some of the best homes at the South. Literacy for Negroes was against the law, but many addle-headed owners, acting against their own interest and the interest of every white man at the South, had allowed their slaves to learn reading. Now, nothing could prevent copies of the Garrison rag from falling into the Negroes' hands.

The literate read to the illiterate, and all of them got more and more worked up about freedom, a better life at the North and eventually full rights as American citizens, and an end to racial prejudice—which, of course, was completely insane! But the Negroes believed it.

So here was the world of the South, running exactly as God intended, yet being threatened because of the lies of abolitionists and Republicans and the greedy grasping of the blacks. It was all an utter scandal. And the ingratitude of the slaves! That was beyond the power of words to express.

And now, even niggers were publishing newspapers! The black scoundrel Frederick Douglass distributed his treasonous *North Star* everywhere, undermining white authority and duping the ignorant blacks with completely fantastic ideas of freedom and equality.

All of this was very upsetting, painful and dangerous. And, of course, as the destined war for southern independence approached, the blacks became more turbulent as the Yankee demand for their emancipation grew. A widespread distemper was in the air—some of it bracing, as the white men of the South reached their breaking point, and some of it alarming, as now could be glimpsed by the masters the utter poisonousness of a world the Yankees would make if they won the war.

And yes, it had to be admitted that Young Sally no longer pleased Young George as she once had. That was exasperating too, since he had promised her that he would never abandon her. But it was beginning to look as though holding allegiance to that promise was unwise. She had so changed from the simple, shy, money-hoarding girl she had once been that he could no longer enjoy his time with her. Especially since the sexual flame had begun to gutter. He could feel the time approaching—rapidly—when it would go out.

Then what?

There was this girl called Cordelia, seventeen but wise for her years, who made no secret of her intention to attract Young George. She was the opposite of what Young Sally had been. Instead of being shy, fearful of hell, frightened of Elizabeth and Black Sulla and certain that Young George would abandon her, Cordelia actually asked him a question one day, when he met her by chance on the path to the South Field.

"When yo gon git done wid dat snooty bitch yo spoilin an git yosef a *real* woman, Young Marse Geo'ge?"

As Cordelia spoke, she pretended indignation in a cute way by putting her hands on her hips. But then she hugged herself and burst out laughing, covering her face with both hands and peeking at him between her fingers. Young George was charmed, had been charmed by her for some little time, her boldness and flirting having not gone unnoticed. He liked her playfulness, and she had a beautiful smile. Her features were odd in that they were not especially Negroid, but her skin was very dark, making Young George think of chocolate—a rich and hearty chocolate, such as thickened the blood and fortified a man against the weather.

He said teasingly, "My goodness, little girl, how *forward* of you! Did you have someone in mind as this *real woman*?"

But she went serious and reached out her arms toward him, as if to embrace him, but then spread her fingers wide and drew back, and again laughed in that attractive, musical way she had. "I could give yo a name, suh, if yo was ter want one."

"Let's say I *did* want one."

"Den I gots ter say a girl name of Cordelia would be jes right fer what yo be needin."

Her laugh rang out again, but Young George could see a bold seriousness in her eyes. They were beautiful eyes, come to think of it, not the mulatto hazel or green but a deep brown, dark and shining.

Young George glanced around him. The way to the South Field led through a stand of some trees and tall grass and weeds, which concealed the path and anyone using it. He reached out and pulled Cordelia to him. She was slim—slimmer than Young Sally had been at the beginning—slim and sweet and very daring. She threw back her head and laughed again when Young George drew her close, but she let herself be drawn.

As she came into his embrace, she dropped her arms to her sides and let him enfold her. He kissed her throat, she giggled; he raised his hand to touch her face, and at once she stopped giggling and stared into his eyes.

He felt suddenly and deeply stirred as he saw her fearlessness and the raw sexuality that she was placing at his disposal. Of course, she would expect something in return. And why should she not? He saw that she would not be like Young Sally, attracted by the sight and security of gold coins. She was surer of herself than that, more grown-up. She would not have to be coddled, instructed, reassured.

He could see that, if anything, Cordelia would reassure him. Every moment he was with her, she would be entrenching herself in his life and, as inconspicuously as possible, extracting from him everything she possibly could. Which was normal! She was just Missy's age, was she not? Even Missy's "friend"? Did it bother him that he was drawing close a girl the age of his own daughter?

Well, the thing was that, with niggers, it was never the same as it would be with whites. You simply could not make direct comparisons. It was nonsense, like comparing cows and horses. Just fundamentally different things. It made no sense to tire yourself out having scruples about niggers. If Young George didn't know that before, he knew it now. Young Sally had proved it, had proved what every sensible white man knew by instinct. He had known it yet ignored what he knew, thinking himself in love. My God, what madness it all was. What terrible, futile madness! Well, it would never happen again. Never in his life would he take a slave so close to his heart. *Never!*

He put a forefinger under Cordelia's chin, tilted her face up. She still stared boldly at him, holding his energies fixed upon her alone. He pulled her into a kiss and she came, with all of herself. He loved the feel of her slim body and small breasts, loved the passion of her as she opened her mouth to his kiss, welcomed his tongue.

Ah, this was more like it! Such a lovely, such a harmless new road to explore.

"I take your suggestion, my sweet one," he said.

And Cordelia replied, "Yo ain't gon be sorry, suh. I kin promise yo dat!"

He decided on the spot that she would not have the cabin. No more cabin niggers for him. No, he would arrange it differently, not quite sure how yet, but under no urgency to puzzle it out. Actually, he had gotten somewhat attracted to Elizabeth again lately. She had lost so much weight, was so slim and light on her feet again. That lightness had translated to her speech, her voice, her manner.

In a way, Elizabeth was much like she had been when he courted her. She had stopped nagging and now had regular conversations with him, very much like conversations he would have with anyone else. In these conversations, she behaved more like a consultant than a wife. This both pleased and alarmed him. For he was and always would be alarmed by anything he could not understand.

As these conversations with Elizabeth became more frequent, Elizabeth herself seemed more reasonable. She did not argue or nag, merely held before him a truth and let him, if he chose, grab for it, like a trout leaps at a dragonfly. Over time, her attentions to him in this way built up a base of a new and very different credibility.

Ever since she had decorated Wilkenson's house, she seemed to be in much better spirits. Perhaps that sort of useful employment was good for a woman. Young George had asked her if she wanted to redo the Big House too, but she said no, she was happy with the House as it was. Which seemed surprising to him. If the overseer's house, why not her own as well?

And she had gone back to riding. She had Wilkenson accompany her, which was a good thing because a woman of her class riding alone was not approved of at the South, as he had heard that it was beginning to be at the North. The South still held fast to principles of gallantry long ignored above the Mason-Dixon Line. Among the many things the South had to teach the arrogant North was the meaning of real gallantry. This fast-coming war would be a fit occasion for the North to learn that. And it would not be the only thing the goddamn Yankees would learn. *No, sir!*

But, as to Elizabeth ...

She went much more often into Richmond than she had in recent years and bought little doodads for the House. She also brought things like pen nibs and pencils and notepaper for him, which he liked and even appreciated, though he wondered why she did it now but never before.

Wilkenson was away more often than he liked too. But Wilkenson was such an excellent overseer, and Young George had found a way to turn Wilkenson's absences to his advantage. Many times, Wilkenson had to go to Baltimore about his goddamn mysterious law case at the same times that Elizabeth went to Richmond, so Young George saw to it that Wilkenson escorted her there before taking the train of cars on to his destination. This was a comfort to Young George and relieved him of the need to send a nigger or two with her, who could better be used at home. It completely excused him from any need to squire her about, which was a brutal waste of his time, although he never said it in just those words.

Among the many things she purchased, Elizabeth now bought material and dress patterns for Missy. The girl had become a wonderful seamstress. And now that Elizabeth had ceased fighting against her, and accepted the girl's sweet agreeableness at face value, she made all of her mistress's clothes. Elizabeth's friends, seeing the lovely dresses Missy made, wanted her to make clothes for them too, but Elizabeth refused to allow it. Missy had all she could do in looking after the needs of little Peggy, making dresses for her and acting as the de facto upstairs maid.

And, as to Cordelia, Young George suddenly realized that he could evict Little Master Will from the attic room and outfit it for Cordelia. Of course, Young George knew about Little Master Will and Missy. Well, in short order, Little Master Will could have the cabin. And why not? May it bring Little Master Will less trouble than it had brought him!

And Cordelia … Make her the upstairs maid, and tell Missy that she had enough to do looking after Peggy and doing her sewing. Then Cordelia would be handy to him when needed. Certainly he would give her money, but nothing like what Young Sally had got.

He kept track of his gifts to Young Sally in the plantation's books under "Miscellaneous Slave Expenses." In the years he had kept her, he had given her upwards of three thousand dollars—and that did not include the cost of building the new cabin! Well, he would get much of that back. He knew where she kept it, of course. There was only so much of it a slave could spend anyway. He knew that she had given some to Sally, and that the old bitch had often urged Young Sally to use her money to run away.

"My momma said wid money lak dat, I kin git Norf prac'ly in de style of white womens. I could buy a freedom letter"—called a manumission certificate—"dat I heah niggas kin git some way dat gon set me free. Wid enuf money, yo kin git anyting yo want."

That would not happen with Cordelia. He would give her a few double eagles or rather the Confederate equivalent. (Yes, that glorious day was approaching when the goddamn Yankees and their gold money would be curiosities of history!) Cordelia would be happy with a tenth of what Young Sally had extorted from him. Nay, a *twentieth!* Yes, and grateful for it. Not sulky but charming as she received him, respectful of him and not liable to gloat or hold herself high. For, if she did, he would let Black Sulla teach her better manners.

Yes, by God! Never again would a nigger own him.

Never!

1861

PINEWOOD PLANTATION, VIRGINIA

It was late at night when George decided to tell Black Sulla what he wanted him to do with Sally. This message he wanted to deliver himself. There was an obscure excitement to it, even though the frailty of age made it a challenge. He lit a lantern, went out and made his slow way past the House slave row, through the gardens, past the wash house, dairy, smokehouse, the barns, the high grasses and scattering of old trees to the field slave shacks. He found Black Sulla's and, without knocking, walked in.

Black Sulla sat up so quickly that it alarmed George. Moonlight spilling in behind him, his lantern's light revealed the scene. In the thick-shouldered slave's hand was a large knife.

"Who *dat*? Don' come no closer now. *Stop!*" Black Sulla leaped out of bed and advanced toward him. "Lift up dat damn lant'n so I kin see yo face. Who *is* dat? Speak *up!*"

George said, alarmed, "It's your master. Simmer down."

"Yas, suh. So yo say. But hold up dat lant'n so I kin be sure. Yo got me blinded."

George did as Black Sulla asked, revealing his face in the light.

"All right, suh," Black Sulla said. "I aks yer pardon fer bein so tetchy, but yo bes not walk in on no nigga out'n de dark lak dat."

George did not reply. He had never in his life accepted correction from a Negro—except from *her*. But that is what he had come about.

"Are you wide awake?" George asked his driver.

"Yas, suh," Black Sulla said, his voice again flat, toneless.

George's voice was calm but it had an edge no slave could miss. "Then listen to me well. I will hold you responsible for doing exactly what I am going to tell you. Do you understand me?"

"Yas, suh."

"Sally is a field slave now."

"I knows dat, suh. She come ter me ter find out which shack she could stay in. An I bosses her in de fields ev'ry day."

"Are you curious why, at her age, she has been sent out?"

"No, suh. Dat ain't none of my biniss."

"Good. Nor the business of any other nigger. Just remember that."

"I membuhs dat, suh."

"Very well. I want you to put her out, hoeing weeds in the tobacco rows. All the fields are in the grass now. It's time to plough. Planting begins in a few weeks. Keep her hoeing in the rows all day, but give her a row of her own and make her responsible for it. Keep everyone else away from her. Nobody is to offer her the slightest assistance. Are you understanding me?"

Black Sulla grunted, his face unreadable. "Yas, suh."

"Refuse water the first time she asks for it. Make her ask two or three times. Inspect her work. Keep up nagging and bullying her. Don't let her come in from the rows for the noon meal. Feed her where she stands in the rows. Feed her only half of what the others get. Don't let her sit down. If she defies you and sits, whip her back to her feet. From the time she arrives in the field after first light until the bell rings at dark, give her no rest. After supper, get her some harness to mend, old clothes to patch. Do you see?

"Keep her busy until you go to bed. Tell her that she must have the mending work done by morning. If she does not have it done, whip her. Give her ten lashes with the bullwhip. Let her stand and take the strokes on her bare back with nothing for her to hold onto.

"Do not let her eat breakfast. Take her at once to the fields and keep her hoeing her own row and on her feet, just as you did the day before. At night, give her more work. If it is not done by morning, use the bullwhip. Ten lashes. Do you understand? Then right to the fields."

George stopped speaking and stared at Black Sulla in the garish lantern light. His face was grim.

"Yas, suh," was all Black Sulla said.

"No questions? You understand *everything?*"

"Not much ter unnerstan, suh. Jes bring hell ter her feets an make her stan in it."

George's grin was fierce. "Good man! I knew I could rely on you. And let me tell you something else …" George's face went solemn. He put a hand on Black

Sulla's big shoulder. "I have put it in my will that, after I am gone, you are to be freed and given two hundred dollars. I know my son will not like it, but that is what I am going to do. I don't think that day is too far away either. But I do want to be sure she goes before I do."

Black Sulla was slow to reply. George could not tell what he was thinking because his broad, flat face remained unreadable.

Finally he said, "Dat be true bout yo freein me, suh?"

"Of course. Why should I lie to you?"

"You din nevah lie ter me afore, suh. Dat I knows bout."

"No. And I'm not lying now. But tell me, how long do you think Sally can last under the treatment I have described?"

Black Sulla pondered. "Old lady lak her? Two day, suh. Den she lie down an cain't nobody whup her back up. She jes lie dere an stare at yo. Yo kin whup on her all yo wants. She won' move past blinkin or say nothin past groanin. Den she die."

"Good," said George. Then, in a louder voice, edged with passion, "*Good*, by God! Good! But don't start on her tomorrow. Wait a few days. Let her wonder. Tell her I called you in and told you that she deserved a little rest."

George let out a little chuckle. He picked up his lantern and went out.

As he walked away from the field slave shacks, he knew which one she was in. Sleeping in peace, no doubt, not knowing what awaited her. He felt the warmth of the old anger in his chest comforting him.

This hour a few days from now, she'll be broken, he thought. *Terrorized, her body exhausted and her mind numb, looking death in the face. Only one such day in the fields could likely bring her to her knees. At her age—and with the rheumatism—how swiftly now will the debt be paid and the books balanced!*

And, of course, there was no question of freeing Black Sulla. Even if he left explicit instructions about it in his will, which he would not, Young George would ignore them. What else could he do? Black Sulla was the best driver in the district. You never freed a man like that.

Never.

1859

PINEWOOD PLANTATION, VIRGINIA

The very next time that Elizabeth came to Wilkenson's house, the intimacy sprang up again like a bed of beautiful flowers. They talked, she wept, he dared to comfort her by taking her in his arms, there was a chaste kiss, he stood back astonished at himself, accusing himself.

She murmured "No, no, you mustn't. I am to blame."

The next time, the kiss was deeper. She clung to him, but they broke away and he said, "I have betrayed my employer. I am such a scoundrel. All you wanted or needed was kindness, yet look what I have done!"

And she cried, "Oh, never say so. It is *all* my doing. I am the betrayer."

And she put a gentle hand to his face. In an instant, they were kissing again, and he touched her breast, she quivered and wept, and he held her.

The next day, when she returned to discuss the redecorating of the house, it was not a minute before they were in each other's arms. He looked deeply into her eyes, wondering if he dared. And she understood him and made the tiniest nod.

He stepped into the next room where his Negro woman Dulcie sat, mending a shirt of his, and said that he needed her no more until tomorrow. Wilkenson watched her leave by the kitchen door, returned, took Elizabeth's hand, led her through the door to his bedroom, closed and locked it.

And, as they lay in each other's arms—on but not in his bed—he said, "This sort of wickedness, of men tempting good women astray, leads to hell."

But no more did he say it than she kissed him and whispered, "Then we shall be in hell together."

She removed only those garments that permitted him entry. Their lovemaking was brief, more desperate than passionate, and afterwards they hurriedly rearranged their clothing and she wept, this time in shame. And there were tears in his eyes too—tears of shame, anger at himself and joy.

"I never imagined that, after Constance died, I would ever love again. But I love you."

And she said, her eyes cast down, "I feel the same. Otherwise I could never …" She broke off, raised her eyes, tears on her cheeks, looking at him.

"I know, I know. Please—my dear one—I know what a pure … what a beautiful soul—"

"Oh, please do not call me pure," she cried out. "I am just the opposite!"

"No, no, you most certainly are *not* the opposite. You are the kindest, dearest—"

"Jared—here I only now for the first time speak your Christian name yet have had you for a lover! Dear God, I am wicked, but I love you. I do love you."

"Elizabeth. I too speak your beautiful name for the first time. Elizabeth …"

"But it must be the last."

"Of course. I know it. I am relieved by it. There can be no more of this sinning. Never, *never* again. This is the end of it. After this, you must never come here again."

"No, and I shall not. I must forget how I love you, how I think of you, how dear you have become …"

"And I, dear Elizabeth, must never again speak your name aloud. All this must be ended and forgotten."

The next day, she undressed completely. There was a short coupling, kisses, tears, then a much longer one. And, for the very first time in all of her life, Elizabeth Gwendolyn Jerrold Leyland came to climax. She welcomed it with trembling and sighing and weeping, clinging to Wilkenson's neck and telling him that she never knew such happiness as this could exist in human life.

And Wilkenson now knew that they must be together somehow, though he had no idea how, and realized in his deepest heart that God would not be against it.

And Elizabeth said, "You are my one and my only love."

Eventually, she made her plan for the redecoration. She cast out all the old furniture and brought in new; ordered caulked and painted the walls and ceilings; had the cracked wood floors replaced; obtained lovely new carpets that highlighted the surrounding new blond oak floor; and replaced the old-fashioned, light-distorting glass in the windows. In the end, she created as lovely and congenial a little home as could be imagined or desired.

She bought paintings of hunting scenes and an expensive, original (and very daring) Thomas Rowlandson art piece, depicting randy British lords and their trollups for the bedroom walls, and flowers and seascapes for the parlor. The kitchen, with its old shelves, was gutted, and new cabinets with glass-fronted doors were put in, together with tiled counters.

Elizabeth provided one of the best cooking stoves for the kitchen, a new set of dishes, tinware, pots, casserole dishes, sharp knives and china, and gave all the old things to the slaves. She had a pantry built in, and outside a root cellar sunk in the ground and lined with finished stone, a stone stairway down and the entry through a new shed, painted white with a dark green trim. She paid for much of this out of money left her by her mother, charging only the furniture and carpets to Young George.

When it was finished, Young George came in to have a look. He was elegantly dressed, having important business in Richmond.

Looking around the stylish parlor, he said, "My God! You could snatch the Queen out of Buckingham Palace, put her here and she'd never know the difference. Who's to stay here, President *Buchanan*? I thought an overseer of niggers lived here."

Elizabeth ignored his sarcasm. "I believe you value Mr. Wilkenson, do you not? I have heard you say that he is the best man you ever employed. You have told me that the Negroes are in a better way of work and obedience than ever before because of the evenness of Mr. Wilkenson's temper and his firm hand in discipline. Why not make happy the man who makes *you* happy?"

"Hmmn. Now you sound like him. Don't let him seduce you on those rides you take with him."

Elizabeth paled; inside she went weak.

But, striving to remain outwardly calm, she asked, pointedly, but trying to sound amused, "Whatever can you mean by *seduce*?"

Young George snorted. "Well, not the *literal* meaning. Dear God, the very *thought* is hilarious! A landless, rootless interloper in your bed? No, I meant, of course, seduce you to his way of egalitarian thinking. Oh, he claims to be a master's man, but he asks plenty in return for it. This is most certainly a part of it," he said as he resurveyed the exquisite room.

Elizabeth began to protest, but Young George waved his hand as a sovereign does to a lady in waiting.

"No, no, never mind. It's all right. Let the rascal have his comforts. As long as he keeps the niggers sweet and tamed. But, if they slip from his grasp, then we push him from ours. Remember that. An overseer is never more permanent than a single season's crop. As quick as that crop is poor and insufficient because of his own lack of application, that quickly an overseer can be gone. He serves at my pleasure. Just now he has it. I don't guarantee tomorrow."

With that, Young George walked with great self-satisfaction out of the overseer's house, mounted his horse and rode off toward Richmond.

Elizabeth immediately sought out Wilkenson's slave woman.

"Dulcie," she said, "go up to the House and send a boy around the fields to find Mr. Wilkenson. Ask him to come here. And, while you are up there, ask Missy to show you the old linen bedsheets I mean to give to Mr. Wilkenson. They need a bit of mending. The matching thread is in the same closet with the sheets. Missy will show you. You might as well do the mending up there. Then, when you've mended them, take them to the wash house. Stay to be sure that they don't scrub them too hard. After all, they are old."

But Elizabeth had no intention of giving him the old sheets, having already bought him new ones. She wanted only dependably long occupation away from Wilkenson's house for Dulcie.

"Yas'm," said Dulcie, an aged, heavy-bodied and mild slave used to unquestioning obedience. Dulcie went out, walking slowly due to lumbago. Elizabeth felt elated. That was the moment at which she realized that she must occasionally sleep with Young George again, for she felt sure that she must soon become pregnant.

As soon as Dulcie was well started up the carriageway, Elizabeth slipped into the bedroom and began to undress.

And when Wilkenson, on his horse at the edge of the South Field, watching the gangs weeding in the rows, saw the boy running toward him, he reined Jupiter around, waiting, for he knew what the message would be.

As soon as the panting boy stood at his stirrup, he listened, nodded and said, "Hop on behind me, youngster."

With the delighted slave boy pressed closely behind him, holding on to Wilkenson's waist, he nudged Jupiter into a trot.

And Wilkenson was thinking, *God knows I must find a way to be with her. I must. I must. I must be with her. I shall be with her. I SHALL!*

1860

PINEWOOD PLANTATION, VIRGINIA

Cordelia was sweet, eager, practiced, ambitious, intelligent, old beyond her years and a skillful mistress, despite the almost insuperable limitations of a slave's condition. Young George felt the way a man feels who has just ridden away from the livery stable on a new horse with which he is enormously pleased.

"By God, this mare rides well, and I believe she'll do!" Just so did Young George think about Cordelia.

And, against former practice, he liked her blackness. He liked the contrast of her dark facial skin and the pinkness inside her mouth. He liked the smoothness of her slim, muscular body and the firmness of her buttocks. He was especially pleased and stirred by her shining, dark brown eyes. He never tired of examining the palms of her hands and the soles of her feet because of the contrasts they made with the rest of her. She wasn't old enough yet to have developed the great, flat, ugly feet of the field slave. Now that he had her in the House, he'd see that she wore shoes and soon enough she would be soft as Young Sally.

And he liked that she was seemingly fearless, laughing and teasing him for his fascinations. Suddenly the years-long climb into sexual intimacy with Young Sally seemed like a colossal waste of time.

Here, in Cordelia, was the perfect slave lover. Indeed, she was the best lover of *any* color a man could want: nubile, trouble-free, passionate, humorous and, he believed, discreet—well, as discreet as a nigger could ever be. Even the old House niggers began their blabbing the instant they had bowed their silent way backwards out of your presence. But what of it? She would have far less to tell anyone than Young Sally ever had.

It had been simple to remove Little Master Will from the attic room.

"I won't ask you your business, son," Young George said, "though I know some of it. I do find it in me to wish that you had let Missy alone, but then what's to be done?"

They were walking slowly together down the carriageway toward the overseer's house and the Richmond Road. Young George had called his son to join him for a talk. He had his arm around the younger man's wide shoulders, mentor-wise, for the place along the road of life his son had now reached was a place he knew very well.

Little Master Will stiffened. Young George could read his thoughts by his body. He was a little amused.

"Now, now, you needn't weave me a web. I know the truth and, as I have said, though I might like it otherwise, things are as they are."

Little Master Will stopped and turned to his father. His face betrayed his uncertainty. He did not yet know how intimate and shared a part of the world of men this sort of roguishness was.

"I see you know *everything*?"

It was phrased as a question in case his father didn't.

"Well," said Young George comfortably, "we never know *everything*, do we? And thank God for that! But the outlines, yes. The attic room certainly. Well, I will tell you a nice secret. The cabin will be available soon. It will take a bit of doing to dislodge her, but Young Sally is going back to live with Decatur in the House row.

"All her furnishings, clothing, doodads and so on will of course be left behind. Oh, I may let her take a trinket or two, to keep her from howling the heavens down. But, for the rest, it all stays. I'm sure Missy can put those lovely things to a much better, much more circumspect use. Young Sally has got quite tiresome and above herself, as I am sure you know. Getting her out of that house is going to be like prying open a clam. But I'm determined to take it slow enough to let her get used to the idea. Otherwise, she'll bellow and bawl till hell won't have it, and the countryside will be more diverted by us than they are already."

He took Little Master Will's arm and they again set out, walking slowly.

Little Master Will hesitated, then said, "Yes, I know. She's a scandal, sir. We—" But here he broke off. He was about to say, "We are a scandal."

Young George knew without being told. "Yes," he said. "That must end. In the future, we must be blameless before the public eye. Well, this war is coming at a good time. Fighting for our Virginia will redeem whatever is clouded as to reputation. Now, new and loftier reputations are to be made.

"I know that I can raise a regiment in a few weeks. We'll form without proper Confederate uniforms and begin our work. The uniforms will come, each properly sized as soon as may be. You'll have a company, lad.

"We'll punish those goddamn philistine northerners as they deserve, then come home to a restored and renewed Virginia—with growing markets for our tobacco; with industrial enterprises springing up in Norfolk, Richmond and elsewhere; with slaves as the laborers; with the state established as the ideal political entity instead of the so-called nation; and with the confederacy continuing to provide services to our whole and newly freed region to link all the southern states together in purpose and thought, and confirm slavery as the will of God and the salvation of the Negro people for all time to come!"

At the front gate, they turned and walked slowly back toward the House. Little Master Will had spoken this intimately with his father only a few times in his life. He was enjoying this talk but wondering how honest, how disclosing he could be. He decided to take a chance.

"Missy is my half-sister, is she not? I can't bear to think so, but everyone says it's true. Mother certainly thinks so."

Young George's face darkened as he thought of all the mischief Elizabeth had caused him by her endless complaining, at home and among friends, about Young Sally and Missy—though lately, thank God, she had become charmed by the girl and accepted her, apparently splitting off in her mind the Missy of flesh and blood from the mythic Missy born to do her hurt. But why now?

Though neither Little Marse Will nor his father knew it, now was when his mother had found such blissful comfort in the arms of Jared Wilkenson that all other preoccupations, once so important, had become all but irrelevant. And her campaign against Young Sally had, in the last two years, become much more indirect and sophisticated, as Elizabeth herself had grown obviously happier.

So things were actually getting better, Little Master Will thought. *My mother had even lost weight. But this damned sister thing...*

Young George looked at his son out of the corner of his eye.

"Your *sister*? What nonsense! Young Sally is Cicero's child and Missy is Decatur's. As to the white in her, who knows? We've all seen niggers who could pass, with parents as black as coal dust. These are the kinds of mysteries that can't be understood yet do a world of harm because of the assumptions of ignorant people."

Little Master Will had never in his life seen a Negro who could pass with parents black as coal dust and was sure his father had not either. But these were the sorts of extravagant things that needed to be said in a situation like this. He felt comforted.

"So I may have the cabin?"

"Absolutely, you may. Starting next week. Depending on how quickly I can get Young Sally out without her causing even more uproar. I hate to have her whipped, but I may have no choice. Of course, she's got to be sold. I'll send her up to Richmond. There's a broker up there who does a lot of trading for the Mississippi, Alabama and Texas markets. I want her as far South as I can send her. And, after all, she's still in fine condition. If she behaves herself, she can be a House slave again. But if she goes on playing the Great Lady, she'll end her days in the cotton rows—and serve her right, for all the ingratitude and trouble."

Young George's voice was strong and loud. It felt very good to have made up his mind; to be in such manly rapport with his grown son; and to discuss matters as intelligent, educated and masterful men discussed them.

"But won't this make mother angry all over again? She thinks Missy and I are brother and sister after all ..."

"Ah, God. Your *mother*. Well, of course, there will an upheaval. It's in her very nature. You have noticed that, surely. Your mother is an unstable woman. There may have been madness in the Jerrold family. I would not be surprised to have it confirmed. Not that it would affect you or your sister Peggy in any way.

"And, of course, we must humor her by tut-tutting her and certainly not taking her seriously. She has by now lost all right to be taken seriously about anything. Bear her like you would the onset of a winter storm that catches you mounted and out of doors. Just pull down your hat and ride it out."

But, even as he said this, Young George did not believe it as he once did. His wife's recent and warm attentions to him, combined with her ability to discuss instead of scold, had attracted his interest again. In fact, he was on the point of returning permanently to her bed. She had, he thought, given him encouragement in that direction by her recent renewal of sexual interest. Now that she was slim and sweet again, but also more mature, perhaps she could permanently provide him a warmer pair of thighs, a more slippery thrust. Time would tell. As yet, she was less passionate than insistent. And, of course, there was now Cordelia. And with Elizabeth riding again, and more often in town, why could he not learn to balance his pleasures perfectly and have the best of both?

Walking up the carriageway with his son, Young George was pleased at the thought. And then he realized that soon there will be a war, and who knew what novelties might await a man of his tastes in the great world beyond his plantation?

How very well, he thought and smiled. *How wonderfully well do things always work out for intelligent and careful men!*

1861

PINEWOOD PLANTATION, VIRGINIA

Young George made a promise, which he wrote in his journal:

How sweet my dear Young Sally has become. Of course, she knows
how Cordelia is growing in my affections. Not being a fool, she must
certainly be sobered by this and yet reminded of where her true interests
lie.

As evidence of this awareness in her, she now spends plentifully and
clings to me and says she loves me, and calls me "My darlin Young Marse
Geo'ge" and "My sweet, lovin Young Marse Geo'ge." I know that is a very
odd address, but it pleases me much. The perfect balance of deference and
affection. Was ever man luckier?

Her fear is covered by the appearance of contentment, her diffidence
by her keen intelligence. Yesterday, as we rose from bed, and I dressed
whilst she boiled coffee, I was mulling over a problem and soon was
muttering it aloud.

Barton, a younger field driver, had asked to marry Lucinda, and I was
not disposed to allow it since Black Sulla coveted Lucinda and everyone
knew it. Black Sulla never wanted to marry, and I would never press him.
But he has had Lucinda many times and would not cease his attentions
merely because she was married.

He is not a man to veer from any purpose he sets himself, no matter
the promises he makes to me. He has subtle or brutal ways of his own
and rightly knows that I would never truly chasten him. Warn him, yes.
Show a lukewarm discipline, yes. But the thought of losing his perfect
confidence makes me ill to contemplate. He is the best nigger in the world.
I sometimes wonder how I deserved the gift of him from God.

Young Sally listened to my fussing about it and said, in a quiet voice, "Yo gots ter stand up tall wid Black Sulla, else he gon run yo lak yo was his nigga. I don' mean yo ter scold him cause dat won' work in yo favuh, but if yo don' bring him down, he gonna be makin yo decide whut's best by whut suits Black Sulla, not yo.

"Bestest ting yo kin do is say ter him, 'Black Sulla, Barton is gittin married ter Lucinda cause yo don' wants ter git married ter her.' Say ter him dat marriage is whut yo gots ter have on dis plantation, cause sparkin widout it is gainst religion.

"Den he'll look at yo wid dat devil's stare of his, an yo kin aks him, 'Well, wait now. Did yo change yo mine bout gittin married? Cause yo knows yo gots first choice on any of dese nigga womens.'

"Den he gon shake dat ugly haid of his an walk off, grindin he teeth. But yo done showed him in a kind way who's de owner an who's de driver. An dat way, yo done made up de marriage yo own sef, not Barton, so Black Sulla won't have no grief gainst him.

"Still, soonah or laitah, Black Sulla gonna hurt Barton. Yo knows dat. It jes be dat wicked man's way. But maybe it take a while ter happen. Dat be good if it do. But whenevah it be, jes take Black Sulla out'n his driver's pretty cabin an put him in de shack row fer a month, widout carpet or nice bed or oil lamp or stove or nothin, jes lak de othuh niggas, but keep him at his drivin. Don' nevah put no man ovah him less yo wants dat man daid. Den Black Sulla see yo be a serious, strong man, an he let up on wickedness awhile. Course, he gon' go back. Yo cain't keep a bobcat in de house. Dey always gon be wild."

I said, "My dear girl, what wisdom you have! I keep thinking that Black Sulla can be cured, but you remind me that he can only be tempered—slightly, and for a short time. So I must always plan to thwart him only temporarily since he will not and cannot change. Yet, if I keep a close eye on him, I may be able to head off his worst rampages. You are a clear-sighted girl."

"Yas. But jes member, darlin Young Marse Geo'ge, dat he a wild ting dat gon jump free of yo when he gots a mind ter. He know how much yo loves him as a driver. He depend on dat. Onliest way yo kin really deal wid him is ter sell him. He know yo won't do dat. He know he above bein a reg'lar slave. De onliest chain he wear be a daisy chain—yo love chain. It's lak he yo woman. He know yo cain't nevah pull him up tight lak he deserve. If'n I was yo, I'd trade him down ter Norf Car'lina. Yo could git three good niggas fer him. He prac'ly famous. Ev'body know he de same lak two good men in one big body.''

Within minutes of her saying this, the agreeableness between us had moved to sweet, soulful love. Once more, I undressed.

And so pleased was I by her, and so touched, I whispered "My darling girl, never will I desert you, never hurt you. At any time you like, I will free you and Missy, send you North, pay for a house for you, and keep you and Missy in comfort all your days. I will come to see you and renew our love. But you will be free, never again to know fear or doubt. Never again to be a slave.''

And she said, making my heart leap for joy, ''Well, I sho don' wants ter go up Norf right now. Yo as good ter me as if I was yo wife. Yo good ter Missy too, tho yo don' let on she your'n. Up Norf, I'd have de monies yo promise, but I won' have yo ter see ter me an perteck me lak yo does. An I loves yo now. I don' wants ter be away fum yo. Not even a day.''

I had made such a promise to her before, and she had listened in silence. Perhaps she knew, even yet, deep in her heart, that I could never do such a thing as free her North. But telling me that she could never leave me cost her nothing and was certain to flatter me. She could afford to invent tactics useful just in this moment, leaving aside any future ones as meaningless.

So now she spoke her love and her allegiance. Yet, despite what I take to be her art, never have we been so in love and so perfectly happy together. And it can only deepen, only grow. It is up to me alone to now skillfully manage what I have myself created. I know all this is still tenuous, yet I cannot but feel it is how things will go on. Every step away she takes from the wondrous life she enjoys must ever seem poisonous to her. Without planning it, I have surrounded her with choices to make that are all of them repugnant to her needs and her self-love, except the single one of pleasing me and binding me ever closer to her heart.

Ah, how I am blessed!

And yet … I am not a fool. The wear in the fabric that we have woven together is growing ever frailer, ever more noticeable. At some point—and that point is nearly within sight—my confidence in Cordelia will fully replace my habits of life until now centered in Young Sally. Then there must come a break. And I will be free again in a way I have not been these seventeen and more years. How this will bolster me, enspirit me!

I had a liberating thought so strong that I wish to write it down to preserve its potency in my mind: Sadness today but glory tomorrow!

In late March, Young George had reached the end of his patience. Somehow, Young Sally had got ruined by his indulgence of her, had turned scold, thought she had the right to chasten everyone and behaved as if she never could be disciplined. He now realized that he had never really been in love with her but was only under a delusion, which had lifted off long before he took any action against her. For the truth was that, though few people knew it, he was one of the kindest men in the world.

Now he made a list of Young Sally's crimes, taking his time and thinking back, so that, when he confronted her, he would have a sheet of evidence against her and, no matter how she whined, she could not whine away the truth.

First, Young Sally gave her mother Sally money but did it in a high-handed fashion and at the field slaves' quarters. The two of them got into an argument inside the shack, but it carried outside.

With a dozen slaves looking on, Young Sally shouted, "Dis heah be de monies yo oughta have got fum dat scrawny tom turkey of a Marse Geo'ge. He bout wore out yo lady hole for a long damn lifetime. But all yo evah done was sneer at him. Yo shoulda look out fo yo'sef an yo daughtuh, but yo din nevah look out fer nobody. Not even yo own sef. Yo life din end on dat slave ship, but yo a'ways ack lak it did. Now I gots ter hep yo, even tho yo nevah hep me or nobody."

"Yo don' got ter hep me," the old mother yelled. "I nevah athked anyting fum yo. Ath far ath I care, yo kin thtick thith money up yo white-man-lovin ath!"

Second, Young Sally was standing in the garden one afternoon, wearing a red silk dress. I had expressly forbidden this outside our cabin, but she defied me. Just then, Elizabeth came strolling toward the garden with our near neighbor Mary Wilson on her arm, to look at the flowers. Mary saw Young Sally and let out an audible gasp. Here was the slut *who was the talk of the countryside, openly lording it! Young Sally had not even the decency to flee but instead put her hands on her hips and smirked at Elizabeth.*

Mary turned away from her as from a naked madwoman and said, "Come, let us go."

Elizabeth was mortified. I was furious. I spoke to Young Sally. It did no good.

Young George had many instances of this kind. He wrote them all out, then read them over several times. That night, he took them with him, as a kind of ammunition, to the cabin. He walked fast, making his mind race, forcefully building up a great, thick resentment, immune to mercy—though, even after all her lapses, he still regretted having to do this.

Well, the only remedy for that was a refractive hardness that bent every ray of kindness into anger. He would not let her deflect him from his course. He absolutely would *not!*

It was late when he arrived, and Young Sally was already asleep. This pleased him, for now she would be groggy and easier to deal with. His will to be impervious deepened. When he arrived, he slammed the door with a great, loud bang and lit a lamp.

Young Sally sat up, rubbing her eyes and said, irritated, "Whut yo gots ter come bangin in heah so late an light up a lamp? Cain't yo jes git on inter bed in de dark?"

Ah! The bitch was playing right into his hands. Such mean-spirited selfishness further relieved Young George of his qualms.

Instead of pulling out his list, he simply said, "Get out of bed, get dressed and go to Decatur's shack. You are finished living here."

Then, with an ill-tempered satisfaction, he turned up the lamp's wick to more clearly see her expression. It pleased him that her face had paled, and her lips had gone nearly white and begun to tremble. He refused to feel pity, considering all the mischief she had done.

"*Whut?*" Her tone of voice was instantly altered. "Yo cain't be *serious*, darlin Young Marse Geo'ge. I'se sorry I be so bad sometime. Come on inter bed, darlin Marse. Come on in an snuggle wid Young Sally."

But the tone of it was shaky, not sweet—nothing like what he wanted from her; nothing like carefree, sweet-tempered Cordelia. Or for that matter, nowadays again, Elizabeth. Suddenly, it pleased him to be harsh. What a wonderful opportunity this stupid black cow had thrown away! His determination deepened, and he felt manly.

"Get dressed, or go in your nightclothes."

Young Sally gasped and sat up straight, holding the bedsheet to cover her breasts. "No, honey, yo don' mean dis. I know yo don'. It be all right termarra. I promise yo, nothin bad lak ter happen evah agin …"

In the harsh light, he was pleased to see tears in her eyes. Yes, and fear, for the first time in years. Real, visceral fear. Why had he once worked so hard to comfort and reassure her when all it had done was work against his interests? It seemed inconceivable now…

"Get up, or I will bring Black Sulla in to *get* you up."

Young Sally gave a little cry. "Black *Sulla!* Oh, sho'ly yo cain't mean yo'd bring in Black Sulla. Yo knows I hates dat man, suh. I hates—"

Young George lost his temper. Or rather, forced a temper the better to force Young Sally. He bent over where she lay on the bed and gave her a hard slap. She screamed. He felt like a man suddenly entered on a risky course that he dared not change.

He slapped her again. Her next scream was so loud and screeching that the very timbre of it entered his flesh and infuriated him. As she tried to burrow under the covers, he ripped them off the bed, exposing her trembling, still-sensuous body in her nightgown, a flimsy red one he had once loved seeing her in. He seized her hair and dragged her onto the floor.

"No!" she screamed. "NO! NO! NO! NO!"

Young George was panting with exertion now. It had gone further than he had expected. He hated violence. And it was all Young Sally's fault!

He shouted, "You've only yourself to blame for this!"

He turned and left the cabin.

As soon as Young George had slammed his way out, Young Sally leaped out of bed, panting, sniffing and sobbing, and began trying to muscle a chest of drawers to block the door. But it was oak and filled with her belongings and very heavy. When she finally got it into place before the door, she saw Black Sulla peering in at her through the window. A crooked smile was on his face. Young George was nowhere to be seen.

Black Sulla moved to the door and, with one powerful shove, pushed the dresser aside like a wicker basket and stepped into the room. The look on his face revealed her future.

He crossed the room to where she stood trembling and, as she screamed again, he slapped her face with his thick hand so hard that she fell insensible to the rug. When she came back to full awareness, Black Sulla was on top and inside of her, right there on the floor.

Something in her let go then. It was a feeling like having her chest torn open and her heart crushed. So quickly and catastrophically had her rose-garden world collapsed that her reason blurred; everything felt tilted and sharp-edged. There was nothing she could do—no act, no plea, not even a thought—to mediate the awful soul-pain that was flooding her.

Young Sally saw Black Sulla's flat face go soft with pleasure as he rammed harder and harder, then climaxed. She felt dazed, dirty, sick. Above all, she felt helpless. Sudden as a summer squall, Young George had in the middle of the night broken violently into her safe world, with Black Sulla behind him, knocking down in seconds every good she had so patiently built up over the whole of her adult life. She was like a woman thrown from a mid-ocean ship in the starless dark, with nothing to hold on to …

After Black Sulla was finished with her, he stood up, retied the waist straps on his baggy pants and said, "Now, girl, dat was wert waitin fer! An dey gon be a lot more times a'comin' right behin *dat* one."

When Young Sally stared at him, blank-faced and unspeaking, he pulled her up by the hair and gave her a rough shove in the direction of her dresser.

"Git movin now. Go on. Git yo tings tergetha."

He told her that she could take with her whatever she could carry but, when she pulled out the brick chink in the chimney, she discovered that Young George had already removed the soiled bag with the money in it. It sank in even deeper now that she was truly adrift, with no friends, no money, no security and no certainty but that of suffering till she died or was sold.

Young Sally's body went limp; her hands and arms felt useless. It was as if darkness were seeping out of her ruined heart, dribbling its poison into her bloodstream. The feeling was what she had always imagined death would be like.

She began to wail.

Cursing, Black Sulla snatched up her body in his arms, blew out the lamp and walked out of the cabin, slamming the door. He marched with her out of the West Woods and down the House slave row. All of the slaves were standing, alarmed in their open doorways, awakened by Young Sally's unearthly screams, as she arched her back across Black Sulla's thick arms and yowled until she lost her breath and seemed to faint.

Black Sulla stopped in front of Decatur's shack where the thin, graying slave stood in a tattered nightshirt, holding a candle, staring at the driver and at the maddened, breathless Young Sally, a look of horror on his face.

"Well now, stud," Black Sulla said, chuckling. "Heah be yo pretty wife back." He pushed past Decatur and dropped Young Sally like a hay bale on Decatur's bed. "Lookie heah, dis be a good night ter mess wid her if yo gots a mind ter, cause she already be all greased up." He turned and walked up to Decatur, grabbing the frightened slave's nightshirt and pulling him close. "Tings be a'changin now, stud. Young Marse Geo'ge done give de word. Don' yo git in de way or yo gonna git run ovah lak a weed by a water wagon."

Black Sulla pushed Decatur so hard that he fell, then turned and walked away into the darkness. The House slaves came hurrying from their shacks to Decatur, helping him to his feet, murmuring their sympathies. Holding candles of their own, they crowded into his shack and looked with a mixture of pity and satisfaction on the crumpled form of Young Sally, who was beginning to stir and moan on the bed, snatched now from her high place and thrown down beneath the feet of the lowest and blackest slave on the plantation.

In the yellow light of a tallow candle, she opened her eyes, looked at the dark faces staring down at her and began to cry. It was not the cry of a woman so much as a child, and not a normal child but a stupid one, a near idiot. And it went on in a barely audible whimper all night and into the dawn of the next day—a mindless snuffle with little moans and hiccups.

All along the row, the slaves returned to their interrupted sleep, then rose with the sun, made hearth fires, dressed, boiled chicory water, ate fried grits and went out to work. Decatur sadly stroked Young Sally's hair before he left. He found that he could not bear to stay alone with her, but she did not seem to notice. The crying went on in the silence of the empty cabin until, at midday, Black Sulla came in.

Then it stopped.

And after that, being now lost to herself, Young Sally never cried again.

On April 12, riding a hired horse through an aroused, exhilarated Virginia countryside, Thomas Bradford—the would-be cigarette maker from Chicago—arrived at Pinewood.

Earlier that same day, Jared Wilkenson had taken the train to Baltimore. Tomorrow, the judge in his lawsuit would render his opinion in the case, which had already been through trial where it had been decided by a jury in Wilkenson's favor. Now, having climbed through state courts to the state supreme court on appeal, it was returned to the trial judge, who was ordered to act on the jury's findings.

The defendant was a Maryland tobacco planter named Ronald Sharp, who ten years ago had held back from his overseer Wilkenson two whole quarters' wages on the grounds that Wilkenson had done shoddy work and deserved nothing. To Sharp's astonishment, Wilkenson had sued—to recover what was owed as well as punitive damages for the harm Sharp had done his reputation. (Because of the suit, Wilkenson had become unemployable in Maryland, for even if none of the planters believed Sharp, they were horrified that Wilkenson would dare to sue him.) Finally, Wilkenson had given up and gone South to Georgia to find new work and wait out the delays and appeals in his case.

Plantation owners were so accustomed to using overseers as they saw fit that it never occurred to Sharp that he would be hauled into court for his larceny. Alarmed at Wilkenson's suit, he offered to settle with him for the sum actually owed, but Wilkenson refused. That amount was six hundred dollars. But Wilkenson was suing for punitive damages of ten thousand dollars, and the jury, disgusted at Sharp's dishonesty with the likeable overseer and offended by the lies the testimony revealed he had spread about him, awarded it. Sharp had used every delaying tactic available to him.

But, at last, it had all come to an end. When tomorrow the judge ordered implemented the jury's decision, as was expected, Sharp would have to pay, and Wilkenson could, satisfied and well fixed, take Elizabeth Leyland and her daughter Peggy to New York City. There, Elizabeth would divorce Young George and marry him.

Wilkenson felt optimistic and secure. He was sure that there would be enough money to keep them in comfort until he could find a position in the city that would use his considerable organizational talents and good sense. And he was relieved that he would not need to depend on Elizabeth's money for anything. In fact, Virginia law being what it was, there was no certainty that she would be able to claim much of it. Under the law, if her husband died, he was not even required to leave her own dower lands to her but could entail them on his son or any male relative he chose. She, being a woman, had no standing before the law.

That being the case, neither she nor Wilkenson had much hope that she would salvage anything substantial. But she did not care and neither did he because, for the first time in her life and the second time in his, both were in love. They would go to New York together no matter what, and make a new life that held the meaning and passion both of them craved.

Peggy had immediately taken to Wilkenson the few times she had spoken with him, though of course she had no idea how things stood between her mother and him. Naturally, Young George could be expected to take legal action to reclaim Peggy, but that was a trouble better left for another day. If needs be, they could go to Canada or even England. There were no longer any limits for a woman who had finally claimed her freedom.

All Elizabeth knew was that now she looked forward to great happiness and peace at Wilkenson's side, whether at the North or in a foreign country, away from the narrow-mindedness and jingoism of the planters and the deadness of her marriage, at liberty now to build a life together in any way that suited them. Neither Wilkenson nor Elizabeth voiced the slightest fear to each other. Both were grateful and eager for the change. Both had got over their scruples against deceiving Young George, whom they now agreed deserved every misfortune that befell him. In fact, to further deceive him, Elizabeth had begun behaving with friendliness—even affection—toward her husband, making visits to his bed, which disgusted her but were vital to explain any possible pregnancy that came before she was ready to get away. Of course, that did not matter now since, against her original intentions and because of the onset of the war with its turmoil and uncertainty, she would be leaving sooner than she had imagined.

After receiving his settlement, Wilkenson would go to New York City, register at the National Hotel on Broadway and await Elizabeth's arrival.

All along, being a careful and prudent woman, Elizabeth had set aside as much money as she dared, and tried to foresee every consequence of every event or act and allow for it.

But consequences that cannot be foreseen cannot be allowed for …

For some days now, Young Sally had been coming out of Decatur's shack and wandering the grounds of Pinewood Plantation. She sometimes walked with her eyes closed but did not stumble. She spoke aloud to herself in a quiet, intimate tone, as to a dear one or a child. She would go to the wash house but not enter it, go out to the fields and walk along the rows where the astonished field slaves moved aside to let her pass. They shouted at her if she trod on the holes they had made for seedlings, and she took notice and corrected her walk, but she was obviously not in her right mind, and not only Young George but the slaves wondered if there was any way he would be able to sell her. It was seemingly a visit to her House row shack by Young George that had launched her into constant roaming.

Little Sulla, weeding in the kitchen garden, saw Young George go into Young Sally's shack, then a minute later heard his voice raised in an angry shout. Too curious to resist creeping closer, Little Sulla came around behind the shack where a battered window shutter stood open. Crouching there, the young mulatto heard Young George's voice again but now could make out the words.

"Listen to me," the marse was saying. "Tell me what you've done with the money you had hidden in your chimney. I won't punish you. I'll even let you keep a little of it. But it was given to you as a gift when you were a kind and grateful person and was never meant as a permanent endowment for the shrew you became. But what's done is done. I harbor no ill will. Give it back, and you may keep a hundred dollars."

Little Sulla heard only silence in reply.

After a moment, Young George spoke again. "Do you *hear* me, you stupid nigger? Goddamn it to hell! That is *my* money you're sitting on! Give it to me at once or Black Sulla will be paying you a visit!"

"He a'ready payin me visits, suh, cause yo done turn him a'loose on me," Young Sally said softly. "He visit me ev'ry day an make me sicker ev'ry time he come. All I wants now is ter be gathered up ter God in heaven. If'n Black Sulla kin whup me ter death, I be glad …"

There were sounds of thick-soled boots pacing the floor. Then, a rush of steps and a loud slap and a scream.

"WHERE IS THAT MONEY?" Another, louder slap. Then a grating shout, "WHERE *IS* IT, I SAID!"

Young Sally's voice floated out to Little Sulla, odd and slow. "I din fine no money in dere. I done tol yo dat. Somebody done got it. I b'lieved it was yo. But, if it ain't yo, den I don' know who. I done tol yo."

More silence.

Then, "One last time I'll ask you: *WHERE IS THAT MONEY?*"

No reply.

Then a great commotion broke out. Little Sulla heard strange crashing sounds, Young Sally's screams and the marse's grunts. He dared raise his head to look in through the open shutter. There he saw that Young George had dragged Young Sally onto the floor and was shaking her as hard as he could. Her head flew from side to side, her body following behind like a kite's too-heavy tail. The marse began kicking Young Sally's belly and ribs with his big boots, still shaking her by the hair, grunting, while her voice rose in a terrible wail, eerie and empty.

Little Sulla's mother had told him when he was a child that, if he was wicked, the devil would come and pull him down to hell, and the boy would realize too late what his sinfulness had caused. This memory intensified the horror he was feeling as he witnessed what was happening in the house.

"Den yo gon make de cry of de damned, boy," his mother had said. "Yo gon be lak a dyin dog, wailin an howlin, an dey ain't nothin lak ter save yo ..."

Little Sulla thought that was how Young Sally's voice sounded now: like the cry of the damned.

Little Sulla dropped down from the window and hurried away. Young George was angrier than Little Sulla had ever seen him. If the marse found him spying, raging and crazy like he was, he was sure that the marse would have him whipped so bad it would be better not to survive it.

Later that day, Young Sally emerged from Decatur's shack. Her hair was down, her face bruised, one eye swollen shut, her lips cut and bleeding, her dress torn down off one shoulder. She wandered to the fields. She drifted to the woods, to the work houses, to the garden, murmuring to herself in a sweet, confiding voice. She did not go near the Big House.

The other slaves, leery of mad people, kept their distance. Only Decatur went to her, led her home, gave her food to eat, tried to engage her. She ate a little but would not speak to him. After that, she never spoke to him or to the other slaves again. And every day, she wandered.

Young George thought, *If God is kind, she will wander far off into somebody's wood lot and die in a dry creek bed. But this cannot go on. I simply cannot let this go on.*

But, as in most things, he took no action; in a few days, the situation resolved itself.

Little Master Will was so smitten by Missy that it was getting very hard to remember that she was a slave, a Negro and beneath him. He had read the word "courtesan" in a book and had never grasped exactly what it meant until now: "a woman who lavished every charm and thought on her protector, and satisfied him so utterly that his formerly limited inner life expanded to degrees of spaciousness unimaginable before."

He trusted Missy more completely than he had ever trusted anyone. And he fantasized that, after the coming war, he would claim her for himself and move to some country like Morocco or Spain where he fancied such relationships might be tolerated.

In her mother's (and her own childhood) cabin, Missy made herself immediately comfortable. Never once did she refer to its earlier use or lament her mother's fall. Here, as a child, she had sat on the lap of Young George while he read to her. Here (as well as at her grandmother's shack), she had been raised.

But Little Master Will was relieved to discover that she was a realist. She did not sentimentalize or mourn the past, especially her own. When she walked into the cabin with Little Master Will that first time, self-possessed and cheerful, nobody would ever have guessed that she had spent half of her life there. Very soon after their beginning, she took to calling him "dearest angel Little Master Will," and he treasured the sound of her soft, clear voice and the look on her face when she said it.

He sometimes called her "my own Missy." Every time he called her this, she glowed with pride and pleasure, as if it were the first time he had ever said it. When they made love, her kisses were so deep, so intimate, so soft, that it seemed he had never really kissed a woman before. Also, her unreserved love for him seemed to be opening secret sexual places inside her, places unknown before but that now, because of her pure, unstinting love, were instructing her in sexual arts that bonded him to her in ways and at depths he had not believed could exist.

The day his father called for the formation of an infantry regiment, and he was given a captaincy and command of a company, he could not wait to go "home" to tell Missy.

He never thought, *Oh, she is a slave and will be Unionist in her sympathies and against the South.*

Instead, he thought, *How proud she will be of me! How dearly I want to please her and make her happy!*

He told Missy, "As of today, I am a captain of Virginia volunteers. We are to start drilling at once. The war can be only days away. We must ready ourselves. What do you think of this?"

He held up a sword to show her. It had been his great-grandfather Robert's sword, the one he had carried in the Revolution. Never mind that it had been at the service of the British king. What mattered was that it bore the glory of the Leyland family honor.

"You are to carry it, dearest Little Master Will? I would have thought that your father would want it for himself." Her eyes shone with admiration, excitement, wonder.

Ah, how good she made him feel! Everything he did, she supported, believed in, loved! She was like a part of himself that had been missing for a lifetime but now had come to him at a miraculously perfect moment.

"No, my sweet one. He is having one made with the family crest and the family motto engraved on the blade: *Per bellum ad gloriam.*"

"Oh, how wonderful!" she cried. "What does it mean?"

Little Master Will smiled. "'Through war to glory.' How I hope I shall live up to it!" As he waited for her reply, a little uncertainty crept in.

At once, she noticed and cried out, "Oh, how could you *not*? You both are such brave, good men. The South will have none better to defend her." Missy took his face gently in her hands, kissed him and whispered, "I shall think of you every minute of every day that you are gone. You are my inspiration."

He put his arms around her and drew her to him, kissing her hair, her cheek, taking deep comfort in her warmth, her scent, her unstinting love.

While he yet held her, she asked softly, "Is the Chicago man to come today? If he is, you will take supper at the House, won't you?"

"Yes, more's the pity. We heard this morning. He should be here any time. He was to have come days ago. We'd about given up on him. Mother's had to put off going to Richmond for a day because of it. Father ordered her to remain at home to entertain him. Of course, I must be there. But I'd rather be here with you."

"I know, dearest Little Master Will. I would rather you be here too. But you have your duties to your station and your family. Those must always come first."

Hearing her say this, he tightened his embrace. "Ah, you are so sweet, so very understanding. I do not know how I have deserved you. I so deeply regret that you have ever been a slave! But now, everything will be different. My grandfather willed me money that is being held in trust. We will go away. We will be together."

They were silent a moment. Then she said, "What is it you have under your coat? I can feel something there."

Little Master Will stepped back, opened his coat. The butt of a pistol stuck out of his belt. He removed it, smiling, to show her.

"Look here, my love. It's a Kerr. The best pistol made in England and one of the best in the world. It's a .44 caliber, five-shot revolver. An arms dealer in Richmond got a dozen of them in January. I made sure I got one for myself."

"Oh," Missy said, "I never saw a pistol so close before!"

"Here, take it in your hand. It's very easy to hold, isn't it? I tell you, there's no revolver better than this one."

Missy cradled the weapon awkwardly against her waist.

"No, take it in your hand as if to use it. That's it. Just hold it out at arm's length. Pretend you're going to shoot that chair there. You see? It's very nicely balanced."

"Yes," she said, concentrating. "What must I do to fire it? Of course, I don't intend to, but ..."

"No, of course you don't. But if you did, it's single or double action. If you want, you can just pull the trigger, and it will fire. But, if you want to aim it more precisely, then you draw back this piece here—the hammer—until it clicks. Then there's a much easier pull on the trigger and a better chance you'll hit what you aim at." He laughed. "Just imagine! Me, standing here, instructing a slave in *fire-arms!* I'd be hung for this in Mississippi."

Missy laughed as merrily as he did. That was the wonderful thing about her. She never had a sulky slave attitude about anything. She was as white inside as she was out.

She asked, "Do you want to keep it up at the House or here? If you keep it here, we'd better find a safe place for it."

"No, not here. I'm going to keep it in a desk drawer in my father's den. I'll have a belt and holster for it in a few days. The Virginia quartermaster is sending uniforms and weapons for our regiment. I think my father intends to ask you to sew uniforms for us two."

Missy's smile was radiant. "He is? How *lovely!* There is nothing I would be more pleased or honored to do. Any small way I can help will be so satisfying for me."

"You are so good," said Little Master Will.

Missy hesitated, her face serious. Then she said, "Truly, you can have no idea how I feel."

At last, on April 12, General P.G.T. Beauregard had given the order for the Confederate batteries to open fire on the little Yankee fort in Charleston Harbor.

At 4 a.m., the big shells from the batteries of naval guns screamed over the water and exploded against the casements of Fort Sumter. The Federal soldiers ran to their guns to return fire as the first shells crashed into the walls and plaza of the Union fort, shaking the ground and filling the air with smoke, dust and the smell of burnt gunpowder.

Days earlier, the resupply ships sent by President Abraham Lincoln had been turned back by the Confederates, and there had been several parlays between Major Robert Anderson, the fort's commander, and officials of the Confederate government. The latter had rowed out the mile that separated fort and shore, but Anderson would not surrender. The Confederates told him they had no choice but to fire on him, for he was, in their eyes, occupying with a "foreign" army property belonging to the State of South Carolina, which was now under the jurisdiction of the new nation called the Confederate States of America.

Rebel shells then pounded Fort Sumter. Anderson kept up his return fire as a symbol of resistance, but it had no effect. Finally, aware that he had done what he could, and had above all preserved the honor of his country (though himself a southerner), Anderson surrendered. He and his men were given safe conduct North where they were received as heroes, and the war—which the North would call the Civil War and the South the War Between the States—was launched.

The news, like a huge wave breaking over low-lying country, spread across both North and South with great force, carried along by the telegraph and by riders, who set out to inform the many towns and settlements not connected by the wire.

At about ten in the morning, the news reached Pinewood Plantation—a few minutes before Thomas Bradford, the Chicago businessman, arrived. Young George was polite but distracted when he received Bradford.

Elizabeth, though showing a lovely smile, had but a moment to spare as she instructed Decatur—dressed formally in white shirt, cravat and black swallowtail coat—to show Bradford to his room, then hurried off. His luggage was carried in the hands of two young male slaves, who could not stop smiling and who stared at Bradford as if he were a kind of angelic visitation. The slaves went ahead upstairs, but Bradford remained behind in the entry hall with Young George, and Decatur waited with him.

Young George said, "Well, sir, the war has begun at last. I think you and I must put off our business a few months until we settle with the Yankees. There are two things I am certain they will not permit us to export: cotton and tobacco. I have no idea what conditions at the new border will be like. I deeply regret that we cannot accommodate you for the length of time we would have liked or discuss business, for that would seem to be actual treating with the enemy— though, of course, you know I mean no personal reference."

Bradford, stunned and disoriented, could say only, "Well, sir, I admit that this has surprised me. I did not think it to be in your interest here at the South to secede, let alone go to war, and I persuaded myself you never would. I suppose there is nothing for me to do now but return to Chicago as soon as I can."

"In that I agree, sir, with great regret. But your opinion is ill informed about secession. The truth is that we have everything to gain by it and are the losers only if we continue on as citizens of the grasping, autocratic United States. We ask nothing of the North, sir, yet they dare to challenge and threaten our very way of life—a way that has existed unchanged and perfect in its social symmetry for over two hundred years."

"By 'way of life,' you refer to slavery, sir?"

Bradford felt very odd, standing in the entry hall of a southern plantation on the first day of an inconceivable civil war, having such a discussion with this slavekeeper who was a stranger, while actual slaves in worn, dirty clothing moved through with his luggage, and the slave butler Decatur stood nearby looking dignified. He had no idea what "social symmetry" was (though, to be truthful, neither did Young George, who had read the phrase in a Richmond newspaper). This whole thing was very, very odd. Bradford's wife had been right: This was not the time to come South.

"Yes, of course. What other dispute have we that matters? Secession? That would not be an issue at all were it not for slavery. No, it is African slavery that eats at the small-minded jackasses up North who neither understand its utter necessity nor appreciate its sound basis in both scripture and in the Negro's own passive, unintelligent nature. And it would not be amiss if you called me Colonel Leyland, sir. For our regiment of Virginia volunteers is in the process of formation even as we speak and within a very short time will be ready to fight for our freedom."

"I see," said Bradford.

What an ugly thing this trip had turned out to be! Bradford felt a little sick. This Leyland fellow seemed a bit mad. Those blazing eyes of his. And now a colonel. In the Virginia militia? What sort of army could these Confederates have? Who would direct it? Their so-called "national" government? The state government? If all the states had separate commands, how could they coordinate anything?

And these scurrying, smiling Negroes seemed happy enough, didn't they? Why else smile? Why was the North insisting on meddling with them? And now he had to spend an evening with these Leylands, sleep here and make his way the next day back to the train station in Richmond, through what surely would be mobs of shouting, threatening southerners, gloriously at war now, perhaps even glad of a handy Yankee to maim and kill!

Well, he would demand that Leyland accompany him to the depot and see him safely on a train to Washington City from whence he could make his way back home to Chicago, having learned another lesson about the blindness and stupidity of which human beings are capable. But first, he would get through this night somehow, say as little as possible so as not to disturb these lunatics and, as early as he could the next day, depart.

Led by Decatur, Thomas Bradford made his way upstairs. In the room assigned him, he stood uncomfortable and irresolute.

Decatur, perhaps recognizing his plight, smiled sadly. "If yo needs sumthin, suh, jes aks." Then he departed, quietly closing the door.

Bradford looked about him. It was a large, airy room, the windows clean and covered by muslin curtains. The furnishings were old but in excellent condition. The bed, side tables and dresser were of what he took to be cherry wood, in the eighteenth-century style. Two armchairs, likewise of an antique design, faced the ample hearth. The dark green carpet looked newer, as if it would be comfortable for bare feet.

Having no other plans as yet, he undressed and had a leisurely sponge bath, using the basin of warm water, scented soap and large, white towel supplied for the purpose. He took his time putting on fresh clothing; buffing off the marks of travel from his nice brown shoes; glancing into an oval mirror to approve of his dark, good looks, fashionably long hair and closely trimmed beard.

He was preparing to go downstairs to the noon meal, which Mrs. Elizabeth Leyland had, in her hurry, described as a "light dinner," when there came a quiet knock at the door.

Assuming it was Decatur, back to see that he was properly settled, he called, "Come in."

The door opened slowly, revealing to Bradford's sight the most beautiful girl he had ever seen. She wore a white blouse and blue skirt, and her long, soft, brown hair fell to her shoulders. Her features were in exquisite proportion. She was a white girl, but her skin was, he noticed, the very lightest, creamiest tan. He wondered if she might have Mexican heritage perhaps, or something similar. Not that it mattered to him. Hers was the sort of beauty that honors a man by its simple existence. Just the sight of her improved his mood.

He smiled.

"I am sorry if I disturbed you, sir," came her soft voice, without any trace of the typical Negro-ese—another testimony, should he need any, that she was white.

"*Disturb* me? I should say not! Just the sight of you cheers me. To what do I owe your visit?"

The lovely girl laughed, as if a cleverness of which he was unaware had produced his words. "I am the upstairs maid, sir. I came to see if you want anything."

His face showed his shock. "*Maid?* But the maids here are Negroes, are they not?"

Again she laughed, and he felt warmed. "Yes, we are, sir."

"You are *Negro*? It isn't possible! You don't look it."

As if what he had said was a great compliment, the girl clasped her hands together and cried, "Oh, *thank* you, sir. You are so very kind!"

"Well, it's only the truth. But you say that you're the upstairs maid?"

"Well, in a way, sir. Another girl named Cordelia does much of the work. But I am also the nanny of Miz Peggy, Young Marse George and Miz Elizabeth's daughter. That takes up a great deal of my time."

Bradford shook his head wonderingly. "My God. Just imagine that. Why, you've as much presence and intelligence as any white girl I've ever seen."

At this, the girl flushed, as if with pleasure. "Sir, I do not know who you are, but I must tell you that your words move me in ways I could never truly explain."

Bradford, taken with her seemingly sweet way, smiled and held out his hand. "I am Thomas Bradford. Manufacturer from Chicago."

"Oh, sir," she said, lowering her eyes, the merest shadow of trouble passing over her face. "I am not permitted to shake your hand. That is too great a liberty for a slave. But I may curtsey." This she then did, and with such elegance that he was charmed.

"What is your name? Can you tell me that?"

Again, her appreciative laugh, which made him feel wise and powerful. "Of course I can, sir, and with great pleasure. It is Missy. And I am at your service, however long you will be here."

Bradford's face clouded. "That, I fear, will not be long. I leave tomorrow. The outbreak of war has destroyed my basis for business here, and I must go back to Chicago."

Missy frowned. "Oh, how *awful* for you, sir. To have come such a long way for nothing!"

My God, thought Bradford, *what an exquisite creature she is!*

He said, in the cheeriest voice he could muster, "Well, I must hasten to say that it was not for nothing. To have seen and met you more than rewards me for my trouble."

He closed the distance between them, and (seemingly against her better judgment, though she struggled but little) she let him take her hand.

"Ah, sir," she said, "This sort of thing is not done at the South. The men here would take it much amiss. Slaves are meant to keep their place ..." Her shining brown eyes showed him her regret and her sincerity. But she did not pull away her hand.

He kept his silence a moment while he held her eyes, being drawn by her soft openness, as if the mere sight of him had revealed to her his worth and his superiority over other men. He squeezed her hand and, to his gratification, she squeezed his. He was astonished that, in a minute or two, his despair at being at Pinewood was replaced with a powerful regret that he could not be here longer.

But now a rueful, hesitant look came on her face, which suggested to him that there was something she wanted to say, if only she dared.

Still holding her hand, he asked, "Come, don't be shy. Say whatever you've a mind to. I would never mention anything you say to anyone else. I am against slavery and would not aid it by any word or deed."

To encourage her disclosures, he stepped a little closer until his clothing almost touched hers. He found that she had a light, fresh scent. He did not expect that from a Negro. But then he realized that he knew little about Negroes—at least the Negro slaves—neither what to expect nor what not to. Here, at Pinewood, he had already seen some who were dark, others lighter, and now there was this Missy. Looking at her, seeing her kindness, her sweet smile and light skin, he had the sense of entering into a very wonderful secret.

Missy hesitated. Her face lost its smile and turned serious. She searched his eyes, as if looking for something to trust.

Then she said, "I would like very much to talk to you about Chicago. I want to know if Negroes there are really free. If they work at jobs for pay. If they are free to live in their own homes unsupervised. In short, are all the stories I have heard true?"

He was touched. Also by now stirred. Her nearness, beauty, scent and trustfulness had his manhood on the rise.

"Yes, that is all true. And there are many jobs for them there. In the stockyards, of course, and at the grain yards. I have a tool-making shop. I have hired a few Negroes in the past myself. Never got to know any of them, it's true, but they were good workers. Unfortunately, white workers resent the blacks having jobs they think are rightfully theirs. You'll always have that, I suppose, the friction between black and white."

Missy's face, so close now, registered only a concern for his problems as a white employer and gratitude for his generosity.

"We two standing here, sir, have no such friction. I wish it were this way in Chicago. I wish it were so everywhere."

Her deep brown eyes took him in.

He felt completely understood and approved of. Still holding her hand, feeling the rush through his flesh of her attraction, he drew her gently toward him. For a moment, concern flashed across her expressive face. She glanced behind her as if to see that the door was shut, then she let him pull her into his arms and into a kiss.

"Ah," murmured he, drawing a little back, "I can scarcely believe this is happening to me. First, a terrible war puts me at risk, then a beautiful woman puts me at ease."

Missy whispered, "Oh, I cannot think what has come over me. I must go, sir. Truly, I must!"

She made as if to draw free her hand but, when he held tight, she did not resist. She looked at him helplessly and let him lead her into another, deeper kiss.

In a minute, he had taken her to the bed and in a minute more got beneath her skirt, she all the time murmuring, "Oh, this is wicked, sir. I must go. You must let me ..."

He pushed his trousers down and rolled on top of her.

She cried out in a soft voice, "Somehow you know me so well. Even had I the will to resist you, I could not."

And, as she said this, Bradford, deliriously happy with this sudden and wonderful good luck, attempted to slide inside her.

Missy gasped, then expertly and instantly shoved him off her and jumped to her feet.

"*What?*" asked the confused Bradford, pushing himself into a sitting position at the edge of the bed. "What is the matter, Missy? I thought you liked it!"

Missy stood, looking tense as a startled deer near the door of his room. One hand was on the doorknob, but she did not turn it.

"I cannot go on, sir. I simply cannot. You will leave here tomorrow. And what will become of me? Supposing I were pregnant? Do you know what would be my fate here? As you would soon have found out, being a man of the world, I am not a virgin. These white men here have had their way with me since I was a child. Only imagine what would be done to me if I bore a child that looked not like them but like you.

"You do not understand, sir, coming from a place where men are kind and generous to the less fortunate. Here, sir, the men are different. I will tell you this. If I had your baby, they would kill me and the baby together! Oh, I must go. I will be missed. I regret what has happened between us, for I am sure that I have hurt you. I apologize with all my heart. But I cannot delay. *Goodbye!*"

At this, the dumbfounded Bradford jumped from the bed, pulling up his trousers as he stumbled his way to Missy's side, grasped her arm as she was opening the bedroom door, reached across her and closed it while drawing her back toward him.

"My God, girl. Whatever is all this about babies and murder? You shock me. I had not thought beyond our being in a romantic way together ..."

"I know, sir. I know. But I must think beyond that. Women have to look out for themselves, sir. Slave women especially so. Things between us went too far too quickly. Now, please allow me to go. Think no more about this. Go home tomorrow and forget Pinewood and forget me."

Again, she turned to the door, again tried to open it.

But Bradford held tightly to her. "Oh, come now, please, cannot we at least discuss this? I am willing to do anything I can to set your mind at ease. How can you, having charmed me, abandon me so coldly?"

Missy went a little limp in his arms, then straightened, looked at him with strangely troubled eyes, amazed him by touching his cheek, then said, "I have never seen a stage drama, of course. But Miz Peggy has been taken to Richmond to see them many times. She has told me all about them. We two now seem like we are one. It is very odd ..."

Bradford tried to follow what she was saying, but her words had confused him. And, before he had sorted it out, she raised her hands to her face and began to weep. He could feel her shoulders shaking ever so slightly as apparently she contained most of her feelings within.

And what else was a slave free to do? he asked himself. *How openly could she ever reveal herself and her emotions? I had come, blundering my way into this girl's life, knowing nothing about all that she was faced with, making demands on her. And now she was so torn and fearful that she had broken down. Dear God, forgive me my selfishness!*

"Oh, Missy ..." he murmured, feeling tenderness for her. "Tell me, what is it? Why are you crying? How can I help you?"

"There is nothing you can do, sir," she sniffled, keeping her face covered.

"Must you keep calling me sir? Please call me Thomas. At least here, if not in front of the family downstairs."

"I do not talk to the family downstairs ... Thomas. That is not my place. I go down only if I am accompanying Miz Peggy. Otherwise, I simply pass through."

"*Pass through*? Going where? Surely they have a room for you up here?"

Missy permitted herself a dry little laugh. "Oh, you are an innocent, Thomas. It is clear to me that you know nothing about the ways of slavekeepers."

She drew a handkerchief from her sleeve, wiped her eyes, blew her nose. Then she revealed her face to him.

He was surprised that her eyes were not red nor did they show much trace of tears. And immediately, he thought, *She is obliged to hide even her tears. What a very cruel thing this slavery is!*

As their conversation went on, it slowly became clear to Thomas Bradford that this girl Missy lived a terrible life here in the hands of the Leylands. For years, she told him, she had yearned to go North but no way had ever opened itself for her. Now, with the war breaking out, it would be harder than ever, for all slaves would be assumed to be Yankee sympathizers and from now on would be much more closely watched.

Ah, if only she could find a protector: a high-minded, courageous white man who could accompany her, posing if need be as her master, as far as Baltimore. From there, they could cross the nearby border into Pennsylvania—not at a main road, of course, but someplace in the woods. And then she would be free! She would make her way to Philadelphia. Along the way, she was sure there would be abolitionists willing to help her. In Philadelphia, a goodly number of former slaves had begun a community that she had heard about. There, she could find work and begin a normal life, rid of the stink and imprint of African slavery, get married, start a family, be happy. If only such a man could be found!

And, even as Bradford stood there stunned and excited by her words, Missy turned and slipped out the door, closing it quietly behind her.

On April 12th at noon, they assembled at the dinner table. Bradford, still bewitched by Missy and a little dazed, was joined by Young George, Elizabeth (his wife), Little Master Will (their son) and nine-year-old Peggy (their daughter), who, despite manners, ignored him. (George, unseen by Bradford and seventy-nine years old, had been dyspeptic for two days and had not come down to dinner but was served broth and milk in his room.)

Two slave women stood in attendance, one at either end of the large, oval, walnut dining table, wearing the same white shirtwaists and blue skirts that he had seen on Missy, both showing him deference with smiles and nods as he entered and took his seat.

An awkward moment ensued.

Then, Elizabeth said, her voice quiet and apparently sincere, "How I regret all this difficulty, Mr. Bradford. You are our guest, after all, which at the South counts for a great deal. Only such a grave political situation as confronts us today could turn us from the duties of hospitality that you have every right to expect from us. But the truth is that none of us have any idea what will come of this war, whether it will be with us for days or years. We must act prudently and help you get back North as soon as you can, for we cannot guarantee your safety under the present conditions."

Elizabeth broke off and looked at Bradford with regret and sadness. He thought for a moment that he saw something else there too—something more personal expressed in her detachment, her look of being occupied inside herself, a look almost of impatience having nothing to do with him, but he could not tell what it was.

One of the slave women brought him a bowl of hot soup. It had a good aroma. He suddenly realized that he was hungry.

As he dipped his spoon in the soup, Young George said, "What I wish is that we could gather together a great auditorium full of northern men—just like you, Bradford—so that the South could explain herself directly to you without the mediation of the biased northern press or the abolitionist fanatics."

"Indeed, yes. Our true story has never been told. Instead, you have claptrap like *Uncle Tom's Cabin*—a lying screed from that abolitionist bitch Harriet Stowe—put before you as if every word of it were true. But look around you, sir. Look at these Negroes you see standing in this room. Do they look abused?

Do they look unhappy?" The young man made a sweeping gesture toward the blacks, and then cried in a loud voice, "Tell this man the truth, girls! Are you *unhappy*? Are you *mistreated*?"

This unexpected challenge to the slaves made Bradford very uncomfortable. He was still full of Missy, still imagining that he could hear her voice and smell her scent. And he remembered she had told him that these men had taken her by force since she was a child and that, if she should become pregnant by any other man, they would kill her. He frowned.

Young George, taking the frown for skepticism, said, "Go on, Phoebe. Tell him the truth."

Phoebe, a sunny-faced woman in her twenties with a thin, lame left leg and crippled left arm, replied, "Oh, suh, y'all is de bestest mastuhs us niggas could evah git. Jes look at me. Some othuh white mens be lak ter put me out in de terbacca fields ter die, but y'all gots me in heah servin de table, an I kin do dat as good as de no'mal womens cause my strong one arm be as good as dey two!"

Phoebe burst out in merry laughter while both male Leylands chuckled and Elizabeth smiled. Peggy slurped her soup. Bradford nodded.

"Thank you, Phoebe," said Little Master Will.

Although Bradford knew that these southerners probably meant well, he was developing a dislike for them. He definitely did not want the Negroes forced into further pro-forma disclosures. After all, what else could they say?

Bradford ate his soup, which was a rich blend of beans and ham and very tasty. Then there was beef, sliced from yesterday's roast and reheated; fresh cornbread, cut thick, with butter; preserved tomatoes and beans from last year's kitchen garden; cold, sweet tea in a pitcher; and rice pudding.

After dinner, Young George rose and invited Bradford into his study.

"Come along, sir, and let us talk. Perhaps we can build bridges that are beyond the powers of politicians to fashion. I shall put forward the South's case for you, so you may return home more enlightened than when you came."

Thomas Bradford, feeling that he had no choice, slowly stood up. He was not a glib man and had no idea how to mount an effective antislavery argument. Nor, truth to tell, was he anxious to do so here in enemy country. He kept thinking of what Missy had said about these men raping her and being willing to kill to protect their honor.

But finally, Bradford gathered enough nerve to ask, "I wonder if you have ever listened to the North's case, sir?"

Young George's smile disappeared. He gave a low, humorless laugh. "Indeed I have, sir, for these many, many years. Now we at the South have listened to it enough. We have our own case to make. I hope you will be good enough to hear it."

Bradford did not like the look that had appeared on his host's face. His timorous rebellion ended at once. "I would be honored, sir," he said in a thin voice, his face pale.

Immediately again, Young George smiled. "Then come along, sir. Come along!"

And, placing his hand on Bradford's shoulder, he steered the unwilling and nervous man into his study and closed the door.

It was 2 p.m. on the second day of Sally's purgatory in the fields. Thus far, she had been bullwhipped twice by Black Sulla, both times coming early this morning, first for not having done her overnight harness mending and later for sitting down in the rows to drink her water. The first time she took ten hard lashes; the second five.

Sally had never been bullwhipped before because George would not allow it. She had felt the pain of thongs and switches but, next to a bullwhipping, they were nothing. Each stroke of the bullwhip cut into the skin. The more expert the wielder and unfriendly the intention, the deeper the cuts.

Black Sulla had the grace of a dancer, feet that glided upon yet held to the earth. His thick chest and massive arms were perfect equipment for a handler of the great whip. He had the touch that raised what he did above work, above punishment. Perhaps it was art, if art were ever meant to maim and kill—or else something utterly unique, a medium for the perfection of pain.

The pain of these cuts was no different than the pain of knife slashes or the raking of iron hooks. Black Sulla could make them go deep, so that flesh lay gaped and running blood, or flick them at the very surface, leaving bloody stripes. But George had told him that Sally was to know real suffering—suffering that endured—so Black Sulla made every stroke one that bit and ripped muscle, like the track of a ploughing bullet.

Sally's dress had been pulled down to her waist by Black Sulla both times, so he would have her bare skin as canvas. He had to admit to himself that, though her face was wrinkled, the skin of her back was comely. She was still a beautiful light golden brown; still clear and smooth, though sagging at the waist.

In the early morning along the field slave row, as the slaves were assembled and forced to witness, Black Sulla said, "Turn round heah dis way."

She did, knowing it was so that he could see her breasts. It had never occurred to her that he might whip her there. As it did, the first flicker of dread fired inside her belly, along with an unflinching determination to bear all without a murmur. Years back, even though she was George's woman and Black Sulla barely out of boyhood, he had once tried for her, knowing that she was not the sort of woman to tell on him. But she had made her rejection of him physically painful and a humiliation besides. Now he could make her pay.

Black Sulla said, "Yo still a pretty woman. Ain't yo, Sally?"

Then he turned her again and laid the ten strokes on her back, exactly as George had directed, cutting at depth. The first stroke raised such a clamorous pain that the image and presence of the stripe-faced captain's knife vomited up from memory. This was a pain very like that ancient one, with a screaming voice in it. But she bore it in silence, even relief, for now the doorway to death at last stood open before her. Soon she would see *him*—Kano. He would embrace her, his dark eyes shining.

Kano would say to her, "You have defeated them. Never did they break you. Never did you swing with their moods, satisfy them, notice them. You have been a rock in a great driving storm that blew across more than a half-century of the white man's time. Never did a single one of them smile because of any kindness from you. You have been a goad at their backs and a worm in their guts."

Saleh thought, *But wait!*

The rush of her euphoric imaginings ceased as she realized *he* would know what she had left undone and, by leaving it, had broken her silent promise. The one hardness he had asked of her she had not given him, and this lack made all the rest of no account. Instead, she had lived and lived and lived; had a white man's child; been merciless, yes, and cold, but still had never done that one thing he had asked of her in his dying thoughts that went deeper than words.

Now, her body being broken and her will dissolving, she must seize the time or her last hope would escape her. She would die as nothing more than a cranky old bitch and, against the backlight of Asante heaven, be exposed as trivial, stupid and a failure. He could not consent to walk with her by the rivers and forests of heaven, present her to the Fulani and Asante ancestors or to the gods. Instead, she would spend not just the already vanished years but eternity parted from him, but now in great soul pain. For she would be able to see, for all this great endless while, him from whom she was parted.

"*Mama!*"

The eerie voice of Young Sally floated out over the rows. The bending slaves raised up to look. Black Sulla, standing among them, turned.

Sally straightened, the pains in her back from the bending and from the beatings flowing together violently, like waters colliding. She looked over to the field's edge and saw her daughter—or rather this woman her daughter had become—with her wild hair, torn dress and empty eyes, bare feet that for years had worn pretty shoes. She saw Young Sally through the screen of her own great pain but also through the resolve just now confirmed, the decision that accessed for her the last of her strength. She said nothing, only gazed at this ghost who had come calling to its mother.

"Mama! We's both fixin ter die. Yo know dese Leyland mens done kilt us. We gon rise up on high tergetha. Dey ain't no slaves in heaven, Mama. Black be as good as white in heaven. An de white mans got ter pay up fer his sins, an de niggas gon watch an be satisfied. We gon be satisfied in heaven, Mama. Dis day or termarra."

Black Sulla shouted at Young Sally, raising high the coiled bullwhip he clutched in his big hand, "Git along now, yo damn fool bitch! If I got ter come ovah dere, yo gon have de same stripes in yo back jes lak yo mama, an den y'all kin die tergetha."

Sally stared but did not speak.

Young Sally turned slowly away. Like a dancer in the ballet, leaning into a graceful move, she drifted along the margin of the field to the wood and disappeared.

Black Sulla turned to the old woman. "Git yo damn face back down in de weed row, woman. Don' yo stan up straight no mo." He grasped Sally by the back of the neck and shoved her head down so roughly that she pitched forward, her face in the dirt. "Git up. Git on up an do de marse's work. I say, git up *now!*"

Slowly, Sally rose but only into a bending stance. She reached for a weed and pulled it. With her free hand, she brushed the dirt from her face and spit it from her mouth.

With painful slowness, the day passed ... the second day of her purgatory.

And Sally survived it.

"Grandmomma, how are you?"

Missy stood just inside the door of Sally's cabin on the field slave row at 7 p.m., right at dusk. It was nearly dark inside but Missy could see her grandmother, lying asleep on the floor. Black Sulla had given her only hay to sleep on, no table, no chair, a candle, a tin plate, a cup and a spoon, some beans, pork fat and a few greens. Sally, too exhausted to make a cooking fire, lay asleep on the hay, her face on an old shawl. At Missy's entrance, she opened her eyes but did not speak or move.

Missy came further into the room, closing the door behind her.

"Grandmomma, how are you?" the girl repeated.

At first, Sally made no effort to reply. But, as Missy waited, she finally said in a hushed croak, "Fixthin ter die." She raised herself slowly on an elbow.

"I know, Grandmomma," Missy said quietly. "It's your time. I hope you die tonight. But if not, you will tomorrow."

"Yath," the old woman said.

"I'm leaving tonight, Grandmomma. I just came to say goodbye."

"Good girl. Yo got hep?"

"Yes, but I won't tell you about it. They'll come to you first, before anybody else, and they'll bring Black Sulla. If you don't know then, you can't tell."

"Thath right. Good. Broke an tired ath I am now, dey mighta been able ter get it outta me."

"I don't think so, Grandmomma. They've never broken you before. Not even on the ship. But I'm not telling anybody. That's safest and best. Only the one helping me will know—at the right time." Missy knelt in the hay beside the old woman, and bent over to kiss her cheek. "Goodbye, Grandmomma. We'll meet again someday."

She rested her head next to her grandmother's dry cheek for a moment. Then she stood up.

"I hope dat we do, girl. Yo be thtrong."

"I *am* strong, Grandmomma."

Sally nodded and slowly lay down again. Missy knew that she would speak no more now. She turned and slipped out quietly, disappearing into the shadows along the path to the Big House.

In her shack, Sally closed her eyes. But, despite her exhaustion, she did not go back to sleep.

Thomas Bradford had eaten a large supper and at 8 p.m. was a little sick—not from the food but from the idea of it, the awareness in depth of the slave hands through which it had passed. The thought of driven captives cooking his meat, kneading and baking his bread, made his stomach queasy. He could not imagine how these white people here could bear to live with such a dreadful strain on their humanity as slavery was.

Yet it was this way all across the South, down as far as the Mexican border and out across the Mississippi into Arkansas and Missouri—hundreds of thousands of square miles filled with white people who were easy with slavery, and millions of African slaves bent under it to the point of breaking.

That Phoebe. She looked and sounded like a simpleton and was a cripple besides. It was not his imagination that she smelled ripe. Was that what slavery did? Twist you out of your normal shape and into another one to suit a man like this Leyland and his handsome, pudding-brained son?

The reality of all this, Bradford thought—though it surprised him to think it—*must be carried as anguish in the slave-prepared food, and accordingly the food made me a little sick because of it!*

Elizabeth Leyland was a beautiful woman but could not hide a restlessness whose cause he could not guess. But, if he lived here, would he not be restless too, restless to be away from this slavery madness?

And Missy … Dear God, what was to become of her? Would he see her again? Could he dare to help her escape? His stomach heaved at the thought, as he imagined being caught by these southern oligarchs and, after a good beating, hanged from a tree. But he was likewise sickened by the thought of doing *nothing,* simply riding away and leaving this lovely, almost ethereal girl in the hands and at the mercy of these brutes!

And she was so *beautiful.* The warm turning over of sexual sensations in his belly instantly replaced the confusion and doubt. Ah, if only she could come to his bed even a single time, how touched he would feel, how sweetened and blessed at the very taproot of his genitals. Oh, to snatch her away from these Leylands and lie with her in northern peace somewhere clean and safe! No sickening dinners, gab, slavery and the black hands that carried and served.

Phoebe, looking thirty but a crippled child of what, effectively ... *thirteen*? Raggedy Negroes, peeping in the dining room windows at the northern man. Smiles, obeisance. Neglected teeth. Nasty, nasty stuff this human bondage.

The male Leylands, speaking in a meaningless bark: "Parp de parp, parp de parp parp ... niggers niggers niggers ... the South ... our heritage history ... the *real* meaning of freedom ... launching a second American Revolution ... we know what's best for the blacks ... damn the meddling abolitionists ... Yankees ... Republicans ... Lincoln ... William H. Seward ... Salmon P. Chase ... Hannibal Hamlin ... parp de parp ... parp de parp parp ..."

Nor was that all. After the dinner at midday, Colonel Leyland (Young George) had been obliged to look after military affairs to do with the formation of his regiment of Virginia volunteers, who were the thundering horsemen and who, all that day, came and went. So, heated by the flash of militancy in his blood, Young George now expected Bradford to listen to the formal presentation of his pro-slavery rant after that nauseating supper.

Much of the afternoon, Bradford had searched as discreetly as he could for Missy but was unable to find her. Decatur claimed not to know her whereabouts but said he would tell her, if he saw her, that Bradford was seeking her. And, of course, it was unthinkable to so much as mention to this Young George person or to the mistress of Pinewood—his wife Elizabeth—Bradford's interest in the girl, even supposing they had a moment to spare from their delirious excitement over the war. To so much as hint that he had experienced a personal encounter with her would, he felt sure, seal her doom.

So the afternoon had passed slowly. Bradford strolled the plantation, avoided the great chaotic bellowing at the front of the house as the young mounted men dashed in and out, watched the Negroes at work and noted their ragged and distressed-looking condition, rested in his room, felt immensely aroused by Missy's memory—and, he thought, her lingering scent. Having privacy and time and a great lust, besides the sort of borderline anxiety that sexual pastimes usually relieved, he wanted badly to frig himself but instead bolted from the room to carry his search for Missy to the limits of seemliness.

But everywhere Bradford failed and felt vulnerable and dejected, and frightened by the clamor at the front door, the steady arrival and departure on horseback of dangerous-looking, bearded, cavalry-boots-and-saber-wearing southerners in huge slouch hats, shouting gleefully at a beaming Young George, who stood on the porch, a clearly uneasy Elizabeth standing with folded arms behind him. They dismounted in the carriageway with a great spring from the saddle while their mounts were still moving and just let their horse run till a slave seized the bridle.

One of them cried, "By God, at last our day has come to whip those sanctimonious bastards from the North—excuse me, Mrs. Leyland, but I am sure you share my great joy on this day of days, when we have passed the brink and can no longer turn back from a war that God himself has created to justify and sustain us!"

To distance himself from these shouters, red-eyed with war lust, Bradford went out to the far fields but found the condition of the shabby, unkempt, bent-looking slaves he encountered there disturbing in a different way. Indeed, seeing the general run of motley field slaves and contrasting them with the dolled-up House servants brought on an aching melancholy.

He felt ill and angry. He wished that one of the large gas balloons, which he had seen demonstrated at the Chicago Fair the year previous, could scoop him into its basket and whisk him to Washington City and the train for Chicago. Being at the South on this day and under these conditions was becoming increasingly ugly and wearing badly on him. He felt an ache starting deep in his chest.

Oh, dear God, he thought, *to be away from this place and be home!*

Then he detected movement out of the corner of his eye, and he turned to behold a light-skinned black woman in a ripped and dirty red dress approaching him with uncertain steps. She stopped and gazed at him with haunted eyes. He too stopped, taken aback, amazed, even frightened at her appearance.

The vision drew nearer. As he saw her more closely, he thought that she may have been beautiful once, long ago, but she certainly was not beautiful now. She actually was … in a way … *horrifying!*

She opened her mouth and uttered a wail that seemed to enter his flesh and pollute it. He stepped quickly back, alarmed and glancing quickly around to see if there might be any help at hand. But Bradford and the apparition were alone at the edge of a field still in the grass.

She abruptly ceased her wail and called out to him, as if he stood far off and not thirty feet away.

"Dis de risin time, suh," she shouted in a shrill, deeply unsettling voice. "All dem nigga gods of my momma's gon rise up. De Jesus god gon rise up. Dey gon be all round me an carry me up wit dem. We goin ter heaven."

The Chicagoan's throat felt clutched, as if by hands. Snatching a breath, he began to back further away from this terrible harpy.

"O-dear-god-of-ages-past … perteck-yo-chile-terday!"

He was on the point of turning about and running blindly, full out, toward anywhere but here …

At that moment, the madwoman veered away and started down a crossing path, her voice rising not shrilly now but sweetly, in song. It was a song without any tune, seemingly, yet was compelling all the same.

"Oh, gods, come an git Young Sally. Oh, Jesus, where yo at? Lif me up in yo lap, darlin Jesus. Yo pretty smellin white man's lap, lak my daddy's in de long ago. Daddy Jesus … daddy Jesus …"

Bradford watched her, repelled but fascinated, as she drifted down the path and disappeared into a stand of trees.

When she was gone, he rushed back toward the House, intending to spread an alarm about the gruesome figure who had just so horrified him. But, even before he arrived, he had realized that not only would he *not* tell these awful slavers about this wretched slave woman, whom they had apparently driven mad, but that he would go to his room, gulp down half the bottle of sherry he knew was on a tray with a glass and fall onto his bed, wishing he could crawl under it and vanish from the South that instant.

This he did, and quickly felt the wine doing its restorative work. Tomorrow, he would be gone from this awful place forever.

Oh, God, his heart cried out, suddenly engulfed in a spiritual passion he had but rarely experienced, *keep me in your divine embrace, and I will be forever true to your commandments! Forever, dear God! Forever!*

Then, increasingly oppressed by a sickening dread, he arose and made his way down the stairs.

Now, he sat like a man under a curse in Young George's den, awaiting the arrival of the planter and the launching of his lecture on the rightness of slavery. But, despite everything, with his mind still darkened by the memory of the madwoman, thoughts of Missy's succulence oozed through him—sexual syrup. He considered asking God to relieve his mind of lustful obsessions. But, being conscious of having already placed a substantial claim on God's assistance and fearful of risking possible divine annoyance, he bravely forbore.

Soon enough, Young George came in and went directly to a small, oak cabinet, which, once its doors were opened, was seen to contain bottles of fortified wines and whiskey.

"What's your preference, Mr. Bradford?" Young George called out cheerily. "Some good Lisbon port or this fine Tennessee whiskey?"

Bradford spoke automatically, having been trained by his wife to regard himself as "woefully vulnerable" to the stronger drink, though he preferred it. "I'll try the port, thank you, sir."

"And I the whiskey," Young George replied, pouring tumblers of each and carrying them to the chairs that flanked the unlit fireplace, in one of which Bradford already sat.

At least, Bradford thought, *Leyland's idea of a proper sized drink matches my own.*

Handing his guest his drink and himself sinking into the other chair, Young George raised his glass in a salute. "Here's to an early and just end to the war, and to a strengthened South."

Bradford, who could endorse only part of that proposition, nodded, and both men drank. Then Young George set his glass down on a side table, folded his hands across his stomach in the manner of an indulgent uncle and gazed at his guest. Bradford sat, clutching his wine glass as if for security, and stared at Young George with barely disguised discomfort. But Young George, enjoying the flow of agreeable ideas within himself, did not take notice.

"Mr. Bradford," Young George began, "I would like to do you the favor of educating you about slavery. And the first thing you must know is that the Negro is peculiarly suited to bondage. Indeed, he is improved by it far more than he would have been benefited by remaining at large in Africa. He is, in fact, as naturally fitted to be a bondsman as the white man is to be his master. So this whole master-slave relationship is really just another instance of the mysterious yet perfect ways of God."

Listening to this, Bradford, though a timid man, was annoyed, both at the complacency of his host and at his effortless assumption of superiority.

Gathering his courage, he spoke up. "Excuse me, sir. I mean no disrespect to your long-observed habits and traditions. But just how is it that Negroes are, in your opinion, so very suited to be slaves?"

Laughing, Young George replied, "Oh, dear Lord! If you were to live here a month, you'd not ask. Only the shortest acquaintance with Negroes reveals the truth about them—that they are savages, barbarians. They could no more live peacefully under our laws and customs than a tiger could be a house cat. You can't change a tiger's nature nor can you change a nigger's. Oh, you could stroke a pet tiger and teach him tricks, but let him loose and your head will be in his mouth quicker than a minute."

Young George broke off, leaned a little forward and looked penetratingly at Bradford. His guest could tell that he was being scanned for a positive reaction and, feeling progressively more ill at ease as every minute passed, tried bravely to look receptive without looking convinced.

"Have you ever heard of Nat Turner, Mr. Bradford?" asked Young George.

Bradford wondered if his host realized what a strong flavor of demand came with the question.

Ah, well, he thought, *let me have patience. It will all be over tomorrow.*

"I take it that your silence means no? Well, he was a slave who broke loose with a gang of other niggers in the Tidewater back in the 1830s. All he did with that freedom he'd stolen from his owner was rape white women and kill white people, including children. That's the savage in the nigger, you see. And there, in a nutshell, is your free nigger. He can't hold back from mayhem any more than a drunken sailor can hold back from cussing. It's in his nature, just as temperance, kindness and orderliness are in ours."

Young George looked closely at Bradford to assess the effect of his words.

Bradford pursed his lips. He did not want to argue with this strangely violent yet outwardly civilized man. But a voice in him suddenly wanted to be heard, and he allowed it.

"I just don't see how you can call an escaped slave a free man, or wonder that he attacked the people who had held him and all his kind in bondage for their whole lives." Downing the rest of his drink for courage, he continued. "It would be like putting a muzzle and bit on a hungry mare and turning her loose into your hay barn. She'd be so frustrated and mad she couldn't feed that she'd kick and try to bite. And who'd blame her?"

Bradford, a little roused by his own temerity, looked Young George in the eyes but was distressed to see those eyes narrow. He saw that the planter was not sure what Bradford intended to say with this odd metaphor but, whatever it was, it had failed.

"Oh. I see that you choose to quibble, Mr. Bradford. But let me tell you, sir, that this problem was not just discovered today. It goes back to the early times in our colonies. Just look here."

Young George broke off, turned and pulled an old, leather-bound book from his book case. He leafed through it, looking for the passage he wanted, continuously glancing up at Bradford with a just-wait-until-you-hear-this look on his face. Presently, he located it. His countenance brightened.

"Now, just listen to this, Mr. Bradford. This goes back a hundred and fifty years. It's the South Carolina legal code of 1712. Here's what it says: 'Negroes are of barbarous, wild and savage natures, and wholly unqualified to be governed by the laws, customs and legal practices of this province.'"

Young George looked at Bradford meaningfully. Bradford struggled to retain a bland expression.

"And you see, sir," Young George continued, "that's not all that's written here. It goes on to say that they—the Negroes—need to be governed by special law 'such as may restrain the disorders, rapines and inhumanity to which they are naturally prone and inclined.'" Young George raised a triumphant face to his visitor and slammed shut the old book.

"It's in the nigger's skin, flesh and blood, sir," he continued. "His darkness goes right to the bone. Don't think I haven't seen it myself!" Here, Young George thought of Young Sally's willfulness and ingratitude, and a burst of resentment shot through him. "I've lived here among them my whole life, Mr. Bradford. Niggers are sly, uncivilized, ungrateful, lying and violent creatures. And, as much as they laugh, dance and carry on, if you lower your guard, why, lickety-split, there'll be a hoe buried in your neck."

Here, Young George knew that he had just told a terrible lie, but also knew there was such a thing—he had read it someplace, or perhaps someone had informed him—as symbolic truth, which recognized truth for the master universal force it was, fully liberated from niggling snivels over "rights and wrongs" and "facts" that never approached the realm of eternal perfection found only in symbolic truth.

Avowing that any nigger would kill you with his hoe was not piddling truth but symbolic truth—truth raised above sense to essence; truth that demonstrated a spirituality far beyond words and opinions, actually touching on the very central, very subtle meanings of things and, in fact, provided the light by which the South is able to perceive the highest truth! Young George communicated all this to Bradford as best as he could, swallowed some whiskey and waited.

The tool manufacturer pondered this, daring to permit his skepticism to peep through. "Well, Mr. Leyland," he replied, "we also have Negroes in Chicago. I admit that I am uninformed about that race. But I must say that the freedmen I've seen—and even employed—are hardworking, like everyone else. As I say, I've hired some at my tool manufactory. Fact is, I use a black carpenter when I've the need instead of the white one I had before because the Negro is just as quick, just as good—and he's sober."

Young George shook his head, like a long-suffering teacher at the class dullard. "Well, of course you'll have your exceptions. There do exist a few variations from the norm. Down here, we call them 'good niggers.' Pretty near everybody's got at least one they know."

At that, Bradford sat up straight. His face grew slightly flushed. "Fair enough. So, adopting your terminology for a moment, Missy just has to be one of your so-called 'good niggers.' She certainly is a beautiful one."

Bradford's mere mention of Missy's name flooded him anew with memories of her sweetness and attraction. He realized that, just in their few minutes together, he had almost fallen in love with her and now wanted to find out as much as he could about her, though he feared that the man sitting in the next chair, who had suddenly grown tense, had surely been one of the white men who had taken advantage of the poor girl since her childhood. The thought of this caused him to frown.

To his alarm, Young George sprang out of his chair, folded his arms and stood, staring down at Bradford, his face gone suddenly blank. "Well, Missy's a whole different thing," he said in a loud voice. "She does not enter into our discussion."

Bradford, though alarmed, could not let the subject drop. "She doesn't? I don't see why not. I think that—"

"Well, sir," Young George interrupted, "let's just get off of niggers and back to my being a good host to you. I doubt we'll come to any sort of agreement unless you spend some time around slaves and begin to perceive their true nature. Meantime, I'm about ready to move up to some of the good French brandy I've got in that little cabinet next to your chair. How about yourself?"

Startled by Young George's abrupt ending of their discussion, Bradford nevertheless accepted the offer of brandy and, suddenly feeling nervous about his journey home through enemy country the next day, was gratified to see another large glass—a sure tranquilizer—being handed to him.

Young George standing, Bradford sitting, they both downed big mouthfuls. In the silence, Young George's swallowing sounds were annoying and ominous to Bradford, since all human things about slave owners had suddenly become strange, though he was grateful for the warm flush brought into his body by the port and the brandy. Bradford realized that he had already gulped down half of the large glass, having also had a goodly measure of port just before. Without waiting, as if rushing to the head of a line, he quickly drank the rest. Young George did likewise and offered the bottle to the Chicagoan. Wordlessly, Bradford held out his glass.

As he refilled it, Young George said, in a quiet, somehow sinister voice, "There's nothing about Missy that you need to tell me, is there, sir?"

A bolt of panic shot through the toolmaker, but he managed to deny its power with a quizzical look. "I have seen the girl but once and that for two minutes. What should there be for me to tell you?"

Young George relaxed. His face softened. He turned a little aside, was silent and then spoke in philosophical tones, as if to the muse of history.

"Mr. Bradford, if you take nothing else North with you, take this: The Negro is the burden of the South. It is he who has thwarted and burdened us from the day he came to our shores. He has made himself indispensable to our way of farming by insinuating himself into our lives in every possible way while still remaining hostile and obdurate. He builds with one hand but destroys with the other. He has fastened himself to the white man like a great black leech, promising fidelity and industry while providing instead duplicity and sloth. You at the North view him as our victim. Not so. *No*, sir! He is not our victim. He is our *affliction!*"

Bradford now also rose to his feet, drank half of his second glass of brandy and stared earnestly at Young George. The well-being that was arising in him with the increase of consumed alcohol made him bolder.

"Sir," he said, "I would understand from what you say that you consider yourself to be in the Negro's power and not the other way around?"

"*Absolutely!*"

"That is what you mean by 'affliction'?"

"Yes, it is."

Bradford downed the rest of his brandy, set down the glass and turned to leave the room. He was suddenly conscious of, and grateful for, being drunk.

"I thank you for your hospitality," he said. "But I confess that I hardly know how to address a point of view as far removed from my own as yours. But one thing is clear to me: The Negro is not your affliction. *Slavery* is." With that, Bradford bowed to his host and withdrew.

From behind him, he heard the agitated voice of Young George: "I pity you, sir! Naïve as you are, it is well that you are leaving the South, for your life would be in danger here!"

Bradford ignored him. But feeling that he could not simply go to bed without a proper goodnight, he went to the parlor where Elizabeth was distractedly turning the pages of a magazine. She glanced up at him and struggled to seem friendly to their guest.

Just then, Young George entered, and the appropriate courtesies were exchanged. Elizabeth seemed to look right through him, though expressing regret at the troubles that shadowed them all just now. Young George said that he hoped nothing he had said could ever be interpreted by Bradford as anything but the most congenial offering of his opinions. Bradford declared that, if only the whole country could get on as nicely as they had, despite the fury of a new war, no war could ever have broken out in the first place. Elizabeth rose and curtsied, offering Bradford her hand, which he lightly kissed. Young George bowed, and Bradford withdrew and made for his room.

Bradford had no more left the room when Elizabeth rose and glanced over at Young George.

"I must likewise go to bed, dear Georgie," she said.

A key element in her deception of him in the service of her love affair with Jared Wilkenson was, she had discovered, resuming use of the pet names for her husband from their early marriage, and routinely saying them once again in the loving tone of voice that had all but disappeared from their lives twenty years since—he being, as she rightly thought, such a dullard, even a fool, and easy to dupe.

Moreover, she had discovered in herself, to her amazement, a marked skill as a dissembler and an adulteress. Her guilt and shame melted away almost immediately after she became physically intimate with Wilkenson and was replaced by what to her seemed a savage exultation when he both moved voluptuously inside her and, later at many times all through the day, when she remembered it and felt aroused.

In those moments, she had no more concern for her husband's feelings, or shame at her own wantonness, than would arise from slipping out of a heavy coat on a lovely spring day. The sense—overwhelming and beautiful—of being at last in the springtime of her own life so filled and energized her that she was gratefully, and almost continually, lost in her passion by day and by night. She was now aware of her sexuality as an utterly new force within her.

Before, it had been a homely handmaiden in her efforts to rouse herself to Young George's insistent needs. She never climaxed in her life before she did so with Jared. She had not even known that women *could* climax, as men did, until now. The simple magic of this had so completely altered her life that it was as if there were a clear before and after, which had swept in upon her like an unexpected fragrant wind, lifting and moving her gently into full womanhood. She barely had words for her happiness, so powerfully did it press outward inside her. Yet she watched and tended it so resolutely that she automatically found herself living two opposite lives with such perfect surrender that there was not the smallest hint in how she looked to betray how she felt.

Elizabeth often thought, *I have never been so happy or known that there was so much happiness in the world. I never felt ruthless in my life, but now I feel nothing else, and it is what all my hopes and all my soft and selfish dreams are wrapped in.*

Elizabeth and Wilkenson had, within a few months of being swallowed by the erotic quicksand, known beyond any possible doubt that each was willing to sacrifice anything—*anything*—to be together.

She said to him, "We cannot remain at the South. That would only make what is already difficult impossible. The laws of Virginia offer us no protections whatever but hold out disgrace and social and financial ruin. I have never been at the North, yet I know it is where we must go and not allow our self-defeating sentiments to dissuade us ..." She looked at him steadily but softly as she spoke.

They were in Wilkenson's bedroom, where nearly all their serious talks had to be held in quiet voices to defeat, as far as they could, the efforts of spies. Of course, in other ways, being so much in the bedroom all but announced their love affair. They had agreed that they could no longer bear to live such an empty, unfulfilled existence, but must, come what may, go together North and join themselves in the deepest, most public love ... forever.

As he slowly trod the risers, the aura of Missy again enveloped the Chicagoan. He forgot his discussion with Young George. Most of his fears were now quieted by drink.

A truth he had never accepted about himself was that he was a fantasizing, weak-willed man, who felt lost without a strong attraction to a woman. The identity of the woman could change frequently, but he had to have at least *one* upon whom to lavish his sexual imagination.

His wife, once juicily attractive, had become a Baptist and had turned to a brood mare in his mind, thinking sex for pleasure a sin. She even thought of him as "sexually insane" because he had once mentioned that he had recently read about masturbation being part of some people's "intimate arrangements." Her angry reaction to him about this seriously chastened his attentions to her. But his serial lusts comforted him, especially when he had nerve enough to carry one into action.

However, fear of God's punishment was never far from his mind, but blessedly this set in, full force, only after—and not before—he had committed his sexual sins. And, in the case of Missy, as beautiful and agreeable a woman as he had ever seen, the depth and intensity of the attraction was all the greater for his having already kissed and fondled her.

She had not been far from the center of his romantic mind since she had left his room that morning. The desire to bed her and the desire to save her lost distinctness from each other. Nor would alcohol, in the quantity he had drunk it this night, bolster his natural discrimination. No, Missy, the good and lovely victim of these slaving scoundrels, needed and deserved a savior, and his heart expanded as he realized that she perhaps had found one—*in him!*

But immediately then, good sense penetrated the alcohol fumes in his brain, and he backtracked. My God! How the mind can run wild and thus put even the most temperate man in jeopardy. What madness!

In this moment, he thought with alarm, *I can scarcely recognize myself! But never mind. Tomorrow, I will take the train of cars North and think no more of this place or what happened here. Yes, a good night's rest can remedy everything.*

His hoped-for business arrangements must be sadly abandoned. But there will surely come a time that sanity will have returned to the country, and that will be the appropriate time to revive them.

1861

BALTIMORE, MARYLAND

Alone in Baltimore on this April day, Jared Wilkenson, though a patient man and not usually given to anxieties, was worried. The outbreak of war had cast shadows across every life in the country. From days that unfolded with a general predictability, everyone had been plunged into a dismaying newness where nothing could be assumed and every plan and arrangement was threatened.

Elizabeth had no way to contact him or he her. Had she gone as planned through Richmond by train to Washington City and thence to New York, taking Peggy with her? Or had Young George forbade her to travel in such tumultuous days, and was he now keeping her against her will at Pinewood? Or had she left as agreed and was now well on her way to New York, and soon would be feeling shocked that there was no word from him?

He had tried to telegraph Young George to tell him that he was "delayed," so, if Elizabeth were there, she would know. But someone, almost certainly Confederates, had cut the wires. Union troops were being moved into position to restore and guard the telegraph lines. He could hear companies of them being marched through the streets to the railroad depot.

He was now two days behind schedule in the final stage of his court case, with the judge sick and the hearing put over on successive days. Ronald Sharp's attorney had moved to set both ruling and penalty aside and to have a new trial. His grounds for this were, to Wilkenson's lawyer, "laughable," and he had assured the overseer that it would be overruled and the appeals court would reaffirm the original verdict.

Wilkenson felt upset and restless, not able to sit in his hotel room and read or in the lobby to observe people's comings and goings. He had taken to walking about the streets of the city, from one end to the other, trying to decide what to do. He began to think that he ought to leave tomorrow, whether or not the case was finished. His attorney could appear for him, and he would lose nothing by it except the satisfaction of seeing Ronald Sharp's face when he realized that he was ten thousand dollars poorer. But that scene, even the judgment itself, meant less as the hours passed, and his need to be with Elizabeth in New York grew.

So he came to a decision: He would take the very next train of cars to Philadelphia and thence to New York. When the telegraph lines were repaired, he could send her a message at the hotel in New York where they had agreed she would be waiting. And, if she had been held at home by Young George, he could find out about that too. And, if it turned out that she had already left Pinewood when she had told him she would, then he could reach her in New York so she could be relieved of her anxiety at his delay and expect his soon arrival. The more he studied on the problem, the more certain he was that this was what he wanted to do.

He did regret, though, that they had decided *not* to rendezvous in Baltimore since it was impossible to be sure they would not be seen by someone who knew them, which could then set Young George on their trail. But now, with this sudden outbreak of war and the frenzy in which the southern countryside had erupted, the best arrangements could collapse amid the chaos. There was no way they could have predicted that the war would start on the exact day that it did—the very *worst* day, for them.

He found himself longing for Elizabeth almost desperately but kept reminding himself that he must deal with these unlooked-for breakdowns in their plan with calmness. He must discipline his mind not to roam about, attaching itself to every negative possibility, but instead continually remind himself that, in only a few days, he would be with his beloved again—and this time, forever.

He had not yet quite accepted how utterly his whole life had changed in just a matter of a few weeks. For, once they had decided that they must leave, and take Peggy, and live together at the North, regardless of any and all obstacles, it was as if, for both of them, there had never been even the faintest chance that they could have done anything else. And the need to now escape—as they both thought of it—grew ever stronger with a force and a rapidity that stunned them.

There were so many possible blockages in their way. To begin with, what they were doing was repugnant to everyone of Elizabeth's class. Adultery, the desertion of a "loving, decent man" (as the community thought) and the pulling up of a young child's family roots to suit the wicked fancies of her mother—who was, after all, a woman of social substance and financial means, and of whom so much better behavior than this was demanded, all in service to an illicit love affair with a man, who was practically a day laborer—was sickening. But this, they both knew, was the way they would be perceived and would create the forever-shadowed life they would be forced—and gloriously privileged—to live.

But, almost incredibly, neither cared. Each was the other's ideal and, when they had met, it was not for Elizabeth a doorway to humiliation, remorse and grief but a miraculous fulfillment of a dream long suppressed, and was now all the more powerful, more insistent, because of it. And, for Jared Wilkenson, it was a second love as profound as the first, perhaps even more so, and seen by him as a blessing directly bestowed upon them by a loving, forgiving, utterly empowering God.

1861

PINEWOOD PLANTATION, VIRGINIA

The decision to go away together came after making love one April afternoon in Wilkenson's house. They had all along been speaking of being together in a far future but without any plan to bring it about. The tension and hopelessness both felt at continuing as they had been suddenly, with nothing foreshadowing it, collapsed into an irreversible explosion of will between one breath and the next, to end immediately the life they were in and embrace a new one together.

As they lay naked in bed, Elizabeth whispered into her lover's ear, "Oh, how I love you, my dearest one. How I treasure you ..."

And, as he began an equally passionate disclosure of his own, she abruptly burst out sobbing. Not being shocked by this, he found that he had been expecting it, willing it. He realized that, as much as he had loved his late wife Constance, he loved Elizabeth just as much—possibly, against any former expectation, even more—and knew more deeply than he had ever imagined possible that he would do anything she asked of him. He would place his life and his future in her hands and receive hers in his. It was as simple and as overwhelming as that.

He pulled her into a kiss that tried to express more than kisses were meant to, and he stopped. He felt clearly, as if he had stepped into a warm bath, her ardor, her sincerity, her determination, her surrender. He drew back and looked into her eyes, wide and warm, as open to him as plants to sunshine. He saw that something in both of them had given way, and it was now as if she had always known him, and he her. And that he was actually an unrecognized part of her and had always been, and would always be. And that nothing, not even death, had the power to truly separate them. He realized all this, and further, that both had advanced in their understanding of each other beyond the outermost limits of what each had always before thought of as relationship.

1861

BALTIMORE, MARYLAND

In his mulling things over, Wilkenson had walked far from his Baltimore hotel near the railroad station, and now, having decided on a course, turned and started back. It was evening and a heavy fall of rain had started, but he did not care. He realized that he had been wandering about for hours but, lacking better occupation, did not care about that either.

In his impatience, he had actually found out where the judge lived and called at his kitchen door, just at dusk, to inquire from the servants as to his honor's recovery, only to be told by a slave that the illness still lingered and indeed might be typhoid fever. This only solidified his decision: He would leave for New York by the next train. His attorney could appear for him, receive the verdict and arrange for payment of the judgment.

He went by the attorney's closed office, which lay in his way, and slipped a note of instructions and his forwarding address—the hotel he had chosen for them in New York City—under the door. He found that now his every thought was subsumed in his love for Elizabeth, his gratitude that she loved him, his agitation at being separated from her and his not knowing exactly where or how she was.

He even found, not to his dismay but certainly to his surprise, that his very politics had been numbed by his love for her and his need for the two of them to be together. Even though southern born and always sympathetic to the South's defense of slavery—after all, it was slavery that gave him employment—and to his birthplace's desire to secede, he quickly gave up that line of thinking since, if he held to it, he could not in good conscience remove North, and so must lose Elizabeth.

He also, and admittedly under the press of circumstance, decided that he could never raise his hand against his country. So he comforted himself that it was well he was heading North. If fight he must, it had to be on the Unionist side. He had never dreamed before how an overwhelming love like his for Elizabeth could shrink to trivia even strongly held opinions. All he could think about was Elizabeth, and the need to be going continually to the telegraph office to see if the service was restored and to the railway station to see if any new trains had been added to the schedule of departures for the North.

But the night train was fully booked, and no new trains had been added, so he bought a seat on the next day's morning train. And he walked on, too tense to settle, ignoring the increasingly heavy rain.

1861

PINEWOOD PLANTATION, VIRGINIA

It was 9 p.m. in Decatur's shack on the House slave row. Missy's mother Young Sally lay on her back on the bed, staring at the dark ceiling. A single tallow candle burned on a small table, dimly lighting the area where Missy and Decatur sat, close to the bed.

Missy said to Decatur, "This man Bradford has nothing to tell us now, though he may yet be useful ..."

"Yas, de war an him come down heah tergetha," Decatur said. "Man lak him fum up in ab'lition country gots ter git on home now ter save he hide fum dese crazy white mens. How yo reckon he kin be useful?"

Missy did not reply to Decatur but said, "Mama," as she leaned toward where Young Sally lay. For a moment, there was silence.

Then Young Sally whispered, but the words she spoke were not for her daughter. They were the same sort of soft, tender words she spoke to herself now as she drifted aimlessly around the grounds of Pinewood. "Well, now, yo dear lil ting. Yo sweet, sweet lil ting. Come git up on yo marse's lap, darlin. Come on now, Young Sally, an give yo marse a lil kiss ..."

Missy turned away. She looked at Decatur.

"Not much longer now, girl," Decatur said quietly. "Yo kin all but see de life drainin away out'n her. Between de Young Marse Geo'ge an Black Sulla, she done been broke in bits. She fixin ter die, an it gon be soon."

"I know, Papa." Missy rested her hand on Decatur's arm. In the shadowed light, she could see his eyes widen.

"How come yo call me Papa, girl? Much as I'd wish yo was mine, yo ain't, an yo knows dat as good as I knows it."

"Yes," she said quietly. "I know. You aren't my blood papa. But I have always thought of you as my real papa. You are the best man I know. Whenever I think of a father, I think of you."

Tears came to Decatur's eyes. "Well, maybe yo kin find words dat would make me feel bettah den dem ones, but I cain't imagine what dey'd be."

Missy's eyes were dry. Crying was not her way. Instead, she smiled.

Decatur wiped his eyes with his shirtsleeve and said, "Somehow I tinks yo gon be off an away real quick now. Dis war de perfeck time fer dat, ain't it? Wid all dis confusion an folks rushin ever which way?"

Missy's face grew serious. She stared at Decatur without speaking, then looked at her silent mother. She got up, stepped over and kissed her mother's dirt-streaked forehead.

"Yo git on away fum de marse now, girl," Young Sally whispered. "De one he want on he lap be Young Sally. Git on away now. He don' lak de common niggas. He jes love Young Sally ..."

"Goodnight, Mama," Missy said. Then she kissed Decatur. "Goodnight, Papa."

Again, tears came to Decatur's eyes. When he spoke, he sounded hoarse. "Night, girl. I feel rain a'comin. Don' yo?"

"Yes."

"Den jes be careful. If yo has ter be out in it ... be careful."

Saying nothing more, Missy turned and went out.

After drifting in and out of sleep, Sally finally heaved herself into a sitting position at 11 p.m., clasped her knees and waited for the pain in her back to subside. Every movement she made tore at the scabs on the whip cuts, to which her blood-soaked dress back was stuck. She was very thirsty from the heat of the rows and the loss of blood. She reached for a jug of water and took a long drink.

"Up, up," she murmured.

The exhaustion was so deep, the pain in her body so nagging that it was like the ship again. Like on that great, heaving ship at sea, with her tongue leaking blood and radiating a pain that was like chewing on knives. This pain now—in her back and hips, from the bending and the beating, pain shooting down both legs as well—was like that, for it snatched her down into itself until she, as a person, all but vanished.

Sally stood up, not in her right mind but in the reverie that arises unbidden in the midst of terrible suffering. She walked about carefully, step after tentative step, in the pitch dark of her tiny cabin, seeking the full use of every limb despite the hurt. She felt, clearly and calmly, the onset of her death.

I won' wear nothin on my feet, she thought. *No. I'll jutht walk up dere on theeth bare feet ... theeth flat black feet of mine.*

It would be as a Fulani woman that she took her final walk, on the strong feet to which shoes were once unknown, for the sake of the rightness of things.

And for the quiet as well ... for the quiet, most of all.

Back at the House at 10:30 p.m., after Bradford went off to bed, Young George turned to his wife Elizabeth, placed a hand on her shoulder and spoke in a soft voice. "I am sorry that your trip to the city must be delayed by the coming of the war. But I am glad you were here. You provided, for Bradford's visit, as the woman of the place, what was beyond me or any man to supply."

He drew her toward him, but she resisted. He stepped back in surprise. "Well, well. I had thought our connection restored. Lately, you have begun coming unasked to my bed, and I have enjoyed you. I thought tonight to invite you and do not understand why you hesitate."

There was the little sharpness in his voice that Elizabeth well recognized. If not assuaged, it would quickly up-level to pique, then hurt, then anger.

She said, "You know how gratified I am that you have put Young Sally out of that ... house. So much of our proper relation was restored by that alone. But I ask you to forgive me. I had not realized how upset, how almost desperate the outbreak of this war has made me. I keep seeing you and Will having to fight the Yankees and risking your lives. The very thought is making me almost ill. I feel that I want to curl up in my bed and weep."

But the truth was that she did not much care about her husband or her son. Their having both stood against her sensibilities and her dignity for so long had badly estranged her. Little Master Will had even taken up with his sister Missy, just as his disgusting father had done with his own sister Young Sally. And this, despite knowing how she felt and how such things so desperately hurt her.

Now, they both would be at risk in this war, which they and their class had sought, and she found that their fates no longer concerned her. Their "southern manhood" demanded service, and they would joyfully give it. It was only a matter of time before the Yankees came South to punish the Rebels, and there would be battles and dead men on both sides.

It surprised but did not disturb Elizabeth that she really did not care if her son and husband were among them. It was especially odd that she had detached so perfectly from Little Master Will. The fact that his father had turned him into a planter drudge like himself—equally selfish, judgmental, venal, rapacious, unfaithful and unkind to women except those he relished—had operated on her over time. Already, it seemed to her that father and son, Pinewood Plantation, the slaves, Virginia, even the South itself, were parts of a receding dream in which she had little interest and to which she bore no allegiance.

The only part of the dream that kept its meaning for Elizabeth was Peggy. And Peggy would go with her. Everything she was and had been was dissolving and reconstituting itself around the person of Wilkenson. The one thing she cared about now was being reunited with him, unvexed by anything, even the war. The thought of them being lost to each other because of some ugly, random quirk of politics made her feel a little mad. Never in her life had she imagined loving a man as she loved him. This love overrode everything, past and present, that she had thought of as "herself."

Still, it surprised her that she did not care about her son. But what was he besides another of the eternally generated planter-cavaliers whose brains were given to trifling and stupid posturings and whose awareness of the greater world recognized no changes made since the eighteenth century? And, even as she had grown indifferent to her son, so very much less did she want to touch or be touched by her son's father, and realized now that to withhold what he wanted would be a great mistake.

Elizabeth had just told Young George that she wanted to go to bed and cry, and he was confused that he saw no trace of tears in her eyes. But he was quickly distracted when she came and rested her head against his chest. He put his arms about her and held her more tightly.

She whispered, as though to herself, "If only you had been as kind to me as this in years gone by …"

"I wish you had been kinder to me also, Elizabeth," her husband replied. "It seems that much of our married life has been unhappy for us both."

He kissed her hair and was pleased by its fragrance—not the old, long-familiar scent of violets but a new and sensuous one. He embraced her more intimately as he felt the sex attraction rising.

"Come," he coaxed. "Come into my bed tonight, and let us make up for the past. Let us be together again and begin things anew. Do not forget, in only days now, I shall be gone to fight for Virginia."

Once again, she hesitated. The very last thing she wanted to do was to give this man access to her naked body ever again. Having discovered the true and deep joys of real romantic love in the arms of Jared Wilkenson, and feeling for the first time in her life appreciated and loved, the thought of having to receive Young George inside her, even if only once more, was disgusting. Still, she had done it before to advance her purposes and realized that she must do it again now.

She raised her face to his, saw the familiar lust in his eyes and, somehow, pushing aside every authentic feeling, smiled, then hid her face again in his shirtfront. "You are right," she said, in a murmur of counterfeit romance.

For a swift passing moment, she understood what life must be like for kept women.

Young George put a finger under her chin, tilted her face up and kissed her deeply. Imagining he was Wilkenson, she returned the kiss.

"Oh, you have truly come home to me, haven't you, sweet girl?"

His self-satisfied smile awakened memories of his egotism and patronizing airs from their courtship days.

She thought, *Dear God, let us get it over with!*

But she said, "Yes, I truly have."

So, with his arm around her, they mounted the stairs to the second floor and walked past her bedroom on the left—Peggy's was on the right—and entered his bedroom at the far end of the corridor. Elizabeth preceded him inside and Young George shut the door …

Meanwhile, Bradford went to his room in the House's opposite or South Hall, across from what he was told was the old man's room and next to Little Master Will's, though he had seen neither in the corridor since his arrival. He was carrying a lit candle, which he used to fire a coal oil lamp that stood on his bedside table.

Still buoyed and emboldened by brandy, still saturated with thoughts of Missy, his mind turned again to helping her escape to freedom. Of course, he did not imagine that he would ever be required to *actually* help her—believing that he would now merely crawl into bed and fall asleep, warmed by the memories of their encounter, and leave on the morrow, thinking well of himself for his bravery and grateful that such bravery was never tested.

But he kept feeling the softness of her lips on his, smelling her sweet scent, seeing into her gorgeous brown eyes with such voluptuous intensity that his penis throbbed to life. His remembering of her evident attraction to him, and how manly and potent she had made him feel, brought up a great and familiar sexual tension, the sort that was always best eased by a good stiff frig.

Knowing the reality that tomorrow he would bid her and this place a bittersweet goodbye, and that he was perfectly free to feel a hero without doing anything heroic, he let his tipsy, romance-drenched thoughts roam as he undressed and slipped into a nightshirt and lay down on top of the bedspread, it being a warm night—though outside, a cooling wind was arising, along with the glimmers and mutterings of an approaching storm.

Like many other married men, Bradford had three separate sex lives: a meager one with his wife, another much less frequent but more stimulating one with other women and a regular one with himself. Of the three, it was the last one that satisfied him best, since he knew exactly what he liked and felt no shyness in bringing it about. His best spendings were those he had with himself, and the best of the best were driven by fantasies of women who had most recently pleased or attracted him.

Tonight, his mind was heavy with the sensuality, beauty and sweetness of Missy. So it was of her he thought as he lay in bed in the guest room—now sexually stirred but also frightened that he was somehow being spied on.

These mixed feelings created unwelcome tensions, for added to them was the vain hope that God might be unaware of his doings and even of his thoughts. This uneasiness of being in a nightshirt and vulnerable—and with an *erection* in the home of slavers—did, to be sure, retard his sexual energies. It was very annoying to him that masturbation, though such a very pleasant thing, was also a sin that he had been warned was especially toxic in the eyes of the deity. And his wife—when he in good faith proposed to her that they incorporate some harmless, barely noticeable version of it into their intimate life—to his horror thought it filthy, so of course he never brought it up again. He also feared suggesting it to his occasional lovers lest it alienate them too.

Burdened by these conflicting thoughts, he blew out the lamp and, in the complete darkness of the near moonless night, lay quietly, drunkenly, reflecting. Because of the strangeness and uncertainty in his thoughts, and his large alcohol intake, his manhood, though wanting to respond to sexual thoughts, went flaccid as a garden slug.

But still, hearteningly, mixed in with his erotic thoughts of Missy and his fears, were ideas of his great heroism should he help her escape North. Under the spell of liquor and sex, he had fleeting moments in which he felt immensely powerful, immune to the interference of the most wicked and sharp-eyed planter, or of a gang of ignorant overseers with ugly greatcoats, dirty boots, rifles, pistols, slouch hats and shotguns.

He could even imagine himself and Missy, walking carelessly through the mob of them, as the villains sat on their swaybacked horses and glared impotently. He would lead her up the gangway of a ship in Richmond, which would sail on the ebb tide down river for the sea, and thence north to Baltimore, all trains and checkpoints avoided. And, at sea, in a snug passenger cabin, he would have Missy to his deepest content—naked, fragrant and shameless.

Just then, the door to his room opened so quietly that he could not hear it but could only see a widening crack of the dim hall light, a single candle in a wall sconce, partly blocked by a female figure carrying a small lamp. Mortified, embarrassed, he scrambled to cover himself as the figure came over to the bed and sat down on it.

Now he could see her face in the lamp's light. She wore a very grave expression with a certain desperation in it, yet also a steady courage.

"Thomas," Missy whispered. "Your life is in danger!"

The night had grown so dark that nothing could be seen without a lantern or a cupped candle in the thick West Woods where Little Master Will and Missy's cabin stood. There were no lights burning inside. Its fine glass windows, closed and clean, reflected the tiny bit of moonlight that crept between gathering clouds, not enough to see by. But, in the cabin itself, a ray of that weak silver light struck a mirror and, in its spilling over onto the bed, revealed dimly that the sheets and blanket were disordered, and that a human form lay very still, partly covered by them.

The chiming clock was silent, nobody having wound it. Nothing moved in the cabin. From without came the rustling night sounds of the Virginia woods, possums, coons, mice, all moving cautiously over the leaf mold, and the beginning rustle of wind. Inside the little house, these sounds were blunted to a whisper by windows and walls. The form on the bed lay in an attitude of such peace that, even if one stood very close, breathing could not be detected.

Outside, the air was growing thick as the chill and heaviness of rain crept down from the north. An hour earlier, there had been a muttering in the sky from far away and small glimmers of light beyond the horizon. Now, a diagonal streak of lightning flashed in the turbulent clouds and after it a loud rumble, like a packed steamer trunk being dragged, *thump-thump-thump* down a wood staircase. The light wind strengthened, brushing the leaves of the thick-clustered trees. It was April, the time of the good-crop rains.

"Let it come now," the planters said, "leaving May mostly clear or light-rained, so the little tobacco plants can root."

The smell of the air and the feel of the wind now meant rain to any Virginian, slave or free. As the storm neared and the wind grew stronger, it rattled noisily the window panes of the cabin while the trees creaked in their swaying. But the figure on the bed, partly obscured by the bedcovers, was not roused.

The bedspread was an especial favorite of Young Sally's, she having bought it ten years ago and used it sparingly so it would not fade. The pattern was one of overlapping splashes, made in France where dyers worked magic with cloth. The splashes were bright yellow, navy blue, orange, forest green and blood red. If the pattern were studied, it could be seen how the splashes repeated themselves but in a differing order from one end of the spread to the other, with red being the widest splash and the one that drew the most attention, focusing the viewer on the descent of the reds all down the cover's length.

In the flashes of light from the storm, the spread was lit garishly for a few seconds each time—all the colors, especially the reds, though blued by the lightning, still shining out. In the moments of illumination, it could be seen that the figure on the bed was male, then that it was Little Master Will, then that his sleeping was so deep as to be coma-like and finally that the pattern of the bed-spread seemed to have more of the red surrounding his head than elsewhere.

Minutes passed as the storm clouds rushed overhead, the frail moon vanished and the flashes of light and the crashes of thunder increased. The thunder grew so loud that, all across the district, horses stamped restlessly in their stalls, hogs pushed down into the deep straw of their barn's floor to escape it and children—slave and free—sat up in their beds, crying out for their mothers.

A bolt of lightning struck a dead tree near the cabin, severing a limb and leaving a hot, springing fire in the splintered socket. The fire rose quickly up the dry trunk, caught the crisping branches above it and, with a roar, burst out in a globe on the dead crown.

In the rising, brilliant light, Little Master Will's body remained utterly still. But now could be seen a cleavage at the side of his head, too wide and too deep to stanch blood or retain life. The presence of blood next to his head suggested that he had, after being struck, made a lunging effort sidewise to escape but had only collapsed again, a bit closer to the edge of the bed, so that blood had made for him something like a half-halo, though life was quickly gone. And now, in the illumination from the burning tree, an axe could be seen too, its bloody blade resting on the corpse's leg and the red-streaked handle angled outward.

Burning twigs fell onto the cabin's roof and sputtered on the wood shingles. Then a big, burning limb—like a man lowering an arm wrapped in fire from the shoulder to the waist—crashed downward to touch the eave. In only minutes the cabin was ablaze, and the living trees around it were growing sere and, one by one, catching fire.

Very quickly, the whole structure was embraced by flames, burning like a toy house on a giant's hand of fire. The furniture, bedspread and body smoked and erupted. Little Master Will's long, blonde hair crackled in its sudden, swift burning. Then his body was lost in the uprush of roaring fire as everything under and around him burst into flames. Fanned by the gusts of wind, the West Woods caught and burned, tree by tree, sending up enormous shafts of fire and creating a bank of smoke, which drifted south with the wind, away from the quarters and the House.

Because of this, it was some time before anybody realized that, in the West Woods, the marse's special cabin was on fire.

Missy stood in Bradford's room and exclaimed, "You … we … are in great peril. We must leave at once. You have no idea what these awful slavers are capable of. Please pack up just a few things—in that valise and leaving every-thing else—so that we may be gone. Oh, please, *don't delay!*"

It is a sad but essential truth that, had Bradford succeeded in producing the calm-restoring sexual release he had intended, the combination of alcohol, relaxation and self-satisfaction might have provided him with a sleepy lack of interest in the face of the urgency in Missy's harshly whispered warnings. But, as things stood, a very different constellation of feelings had hold of him.

First was shame, since Bradford believed that God stood against sexual entertainment of every sort and against masturbation most of all. It seemed especially wicked to him to have fantasies about a Missy of the mind just as the Missy of the flesh walked into his room. Every time such a thing had happened to him—which had not been often, thank God—it had always concerned only his wife. And he had never been actually exposed but had felt chagrined, guilty and brutish. It was the sort of thing that, if he were caught in it here, would cause him such mortification at the thought of his ruin and would consider suicide. He had never uttered aloud the word "masturbation" in his life, never discussed the practice with even his closest male friends and was deeply regretful that he had ever mentioned it to his wife—though he had managed without using the word itself.

She had said, once she grasped what he wanted, "*What?* How *dare* you ask me to engage in such filth! That is the most evil thing I have ever heard. You don't mean to tell me you do that, *do* you? And you, a married *man!* Dear God, if I thought you did that when I am away from the house, I would end our marriage at once, and no court in the land would deny me that right!"

Her mentioning divorce and court chilled his blood horribly as he imagined the Chicago papers' headlines: "RESPECTABLE WOMAN SEEKS DIVORCE OVER HUSBAND'S UNNATURAL SEX HABITS! Tool Manufacturer Thomas Bradford Named in Sensational Suit!"

He hastened to say to his wife, "No, no. It was only a momentary aberration. I have never done such a thing in my life! I can't imagine why I even *thought* of it or mentioned it. Please forgive me."

As he had felt about his wife, he now felt about Missy—that he owed her a special consideration for having, so to speak, affronted her. He always felt guilty the next time he saw in the flesh any woman about whom he had fantasized. Yet, at the same time, he felt again the throb of yearning that had caused her to be his mental object to begin with. It was confusing, to say the least.

Also, there was the unslaked sexual desire itself, which was doused upon Missy's arrival but was now creeping back. With it came a return of his nerve.

An old scoundrel of his acquaintance had put it thus: "Fresh cunt, fresh courage."

Bradford was now feeling just so. Missy's closeness, the congested feeling in his loins and the residual well-being of the brandy caused a rapid discharge of ideas, even as he sat up in bed and stared at her.

"Missy! I am glad to *see* you!"

"And I you, Thomas. But please don't waste time. I do not know how long we will have before they …" She broke off, looking at him as if confused.

"They *what?*" Bradford asked, alarmed but not panicked. For what had he done to inflame the planters against him besides attempt (without even succeeding!) to frig himself under their roof and about which they knew nothing?

Then a terrible thought struck him: *Or did they? My God, did the devils have a way of spying on him?*

In the lamplight, Missy looked pale, drawn, very frightened. "Kill you! Kill you, Thomas, for what you have done!"

At the word "kill," Bradford's stomach heaved. "*Kill?* You must be mistaken, Missy. I—"

"Thomas, you forget where you are. This is the *South*. These are *monsters*, Thomas, not men like you."

"But what do they imagine I have done?" he cried, swinging his feet off the edge of the bed and standing up.

"They do not *imagine* anything. They know that you have kissed me, felt under my dress and lay on top of me on your bed."

"*What?*" cried the suddenly astonished Bradford. "How in God's name could they know *that?* Did you tell them?"

"I? Are you mad? It was that wicked nigger Decatur. He spied on us through the keyhole and went right to Little Marse Will, who is very possessive of me and hates any man who so much as looks at me. Once Little Marse Will found out what you had done, he went into a rage."

"What I had done? You *encouraged* me! You know you did!"

Missy ignored this. "Cordelia the maid told me all about it. She says that Little Marse Will is in his cabin in the woods, drinking whiskey and brooding. She says that he's held back from shooting you because you are a guest and are to leave tomorrow, and Cordelia said that he excuses me because he seems to think that you must have forced yourself upon me against my will—"

"*Forced?*" Bradford cried in a loud voice.

Missy put a finger to her lips, looking terrified, even hunted. "For God's sake, Thomas," she said, the tiniest quiver in her voice, "speak softly. He may be convinced that I am guiltless now but, by morning, he will be wanting my blood as well as yours!"

"But this is madness! All this talk of murder. Good God! I can scarce believe this is happening ..."

"It is, Thomas. It *is* happening. You must dress quickly, and we must leave. I need you, Thomas. I need you to help me find my freedom." Her low voice took on a plaintive, beseeching tone. "On my own, I should be snatched up like a stray lamb. But, with you, I will be safe. I can pose as your slave, and who will there be to deny it?

"You are a well-dressed, self-possessed white man. No one will suspect you. But we must avoid Richmond and the railroad. We shall pass through most safely if we take the packet steamer from Norfolk up to Baltimore. Nobody here will know when we left or where we are going. And, before they realize that we are gone, we shall both be out of this horrid place and safely sailing North.

"From Baltimore, we can cross easily out of the South. Once in Pennsylvania, you may go your way, and I shall go mine—if you like. But I am anxious to show you my gratitude in any way I can. I would wish to be with you in Philadelphia where we could finish what was so sweetly begun this morning ..."

Missy's eyes were expressive in the shadowed light. She reached for Thomas's hand. And he—stunned, disoriented but still lustful, the more so for her naked promise of what might pass at Philadelphia—let her take it.

"Only remember, dear Thomas, remember that it is not I alone who is in danger. You are in worse peril. Little Master Will's wrath is a terrible thing. He has killed twelve men in his life, and he but twenty-one years old. Oh, you poor, dear man! Look what your kindness to a friendless slave girl has cost you! But we must hurry. As you value your life, *hurry!*"

Twelve men! Dear merciful God!

Confused, frightened, lustful and suddenly burdened with a mission as a redeemer of maidens, Bradford was morbidly aware of how small-statured and thin a man he was, and that he had no gun with him and indeed had never so much as held a gun in his hand in his whole life.

He gamely set about dressing. The peculiar constellation of feelings in his breast urged haste on him. Already he was fantasizing Philadelphia, a suitable hotel, how long he might legitimately prolong his stay with the girl, what to say when he telegraphed his wife (besides that he had sidestepped the war and was safe at the North). But, most of all, imagining with dread the fire-red face of a furious and lethal Little Master Will, husky as a gorilla, bearing down on him with a whip and a gun.

"How shall we get away?" Bradford asked Missy as he jammed his belongings into his valise.

"I have already been to the stables." she replied. "I have hitched a gig to a fast horse. We will leave Pinewood by the Lower Road and not drive past the House at all. I know a fisherman, a free Negro, who lives not five miles from here, right on the James near Charles City. His boat is stout. He can take us to Norfolk.

"We must avoid Richmond and the railroad. There is too great a chance that I would be recognized and you arrested. But, riding with the current and under sail, we can arrive by mid-morning in Norfolk, and then take a packet steamer to Baltimore. I wish we could simply sail North, directly to Philadelphia or New York, but we would be so much more closely examined if we tried that. But never mind. At this time, only two days from now, we will be in Pennsylvania!" Missy squeezed his hand.

"How much is all this to cost?" Bradford asked. Fear flashed in him. "I have a round-trip railroad ticket after all. I do have *some* money, but …" He sounded suddenly doubtful.

Missy moved quickly to reassure him. "Don't worry. I have saved all my life against this day. I have enough money to get us both to Philadelphia." Missy looked firm and brave.

Bradford took heart. A trace of chivalry reappeared in his voice and manner. "Well, I certainly did not mean for you to pay *my* way. Of course, I shall pay my own. And, uh, all our expenses in Philadelphia." He gave her a meaningful look. And his heart leaped when it appeared that she took his meaning!

Oh, Thomas, her eyes said. *You are so good, so brave, so very kind.*

Despite his fears, and her hurry to be gone, she gave him a warm tonguing kiss, holding herself close against him.

And this, as she had believed it would, quieted him.

They put out the lamp, crept out of the room and down the servants' back staircase, where Missy made Bradford wait. She hurried through the entry hall and into Young George's den, then came back, tucking something into her large, straw, purse-like bag. They went out through the scullery door, then the kitchen garden, along the dark paths, through the maze of outbuildings, until they found a path, and followed it toward the tall grass.

Because of the slave Nat Turner and his murdering Negroes, Young George had at night for some years locked and bolted both the doors and the windows on the first floor of Pinewood Plantation. But Missy cared nothing about locks and, after the passage through it of herself and Bradford, the scullery door remained unlocked behind them.

As they neared the grass, a heart-stopping howl suddenly erupted about a hundred feet ahead of them, followed by waves of drawn-out, warbling wails.

"Dear God!" cried Bradford, stopping in his tracks, alarmed and again gripped with fear. "What is that awful *screeching*? It sounds like a soul lost in hell."

Missy hesitated. Then said, "It *is* a soul lost in hell."

"*What?* You know her? Who is it? And why is she *screaming* so?"

He was troubled, and she could see it: how deeply, how quickly things unsettled him, letting loose all his anxieties. And he must be still at least a little drunk, mustn't he? What would she have to contend with when he was truly sober?

"Never mind," Missy said, not slacking her pace but taking his hand and urging him along. "It's only a girl who works in the laundry. Most of the time, she is quiet and shy but, when her madness takes her, she does this. Nobody pays her any attention."

Suddenly, Bradford realized who the screamer must be. He took hold of Missy's arm and squeezed it hard, again coming to a stop.

"Today," he said, excitedly, his voice rising, "I met a madwoman out near one of the fields. A light-colored slave woman. I was out walking about—looking for you, in fact, though I never found you—and this, I would have to call it an *apparition*, materialized before me, by turns howling and singing. She was clearly quite mad. I admit that she made me uneasy. Well, it was beyond uneasy! I truly thought she might be dangerous. I did not know if she might have a knife, even. You see, we at the North—"

"Hush, Thomas," Missy interrupted, her voice a harsh whisper. "You're speaking too loudly."

She freed her arm from his grip, then brought his hand to her bosom, as if in comfort. At that moment, another shriek arose but now further away.

The madwoman must be moving away from us, Bradford thought, relieved. *Thank the Blessed Christ!*

He sucked in a little breath, as if to call back his outburst, and murmured, "I beg your pardon. I—"

"That is just a woman named Sally, who is harmless," Missy whispered, now brusquely. "Young Marse George lets her run loose when she's like this. She's none of our concern tonight, Thomas." Here, Missy took a breath, willed herself to softness and hugged Bradford's hand gratefully, lovingly against her breast. "Tonight," she whispered into his ear, "you are joining the heroes of this age. Your great courage in helping a poor slave girl escape to freedom will be remembered forever. Your name will be honored across all the coming generations."

Missy's words touched Bradford … a little. But his effort to brace himself, like a warrior for God, did not succeed. He stood up a bit straighter, but that was all. A sense of dread suddenly expanded inside him. It was the fully formed sense—and, in this moment, unopposed in his mind—of having been thrust into a horrible and unnecessary plight against his will, against his better judgment. And now he might be trapped in it with no way out. If only he had not been caught up in lust!

"Well, she was going on and on about it being time for her to go up to heaven," Bradford said, still speaking too loudly as his attempt to moderate his voice was defeated by his fear. "She said it was the 'rising up'!"

"Well, don't let it concern you," Missy whispered, touching his cheek with a warm hand. "We have important tasks ahead of us, and you must remember what brave work you are doing."

Seeing this as a clear reference to danger, Bradford immediately forgot about the madwoman, and about everything else, and his mind focused only on their precarious situation here in the Virginia woods in the very heart of the slave-holding South, trapped with a slave woman escaping North in the middle of the night. For the first time, the actual horror and magnitude of what he was risking overwhelmed him.

He gasped, "My God, Missy! What have I let you talk me *into*?" As awareness of the true peril in which he found himself cascaded over him like a wave of ice water, it was as if, in that moment, he had shrunk to infancy and suddenly could feel in his gut the unmerciful danger. "How can I have been just romping about like a fool with you in the night in this horrible, so-called Confederacy, when my very life could be forfeit at any moment between now and my very doubtful salvation, which I clearly see may *never* come, and instead you will be recaptured by Leyland's men, and I shall be murdered!"

His agonized cry so alarmed Missy that she pulled Bradford's head to her bosom and began whispering reassurances. "Oh, Thomas, my dear friend, please do not think we are in such peril as that." Here, she turned his head more toward her, so that her clothing muffled his mouth, and embraced him more firmly. "We shall be fine and safe, I promise you. I am certain that we will pass unnoticed tonight, and all will be well.

"Please, never think that I would expose such a fine man as you are to danger. This little trip we are taking has been taken hundreds of times before, when courageous and kindly white men have brought colored folk to safety and freedom ..."

Her voice softened further, and her hand stroking his face was now a mother's touch. He began to relax in her arms. As he did, she reintroduced what she knew was the one central inducement to him for ever becoming involved with her in the first place.

"How sweet it will be when, in only a day's more time, I can lie with you in a soft bed and lavish on you the ... tenderness ... we both so desire. Oh, that will be so lovely, Thomas, and I shall feel so deeply consoled. No one is pursuing us. Truly, we are no different from any other travelers. All is well."

She drew him into a deep kiss, which she prolonged until she had coaxed all of him into it, and he was moving from fear to arousal. Thus realizing that he was not surrounded by a great outrush of planters with whips, Bradford allowed himself to be comforted. But then he noticed the clouds lit red from below by a great light in the West Woods.

"My God, what is *that*? What is on fire?"

Missy glanced toward where his finger was pointing, then again pushed him on.

"Oh, *that*. They are burning the field stubble before the planting."

"What? Surely that is too large a fire for that! And do they burn the stubble in the middle of the night?"

"Yes, of course," Missy said, showing him impatience. "That is the custom amongst tobacco growers. I thought you must know something about tobacco farming since you want to be a cigarette maker."

Fresh lightning lit the sky as she spoke, and a wind came up. Rain was so near that its taste was in the air. Bradford, puzzled and embarrassed, fell silent. He still believed that everything Missy said must be the truth. But, in that case, why was he feeling confused?

He and Missy, still hearing the screeching that rose from the high grass they were approaching, turned left and away from it on the path to the stables and were soon absorbed into the trees.

And Missy kept it unspoken within herself that this would be the last time she would ever hear her mother's voice.

Young Sally had begun singing. For two days, it had gone on. The slaves thought that this might be the last straw and Young George's patience would certainly crack now. Humming, murmuring were bad enough. But everyone believed that to go about the plantation slovenly, her dress filthy with dried blood, her body running to gauntness now that she had forgotten food, and singing insane songs in a loud voice would surely prove too much.

It was known that Young George had sent Black Sulla to quiet her. The marks of the fresh beating were on her face—raw, red places; a newly torn lip; a puffing under the eye. But it changed nothing. She still walked the place, singing—howling, really—the words jumbled and the tune flat but easily recognized as the story of Young Sally's own life. And, because of that, at least some of the other slaves judged her less harshly once they glimpsed the inner world from which the bitch in her had emerged.

Young Sally sang many songs now, but one she sang more than the others. It began with sensible words and a proper tune:

Long days gone in dat time befo,
De Lawd bring a girl baby ter Sally's door.
Sally yell, "Take dat baby an trow her way!"
But de Lawd say, "No, ma'am, Young Sally, she gots ter stay."
An Sally say, "Well, den, I drown her in de creek.

Dat wicked white man's chile, she won't live a week."
But Marse Geo'ge he go pick up dat chile,
He say, "Hush! Dis babe she gon stay awhile."
Den he take Young Sally and hole her tight,
And say, "Ev'ting gon come round right."
So Marse Geo'ge he cradle Young Sally an kiss her
An he say when he away he pow'fly miss her ...

Young Sally would sing this part of the song sweetly, with a tune that was not especially melodic, or even the same from one time to another, but serviceable as a frame for the words. But then, her voice rising in agitation, jumbled verbiage poured out of her, and the tune faded to an irregular chant that was half-scream. This was the part people hated.

More than one slave went to Young George and—respectfully, hesitantly, in a very soft, diffident voice—told him that Young Sally had gone mad and needed to be dealt with.

But Young George always said, "Shut your damned mouth, or I'll show you what mad is," also applying a slap, punch or kick, depending how liberal he felt just then.

But, when Little Master Will had once broached the subject of Young Sally's strange behavior to Young George, he said, "Well, you can't put crazy niggers in with whites and, as far as I know, there aren't any lunatic asylums for just niggers alone. Why would there be, after all? What would be the point of it?

"I'm looking into sending her down to Texas. Certainly getting her away from here will be a good thing. Can't get a red cent of money for her, of course. That's a dead loss. But there must be plenty of men who would take her for nothing on the chance that she'll snap out of it. If the shoe were on the other foot, I sure as hell would take her. And, if things work out, then whoever gets her has got them a new thousand-dollar nigger. And, if they don't, all they've lost is her keep. For the chance at a thousand-dollar nigger, who wouldn't take a little risk?"

Late on the night of the day the war started—about 11 p.m.—and the man from Chicago came, and Elizabeth put off her trip to Richmond, and Missy had come and gone at Decatur's shack, Young Sally went out wandering and singing.

To her, the nicest thing about the kind of singing she did now was that, at the center of it, she could hear a clear, sweet voice directing her. It was the same voice that spoke to her of George's affection and the lovely times of her childhood. But, in the depths of her singing, it had a sterner tone and gave not so much comfort as direction.

Young Sally listened to the direction now, just as she had the comfort. Her life had slipped out of her hands. She felt herself in a body that floated all on its own to the very places it needed to see and be, for reasons unknown to her and unimportant. She heard the voice with especial clarity at moments when her song was most rageful and her own voice most screeching, when real words had slipped out of her mind and were replaced by sounds that stood for her feelings better than the words themselves ever could. These sounds brought her pictures of the past and the future and instructed her about what she realized were her ... duties.

Tonight, in the dark of the sliver moon, an eyelash of light in the sky swiftly being covered by clouds, she heard new things as she wandered. She sensed that she must get far away from the House to listen carefully. So she went halfway to her mother's shack on the field slave row, stood in the tall grass and screeched the wordless words until her mind started to ... fill up.

From the field row and the House row shacks came the agitated voices of slaves shouting at her, but they were no more to her than cricket sounds. Fireflies to the ears. For this filling up was a new and wonderful thing, to be encouraged, honored. Not just any nigger would have this voice at the heart of singing or this filling up—only one who had sat on a great man's knees, been loved by a white father whose word or look shook other niggers down to their flat, black feet. She alone could be calm and safe in the swirl of tensions around this powerful white father and that hard-faced Fulani mother. She alone ... she alone had the right and the power ... to fill up.

Momma was dying now. Yes, and herself as well. But the filling up made death a radiant thing, like a god's kiss inside her soul. She let the quavering tones of her voice project truth, like a magic lantern's image on the dark face of night. The smells of flowers, dirt, dried blood, her own body, the odors carried on the coming rain and the wind, the scent-texture of slave life ... what it really meant to be a true white man's nigger in a beautiful tan body, balanced on knees of love ... heart-warmed, hug-warmed, despite skin or history ... my Papa loves me so ... until comes teenage and Papa's distance ... sweet girl's new between-the-legs blood soaking into old rags … new breasts and hips blocking his light … Momma so wicked cold to him whose hands held up the world.

Momma say, "Don' let dem men touch yo. Black or white, dey ain't of any count. Dey will just drag yo inter hell wid dem. Yo see me, don' yo? I don' speak ter dem. I just look at dem lak dey roaches, an I spit on dere shoes. Dey kin kill me. I don' care. Don' yo care eithah. Dere is nothin down heah on Earth fer niggas anyhow cept pain. Get on up ter heaven as soon as yo kin. Don' evah, evah, *evah* trust de white men. Dey be human devils who eat yo tongue an stroke yo lady hole right tergetha."

When at last Young Sally was filled up, the singing stopped. She suddenly felt like a little green leaf on the new, pretty wind rising around her. It hardly seemed as if her feet met the earth, as she drifted out of the grasses and past gardens and sheds and huts of sleeping slaves, and others lying awake, listening for her song, which would come now no more.

She stood at the back door of the Big House, the Fulani gods and ancestors and Jesus and Father God and the Holy Ghost crowding around her, lifting her by spiritual force onto the porch, the first time in many years that she had been as close as this to the House. In fact, since those long-gone happy days of serving at the table, with the white men staying completely in their own world and she thinking of marriage to some beautiful, strong, black man and children, and then freedom, she and all the former bondsmen spreading out over the country, like rainwater in a spring field, and a farm in Maryland or at the North—somewhere. All swallowed by Young George's greedy mouth and paid for in gold now vanished. The lies that oozed from him, tar on her loins and life …

But, in the filling up, everything was at last seen as it would and must be.

Her letting Elizabeth alone was needful for she was a wounded wife. Young Sally was the unwilling sore in that lady's skin, ground in brutally by the selfish thumb of Young George. Young Sally believed that, for her mistress's own causes and private purposes, Elizabeth would never have had Black Sulla whip her. Woman to woman, Young Sally understood.

But Black Sulla! It cracked inside her like his whip, like a wind-bent tree limb, breaking … *Black Sulla!* … How could she have thought that he might be second when, in every way—*every* way—he was the natural, the righteous first?

Young Sally tried the back door.

Open.

In her day, it never was because of Nat Turner. But tonight, the Fulani gods and ancestors and Jesus and Father God and the Holy Ghost had flooded its lock with their love. This she could sing about, if singing were needed anymore. In the scullery, the smell of lye soap; clean, stacked dishes; the fragrant ghosts of old, lost suppers resting on the counters, brought in from the cookhouse by hurrying slaves. Yes, just the same ... same as in the long ago ...

Young Sally, in the inky dark, felt for the drawer she wanted, reached in, found what she sought, took it up against her—a holy treasure—and went out again.

Now she was no longer drifting but walking in long, barefoot strides through the harmless dark, like a driver, like a she-Sulla, her feet seemingly in the last green grass of earth ... the clarity of the filling up, just like peace, just like heaven but sooner, of this world and not the next. And, in the next, a greater filling up would overspill soul and spirit, bonding them with all Young Sally-ness in a ball that bounced high, high through the highest clouds, airs and waters to the very sandaled feet of God on his throne of glory.

And God would pick her up and put her on his lap, and he would say, "Oh, chile, my darlin Young Sally. Yo done come home, ain't yo?"

Coming out of the House, she met her mother, as if prearranged, a God-gifted goodbye. Each spoke to the other in harmony with the truth in them, which was so powerfully pressing out, and Young Sally felt a spirit wind rising under her torn and bloody dress, breezing her along. She moved briskly forward, blessed and smiling in the holy wind.

Black Sulla, she said inside herself. Her heart was cradled in the hands of the one eternal Father who, in the filling up, had told her when and how and who. *Black Sulla, Black Sulla ... I'se gon make yo my man. I sho nuff gon make yo my man.*

George realized that he was dying when the dyspepsia, indifferent to remedies, crept like barometer mercury up his throat.

This is the taste of cancer, he told himself. *It is the bitterness of a wasted life.*

Sleep now came in little groups of pain-bound minutes, resting on sourness, spread out over the course of night. How quickly it had come on! No more had he condemned Sally to death in the rows, made sure of Black Sulla, than he sickened at his next meal and never took another meal afterwards. The weakness, the hollowness he felt did not seem new as much as finally faced.

So much of his life had been spent furiously grasping at the unattainable and pushing away the inevitable. The end of a life lived in such constant grasping and ill temper can bring nothing but regret. Yet he had regretted all along, making regret the prayer with which he greeted and parted from each day. So now, he sat propped by pillows on his deathbed, recapitulating every regret of his long life since it was, as it always had been, his perverse and sole source of comfort.

The most sickening and satisfying thing was that Sally had been whipped down to the cellar door of death and would surely slip through tonight. Perhaps she was dying even now. Perhaps she was already dead and stiffening in the dirty straw of the field slave hut, alone and unmourned, as befitted her. He would see to it tomorrow that the slaves dug a deep hole in the woods and cast her into it, face up in her bloody clothes, then fetch him, carrying him in a chair given his weakness and sudden decline, so he could see the dirt shoveled into her half-open eyes and mouth. He would give orders that her grave be concealed by scattered leaves and remain unmarked. Then, having outlived and at last punished her, he could die.

God was kind. God knew how George had suffered at that woman's cruel hands, despite his generosity, good-heartedness and loving intentions. Just as God had allowed Moses to take revenge on the idolaters who had dishonored him, so God would allow George to possess this final and full justice before he passed. Perhaps, their deaths coming so close together, he would be able to witness her plunge into hell, even her brutal reception there by God's own avenging demons, which did his will for the mysterious higher good of all righteous men. That would be the best thing of all.

In the Bible, Jesus said that the damned in hell could see the risen faithful in heaven. Ah, how George hoped that was true! Then his justification could echo on through all time to come, with a sweetness beyond telling.

Yes, sweet …

And yet …

And yet not even the satisfaction of this, his greatest triumph over her, could completely rid him of every suckling root of love. Lying here now, days or hours from his end, he still recalled the beauty of her face in the slave pen at Charleston, her straightness of carriage and her disdain even under—as he soon learned—the pain of a wicked disfigurement.

And her sweet body that never opened to his love. Dear God, what he would have done for her had she but *let* him! He would have raised her up higher even than their daughter Young Sally would rise. She would have been a queen with a subject people to rule over—all of the niggers and, of course, she would reign over him. She always had done that.

In good times and bad, Sally alone could make him happy by a smile, a kiss, a nod, and would, he knew, have made him the happiest man on the face of the earth. He forgot now the times he had her whipped, cast out into the hot fields; the times he had threatened and cursed her, struck her, shouted into her passive, beautiful face his rage and frustration. He forgot likewise what he had long known. If he had taken her properly, even once, with her spending and melting in his love, he would have fully awakened to the fact that she was nothing but another comely nigger and soon enough discarded her. Now, all he could think of was her refusals and punishments of him and his own steadfastness and unwavering love.

He had not eaten anything and was weak and lightheaded. Nobody came to his room to see him. Not Young George, Little Master Will, his daughter-in-law Elizabeth—nobody but the brassy, laughing, nigger wench Cordelia—the upstairs maid, with whom Young George had taken up after Young Sally and with whom he was now climbing the stairs—the same attic stairs that George had climbed with Sally.

That Cordelia, he thought. *She was a willing, worthwhile girl. If only Sally had been like that. If only …* Nostalgia and self-pity flooded him. *Ah, for those days, empty as they were, because at least then her body was young and fair, her eyes were goddess's eyes and her breasts, her color, her carriage, so regal, so stunning. Oh, for a final taste of that mystery, for the holy frustration of his worship!*

Well, as Edgar Allan Poe had written, "Nevermore." Nevermore would life be as it ought to have been. All hopes, dreams, pleasures—nevermore.

If only she could have seen him … really *seen* him … could have accepted him … accepted his love …

If only she had known *him …*

If only …

Sally found that every step on the House path liberated a memory.

It was a pageant of scenes, like her Kano's death-dream, but from earlier times … from her days in her uncle Tenkaminen's thatch house of mud floors, with the gaunt, old sorcerer squatting in the Fulani way, explaining the casting of spells against enemies.

"… bury the egg three weeks in the soft earth. Then, when it is raised and examined and rotted, break and pour it on some article of the enemy, and bury that in the same hole, keeping in mind the clear intention of what his hurt must be. Invoke the gods and ancestors in your behalf, and a black stinking flower will bloom in his life, and he will know whence it came and oppose it with counterspells but in vain …"

Oh, how she remembered those days:

… her Fulani mother's face placid, despite the dry, hungry times stretching across years.

… the fat cows, when life and rain were good.

… father taking his herd to the Sahel grasslands for the dry months.

… staying behind with her mother and young brother, who was possessed by a dark spirit at his birth, the boy dull but sweet behind his oddly shaped eyes. In the end, the boy wandering heedless and god-lit, far from Tekrur, until after many days, hunters found his eaten-at body in a leopard tree.

… the comely Muslim boy, who came with his father and uncles and slaves from upper Mali through Tekrur, to trade in the south when she was twelve and absorbed by the gods, so drawn to him that her body awakened, yet emptily letting him depart without his ever hearing her voice, despite his words to her and his touches at the well at dusk, for she already knew her destiny.

Remembering all this now, a few steps before the end, seemed in some way sweet. But Sally had never savored the sweet and did not savor it now.

A great sheet of light riding the van of the coming storm flashed on suddenly, showing Young Sally walking in powerful barefoot strides away from the House, her madness somehow taken in by a higher madness that raised her gauntness and wounds to marks of beauty.

Sally stopped. "Where yo goin, girl?"

Young Sally breezed on but turned her face to her mother with a sky-lit smile as she passed. "I'se goin to de blackbird's nest, Mama. I'se gon fix him fer my suppuh."

"What in de hell yo talkin bout, girl?"

There came a deafening thunder crash. Young Sally stopped to accommodate it, still smiling.

Then: "All de ways of Fulani gods an de Fathuh an Jesus an de Holy Ghost, dey be good ways. Dere love gon cook me up a righteous suppuh in de end. De soup of heaven be made out'n blackbird meat, dark an sweet, all de badness bled out. Yo jes wait, Mama. Befo yo rise up to de good niggas in high heaven, yo gon see."

Young Sally's face cleared and a kind, calm look came up, a single blossom in a burnt field. Then she turned and walked calmly away.

Sally, oppressed by her physical misery but caught up in her internal meshing of life ends, the blending together of the world of huts and trees and light and the river with this white man's land of the soul's death, let her daughter go uncomprehended and uncared about. The only love of her life was Kano. Her abiding hate was the white man. Young Sally was no more to her than a bird call, a sunrise, a cold rain.

Mithy, now ... but nevah mine ...

Sally turned away from even the thought of her daughter or granddaughter. A single need possessed her. She found the open scullery door, made her quiet and painful way through a searching of drawers and cabinets lit by lightning. All the while, as if it were through this physical process, she felt the unconnected ends of her life knitting together into a single, thick, unseamed trunk.

Then suddenly, so swiftly and deeply that she was shaken, sixty white years fell away into the blackness of her birth and youth and family. She realized that, to accompany her to heaven, the Great Gods of lightning and thunder had shouldered up past the flimsy white man Jesus, past all the Christians, past even her once-precious Little Gods of river stones and whirlpools, and were lighting her way home. In the scullery of the slaving white man, amidst the shouting of the Big Gods, Sally stood stiff and absorbed, her mind steadied as if at the river beside the great stone. A whirlpool of sweet memory circled her heart, the Little

Gods sparkling flakes of light in it. And, for the first time since her childhood in Tekrur, happiness flooded her.

All dith ugly thlave life ith only a dream aftah all, she whispered in her spirit. *An ev'ting I catht away in anger still gone wid me even tho. An all dat I am, an wath, ith de thame ath evah. I come forward in time an thpaith, but thith body dat I flaunted an denied ter dem, an thought wath mythef, ith a dyin leaf on an ugly tree.*

Thith body dat de demonth took an broke an raped ith truly nothingneth. Now I know dat, in the rithing up, all thingth real are rethtored an made whole, though in fack dey never was injured. All thingth truly are ath dey was at de river by de great thtone in de watercourth an de whirlpool below, where one worl move eternally, even now, into an out of de othuh.

But I mithed ev'ting. It mutht have pathed me by while I wath angry cauth then, even if I looked, I could not thee it. Yet now, I kin be it. To thee it ith to be it. How thtrange an heartbreakin an good. But, to thee it, I need ter thtand in rithen truth ath in a well of thweet water, ter de mouth, de earth, de eyeth. Den be thubmerged an breathe it. Den ev'ting will change. An nothin ith changed.

For the first time since her childhood, Sally wept, a soft weeping such as she did when leaving her uncle's house the day she realized that she knew her destiny, and accepted it, and her child-self vanished. Nor was it her child-self weeping now, but herself wrenched into humility by Kano and made stronger than anger and stronger than fear.

This then was the Sally who passed from the scullery into the spoor of the well-known slave paths in the marse's House, up the back slave stairs and down the hallway to the bedroom door through which she had been taken first when her tongue was still healing and George had not yet married Martha.

Sally opened the door, no longer needing eyes since years and suffering had imprinted in her this room's map. But, in the light of the gods' flashing, roaring encouragement, she saw that he—George—was sitting up in bed, perhaps wakened by the gods who had come to bring her home. He beheld her in silence but not surprise. He reached over with trembling hands and lit a candle.

She said in a quiet voice, "Yo know why I come. Don' yo, Marth Geo'ge?"

For a minute, he said nothing. Then, "No."

"Yo din evah exthpeck me ter come, did yo?"

Another silence. "No."

"Yo thought I'd be daid now, thnatched out of thith ol body by work an whipth."

George said, "I thought you would die tonight. I was sitting here, thinking about you. About how I loved you."

"Yath. An me nevah thowin any love back."

"No, never."

Sally hobbled closer until she stood at his bedside. She could see the futility and disappointment in his face as the light came and went, a face now as always hemmed by weakness. She could see that he was a shell, all but extinguished at his core, finished with life. Yet, as her face softened and she leaned closer to him, she could also see the longing for her that he had thought to kill but was brought back sharp and young by her simply coming into his presence—and being, for a single moment, kind.

Sally leaned toward George, into his white smell and his aura of selfishness and danger, watching his eyes widen as she raised a wrinkled hand to his cheek and turned his face fully toward her, nudged open his mouth with her lips and drew him into a deep, soft kiss.

She pulled gently back. She wanted to see his eyes. They were strange eyes now, like windows in a house that was collapsing from within. She could see debris raining down behind them, the sudden violent wreckage of his hatred, of his ancient habit of self-doubt, anger and frustration.

He gasped and tried to speak, was unable to form the words and instead reached out an old, trembling hand, took her arm gently and drew her into another deep kiss.

As she touched his tongue with her split one, he, his voice shaking, murmured, "Oh, dear God, how I have always loved you."

And she replied in the softness of the kiss, "I knowth, Marth Geo'ge. I truly knowth."

Her words brought on a shaking in his flesh, like a weeping child consoled by a good mother after a very bad dream.

"Sally, Sally," he whispered, still engaged, enthralled in her kiss.

"Yath, ith Thally, Marth. Thally an nobody elth."

As she spoke in her intimate whisper, still touching his face as he tried with his skinny arms to pull her yet closer, she raised her other hand. Holding a large kitchen knife, in the smooth flow of naturally unfolding events, she seized his thin, white hair, showing him the knife for only half a heartbeat, only until his face collapsed, only until he was snatched out of her stage play by horrid surprise, only until he saw the same smile on her face that John Potts had seen, only until he realized that she had once again walked with nailed shoes upon his tender guts and was rejoicing.

Then she slashed across his throat, all of her failing strength brought to a high-fixed point of power by this last and best chance to pay her debts and keep her one promise—all in a single, glittering moment.

Instantly, he toppled over toward her and was dead in seconds. In the candle-light, she watched his eyes dim as the life oozed away with his blood. While she watched him die, her weariness and the pain of her body reclaimed her. It was as if she had been on a short leave from a terrible, cruel prison and now entered back willingly into its darkness and suffering.

Sally did not know if George was dead or alive when she cut off the penis that had dishonored and ruined her. His body did not jerk. Still, she was not sure. But the pupils of his eyes were fixed, the lids low when she cut away the lips that had made her kiss them and had parted in laughter at the lisp that white men had given her. She rested the penis against his cheek and reached into the liver-like space of his dead, blood-ringed mouth. Yes, he must have been dead when she cut the lips, for the blood had stayed, glistening in the tissue, and had dripped but not run …

Her light fading, a deep tiredness mixed with a sense of rightness and completion arose from some unknown place inside her. Her strength seemed to drain away, like water in a sprung barrel. Still, she was firm and deliberate in her movements, knowing that the Great Gods, who still celebrated outside this slaving house, would surely allow her to live long enough to serve them to her heart's desire.

Thith moment, she thought, *be all de juthtith I will evah git. It be more den motht thlave women git. Tho let it be done—not only fer Kano, not only fer me, but fer all dem: the thlavery-polluted black womenth who went befo an will come aftah. Let it be fer all dem. Even dat daughter … even Young Thally.*

She cut out his tongue, which had abused and poisoned her with words and kisses. She put it aside on the night table, picked up his old, withered penis and the grotesque oval of his lips and put them there as well. Then she grasped his thin, depleted body by the shoulders and, with the final offerings of her every dying sinew, dashed him down with a rustling thump onto the carpet next to the bed.

She stripped off the bloody coverlet. Suddenly, it seemed to weigh tons; the blankets and sheets as well. She threw them aside, taking care that they did not cover or in any way obscure his body. Inside, the flame of her life burned lower. Every effort now seemed that it must be the last, since the well from which strength might renew itself was dry.

She went to the closet of the room, each shuffling step like a spigot's last drip, for a fresh pillow and blankets. One blanket she spread slowly over the bloody place on the bed. Her arms felt like lead. Out of the corner of her eye, there suddenly swam into view the Fulani heaven, with its trees and streams and gods, its crystal bridge a structure of pure light, rising in an arc that vanished into clouds. She knew it was the bridge to the Asante heaven, and now she could cross it in pride and peace to be with him—her beloved Kano—and together they could pass back and forth through all eternity.

Sally put the pillow on the bed. Outside, the Great Gods raised their voices to salute her. The jagged light, the wind, the booming thunder all embraced her as she heaved herself onto George's bed, taking his place, with him lying sprawled and hapless, without dignity, below the level of her feet.

"You have worshiped the Little Gods," the Great Ones said, "but now, we have come to carry you across. Everything will be answered and set right now. Come, Saleh … come now …"

She slowly drew up the other blanket until it covered her breasts.

When dey fine me, let dem thee dat I done reclaimed my body an my privathy. De dignity dey tried ter take, I held. Not a one of dem evah had a thpeck of it … nevah … not a thingle one of dem …

"Come now, Saleh. This softness rising around you, this is all of us … the Little Gods and the Great Gods, come to carry you across …"

From the corner of her eye, the vision of Fulani heaven shifted dreamily around and spread itself out in front of and all about her. Now she could see the far end of the crystal bridge. At its near end stood Tenkaminen, her uncle the sorcerer. Her heart swelled as she saw his grave smile and remembered suddenly every moment and every word of his teachings.

Then she saw her mother and father. They had a large herd of cows and bulls and a beautiful hut. Beyond them, stretched to the horizon, lush green meadows for the cattle to graze, and the air rich with the singing of birds and warm with a rising sun. She was overcome with the smells of Tekrur: the cattle, the grasses, the flowers, the perfumes of its vast distances and its mysteries borne by the winds.

As her breath shortened, the vision grew clearer. Now she could see a figure on the bridge, crossing into the Fulani heaven. Her uncle lifted his arm to indicate the figure, and he smiled.

His smile flowed toward her like honey. She opened her mouth to receive it and, as it passed her tongue to her throat, she suddenly knew everything she had ever needed to know. Peace was all about her, like a loving gel holding her motionless, and she could see now that the figure approaching over the bridge was a man—dark, powerful, smiling.

Tenkaminen moved a little aside. The man stepped off the bridge onto the blessed earth of Fulani heaven, and she saw that it was he. As she had hoped, as she had believed, as she had deeply known he would—while the white years dragged endlessly on, caking her with their grime until she was liberated and free to rise—Kano had come for her.

He walked on strong, perfect legs, his heavenly body beautiful, ambient smells so sweet, the scene so perfect, that tears spilled down Sally's cheeks, heart-felt tears, which came easily now. Her breaths were very shallow and beginning to skip. The fleshy heart felt like a stone.

As the human body died away, she saw herself projected outward into the body of her youth, the body Kano knew and that knew him. She saw herself standing next to him, very close, where she could clearly see his radiant face and hear his voice, speaking to her in Senegalese. But she could not quite grasp the words. She was in the human body and the heavenly body at the same time.

She could see, standing there by Kano and looking back over her shoulder, a silver cord connecting her to the visible world. She took it up in her hands. It was like holding light. She laughed and looked at Kano. He nodded.

"Break it," he said in that sweet, deep voice—the voice of her wisdom and courage.

She felt somebody's breath stop. She pulled hard on the silver cord and saw it come loose from the body of an old slave woman, who was lying dead in a bed, floating above the body of a demon that was turning to ashes and blowing away in the strong wind. All around her and Kano, the gods' eyes flashed fire and their voices rang out with laughter while she greeted all her loved ones. And then, with her hand in Kano's, she turned and walked with him over the bridge of light into Asante heaven.

And, behind her, reflecting on the windows of the room where the old slave woman's body lay near the torn corpse of the old white man, another kind of fire cast its light across the plantation, as the wind-driven fire in the West Woods blazed hot and bright.

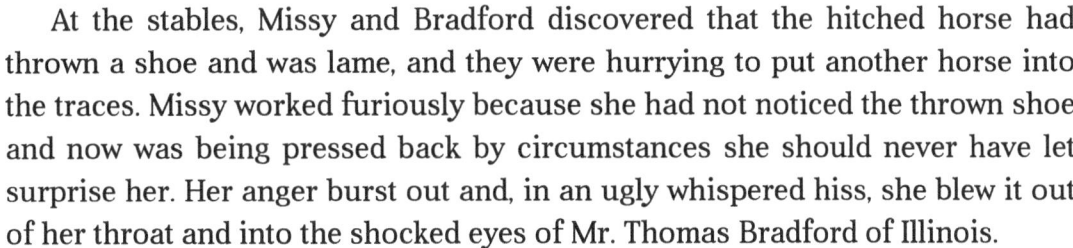

At the stables, Missy and Bradford discovered that the hitched horse had thrown a shoe and was lame, and they were hurrying to put another horse into the traces. Missy worked furiously because she had not noticed the thrown shoe and now was being pressed back by circumstances she should never have let surprise her. Her anger burst out and, in an ugly whispered hiss, she blew it out of her throat and into the shocked eyes of Mr. Thomas Bradford of Illinois.

And, though downstairs in the House swiftly vanished from Sally's awareness, she saw with her inner sight that a woman, whom she knew as her daughter, was coming through the open scullery door.

Upstairs, Peggy, who was not afraid of the thunder but was wakened by it, had lit her bedside lamp and was sitting up in bed, reading a book about happy children in a land of gardens, fountains and light, where no one ever died.

At 11:10 p.m., Young Sally walked swiftly, feeling renewed after so long a time trapped in a false old age. She had the knife out from under her skirt now, loving the look of its glitter under the bolts of light, yet wishing for rain.

She had never been baptized into the white man's Christianity but believed in it as a half of the cosmic truth, with the gods and ancestors of Tekrur being the rest. But, with the filling up, the two faiths had come together. The gods and ancestors and Jesus and his Father and the Holy Ghost were shining together everywhere she looked—even in the darkest places, even beyond the clouds—and were showing her every truth and guiding every action.

She wanted the heavy rain that was coming to be like a waterfall poured out from all the heavens. She would stand in it, take off her bloody dress and at last be baptized in the name of the Father and of the Son and of the Holy Ghost. The healing water would bathe her every wound, seep under her skin and touch her heart. How sweet it would be as all mysteries lifted gravely off, with the majesty of rising eagles, and her last puzzlements, her last fears, would be behind her.

Young Sally stopped on the path to the field row. A single drop of rain had touched her when, as by chance, she had lifted her face with her mouth slightly open. The drop had fallen on her tongue. It was such a holy touch that she spread wide her arms to receive the Christian Three feeling guided by the Fulani Great Ones.

Immediately, more drops fell. Young Sally's heart swelled. After the weeping, the whispering, the singing and then the filling up, now at last had come the culmination as it must have been planned all across human time.

She tucked the knife into a deep pocket and began unbuttoning her dress from top to bottom. She slipped out of the top half, wincing as the whip sores clinging to the cloth were disturbed, holding up the dress with one hand. Pain was a very different experience now. It no longer rang in her as purging or damnation but instead as a wink, a nudge, a giggle from the gods all around her.

"What a joke life is!" they told her, laughing in their beautiful, deep voices.

And suddenly, there Jesus was, standing on the path in front of her, Black Sulla's house visible just over his left shoulder. Jesus was in his church gown and white man's long hair with sparkling African eyes, golden brown skin and his smile.

And Jesus said, "Now yo jes do lak yo s'pose ter, girl, an git all dat holy work behine yo. Den me an all de blessed Fulani nigga gods an de Fathuh an de Holy Ghos gon fetch yo right up ter heaven wid us, an it gon be grander up dere den yo evah magine. Jes wait an see."

Then Jesus broke into a hearty laugh, stood out of her way and motioned Young Sally through, pointing right at the house of the blackbird, which she was going to make her meal.

The rain was wetting her bare flesh now, drumming on her more heavily with her every breath. She took out the knife, slit the upper half of the dress and tied the two ends tightly around her waist so it would not slip down as she walked. Then she set out again, smiling at Jesus as she passed him, her blessed knife back in its pocket, awaiting the holy moment, as the preachers said that Abraham's knife must have done in the long, long ago.

And Jesus said, "'Membuh now, don' try ter stab him in he troat, cause if'n yo be too slow or he too quick, he gon grab yo hand, take de knife, an den he be so mad he cut off yo nose an yo toes an yo tits an I don' know what all. But I does know dat, at de end, he gon gut yo out like a sow carcass. So yo membuh what I's tellin yo, an yo gon be jes fine."

"Yas, suh, Marse Jesus," Young Sally said.

The rain washed Young Sally's shoulders and breasts. She looked down her front and saw a very diverting thing. The rain was running off her nipples in small spouts, like drinking fountains for the Little Gods of the Fulani. Her heart, already touched by the Great Ones, seemed to glow.

Oh, she thought, *to nurse a sweet Little God stead of de snake Missy, who'd had her milk an now would suck de good of de whole white worl up her lady hole cause of de fool Little Marse Will. But tings be as dey be. An, in de fillin up, ev'ting be cancelled anyway an started agin. Dere cain't be no bad in de midst of all de good, even if de bad look real, lak sickness in a dream...*

Young Sally eased open Black Sulla's door just as a flash revealed the house's interior of solid oak table and chairs, an old leather easy chair by a stove, the rug and a white man's bed with a comforter. Snuggled in it, Black Sulla was asleep with just his huge, black head visible on a white man's pillow. Close by, she saw a little table with matches and a candle in a proper candlestick instead of, as she had once seen, in a knothole in a woodblock. She glided across the floor, leaving a water trail, her heart rising yet more as her hands found the matches in the dark and lit the candle.

"Whut?" said Black Sulla, lurching from sleep. "Who de *hell* ... Why, is dat yo, Young Sally?"

He quickly sat up, swung his legs over the bedside and stared at her. He slept naked. His short, powerful body, braced by his thick arms, was frightening.

Young Sally smiled, then broke out laughing. "It be Young Sally, sho nuf!"

Black Sulla blinked. "*Damn*, girl! Whut yo come roun heah fer, runnin in dis cold rain wid yo tits out? Crazy womens brings bad luck ter a man's house. Git on out now."

"Well, yes, I's nekkid at de top of me, but yo seen all dat plenty times befo."

"Dat when yo still had a brain in yo. Now yo ain't no bettah den a biddy hen. Yo brings bad luck now ev'ry place yo go. I says git on out, an I ain't lak ter say it agin!"

Black Sulla stood up. Young Sally gracefully bent to put the candle down, then straightened. And, as she did, it was as if she straightened up into sanity and solidity. There was a shift of her very life energy, so pronounced that Black Sulla could not miss it, though it registered on him only as the awareness that her breasts were suddenly attractive.

A little smile began to tug at the corners of his mouth. "Well, I reckon befo I toss yo out, I bettah know why yo come."

Young Sally smiled a courting smile, with a slight lowering of lashes over her hazel eyes, so beautiful in candlelight. The wounds on her face were not removed by this shining out of her sexual energy but made to glow with mystery. She was looking at Black Sulla's penis—the same large, thick penis she had seen many times before when it had rammed her as if she were not a living thing but a removable lug in a log of flesh.

Black Sulla sensed her, smelled her and his left-leaning penis slid like an opening telescope down his leg and lurched right, then came up like a man's arm, slowly gesturing threat.

He still a Calabar, still eatin babies ter please de gods, Young Sally said to herself in words her mother Sally had once spoken. *Men like dat are all prick. Take away dere prick an dey will go down lak dey be made of dust.*

"Why I come was ter see what I be seein lately," Young Sally said, her voice rising to be heard over the thunder, her glowing eyes still on his penis. "Womens dat once has Black Sulla cain't go back after dat."

Black Sulla smiled, showing his big gapped teeth. "Nothin ter go back ter, is dere, Young Sally?"

"No."

"Yo knows I always had me a yen fer yo, but yo high-yaller ways slapped me back."

"Dat was befo I know'd yo fer what yo is. *Really* know'd yo."

Black Sulla, softening, asked her, "How come yo ran roun actin crazy? How I know yo ain't still crazy but in a diff'rint way?"

"Why don' yo come see if my lady hole feel crazy?"

Suddenly her mother was in her brain: *Dat ugly nigga had me once, or tried. But I stuck a big needle right up he balls when he be leanin down on me, fixin ter shove it in me, an he jump a mile up an a mile off. An I said ter him, right dere an den, "Don' yo fo'get how I knew witching in Fulani times, an I kin witch now. I witch yo black ass right inter de grave. I witch a sickness on yo balls dat gobble up yo prick an belly until yo cain't walk or die. I a'ready put a sweat rag of yourn in a spirit hole dat I dug among de oak roots, an all I need ter do is ter blacken de water round dat stump wid half-burnt wood ter make a evil grow on yo. So don' yo come round heah anymo lest yo come ter kill me. An, if yo does kill me, den it be Young Sally dat pour in de water cause de hole done a'ready been witched. An if not her, den Missy."*

Young Sally had more than a needle to offer and a sweeter way of offering it. "Come on, now."

She could see Black Sulla's little flickers of caution and the rising of his man sap.

"No, yo come on heah to de bed. I likes womens on dey back." His grin was steady. But he was a wolf not sure of its prey, backed against its den, leery. "Let's see yo dress, Young Sally. Dat yo don' got nothin in yo pockets."

Young Sally laughed, throwing her head back and clapping her hands.

Lord Jesus said, "Yo doin jes right, girl. Dis fool gon come yo way befo yo done wid him."

I knows dat, Lawd, she thought. *He be too wicked ter live. An, if he daid, he stink up heaven. Hell's got its mouth open fer him. Ain't dat so?*

"Dat's so," Jesus said, laughing and bending down low to slap his knee, like old Uncle Silas did in her child days, when he was too old to work, and George allowed him to sit and smoke his pipe and amuse the children.

The rain slashed at the roof. This kind of storm usually came in late summer or fall, not spring. But Young Sally loved its seeming rage as matching a center in herself, opened by her singing. Again, the lurid glare of the lightning. The wind rattling Black Sulla's real glass windows.

"Come on now. I wants yo ter take me standin up. Young Marse Geo'ge do dat an git me likin it. Strong man lak yo kin make it good fer womens dat way ..."

In the end—despite his caution, his cupidity, smothered as she knew it would be because of the aura of her exaltation from the filling up—he carefully approached her. And it was easier than it ought to have been or anyone would have guessed.

They were the same height, so the prospect of having her standing up was especially attractive to Black Sulla. Drawn in by it, he lifted her dress hem. Young Sally spread her legs apart with a loud laugh and drove up into his genitals with her knife.

Jesus said, "Don' let him bide, girl. He lak a snake dat ain't been stepped on but once."

Yas, Lawd.

As Black Sulla screamed—a thing surprising to her, given his solidity and meanness—and seized her throat, she rammed the knife home again and again and again. Black Sulla still screamed, tried to knee her and pull her face into his bite, but the stabbing had hit the life centers so strongly that, in seconds, his knees buckled and he pitched down. A thunderclap and his crashing onto the floor sounded together, which Young Sally took as the agreement of the Great Ones.

"How de hell yo evah do dis ter me, you nasty bitch? How de hell …"

He lay almost motionless. She wondered if he were paralyzed somehow by her strikes. Or was he tempting her nearer to catch at her dress and her life?

Young Sally fetched the candle and looked down at him. No, it was not trickery. She could see the film in his eyes, making him blink. She had a sudden inspiration that made her laugh. She hawked and spit at him, an arrow to his forehead.

He blinked again. His voice was surprisingly weak. "I gon be all right, girl. Don' tink yo gots me down. I gits up strong bye 'n bye. Den I rip out yo tits from dey roots. Jes wait …"

Then she saw the spreading pool of blood. He lay on his belly, his head lifted, trying to push himself up with his big hands and failing, while out from under him spread the blood, richly red. Young Sally felt exalted, like a child who has dreamed of flying a kite and now has flown one. She spit again, hit him again. This time he shook his head, as at an impish brat.

His voice was still weak. "Dat jes silliness now, girl."

Then his head sank down onto the worn carpet. Young Sally went to Black Sulla's bed, sat down on it and watched. She heard the gods rejoicing. But she did not take her eyes off of Black Sulla. She could see his back moving ever so slightly with his breath. Then the movement was less. Then she watched very carefully for what seemed many minutes, and it did not move at all.

Jesus said, "Dat's right. He daid now. I see dat fool's soul tryin ter go upward but de air of heaven be too thick. He droppin back down inter hell. Oh, my, dat nigga kin see de little devils waitin on him down dere, an he be a'yellin as if a big dog done cotch he foot in its teeth." Jesus chuckled.

I thanks yo, Lawd. Yo sees whut I cain't.

"Go on now, an git yo dat taste of blackbird if yo's got a mind ter. Shave it off'n he pecker, so what he done yo wrong wit an drove yo down wit an broke yo spirit wit yo kin taste, an de powerfulness he done took away fum yo will all come back, besides all de powerfulness he gots his own sef."

Dat better den shavin he tongue, Lawd? For all de meanness he said ter me?

"Oh, my, yas! Yo don' b'long shavin dis nigga's tongue. Yo gits yo a tongue by 'n bye."

Yas, suh, Lawd.

Young Sally waited another little while, then approached the body, walking barefoot over the blood-soaked carpet, rolled the heavy corpse onto its back, pulled out the still-engorged penis and sliced a thin piece off the tip. Black Sulla's eyes were open, which startled Young Sally but did not deter her. She held up the little piece of flesh so that the gods and the Holy Trinity might see and be satisfied. Then she ate it, mindful of its terrible, writhing vibration as it touched her lips but dying slowly from the wounds her teeth had made as it snaked down inside her.

Leaving Black Sulla and his whole world behind her, and instantly forgetting it, Young Sally went out again into the driving rain, back toward the Big House.

The fire in the West Woods that had lit the sky was gone. The heavy rain following behind the display of the gods fell on a chastened world. Jesus stayed with Young Sally, but the Fulani Great Ones withdrew. Now the powers of the filling up ushered her along like a breeze at her back, promising the redemption of all Negroes through the sacred actions now laid out before her, like a clean altar cloth.

… *Might be,* she suddenly thought, *de gods—all de gods an trinities an woodland spirits an nature gods was what de fillin up be made of.*

… *Might be de fillin up be only de breathin of de secret hidden worl, fum de level below well water an bedrock, an way bove de highest, thinnest clouds.*

… *Might be dat I was breathin de spirit worl.*

Or the spirit world was breathing her.

1861

NORFOLK, VIRGINIA

Having got to the boatman's house and come down river to Norfolk, on this April morning Missy and Bradford set about finding the schedule of the packet boats to Baltimore. Bradford had suffered from severe anxiety the whole way for, as the alcohol left his blood, fear replaced it. He saw very clearly now that he was a white man helping a runaway Negro slave at the South—never mind that she didn't look very black. This was the second day of the war, which generations had predicted, and now his generation was obliged to fight.

The old man at the packet steamer office, white-haired and missing several teeth, wanted to talk about the war. He was a friendly and curious man and was passionate for the southern cause.

"Looks to me like the Yanks cain't dodge us now," he said firmly. "They're going to git their comeuppance." He looked searchingly at Bradford. "What do *you* say about it, sir?" He watched Bradford with a look that suggested he wanted an answer and an endorsement. "This is all folks is talkin' about. Where do *you* stand, sir?"

Missy had carefully instructed Bradford as they came down river in the boat paddled by the silent, free Negro. It had shocked Bradford when she brought out from her straw purse a dirtied little cloth bag full of gold coins (mostly, as far as he could tell, Federal twenty-dollar gold pieces), though Missy quickly closed the bag and put it away after paying the boatman, so he did not get a good look.

But he saw clearly enough how much she paid the squat, impassive black man, who only spoke to say his name—Isaiah—and to name the fare: one hundred dollars. Dear God, what an incredibly huge amount of money for a little boat trip! Bradford was astonished at how readily and unemotionally she had handed it over and at the fact that she had it to give in the first place. He wondered how a slave had accumulated so much, with seemingly a lot more remaining inside the soiled cloth bag. But Missy quickly took his mind off her money and focused it anew on the danger they were in.

"Thomas, you must remember at every moment that you are a southerner," she had whispered to him during the boat ride down the James River. "In Norfolk, the city will be mad with talk of war and of punishing the North. You must agree with all secessionists who speak to you and be joyful with them.

"If they suspect that you are a Yankee and assisting a valuable slave to escape, they will arrest you and put you in jail, give me a beating and send me home in chains to let the Leylands deal with me. Believe me. I would not live out the month." She was too valuable a slave for him to believe this, but somehow he could not speak. "And you, Thomas, if you are not hanged immediately, will be put in prison and not released unless the Yankees win the war. If they do not, you might as well die there, never seeing your wife or children or your home again."

Missy whispered this to him as they sailed down to Norfolk, the stolid Isaiah at the tiller in the rain and Missy sitting very close to Bradford under a leaking canopy. He could not quite accept this as the truth but was terrified by her words nonetheless.

It is very hard, Bradford thought miserably, *to discern any likelihood while in the grip of fear and alcohol.*

"I will do as you say. Don't worry," he answered in the strongest voice he could manage. "I do wonder, though, if things are really as dire as you suggest." He showed her the ghost of a smile, hoping to portray a devil-may-care attitude, which, he saw immediately, was impossible.

Missy's look grew stern. In the dim light, she seemed to draw into herself.

Her tone became impersonal. "Wonder all you like. I am telling you what you must do to save your life. If you are a fool and will not heed earnest advice, I cannot help it. But remember: It is two of us your stupidity will kill, not just one."

Hearing this, Bradford grew more fearful and was suddenly very angry at himself for attempting to be a hero when he was at heart a coward, and for being drawn into this entire nightmare by nothing more redeeming than lust and drunken delusion. He saw, belatedly, that he had been especially unwise in trusting Missy, who was no longer behaving with the sweetness that he had imagined was her true nature.

Apparently, she had skillfully duped him—a man who, in such a childlike way, had always trusted in the goodness of others. It would not at all surprise him if, at Philadelphia, she ditched him at the railway station, perhaps even managing to get hold of his wallet in the bargain. He wished that he was home with his wife, though she was a Baptist and a prude. At least she had never put him in danger of being hanged!

At the packet window, Bradford replied to the old ticket seller in what he hoped was a hearty tone, "Sir, I regret to say that I was born at the North. But, in recent years, I moved South, where I proudly remain. Once I have taken this slave to my brother in Baltimore, who has asked to borrow her to serve his ailing wife and care for his children, I will return home and join a regiment of volunteers to fight for the Confederacy."

This much Bradford had carefully rehearsed in his mind. What he was not prepared for was the old man's next question.

"And where *is* your home, sir?"

As Bradford stood speechless, staring at the man, Missy stepped diffidently forward.

"Oh, if'n yo might s'cuse me, suh," she said in a thick slave accent, her eyes cast down but then raised artlessly to meet the ticket seller's questioning look. "Dis heah be de kin'est marse in de whole Souf. We fum up by Charles City, dis side er Richmon, suh. Marse Thomas Bradford be a modes man, suh, but when Young Marse Geo'ge Leyland git poorly wid de consumshun, he write he blood cousin Marse Thomas, an he come down fum up in Penns'vayna to hep Young Marse Geo'ge run he terbacca farm."

"Pennsylvania, you say?" asked the agent, softening as Missy's eyes and smile won him over. "I thought you said you were from the South, sir."

Even though he had just told the man he was from the North, at this mention of Pennsylvania, Bradford looked stricken. He went numb and stared helplessly at Missy, who, seeing the look on his face, gave out a musical little laugh.

"See dere, suh! He don' wan me braggin on him. But Marse Thomas come down an hep out so good dat de niggas all take ter him strong. So Young Marse Geo'ge know he ain't got long ter live, an he know he son Little Marse Will be more wild den wise, so he want ter sell Marse Thomas Liberty Plantation, Miz Elizabeth's daddy's place dat come wif her in dey marriage.

"But dis marse went back up ter Penns'vanya where he be born'd fer a few yeahs, cause he know terbacca grow good up dere, an dat good farm lan be lots cheapuh den terbacca lan in Vuh-ginia. An sho nuff, he done good an he still do good. Dey uses free niggas up dere, but he lets dem sharecrop some good acres an so he don' pay dem nothin. Marse Thomas, he know dat up dere dey grows as good terbacca as dey grows anyplace. So now he gots him two good farms, suh—one Norf and one Souf, an deserve tree.

"But I tells him, suh," she went on, sounding like a cheerful gossip, "dat I don' wan ter go Norf to work on he place in Penns'vanya, up dere in ab'lition country where de Yankees try ter turn me agin my good marse. No, suh! War or no war, I'se stayin right heah at Liberty soon's I gits back fum hep'in Marse Thomas's big brothuh's wife in Baltimore, who gots tree chillens, an now she gots de scarlet fevuh an cain't do a lick of work or git out'n bed, neithuh one. But I be back. Yo jes see!" Again, Missy's lilting laugh rang out.

Seemingly charmed, the old man said, "Sir, you got you a damn likely nigger wench here. But I didn't know that George Leyland, Jr., had the consumption. Hell, I heard he was getting up a regiment of volunteers."

"Dat he be, suh," said Missy, completely assuming guidance of the discussion but now a sad tone emerging in her voice, while Bradford looked on with confusion. "But dat jes cause he a brave an good man, suh. He ain't gon be no mo able ter ride out wid dat reg'mint den a blind nigga. Cause when he ain't coughin, he sleepin."

Bradford, slowly becoming aware of the role he must play, though still feeling shaken, nodded. The agent let the subject drop.

But Bradford's spirits again plunged when the old man told him that the daily steam packet to Baltimore left at 7 a.m., and there would be no way of leaving town until tomorrow morning unless he took the cars to Richmond, then over to Baltimore. Of course, the railroad was out of the question because of the greater risk of being seen by many more people than on a little packet and, with that, a higher likelihood of being questioned and (Oh, may God forbid it!) arrested.

And the thought of a whole day's wandering about was nauseating. Pretending joy at the breaking out of this wicked, hideously inconvenient war. A night in a Norfolk hotel, where Missy would have to stay with other slaves in rude quarters in the basement, and where he would be obliged to pay for two rooms instead of one and could not dare advance even a single degree in his aim to seduce her.

"But is there no *other* way, sir?" he asked the old man. "My poor sister-in-law is so grievously ill and needs our help so desperately. I cannot bear to waste the time it would take to retrace our steps by the cars."

Despite his fear, Bradford was surprised and proud to hear himself say this since it bespoke a previously unknown ability to lie when cornered. His fanciful nature immediately suggested to him that he become a novelist, tell this story in a book and become wealthy. But this thought, fleeting and silly, was like a worm of good cheer in an otherwise huge and homogeneous apple of fear.

"Well," said the agent, as if pondering deeply. "Might be you could catch on with Cap'n Ross there."

Bradford and Missy both turned and saw a man in a seaman's jacket and cap, standing with one foot on a wooden railing, calmly smoking a pipe as he gazed out into the Chesapeake Bay. His face was tanned and weathered by years at sea, and there was a certain calmness about his stance, facial expression and person that was immediately reassuring.

"Cap'n Ross, you say?" Bradford asked the agent, his hopes rising.

"Yes, sir. Cap'n Ross Carle. He's got his Margaret Arabella in the shipyard, right across the river at Hampton. A clipper. Truth is, she's seen her day, but by God she can still fly.

"I've known Cap'n Ross for years. Seen the Margaret Arabella at least ten times before now. She throwed a lashing low on her for'ard top mast, and then the mast footing come loose. Good thing there weren't much wind out at sea when she done it. That spar swinging wild could of knocked a hole in her hull near the waterline the size of a kid goat. And, with even a moderate sea, she'd of gone down like water in a drain. But he got her in safe, and she's sailing out sound in a few hours."

"But will she sail to Baltimore?" Bradford asked. He could feel Missy, intense and barely breathing though looking cheerfully optimistic, close at his side.

"Better ask him. But I think so. He was bound there when he had to stop in here so's he could get a big crane to hold her mast while they repaired the footing and the spar."

Again, the two turned to regard Cap'n Ross. Still placidly smoking his pipe, he was now aware that he was the subject of their conversation and had turned a curious face toward them. Bradford, growing increasingly charmed by his new-found courage, immediately walked over and held out his hand, Missy following.

"Sir," he said, "I am informed that you are Cap'n Ross, whose clipper ship is in the Hampton shipyard for repairs."

Cap'n Ross smiled and took Bradford's hand. "You are right, sir. And you are ...?"

"I am Thomas Bradford of, uh, uh—"

"Liberty Plantation, suh," Missy quickly supplied. "Dis marse so use ter sayin he from Penns'vanya dat he keep fo'gettin he live half-Souf now." Missy laughed merrily, affection, respect and obedience all implied by the look in her eyes.

Bradford's face grew red. "She is right, sir, I fear," he said. "I am an absent-minded man." But his face once again showed alarm.

"Well, sir," said Cap'n Ross good-naturedly but looking the two of them over with some care, "as long as we never forget those who love us, though hastening to forget those who do not, we shall be all right." He pressed Bradford's hand warmly.

Again, Bradford was relieved by this emerging ability to lie once he had gotten started. He realized that, without Missy, he would likely be in jail now. But then he further realized that, without Missy, he would not be here in the first place!

"I was wondering, sir—Cap'n Carle—hearing that you are bound for Baltimore and sailing today, if you could accept passengers."

"Call me Cap'n Ross. That seems to suit me best." Again, his friendly smile. He had graying blonde hair and a beard that followed the line of his chin, omitting the upper lip, and carried that bit of extra weight that even a fit man past sixty could not avoid. "And, as to sailing with us, why I would be happy to have you as a guest! I rarely take passengers but, this being such a short sail, it would be an agreeable diversion for me—as well as, I presume, a convenience for you."

Both Bradford's and Missy's faces showed immediate relief.

"Sir," Bradford said, his strong feelings evident, "a convenience indeed. My sister-in-law lies ill, and I am hastening with this girl to assist her and her family of children."

"Well, then," said Cap'n Ross, "you are as kind as you look. And, as it happens, you couldn't have found a ship that could get you there sooner than the Margaret Arabella. Have you all your luggage?"

"Yes, sir. We are traveling light."

"Well, then. This must be a meeting blessed by heaven. For I was just getting ready to take the ferry across to my ship. She's repaired. I've inspected her, and she's just now taking on fresh water. We'll sail in less than two hours when the tide starts to ebb."

"But, of course, you will let me pay you, sir," said Bradford, now aware of the surge of gratitude in his bosom for this wonderful stroke of good luck.

"Pay me with your enjoyment of the trip, sir. I've a small cabin for you and a space 'tween decks for the colored girl. If we weigh anchor at two this afternoon, we'll be up the Patapsco River and dropping anchor at Baltimore by five tomorrow morning. And, regarding the cost: As I age, sir, I find that my need to be of service to my fellows grows, whilst my need for more money declines."

Bradford heard Missy's sudden intake of breath. He too was surprised, both at the stated speed of the ship and at its captain's generosity.

"*Five tomorrow!*" Bradford cried. "But how can we travel as swiftly as that? I confess that I am astonished."

Cap'n Ross smiled broadly. His look clearly showed his affection for and pride in his ship. "Suppose I tell you once we're underway? We have a good weather situation just now to aid us. Come, let us take the ferry across and board the ship. Once we're under sail and out in the Chesapeake, I'll explain what I mean."

1861

THE MARGARET ARABELLA

The ferry was a little steamer that cast off her mooring line on the even hour of this April day, and the crossing was quickly made. As they walked toward the slip where the Margaret Arabella was moored, Bradford (who knew little about ships) and Missy (who knew nothing) were both taken by the sharp bow, narrow beam and swept-back masts of the classic clipper ship, past her heyday now but still a beauty to behold. They came up the gangway and the crew shouted out greetings to their captain and evidenced (in other ways) their approval of Missy.

Cap'n Ross said, "She is nine hundred and fifty tons, so she's not the biggest clipper. And she's old and getting tired. I can't keep her at sea much longer. As it is, the boys spend more time aloft than they do on deck, replacing blocks and lines in her rigging. She's wearing out, Mr. Bradford.

"But I've sailed her for twenty-five years now, and they're twenty-five years I'll be grateful for as long as I live. I'm a sailor and always have been, since I was old enough to ship on a merchantman. I can appreciate a good ship! And, by God, sir, she can still fly, even fully laded as she is now and with a sag in her sheer. When she's got the wind, there isn't a steamer yet made that can beat her."

As Cap'n Ross spoke, crewmen came and took away their few belongings. Missy was led below decks while Bradford stayed topside on the quarterdeck, watching the captain direct the final preparations for casting off.

Soon, they were out in the bay. As Bradford witnessed the hoisting of the mainsail, and the tight, quick response of the Margaret Arabella to the wind, he looked down at the water and saw the bow begin to slice through the light chop and could actually feel underfoot the acceleration of the beautiful, old ship through the sea.

A great sense of liberation took hold of him. He felt immensely grateful to God for this deliverance and the seemingly divine intercession of a friendly, generous sea captain at just the needed moment. He now again felt that helping Missy was the right thing to have done; began to believe—as Norfolk and the brute Leylands fell swiftly away behind their wake, and the horizon of the great northern end of the bay arose before them—that they now were safe, that all was well, that all of his unkind perceptions of Missy were only the result of his tensions and fears and that Philadelphia was once again a shining hope.

After his usual fashion, he cast his romantic mind forward. He reclaimed his heroic stature, seeing it now as one that could only grow as he lived out his years, telling his story (well, *most* of it) to succeeding generations.

On deck, his spirits continued to soar with the still freshening wind. The marvelous sea air, streaming over him, felt renewing. This old captain was as fine a man as God in his great mercy had ever made. And, as likely as not, he would set a quite adequate table for Bradford to enjoy, while Missy too would surely be appropriately served. He tried not to think of her alone 'tween decks and, after a very short period of mild disquiet, was successful. Every passing minute out of the Hampton shipyard elevated his spirits more.

He turned to Cap'n Ross and said, "I cannot tell you how I appreciate what you are doing. You will never know how much it means."

The old sailor turned to him with a smile. "Oh, I think I *do* understand. You see, I'm from Ohio. Lake Erie was the first good-sized bit of water I ever saw. It made me long to see the ocean. Once I did, I left the farm life behind for good. But, the thing is, Ohio's strong abolition country. I was raised up to hate slavery. If I were to want to help that little girl you're with get North, I reckon I could do it pretty smooth. I've been South as much as I've been North, you see."

Here, Cap'n Ross paused and looked ruefully at Bradford. "But, on the other hand," he continued, "I don't suppose that's been *your* experience!" Cap'n Ross broke out in a hearty laugh. "You're a tenderfoot, if I ever saw one. Why, if you'd taken that little slave girl on a packet, those southern boys would have had your hide nailed to a bulwark before you'd ever raised the Patapsco River! I never saw a man who looked and acted less southern than you in my whole long life. So, I'm grateful that it was me you met and not somebody else."

Bradford was staggered. "My God! You *know!*"

Cap'n Ross laughed again. He seemed both amused and impressed. "Well, son, what I'm trying to tell you is that you might as well have been wearing a sign."

Bradford felt defensive as well as terribly exposed. "But the ticket agent. We *fooled* him!"

"Who? Old Jim Conway? Hell, he's as abolitionist as I am. Why do you think he steered you to me?"

"Oh, dear God," Bradford said, feeling sick.

"Well, don't let it get you down. We've got a clear sail. You can rest up overnight, and tomorrow you'll just be in Baltimore long enough to rent a horse and buggy, and slip across into Pennsylvania by a back road. Just go on up northwest toward this little town of Lineboro. It's maybe fifty mile or so. It'll be dark and late when you get there.

"Don't go into town. Just leave the rig in the woods, where somebody's bound to find it the next day, and cross the state line on foot. You'll go into the trees in Maryland and come out in Pennsylvania. There'll probably be a fence right on the line, but maybe not.

"Anyway, once you're in Pennsylvania, all you got to do is get up to York and take the cars wherever you want to go. I don't think anybody up North is going to be worrying about the Fugitive Slave Law anymore. Not with this war."

"Fugitive Slave Law?" Bradford asked. He had heard of it but had no idea what it actually meant. And, for some reason, he had thought that, once in Baltimore, everything would be easy, even automatic, and the way would lie open to Philadelphia—just how, he had no idea—but certainly he had not thought of a night ride in a buggy and a furtive crossing of the border in pitch black woods with a Negro woman at his side.

"Well, yes, the slavers got that law passed a while back. They were sick of slaves getting away to the North and the northern states being under no obligation to send them back. So, when the law passed, the northern states had to send back any Negro that a white man could prove ownership of. The slavers just sent their ruffians North with ownership papers, and they brought back the blacks by the cartload. You didn't know about this?"

Bradford looked pale. "Yes, sir. I heard of it. It never concerned me directly, you see. I have never known a Negro personally." He hesitated, and then continued. "Well, I have employed a few, but that was different."

"But you met this one and decided to help her?"

"I—yes, I think you could say that."

"She's a beautiful woman. But she's black. Not real black, I grant you, but anybody who don't have both eyes shut can tell which she is. You wasn't counting on her passing, was you?"

"I—I don't know. I don't know what I thought."

"Well, as I say, you're a greenhorn. But maybe it's just as well. You won't out-smart yourself. But if I were you, I'd let the girl take the lead. She's intelligent. Knows what she's doing. All you got to do is just look as white and mean as you can, be unfriendly and stiff-necked, so folks won't want to talk to you, and you'll get through Baltimore fine."

Cap'n Ross put a comforting hand on Bradford's shoulder. "You're a brave man, sir. Nobody can ever say otherwise after this. You'll get through. I know you will. But don't ask anybody how to get to Lineboro. That's as good as telling them what you're about.

"Go over to the railroad station. They have a big map there, showing the rail lines. It also shows the roads. It's an easy drive and pretty straight. The roads might be muddy because of the rain. Might slow you down some. But that's all. Late tomorrow night, you'll be in Pennsylvania. Then, hire a farm boy to drive you in his wagon up to York, and you can eat your dinner there and take the cars when you're done."

Bradford nodded, trying not to be overwhelmed. But the conversation had grounded him with a crash after so very recently soaring at the heights of gratitude and fancy.

Cap'n Ross, seeing his turmoil, said, to divert his attention, "I told you that I'd explain once we got underway how good a shape we're in weather-wise. Well, the fact is that the Norther, which blew through last night and this morning, has veered to the southwest. I'd bet my shoes and shirt that the wind'll hold steady at twelve to fifteen knots for at least our leg to Baltimore.

"This is a sweet reach we're in now. No need to beat back and forth across the bay with a wind like this. These are pretty near perfect conditions. Maybe you and the girl coming aboard brought us luck! I will tell you one thing: This kind of weather, with everything about it as kind on the heart as sunshine on Easter, is one of the great rewards for a life of sailing to sea and tasting my share of hard times and frustration. On other nights to come, when we're shipping thirty-foot seas, I'll remember this night and be grateful."

Before dawn the next morning, they sailed up the Patapsco River and passed Fort Carol to starboard, whose construction had been the work of a young Federal army engineer named Robert E. Lee. Ahead, they could see the lanterns on the rails of the ships in Baltimore's crowded harbor. For the first time since the boarding, Missy came up on deck. She looked pale and tight-lipped.

"What's the matter?" Bradford asked her. Her hard face and noticeable dishevelment alarmed him.

At first, she did not reply but then said, "The matter is that I am black, and the sailors said I could not be on deck while we were under sail because 'Negroes are not permitted liberty of the ship.' But I noticed that they all thought they had liberty of me."

"I am sorry," Bradford said, shocked by her disclosure. "I don't know what to say. Cap'n Ross is abolitionist. He told me …"

But Missy did not reply as he thought she might by saying, "Oh, it is not your fault, dear Thomas." Instead, she looked at him, her eyes steely. "*You* are sorry? Well, so am I!" She turned her gaze out to the dark river and was silent. Then: "One day soon, they will be sorry too. Sorrier than they have ever been before."

Bradford chose not to notice this remark. As the boarding ramp touched down on the dock, he took Missy's arm, again thanked Cap'n Ross and started across the gangway.

Missy snatched her arm free and sent Bradford an angry look. "You don't *escort* a Negro woman, you damned fool! You let her *trail* you."

1861

BALIMORE, MARYLAND

The sun was coming up on this April morning, and a restaurant they passed was just opening its doors. They went in and had breakfast, with Bradford sitting at a table and Missy being sent into the kitchen.

The waiter gave Bradford some bad news. "Well, sir, I guess you've heard. Some of the niggers are trying to get North. Guess they figure our minds are on the war now. Leave it to niggers to light out just when you need 'em most.

"Well, they won't get far. The patrols are doubled out in the country, and they're riding all night long. There probably ain't a white man in Maryland who won't be willing to help out keeping order. Cain't jest open the borders like a hog pen and let 'em all run out to wallow. Besides, while you're letting the niggers out, you're maybe letting the Yankees in!"

This news plunged Bradford into gloom. Walking out of the restaurant, he again envisioned jail and death at the hands of the slavers. Again, he hesitated, temporized, and Missy had to hide her disgust at her treatment in the kitchen and to talk long and earnestly to get him to continue with their plan.

He finally agreed, but Missy could see from his pale face and shifty eyes that his courage was leaving him, even as sobriety had reclaimed him. She realized that she had to be prepared to take full governance of him should an emergency arise, which, being an unsentimental realist, she was nearly certain it would.

Following the directions given them by a waiter, they found a stable. Bradford hired a rig, lied about why he wanted it and when he would return it, and all but swallowed his tongue at hearing the size of the deposit he was obliged to leave to secure it—which, of course, was now *lost money*. He wanted to argue the amount but realized that would be most unwise since it would likely expose them to deeper investigation.

They mounted the buggy. Bradford listened impatiently to the hostler's long-winded instructions about the virtues and peculiarities of the mare—Robin—that stood quietly in the traces. Then they set off, headed for the train station in the clear, humid morning through the streets of Baltimore, where the gas lamps were being turned off by men carrying ladders.

Fatigue and anxiety seized Bradford again, but he said to himself, *After today, I shall worry no more. And then I shall have my reward.*

At the railway station, he studied the map until he was sure of his way, with Missy standing by, looking stupid but mildly interested. In the warming sun, the roads were drying nicely, and again Bradford's brooding thoughts lightened. He turned to Missy and smiled.

She looked at him expressionlessly for a moment. Then, as if suddenly recollecting something, she smiled back.

1861

PINEWOOD PLANTATION, VIRGINIA

Up the stairs—with her treasured knife back in her pocket, her soaked dress clinging to her body and her breasts still bare—crept Young Sally, mirth music rising inside her like chanting. Oh, the sweetness of all creation, when creation can be added to or taken away from! When the whip of power has passed into the brown hand of woman, man's weakness and his victim ... Fulani blood in clamorous celebration and no longer gelled in its curdled lake of the mind by its leakage from the thousands upon thousands of the dead ...

At the North Hall was Elizabeth and Young George's room, though usually he was at the cabin in the West Woods. But tonight, Young Sally was sure he would be here, though he had stopped telling her things like this. Elizabeth was the mistress whom the slaves knew had long had her legs around Wilkenson, the overseer. They were all pleased to keep Young George in the dark about it. And Elizabeth, though erratic, was mostly kind now and Wilkenson, as always, good-natured and fair.

Young Sally walked to the far end of the hall, next to the wicked room where Young George had first led her, whispered, tricked and pawed her, sung of love, given her gold and jammed himself into her dryness, proclaiming their coupling sweet and she adorable. That same room, where she had wept on the bed and soiled the spread with her blood while he cooed ...

Young Sally thought, *Lawd, sho'ly I kin cut dis one's tongue since he poison de worl wid it.*

And Jesus replied, "Course yo kin, girl. What yo tink? Hogs an toads be closer to God den him. Dis one gon fall ter hell so fast dat he punch a hole in hell's cellar. De blackbird, he done he wickedness wid he pecker. But dis one, it jes as much wid he tongue."

Passing Peggy's room, Young Sally saw a pale aureole of light around the ill-fitting old door and felt a pang that the little girl, who had never in her life harmed a slave, lay awake. Was she a part of the creation that needed to be taken away? In the great rearranging, was her place in the world to be given up in favor of another, more deserving one?

The Lord said, "Girl, don' yo be killin no chile, even if she done pissed on yo haid, which dis chile ain't. She sweet lak summer tea, sho nuf. Leave her be an jes go on bout yo biniss."

Yas, Lawd.

Young Sally paused to listen at Young George's door. She heard the bed making a familiar squeak and clank as Young George was having intercourse with Elizabeth. His grunts and incoherent effusions poured out under the door, but Elizabeth was silent, so Young Sally could not tell who the woman was. Perhaps it was Cordelia. Perhaps even the pig's own piglet—the slut Missy—for where evil is done without effort, as if it were the grinding clockwork of life, there can exist no limits to wrong.

Young George's panting, wordless grunts were as familiar to Young Sally as his smell. Once, in a life lived as another woman, she had liked and welcomed him in his every grossness. Now, she wished that his breath was a graspable thing whose life she could reach for down his throat.

Young Sally tapped at the door. The squeaking and clanking abruptly stopped. There was a silence. Then, "Who is it?"

Young Sally tried the door and, of course, it opened. On this night, when the gods' love lubricated every lock, and Jesus stood by her side giving direction, how could it not?

The door swung slowly inward. The rustle of Young George dismounting and Elizabeth pulling the covers over her nakedness came to Young Sally's ears. And, in the glow of an oil lamp, there was revealed to her the angry face of Young George and the pale, agitated face of Elizabeth. At the same time, hers was revealed to them.

Young Sally heard Elizabeth's sharp intake of breath. Young George pulled his nightshirt down over his erection as he leaped off the bed.

"Now just what in the goddamn hell are you doing in this *house*?" he shouted.

Elizabeth murmured, "Just ask her to leave. Don't upset her. You know she's not in her right mind. Go down and see her out. The scullery door must have been left unlocked."

But Young George ignored his wife and, his voice still raised, cried, "And how did you get *in* here? Who let you in? Did you break a *window*?"

He took a menacing step toward Young Sally, who burst out laughing.

Jesus said, "If'n yo keeps up laughin, he gon strut right ovah heah an give yo hair a shake. But he ain't lak Black Sulla. Dis one don' even magine dat yo would do nothin ter him. Dis one yo kin jam de knife right at he throat. An, if'n yo miss, he won' do nothin but blink, an de second try yo kin kill him easy …"

Yas, suh, Lawd.

"Suh, I come ter tell yo dat some of de niggas in the House row be real sick."

As soon as she said it, Young Sally laughed again—a robust theater laugh that trailed little chuckles after it.

It sounded so strange that Elizabeth felt a chill. Young George held back from whatever chastisement he intended and simply stared at Young Sally. And, while he hesitated, she—with a grotesque little hop, as if skipping rope, and the laugh funneling into a loud shouting "Ha!"—pulled out her knife, drawing back her hand that was holding the blade, like an archer with an arrow on a drawn bowstring.

Then, in a split second, she was ramming home the knife, sharp edge down, as cleanly through Young George's throat as if she had practiced the move under the eye of a dancing master. At the same moment, Elizabeth screamed—a long, grating scream, like the sudden turning of a rusted gin.

At once, Young Sally felt sucked up into demonic anger by that scream, and Jesus tried to interfere but she shushed him hard. She began to saw madly at Young George's neck with her sharp knife, like a demented baker with a new loaf, clear down to the bone notch below his Adam's apple.

And, his voice box instantly maimed, only his eyes and wide-open mouth soundlessly begged and cursed her until, in seconds, he staggered at her, then dropped to his knees and fell forward, out the doorway into the hall, where Peggy, who had come out of her room, saw him land and lie still, the knife still in him. Peggy could not see Young Sally's face but had recognized her voice, and she knew it was her mother who had screamed and was screaming again now.

That screaming maddened Young Sally and undid every plan. She snatched the knife out of Young George's throat, making his head twitch as if in irritation, then glanced down the hall and saw the child. A keening sigh came out of Peggy and rose in pitch and loudness—a child soprano tuning her voice, which blended, a harmonic, with her mother's. Young Sally now felt battered by her anger, as if it stood outside her but was connected, another woman's screams suddenly grafted to her gut.

In this turbulence, things wore a deep red tinge and everything was slow. Young Sally's body felt drugged with a tension that turned her flesh to cords, which screeched with the strain, as if she had drunk snake venom stirred up in stump water, and the devil had whispered in her ear that he loved her.

For a moment, she could seem to see the anger—a red tornado, squashed down to a small size with its power intensified a thousand times. And, when she realized that she must take it inside her, it was a sexual moment, a mating with death, an opening of her mouth to the frenzy and history and madness of slavery, loose in the world and waking her insides to their highest duty, with a surge as strong as if from a swallowed galvanic wire.

"Oh, Miz Elizabeth," said a madwoman's voice, Young Sally a puppet on that woman's lap. "Oh, Miz Elizabeth. Dey ain't no hope no mo now. Yo gots ter go wit yo man, dat's de law. I kin see dat plain as yo face. Difference be he gon sink down ter hell, but yo lak to rise up an kiss de lips of de Lawd Jesus ... jes lak in de fillin up. In de fillin up, ev'ry langwich spoke be heavenly tongues, an holy fire gon rest on yo haid. Fire ... yas'm, it gon rest on yo haid ..."

Then, at the same moment that Young Sally leaped at the bed, Elizabeth rolled off its far side, still screaming but now in words. "Young Sally! *Don't!* I'll free you ... you and Missy ... free you today ... *tonight* ... give you a thousand dollars ... a freedom paper ... take you North myself ... Young Sally! *No! NO!*"

Elizabeth's voice shot up into hysteria, and words became tumbled and queer. From the direction of the hallway, Peggy screamed again, but the sound had dimmed as she flew downstairs, toward the scullery door and the House slave row, where she could find Decatur and other slaves and help.

Young Sally, following the terrorized, naked Elizabeth's every shift and feint, the bloody knife held out like a gift, said quietly, "I don gots my freedom already, Miz Elizabeth."

And she slashed at her with a wide, disciplined swing that caught the nipple of Elizabeth's left breast and took it cleanly off.

Abruptly, Elizabeth stopped screaming, stopped running, looked down in paralyzed disbelief at the blood leaking from her breast. She looked up at Young Sally as at a harpy who was trailing hell smoke and coming straight from the netherworld to eat her flesh.

In that split second, Young Sally had sprung forward, seized Elizabeth by her lovely blonde hair and made powerful slamming stabs in the belly, the thigh, the genitals, the chest and the belly again, so fast that her hand was a blur. And Elizabeth, whining and weeping, slumped down.

Young Sally jumped onto her naked body, straddling very tightly with her comely brown knees Elizabeth's pretty flesh, holding the knife in both hands now. Elizabeth's glazing eyes watched the knife brought down on her nose and cheeks and mouth, both women grunting oddly for the first two blows, then Elizabeth seized by silence, and only Young Sally's passionate, breathy sobs and the squish of the deep-reaching stabs making a fugue in the mysterious and awful music of it.

For a time, Young Sally sat still, not moving a muscle, rapt in a dream or a memory or a trance. She smelled the spilt blood, felt it slippery on her knees and hands and nodded, as to God (the referee of all contests) and Jesus (the book-keeper of heaven).

Jesus said, "Yo done good, girl. Sho nuf, Miz Elizabeth gone straight ter heaven an dat marse drop heavy as de niggas' tears down ter hell. An dat Black Sulla, dey a'ready hired him on down dere. He gon work his way clean out'n hell befo de Judgemint. An right now, he jes be a'waitin fer dat marse wid a pitchfork de size of a young apple tree. An he gon keep up whompin dat pitchfork inter dat marse's belly till kingdom come. Yas, ma'am!" Jesus laughed a merry, contented laugh and looked tenderly at Young Sally. "Now yo jes do de res lak yo s'pose ter, li'l darlin. An, befo de nex sunrise, yo an me gon be tergetha in heaven, a'standing at the right han of de Fathuh. Me an him, we jes a'waitin fer yo ter finish up … dat's all."

Young Sally sat with her light brown flesh touching the cooling skin of Elizabeth. The anger that had bitten into her was drawing back now, its powers spent, an emptied bucket falling back into a well …

Yas, Lawd.

Young Sally got slowly to her feet and went out to the sprawled corpse of Young George, remembering her right to the sacred meal. She bent over his dead face pressed on its side into the carpet. She did not need to turn him but instead pinched his tongue with her fingernails, and pulled it out far enough to cut off a piece as big as the one the white demon had cut from her mother's tongue in the long ago.

She put the piece of Young George's tongue in her mouth. Immediately, her life's energy slumped as she tasted in the tongue she chewed and swallowed its owner's kisses and remembered promises. She stayed forlorn only a minute. Then she straightened up and went slowly down the stairs, leaving behind the knife.

In the parlor, she took the large oil lamp from its oak stand and poured out its contents on the drapes and carpets until it was empty. Then, in Young George's study, she took another, smaller lamp and did the same on his desk and chair. She slipped out of her wet dress, yanked down a curtain and enfolded herself in it. The rest of the coal oil she poured onto herself, wetting the curtain material and soaking her long brown hair.

Don' mattuh dat de rain still fallin outside, Lawd. In heah, de fire gon rise up so hot dat nothin lak to stop it.

"Dat's right, darlin," Jesus said. "Take de match off'n de daid marse's desk now. Retch out yo hans ter Jesus, honey. Come git up on Jesus's lap. Jes strike dat match an den crawl up on Jesus's lap, jes lak on yo papa's, an Jesus will lift yo right on up. All de Fulani gods is heah, waitin on yo too. Yo mama's heah. An yo righteous true white papa. Dey ain't no culluh in heaven, honey. Ain't no sufferin. Ain't no misery. Ev'ting be sweet up heah, darlin. Jes drop dat match an come on an git up on Jesus's lap."

Yas, suh. I gots no place else ter go.

Young Sally struck the match. Instantly, the curtain material and her hair burst into flame. The fire dashed like running, red lightning through both rooms, scooping them into itself. The pain so surprised Young Sally that, without meaning to, she screamed. The fire roared about her ears like a live thing that knew her.

In the far distance, she heard Decatur's voice calling out. It seemed to her, as she gasped and breathed brimstone between screams, that he must be crying, for his voice was thick and agitated and grieving.

"Young Sally! Where yo at? Don' be startin no fire, Young Sally! I kin *smell* it! Put it out, girl! Don' be a damn fool now! *Young Sally!*"

She pitied Decatur even as she could feel her lungs crisping and her eyes searing. And then all the world's pain came to rest on her and breathed her as she breathed it …

As she fell, she realized that at last the filling up was complete. Everything had become transparent though she was blinded. She could see, standing in a cove of peace just beyond her reach, Jesus smiling at her with his arms out. The last thing she knew of body and earth and pain was holding her arms out to him.

But then there descended on her a moment of beautiful, tender darkness, like praying in the slave balcony of the white man's church. Suddenly, she was in the rising up—flexed, bowed backwards, as she had been when her papa would pick her up with his sacred hand in the small of her back, and she would rise as on the wind with legs and arms dangling, laughing with the joy of the effortless magical rising ...

Decatur, slave voices, fire, sound, fading. A stopping now, like the sweet gearing down of the entire world, pouring out love at her feet.

She opened the eyes of her spirit body and, as she did, a spirit sun from before time and after suffering rose in her belly. There burst from her its light. Her earth-self wanted to weep, but her spirit body became joy, melted into the arms of the Lord Jesus, who was sitting in a sweet, brown rocking chair, stroking and kissing her hair, just as beloved Papa had done.

"You are home, my darling girl ... my sweet Young Sally," Jesus said in the voice of her father. "You are home now."

And, around her body, Decatur and a swiftly growing band of slaves beat at the flames with pillows and blankets, poured buckets of water on her and on the wide-flung fire, gradually shoving it back into its seed. Then, the rooms behind them, smoking in ruin, the slaves slowly, fearfully began to mount the staircase.

1861

BALTIMORE, MARYLAND

No sooner had he rented the buggy and joined the April morning rush of jubilant, war-mad people onto the streets of Baltimore City than Thomas Bradford's courage deserted him again, and he knew that this was not the time to cross through the frenzied town from wharf to farms with a slave at his side. He did not know what might happen and rapidly projected many scenes, all of them dire, and so told Missy that they must withdraw until dark.

Missy argued. "Why hide now, when success lies so close at hand? Just make for Lineboro—you know the proper roads now. What makes you so faint of heart? What could possibly happen? Why do you think anybody would notice a man and his slave woman? Simply drive on, for the love of God!"

But Bradford said, logic persuading him, "Town is one thing; the country another. Out there, they will know us for strangers and see a white man they do not recognize, driving a colored woman toward the state line. Do you really think that would go unremarked or unchallenged? We are in the viper's nest now. Shall I let your impatience get me stung-bitten? Not on your life!"

So, despite that, she continued to argue. Bradford drove to a nearby hotel, arranged to have the buggy and horse stabled, got a room for Missy in the hotel's basement and another for himself on the fourth and top floor, from the window of which he could look out upon the turbulent city, hear the rowdy cries of drunken secessionists and be grateful that he had obeyed his instincts and gotten out of their way.

Eventually, he had a meal sent up and authorized one for Missy, and also ordered a quart of brandy, which pacified and comforted him as he steadily worked through it, feeling again the courage and self-satisfaction that had the day before attended the deeper drinking of it. At about noon, he fell asleep and slept until dark, when the discreet knocking of a bellman got him up to be informed that his slave woman had fallen ill and was sending for him.

Seeing the message for what it was—a sign from the girl that she was impatient to leave—he arose, finished his bottle, washed his face, picked up his valise and went down to the lobby. Missy, looking peaked and carrying with her, beside her straw bag, another larger package wrapped in brown paper, awaited him.

Anyone watching this scene saw her greet him with a wan smile and a curtsey, observed her speak a few words to him in an undertone and witnessed his nod and immediate exit out the back door to the stable yard with the girl following. To such an observer, she must have seemed as respectful and compliant a slave as had ever existed.

Earlier, upon arrival, Missy had sat in her tiny basement room, pondering. Since things were not unfolding as she wished, she tried to think of ways she could turn matters to her advantage.

Presently she went out and found one of the hotel's Negro laundresses. Missy had a whispered, intense conversation with her, gave her a double eagle, asked the woman to repeat back to her what she wanted.

Missy said, still in a whisper, "Yo kin keep de monies yo don' spend. Dat be a good size pile, we bof knows dat. An I trusts yo ter hep a culluh'd sistah. But jes membuh dat, if yo speaks bout it ter anybody, I gon' witch yo ass into de shittin sickness, an yo won' git ovah it til death lift yo up. Yo unnerstans dat, don' yo, girl?"

The woman—an older, stout, free Negro—nodded. She was fascinated and frightened by the burning look in this almost-white woman's dark eyes, in which she could find neither softness nor compassion. She did not doubt that this comely woman had witching powers, for she knew that the power always carries fear with it by which it makes itself known. And the laundress felt fear very, very strongly.

"Yas, I unnerstans. I be back ter yo room in a hour. Dis money be a god's blessin on me. Sho nuf, I ain't gon say nothin ter nobody, an dats a fack."

In less than an hour, Missy took the articles the woman had bought for her into her hands one by one and examined them carefully. Then she nodded.

"Dat's good. Yo done good. We be leavin at dark. I don' wants ter see yo or hear nothin more bout yo fum now til den. Jes lookie here." Missy held out to the washerwoman a blue-and-white checked kerchief.

The woman's eyes widened. "Where yo git dat, girl?" There was both fear and irritation in her voice.

"It be yo's?" Missy smiled but not reassuringly.

"Yo knows it be. Now where did yo git it fum?"

"Dat ain't a bit of yo biniss. But jes look close heah. What yo see?"

"Dat … dat's blood. Dat dere's blood, ain't it?" Queasiness and terror showed on her wide, genial face. "What fer yo puts blood on my kerchief?"

"Ter show yo I kin do it. Now yo listen. Dis heah kerchief's already witched. Ain't nobody kin take off de witchin but me. I fin out yo done blabbed yo mouf an inside three days yo gon be shittin out yo own guts on a bed o' pain. An in four, yo gon be plungin down ter de demon swamp, an yo jes bettah hope Jesus kin cotch yo afore yo goes clear on down. Now yo tell me straight out: Has yo told anybody bout me an what I aks yo ter do?"

"No'm," said the older woman, gone grim and tense. Her eyes were diffident, her body showing surrender.

"All right, den. But jes membah whut gon happen ter yo if'n yo lyin. Yo gon puke an shit an blaspheme an cry. An it won' none of it do yo even de littlest good. Yo gon stink so bad dat ev'body gon know yo been witched ter hell. Dey won' even put yo in de graveyard wit de othuh niggas. Yo gon be smelly daid an buried off lone under rocks, like a lather'd up dog. Now go on bout yo biniss, an be grateful fer de moneys yo gots, cause I kin witch dat away too."

After the frightened laundress left, Missy looked over her purchases again. Then she lay down to sleep, awaiting the coming of night.

It was nine o'clock by the time they drove out into the quieting streets, emptied by a strong new fall of rain. The buggy's top was up. Bradford had asked Missy to drive, but she convinced him that a real slave owner would not let a female slave take the reins unless he was ill or elderly, so he continued on. The gaslights were lit, their bright, stark light showing the slanting rain.

The mud streets were puddling fast. Bradford dreaded the drive along country roads where to sink and stick was, in his mind, to die. Yet the brandy gentled his own fearful thoughts, and Missy's mysterious scent reminded him of her promises. So, trusting for the moment in both the seen and the unseen, he drove toward the west ... to "freedom."

But, only a few blocks into the journey, directly in a pool of streetlight, a man leaped out of the shadows and seized the mare's bridle, hauling her to a stop.

"Here now!" the man cried. "What are you about, sir? Don't you know that this woman is a slave and belongs to her master at Pinewood Plantation? Where are you taking her?"

Bradford did not know the man and gasped. Instantly, his guts twisted.

But, before he could speak, Missy said, as if pleasantly surprised, "Mr. *Wilkenson!* It is so nice, sir, to see a friendly face in a strange city."

Bradford, remembering Cap'n Ross's advice to keep quiet and let Missy speak, did not reply. Missy smiled her innocence and sweetness at Wilkenson, but he held to the bridle and did not smile back.

"I don't wish to hear from you just now, Missy. I want this gentleman to account for himself."

"I ... I ..." Bradford began but felt a terrible constriction in his throat and desperately tried to clear it. "I am ... uh ... Thomas Bradford of ... uh ... Chicago ... and am escorting this ... uh, lady ... uh, woman ... to Mr. Leyland's sister's house ... here in Baltimore."

Wilkenson frowned. "I beg to inform you, sir, that Mr. George Leyland, Jr., has no sister or brother, here or anywhere else."

Bradford felt that he had been punched in the stomach. Visions of a southern prison arose immediately to terrify him. He looked over at Missy, helplessly.

She said, composed and even amused, "Poor Mr. Bradford! I fear that he is easily confused. It is not Mr. Leyland's sister to whom we go, but ... well, wait. Let me show you."

Under the light of the street lamp, Wilkenson could see that Missy was still smiling. Standing tensely in the rain, holding fast the mare's bridle, water dripping from his wide-brimmed hat, Wilkenson watched as Missy reached into her large, woven-grass bag. He looked steadily at Thomas Bradford, who was all but shaking, which would have reassured him only a few days ago, but now—dear God, why hadn't he seen this before?—it didn't matter!

Wilkenson suddenly realized what a foolish thing he had done. Now, he would have to take the girl and this white man to jail, account for himself, lodge a complaint against them and leave a trail for Young George to follow. What did he care if Missy was bolting for her freedom, helped by this white fool? Was he not himself doing exactly the same thing?

No, it was nonsense. His years of conditioning to being a master's man and an unquestioning advocate of slavery and all it stood for had blinded him to his own aims and dearest needs. *Good God!* He suddenly realized that, by stepping into this situation (whatever it was) so recklessly, he was actually jeopardizing his own freedom and his life with Elizabeth.

It took Missy a moment to find what she was looking for.

During it, Wilkenson said to Bradford, "Aiding in the escape of a slave has till now been a felony here at the South, sir. But these are new and unpredictable times. Everything we thought true is being upset. As you will soon discover, the Leylands' business is no longer my own. I have no need to interfere with you. Go on about your way, as if we had never seen each other ..."

But just then, Missy said, with a merry little laugh, "Ah, here it is. This will explain *everything!*"

She withdrew Little Master Will's Kerr revolver and cocked it. Then she carefully aimed it at the forehead of the astonished Wilkenson and pulled the trigger. Bradford saw the flame leap from the barrel and heard the loud report. The overseer instantly fell, dead before his knees touched the mud.

The pistol's shot was so loud, and the shock of Missy's shooting a man so great, that Bradford uttered an involuntary little scream. Instinctively, his hands went to his mouth. He then saw but did not understand Missy turn the gun on him, cock it again, aim at his face and fire.

He did not hear the pistol shot or feel Missy put her shoe in his ribs and tumble him out of the carriage.

He did not hear Missy slide into the driver's seat, pick up the reins and yell "Git-ap!" while slapping the horse's rump.

He did not hear the hooves strike the mud or the slosh of the buggy wheels, gaining speed and driving swiftly away.

Behind her, Jared Wilkenson and Thomas Bradford—strangers in life—lay very close, almost touching hands in death.

And, in the buggy, Missy tucked the Kerr back into her bag, urged on the unwilling horse, who wanted her dry stall and hay in her stable away from the rain, until she had put miles between herself and the men's murders.

Missy did not believe that she had been seen but did not think it mattered now. Finding a small city park, deserted in the dark and the downpour, she drove to its far end, where it blended into a wood, and stopped under a wide-spreading oak tree.

Working quickly but carefully, she opened the package brought to her by the washerwoman. It contained a pair of black, thick-soled boots; brown cotton work pants; a gray, long-sleeved shirt; a long, white silk scarf; a billed cap, similar to the kepis worn by soldiers; a pair of cotton socks; and men's cotton underwear.

Quickly stripping off her dress and underthings, and being for a moment naked in the buggy under the heavily dripping tree, she bound her breasts flat with the scarf, pulled on the clothing and boots, tucked her hair under the cap, put her dirty cloth bag containing the gold coins into one pocket of her trousers and the Kerr revolver into the other and jumped down to the ground. She gathered up her clothes, making sure that nothing was left behind, even the woven bag. Then she unhitched the horse, who was now stamping her displeasure, from the traces and, easily rolling up onto her bare back, rode away into the night.

After riding for a few miles on the nearly deserted road, she stopped and dismounted. By tomorrow, the police would likely have pieced together the sequence of events and would be sending out posters, describing a light-skinned, attractive Negro woman. She wanted to give them no clues that she was now traveling as a man. From a puddle in the road, she scooped out mud and rubbed it on her boots, pants, shirt and cap. She dirtied her face and made sure that mud stayed on her hands. The persistent rain carried the mud through the fabric of her clothing; she hoped that it would dry dirty.

Missy pulled up weed clods from the adjacent field, dug down with her hands, buried her woman's clothes and the bag and replaced the earth and the clods. Knowing that the horse without the buggy would make much better time, she headed out westward from the city, looking for the Lineboro road.

But she had not traveled through the countryside fifteen minutes before she saw dimly through the rain on the road ahead of her a group of three horsemen, moving at a slow trot. Instinctively, she knew they were a patrol and quickly slowed her horse lest she overtake them.

But they had heard her, swung their horses about to face her and called out, "Who goes there? Identify yourself!"

Missy called back, in as manlike a voice as she could manage, "A friend, on my way home."

"Why do you not stop, friend?" shouted the man who had called out before. "Come closer and identify yourself."

Suspecting something, the three kicked their horses into a canter back in her direction. Missy wheeled her horse and galloped back the way she had come.

Behind her, she heard the men cry out, "*Stop or be shot!*"

But she only lay forward onto her horse's mane and, in a moment, heard the crack of a rifle. She felt the breath of a bullet as it grazed her shirt, but not her shoulder, and heard the zipping of two more, one on either side of her.

She thought, *If this is what war is, why would anybody be afraid of it?*

Like a soldier in battle, her blood was up. As she dashed through the darkness, having repeatedly to deal with her horse's reluctance to gallop for this stranger on her back, and down a road where there was almost no light, she was planning what she would do if they overtook her.

In only a little while, the men turned back and, for the moment, she was safe. But it was clear to her that an alarm was sure to be raised and that now was not the time for an unaccompanied, disguised Negro woman to approach the state line.

Instead, Missy turned the horse down a lane. Then, after proceeding for about a mile, she rode off the lane into a thick copse of trees with no house-lights in sight. Believing her mount to be well concealed by greenery, she killed her with a pistol shot behind the ear and, before she was fully down, Missy was already running in long strides back up the dark, muddy, pot-holed lane, lest any who had heard the shot come investigating.

Then, keeping to back roads and traveling at night, visiting slave cabins in the wee hours for food and directions, and hiding in the woods by day, she headed slowly, steadily south for a distance of sixty-five miles, toward Washington City. She knew what had to be done to provide for herself and was neither ashamed nor afraid to do it.

Neither shame nor fear had ever meant anything in her life. She was coming to realize—now in this lonely woods, far from her past and her people—that she had never, from her earliest childhood, been afraid of death or been at all attached to anyone, even her grandmother.

And yet ...

On the second day of her journey, passing through woods that bordered a field of clover alive with bees, Missy remembered. And, without love, without even any tenderness she was aware of, it struck her that she wanted to keep her promise.

After peering out from the trees for long minutes, and satisfying herself that there was nobody nearby, she waded carefully out into the clover until she was surrounded by the bees. She closed her eyes and let her breathing settle.

Then she spoke to them: "My grandmother Saleh, of the Fulani people of Senegal, is dead and stands at the gate of heaven and wishes to enter," she said quietly. "Go, all of you, and tell the gods and ancestors that she is waiting."

A sense of completeness and a cold anger beyond all words arose in her. Already the reality of burying the axe in Little Master Will's sleeping head was fading away.

Then, slipping into the deeper woods, she continued moving south, knowing what she must do and thinking carefully about how exactly she would go about it …

www.ingramcontent.com/pod-product-compliance
Lightning Source LLC
Chambersburg PA
CBHW080750250626
47162CB00011B/3081